LOST AND
FOUND

BOOK THREE MY HEART IS YOURS SERIES

TERI MCGILL

Copyright © 2014 Theresa M. McGill
This book is a work of fiction. Names, characters, and events are the product of the author's imagination or are used fictitiously. Any resemblance to real persons, living or dead, is coincidental and not intended by the author.

Lost and Found, My Heart Is Yours – Book Three
ISBN: 978-0-9863645-2-5 (Ebook)
ISBN: 978-0-9863645-5-6 (Paperback)
Published by Teri McGill (Amazon, KDP, CreateSpace)

First edition: 2016
All rights reserved. In accordance with the U.S. Copyright Act of 1976, and electronic sharing of any part of this book without the permission of the publisher or author constitute unlawful piracy and theft of the author's intellectual property. If you would like to use material from this book (other than for review purposes), prior written permission must be obtained by contacting the publisher at Teri@TeriMcGillAuthor.com or at TeriMcG91604@gmail.com. Thank you for your support of the author's rights. Teri McGill is in no way affiliated with any brands, songs, musicians or artists mentioned in this book.

FBI Anti-Piracy Warning:
The unauthorized or reproduction or distribution of a copyrighted work is illegal. Criminal copyright infringement including infringement without monetary gain is investigated by the FBI and is punishable by up to five years in prison and a fine of $250,000.

WARNING:
This book is intended for mature audiences (18+).
Contains Adult Sexual Situations and Language

DEDICATION

The Golden Rule:
"Do unto others as you would have them do unto you."

    This book is dedicated to all the DREAMERS and BELIEVERS in our universe. I am convinced there are more of us out there, and although I have met some of you, I don't know nearly enough.

    The dreamers imagine a planet where resources, both living and non-living, are respected, conserved, and protected. If Earthlings followed The Golden Rule, the words 'war' and 'hate' would not exist in any language. While one of the oldest proverbs, it has sadly been forgotten by much of today's society.

    The believers have faith in the intangible: true love, second chances, soulmates, angels, miracles, and countless other benevolent, spiritual forces that exist without plausible explanation. I have always been and will remain a dreamer and a believer until the day I leave this Earth.

ACKNOWLEDGEMENTS

My sincere thanks and appreciation to the tireless staff at **Hot Tree Editing**: Becky Johnson, Peggy Hurst Frese and all the brilliant editors and beta readers who have offered me their support and encouragement. I am grateful to everyone who read, blogged, and shared my novels or friended me in the book world. Thanks to **Bex 'n' Books** and **Hot Tree Promotions** for their willingness to spread the word and steer book-minded people to my Facebook pages. Many thanks to all the wonderful online book blogs whose mission is to share indie novels with the literary world. I am also indebted to the numerous FB book-related sites that offer authors free 'takeovers' to advertise their novels. I especially wish to thank the many authors — members of the Indie Author Community — who so graciously corresponded with me through email or Facebook and always had time and patience for a new author's endless questions.

My heartfelt gratitude and love goes to my editor and (as of recently) real-life friend (not just on Facebook), **Becky Johnson**. I had the utmost pleasure of meeting her a few months ago, and we spent many hours sharing our love for romance novels, book boyfriends, and red wine. Becky, you are an inspiration!

Another special 'thank you' goes to Sheila Kell, a fabulous author and wonderful, supportive friend. We finally met at the RT Roundup in Houston last October, and now have several more writers' conferences planned for future attendance.

Many thanks to my friends and supporters in SoCal, especially Lynne Tucker — always willing to like, comment, tweet, and share my author and book series FB pages and posts. I also must thank my street team, Teri's HeartBreakers, for their tireless efforts in supporting and promoting my novels.

In addition, I appreciate the friendship of my fellow authors in the RWA (Romance Writers of America), and LARA (Los Angeles Romance Writers).

CREDITS

Editing: Hot Tree Editing
Becky Johnson, CEO
Peggy Hurst Frese, Editor
http://www.hottreeedits.com

Formatting: Dafeenah Jameel at Indie Designz
http://www.indiedesignz.com

Cover Design: Louisa Maggio at LM Creations
http://lmbookcreations.wix.com/lm-creations

My Heart Is Yours (Series)

Book 1 – Signs of a Quiet Heart

Book 2 – Living For Two

Book 3 – Lost and Found

LOST AND FOUND

BOOK THREE MY HEART IS YOURS SERIES

Prologue

Excerpt – Chapter 7 Signs of a Quiet Heart (My Heart Is Yours – Book 1)

*"There is no greater sorrow than to recall
our times of joy in wretchedness"*
– Dante Alighieri (Inferno)

ONE YEAR AGO

It was Thursday night and Tyler's realization that the whole week had passed without a word from Robbi hit him hard. A sick feeling had permeated his stomach and he regretted listening to Tony. *What the fuck am I doing? I like her a lot, and I want to be with her. It's not complicated, but now I've gone and fucked it up!*

An hour later, Tyler found himself at the North Star and Tag was pouring him a third Jack on the rocks. He had purposely sat in the seat Robbi had occupied the previous week, hoping to catch her lingering scent. No luck there.

"So, T-man, where's your girl tonight? And, by the way, you look like shit on a stick, my friend," Tag queried with a lift of his brow. Tyler shrugged, and then let out a menacing growl.

"Fuck you, Tag. First of all, she's not my girl and I don't have a fuckin' clue where she is!" Tyler slammed his glass on the counter indicating he wanted another drink.

Grunting, "Follow me, lover boy," Tag grabbed the bottle of Jack Daniels and two glasses and led Tyler to a small corner table. "I'm clockin' out for the night!" he shouted over his shoulder at the other bartender. Tyler stared at Tag, as he filled both glasses to the brim.

"I've been tending bar for over ten years, and I know that look when I see it. And you, my friend, had that look Friday night. She *is* your girl and the sooner you admit it, the better. So, talk to me. What happened?"

"We saw each other Saturday night and Sunday, the best fuckin' dates I've ever had in my life. There was no jumpin' in the sack, however. We just talked a lot. I mean, like, for hours. I felt like I had known her my whole life. Then I got cold feet and didn't call or text her all week even though I was thinkin' about her the entire damn time. I'm such an asshole. I feel like I blew it." Tag listened intently, nodding at appropriate intervals. Years of bartending had taught him how to be a patient and empathetic listener.

"I know you think I'm a soulless dick — and you would not be wrong — but I am going to give you some advice and I want you to listen to every single word. We've known each other going on ten years, but you really know nothing about me. All we ever discuss are Harleys, booze, sports, and pussy, right? Do you even know my real name or where I'm from?" Tag challenged. Tyler shook his head despondently, scrubbing a hand down his face. "Everything I am about to tell you must remain between the two of us. Do I have your solemn word on that?" Tyler nodded resolutely, as the two shook hands.

"My name is Cole Taggart and I grew up outside of Austin, Texas. I was the star quarterback in high school and got recruited by the Longhorns, ending up with a full athletic scholarship." Tyler interrupted at that point, unable to contain his astonishment.

"But you hate the fucking Longhorns!" Tyler argued. Tag ignored Tyler's outburst and continued; his narrowed eyes wordlessly warned Tyler not to interrupt again.

"I met Miranda the first day of freshman year. We were in the same philosophy class and hit it off immediately — best friends, soulmates, lovers — we had it all. She was the most beautiful soul I had ever met, pure, radiant sunshine. I loved her with every single cell of my body and, miraculously, she loved me right back. Her eyes lit my soul on fire." Tag's bright, green eyes darkened briefly, as he heaved a sigh. After having heard nothing but crude remarks come from Tag's normally filthy mouth, Tyler was taken aback by his sincere, heartfelt confession.

"There was a frat party one night. I participated in a drunken gangbang, which was videotaped, and the following day Randi saw it. I tried to explain, but she refused to talk to me. Two days later, she was gone, killed in a car accident. She had gone out with Jake, one of my fraternity brothers. I found out he was the motherfucker who videotaped me. Apparently, Jake had the hots for my girl all along, and Clark, the fraternity's president, was his cousin, so I could have been set up. Jake also died in the crash, which — thank fucking Christ — saved me from a murder charge. The day after the accident, I confronted Clark, asking questions about his possible involvement and a huge brawl ensued. A few of the frat brothers were around — big fucking tactical error on my part — and they kicked my ass, also fracturing my arm in the process. My *throwing* arm, to be exact. I was looking at surgery for sure with no guarantee I could ever play football again.

"My entire existence, my only reason for living, ended when Randi died. I was broken. I lost it at her funeral, some kind of incoherent mental breakdown. At the cemetery, I actually tried to climb down into the grave with her. It felt like

I died alongside her; but at least, I was able to experience real honest-to-goodness love for the best two years of my life. I threw her away for a ten-second drunken fuck." Tears were in Tag's eyes, but he quickly blinked them back.

"I quit school and aimlessly travelled around the West Coast from San Diego all the way up to Anchorage, where I worked for two years. I ended up here; stayed with a guy I met in Alaska whose dad got me this job. I became Tag Coleman, and I've been living this hollow, worthless life since, because it's what I deserve. It was a conscious choice to become the heartless man-whore you see before you. It was my way of dealing with the guilt and pain. I'm fucking my way into delirious oblivion, drowning my sorrows with my cock buried in a different, nameless pussy every night. I close my eyes and pretend it's my Randi's perfect body against mine, but nobody feels like her, smells like her. I wish I could have met her when I was older. We make stupid mistakes when we're young and don't realize how we alter our destinies forever. Dante said, 'The path to Paradise begins in Hell'. Beautiful fucking words, right? That's how life is supposed to be. You go through years of shit then obtain your reward. That's *your* life, Tyler. Your Paradise is *this* close." Tag held up his thumb and forefinger, barely a millimeter between them.

"I had mine but I lost it; now I'm in Dante's fucking Inferno Hell for however many miserable years I have left. I've accepted my dismal fate; I know there is no happy ending in the cards for me. I'll walk this Earth alone, but you are a far better man than I could ever hope to be. You deserve so much more. Don't blow this, Ty! Do not let her go. Robbi is the real thing, a good girl, a good person, like my Miranda was. She's not one of those plastic Barbie whores; goddamn fuckin' parasites who are always sniffin' around guys like us. Are you trying to convince yourself she's probably just another random, casual fuck? You're not fooling me one bit." Tag's index finger was forcibly jabbing Tyler in the chest, punctuating each syllable for emphasis. "I. Know. That. Look. You were staring at her the same way I used to gaze at my beautiful girl. You do not want to wake up and realize that the best person you ever had the privilege to know and love ..." Tag's voice faltered as he reached to down the last of his drink.

Tyler extended his hand, resting it on Tag's shoulder. "You need to forgive yourself, buddy. Wasting your life doesn't have to be your future."

Tag's laugh held little mirth as his lips curled into a sardonic grin. "I let my future slip through my fingers. I think about Randi with every single breath I take. Forgiveness only succeeds if your memory fails. I believe in the existence of Heaven. When I hold Randi in my arms again, and she tells me she forgives me, then perhaps I will be able to forgive myself."

A high-pitched, female voice broke the comfortable silence between them. Tyler had more questions to ask Tag, but they would have to wait. The determined redhead, a regular customer named Ginger, and her blonde companion pulled two chairs over to join them. Tag tilted his head slightly and gave Tyler a death stare before turning toward the two women. "Speaking of Barbies," Tyler muttered disgustedly.

"Good evening, ladies!" Tag's wide, toothy grin belied the pained sadness in his eyes.

"Hey, Tag, baby. Who's your handsome friend?" The redhead leaned into Tyler, attempting to rub her breasts against his arm, but he pulled away. Endeavoring to avoid her, he stumbled against the table as he shakily made a weak effort to stand.

"I gotta go ... have a busy day tomorrow," Tyler mumbled semi-coherently. Turning to leave, Tag jumped up and grabbed him by the shoulder.

"No way are you driving, T-man. I will not have a DUI or worse on my conscience. Come on, ladies. Let's drop my buddy off, then the three of us are gonna take this party to my place."

Chapter 1

*"For where thou art, there is the world itself,
and where though art not, desolation."*
— William Shakespeare (Henry VI)

TWELVE YEARS AGO …
SAN ANTONIO, TEXAS

Dear Diary,

I'm back in Texas for a week. These past few days have been the worst nightmare of my life … but I can't wake up because it's real. Two days ago, my family buried my best friend … my 'big sister' … my beautiful, precious cousin Randi. She was the older sister I always wanted but never had. Randi was my first babysitter; she read to me, taught me my colors and numbers, played spelling games with me or week-long games of Monopoly. She sang me to sleep while we gently ran our fingertips up each other's arms — our 'tickle time' she would call it. And now, she's gone.

Everyone is saying her boyfriend killed her. Not directly, but he cheated on her and broke her heart; pushed her into some other guy's arms who was drunk and killed them both in an awful crash. I'm not sure how I feel about it … about him, even though I told Randi she shouldn't break up with him because of it.

Please, God. Explain it to me. How could you let this happen? Aunt Morgan and Uncle Victor wouldn't talk to Cole at the funeral, refused to look at him. Cousin Marshall blamed Cole for killing his sister, had even warned him about that 'athletes-only' fraternity he belonged to, told him they were trouble. Uncle Victor had to restrain Marshall. He would have beaten the shit out of Cole otherwise. It was heartbreaking. Cole cried through the whole service. He was so distraught. At one point, he stumbled toward the grave and fell. It had been raining and he slipped in the mud. He was out of his mind, screaming her name over and over, shrieking uncontrollably, "I'm sorry, baby. I am so sorry. Please don't leave me. I can't live without you." It looked like he was trying to reach down and touch her coffin, which had been lowered into a big, gaping hole in the earth. His parents and some other big guy grabbed him and forced him to leave. Marshall told me Cole quit school yesterday morning, cleaned out his dorm room and no one has seen him or his truck since. He didn't even inform his parents what his plans were. He simply vanished.

I didn't really know Cole that well. I would see him at Thanksgiving or Christmas when Randi would bring him home with her from UT. He seemed like a great guy. I always had kind of a little-girl crush on him. I met him for the first time on my twelfth birthday. Randi brought him to my party. I didn't talk to him much until afterwards. I was outside testing my new skateboard and took a nasty spill in the middle of the street, scraping my elbow and forearm pretty bad. Cole came running over and was checking me carefully like the doctors do on TV, evaluating my injuries or whatever. The pain was awful, and I was crying hysterically, although I was trying not to. I think I may have been yelling about it being broken. I was so mortified, acting like such a big baby in front of him.

Then he started talking in a soft, soothing voice and caressing my arm so gently that all I could think about was how pretty his green eyes were. OMG! He whispered, "Emma, don't you worry. I can see nothing's broken, but you might have a few gnarly scars. Show them off proudly when you lie to all your friends about how you fell in the middle of executing a perfect three-sixty on the half-pipe. Even Tony Hawk would be proud." Cousin Randi had joined us and she was holding my other hand. Cole continued with his calming words. I remember still feeling freaked out, as I sucked in giant gulps of air. "When you see that scar in the future, I want you to remember how bright the sun was shining and how beautiful the flowers looked in your front yard," Cole soothed. I scanned my surroundings then managed to give them a wobbly smile. Randi was eyeing Cole, sending him a secret message with her eyebrows. "Do it, baby. It always makes my boo-boos feel better." She giggled, giving me an evil wink. He leaned over and placed a light kiss on my raw, mangled elbow and (I swear to God, dearest Diary) the pain instantly disappeared! Well, not exactly, but it felt a lot better. He then carried me into my house, demanding to know where the first-aid kit was located.

Cole had it all — handsome, sweet, smart, great athlete. They were madly in love, planned to get married when they graduated UT. She even had dreams of what their future kids would look like. God, I miss her so much my heart hurts.

Everyone hates him now, but I can't. A small part of me still cares about him. He was kind to me the few times I met him, even when he didn't have to be — when I was the annoying little kid who followed the two of them around. I will always love him for that and for giving Randi so much happiness. She was her best, her most perfect beautiful self, when they were together.

I have read plenty of tragic classic romance novels and seen *countless heartbreaking movies in my life. Mom and I are addicted to those stories. It started when Mom showed me Romeo and Juliet when I was twelve. It was the more recent one starring Leonardo Di Caprio whose character also died tragically in Titanic. Mom and I boo-hooed together for hours. It was a special bonding time for us, something only the two of us shared. Thousands of tears and tissues later, we still enjoy a gloomy tale of doomed star-crossed lovers: Wuthering Heights, West Side Story, Jane Eyre, Untamed Heart, Legends of the Fall, Edward Scissorhands, just to name a few. The list is endless. Romantic. Tragic. Fiction.*

What I saw was real ... too real, as my heart shattered into a million tiny fragments. The gut-wrenching images I witnessed at Randi's funeral are permanently seared into my brain. Cole's anguish and pain will haunt me for the rest of my life. I can only hope he survives this and somehow can come to terms with what happened. I pray to God ... if there is a God ... please keep him safe. I know Cole wishes he could have died with Randi, but do not let that happen. Please. ~Emma Marie~

P.S. Back home tomorrow. I miss Alex and my friends.

Chapter 2

"The child must know that he is a miracle, that since the beginning of the world there hasn't been, and until the end of the world there will not be, another child like him."
– Pablo Casals

JANUARY
EMERY

"Wake up, sweetie! Randy's been up for two hours already," Olivia Lawson chided her daughter, gently stroking her bare shoulder in a vain attempt to stir Emery out of a deep slumber. "He's searching all my favorite hiding places for his gifts. That should keep him busy for a while, considering his presents aren't even here."

Emery knew how difficult it was to surprise Randy. He was a curious, extremely resourceful boy ... strong, tenacious, and intelligent, just like his father. He shared his dad's good looks as well: olive complexion, dark brown, almost black wavy hair and eyes, and sinfully long eyelashes, which were the envy of every female who encountered the affable child.

Since it was her son's ninth birthday, Emery's dad, Sam, had gone out with Alex, Randy's father, to make sure every detail was finalized for the big surprise at noon. They had plans to attend a closed practice of the Arizona Cardinals, Randy's favorite football team. One of Sam's clients, a bigwig in the Cardinals' organization, had called in a few favors.

Emery was about to roll over when someone jumped onto the bed, effectively barreling into her head.

"Mommy. Mommy! You gotta wake up. Grandma said the chocolate-chip pancakes are almost ready. Now, Mom." His palms cupped Emery's face as his long fingers tapped her cheeks.

"Okay, baby, I'm up," she grumbled, ruffling Randy's bed-head hair. "Happy birthday, my little man. How does it feel to be nine?"

"Mom." Randy's voice was sternly adamant. "No more 'baby' and no more 'little.' I'm too old for that stuff." He pouted, although his eyes sparkled mischievously. Emery played along, grinning inwardly.

"Too old? Oh, puhlease," she retorted. "You're still a whole year away from double-digits, kiddo. You can't drive, you can't vote. The only thing you *can* do is let your fantastic mother, the greatest mom on the planet, call you her baby for as long as she wants. Deal?"

"Hmmm …" Randy mused, pensively stroking his chin with his hand, like a supreme court judge pondering a life or death verdict. This verbal banter was a favorite game of mother and son — one they enjoyed immensely and played quite often.

"I've reached my decision," Randy ceremoniously announced with a flourish of his hand. Emery could hardly suppress her laugh. "'Baby' and 'little man' are out, but you may call me 'babe.' You call Dad 'babe' sometimes, so I'm cool with that. But never in front of my friends, okay? Unless you'd rather refer to me by my new nickname at school. RAZ! Awesome, huh?" Seeing his mother's puzzled expression, Randy clarified.

"Duh … my initials, Mom. Randall Alexander Zamora. RAZ. You like?" His dazzling smile never ceased to light up Emery's heart. He was a sweet, easygoing, loving child, named, in part, after his great-grandfather who, unfortunately, had died a month before he was born. There was a second reason that particular name had been chosen, as well as the subsequent nickname, but the family preferred not to discuss it with the child.

Emery and Alex had never married, but had professed vows to each other nonetheless when she first found herself pregnant at seventeen. They had been best friends since middle school and morphed into lovers, eventually becoming unanticipated parents. They'd never regretted their decision and subsequent commitment. One look at the beautiful boy they had created together was reason enough. They decided immediately that they would not marry, despite parental objections on both sides, and led separate lives, which overlapped when necessary. Emery and Alex pursued their individual career dreams with the assistance of both sets of grandparents, who had fallen madly in love with the little boy from day one. Emery had gone to University of Texas for her freshman year but was not happy, so she transferred to Arizona State University and finished her degree in fine arts there. She joined the ASU faculty upon graduating and became an art teacher. Alex graduated from the Phoenix Police Academy, and he was making a name for himself on the streets. He recently had become a detective, one of the youngest in PPD history, and because he was fluent in Spanish — Alex's parents were of Mexican heritage — and relatively youthful looking, he worked undercover: immigration and drug cartel cases. His job was as dangerous as he was fearless, which had proved to be a lethal combination on more than one occasion.

"RAZ. I love it, babe." Emery nodded her approval, winking impishly at her mother. "And when you turn eighteen, we can all get matching RAZ tattoos using a Gothic tribal-type font." A booming male voice could be heard entering the house. Randy bounded from the bedroom, bellowing, "Grandpa! Daddy! Mom said we're all gettin' tribal tattoos."

Olivia laughed, rolling her eyes at Emery. "He is hilarious. Smart as a whip and a good boy, too. You've done an impressive job with him, honey. I'm proud of you."

"Well, Mom, I learned from the best. And thanks for letting us move in with you for a while. I'll start looking for a new place when I return from San Francisco in June. Maybe I'm finally ready to buy something ... a condo or perhaps a small house?"

"Now, Emma Marie Lawson, you know the two of you can stay here as long as you want. We adore you living with us, and there's plenty of room."

Emery knew quite well her mom was dead serious, especially when she used her entire birth name. She had dropped the name during high school, preferring the sound of Emery. It was the perfect combination of 'Emma plus Marie', not to mention a one-of-a-kind name no one ever forgot.

Following a lavish brunch consisting of Randy's favorites, they retreated to the living room where several brightly wrapped gifts were piled on the coffee table. Ten minutes and a mound of shredded wrapping paper and torn ribbons later, Randy was thanking everyone with kisses, hugs, and plenty of high-fives. A new laptop from Grandpa Sam and Grandma Olivia, school clothes and an official Arizona Cardinals #11 Larry Fitzgerald jersey from Emery, and finally from his dad — head-to-toe gear for the football season, which would be commencing in a few months at a nearby after-school athletic center. Sam motioned for Randy to sit on his lap, after the boy had donned his new jersey.

"Grandpa, your eyebrows look like two caterpillars talking to each other!" Randy chuckled, pointing mischievously at Sam's bushy brows.

"I told you they were in desperate need of a trim," Olivia scolded, wagging a finger at her husband.

"Oh, hush, Liv. Let me announce the big news. We're all going to see the Cardinals today. How about that, Randy?"

Rolling his eyes at his grandfather, Randy countered, "But they're not playing today. You should know that, Gramps. They're playing tomorrow, or did you forget about the playoffs?" Wrinkling his nose, Randy looked disappointed. He loved going to see his favorite football team; Grandpa Sam had four season tickets right on the fifty-yard line.

"Well, the next best thing would be to go to a team practice. A closed practice with only family, friends, and VIPs in attendance." Sam watched his grandson's countenance gradually transform from distress to jubilation as the words sank in. "And I suggest you bring your new football. You never know whose autograph you might get."

Randy's face exploded into a mile-wide grin. "Larry Fitzgerald? Holy sh ... I mean, holy crap, Grandpa. That would be awesome!" Emery smiled as Sam ignored Randy's near profanity. Her father had often been guilty of mild cursing in the boy's presence. "You never know, son. The players often are available during practice to meet and greet their fans."

Emery voiced her excitement as well. #11 was also her favorite Cardinal, a gifted wide receiver who possessed the combined physique of a body builder and the extraordinary graceful leaping ability of a ballet dancer. *I wouldn't mind meeting him myself. He's freakin' hot! I'd better wear my Cardinals hoodie.*

Several hours later, they headed to Randy's favorite restaurant, Alice Cooperstown. It was, by far, the coolest place in Phoenix to hang out, watch a game, eat, drink, and mingle. Alex was a huge Alice Cooper fan, which had always puzzled Emery. Randy loved the place because of the wacky ambiance, the cool kids' menu, and the abundance of NFL memorabilia. He also fancied the wings and sliders while his parents appreciated the microbrews. An ecstatic Randy was clutching his football contentedly with both hands. Signed by his hero, he had not let go of it since shaking Larry's hand. Also in attendance were Emery's aunt and uncle, Morgan and Victor Galloway, who had relocated nearby after selling their house in San Antonio, Texas, the previous month. Uncle Vic was returning to his alma mater — the Sandra Day O'Connor College of Law, at Arizona State University in Tempe — as an adjunct professor after twenty years as a prosecutor. He was happy to leave the unpredictability and drama of courtroom life behind. Besides, Morgan and Olivia, who were twins, missed each other terribly. The two families would only be about fifteen miles from each other instead of over one thousand.

The final chore before the Galloways moved had been to clean out their daughter Randi's bedroom, which had remained untouched since her death twelve years before. When she'd first died, Randi's mother had gone to her dorm room to gather her belongings, which fit into three large boxes. She had also found a decorative wooden box, which had been tucked away under her bed. Clothes and other unimportant things had been donated to a local women's shelter, but the wooden box containing Randi's personal items — jewelry, mementoes, letters, photos, a journal — had been kept for years, hidden out of sight on the top shelf of Morgan's walk-in closet. Knowing how close the cousins had been growing up, Morgan knew her daughter's precious memories would be lovingly safeguarded by Emery, so she had given the treasured box to her when they first moved into the new house.

It had taken a few weeks before Emery could gather the fortitude to open the box, knowing in advance the emotional toll it would take. Although she had mentally prepared herself, the task proved to be overwhelming; she cried over every single item. Randi's boyfriend, Cole, was everywhere: love letters, notes, pressed roses, gifts, jewelry, concert ticket stubs, stuffed animals, and a photo album. Folded neatly was one of his Longhorn jerseys he had given her, and a T-shirt that said "Property of Longhorn QB Taggart #7". Emery had buried her face in the shirt inhaling deeply, but the only scent remaining was a decade of musty old memories.

Emery had smoothed her hand over the suede cover of Randi's journal, opening it gently. The pages had yellowed a bit, but the handwriting was perfectly clear. An occasional tear flowed down Emery's cheeks as she poured over each entry, despite her futile attempts to prevent the moisture from dripping on the fragile paper. Her curiosity got the best of her and she skipped to the final few pages. Sadness overwhelmed her as every word was scrutinized. *Cole Taggart. I will find you. I'll track you down to the ends of the Earth if necessary ... for Randi.*

Emery was abruptly yanked out of her painful reminiscence by laughter from her son. "Did you hear that, Mom? Marina and Sofia are gonna design clothes for twins. How cool is that?"

After a few exceptionally difficult years following Randi's death, Morgan and Victor adopted ten-year-old identical twins from Russia. As young girls, they had always adored fashion and were now enjoying their first year in college at the well-respected FIDM, Fashion Institute of Design and Merchandising, in Los Angeles.

Later that evening, after the festivities had died down and everyone had retired, Emery and Alex found themselves on her comfortable double bed watching TV. He rarely spent the night and luckily Emery's bedroom was on the opposite end of the house if things got hot and heavy. They had known each other since the 7th grade; Alex had been her first and only boyfriend throughout her school years and their strong friendship had never wavered.

"So, Emmie, you've decided on the San Francisco Art Institute? Does it have anything to do with the mystery man whose name you gave me last month? The one you asked me to track down for you?" Alex tilted his head, trying to read her expression. Emery nodded contritely.

"I've been searching a long time for him. He knew my cousin and it's crucial I talk to him. Now's my chance, and besides, SFAI is a great school and this sculpting class is exactly what my résumé needs." After a short discussion about her fast-approaching semester in San Francisco, which included Alex helping her make the drive up north at the end of February, the twosome spent a few minutes indulging in their yearly ritual as parents: sharing a laugh and reminiscing about their beautiful son's birth. Emery would always bring up the excruciating pain of pushing an eight-pound, three-ounce baby's giant head out of her vagina. Alex would boast about being the perfectly trained father-to-be: holding her hand, pressing a wet cloth to her forehead, and coaching her as they both executed the Lamaze breathing technique together.

"Oooh! Oooh! Aaah! Aaah!" Emery reenacted, mock shouting at him, "Alex, don't look at my pussy when he comes out. Promise me! You'll never want to eat downtown again if you see that hideous, gory sight." She collapsed into his arms, giggling uproariously.

Alex waggled his eyebrows suggestively. "As you know, Emmie, downtown is my favorite place to eat. Which reminds me …" He quickly got on his knees, tugging her jeans and panties off in one quick motion. Nudging her thighs apart, he nestled his body in between her shapely legs, which she instinctively wrapped around his lower back, heels digging into his ass.

"God, Emmie. You smell as good as ever, maybe better. I've missed tasting you. It's been a while." Forcefully grabbing her hips, Alex dipped his head down, and licked the entire seam of her slit before he pulled her clit hungrily into his mouth. Knowing exactly what she liked, he alternated nibbling and sucking her sensitive bundle of nerves, and then flicked it hard several times with the tip of his tongue. Her hands were tangled in his hair, pushing his face tighter against her smooth pussy, where the rough stubble of his facial hair was causing a sublime combination of pleasure and pain against her sensitive flesh.

"Alex! Oh, God, right there, baby. Don't fucking stop." Separating her slick folds, he carefully pushed two thick fingers deep inside her, thrusting and withdrawing in time with the frantic pulsating movement of her hips, while his tongue continued its assault on her clit. A powerful orgasm ripped through her, causing her lower body to shudder around him.

"Inside me, Alex. Now!" Alex smirked, then hurriedly discarded his jeans as he obeyed her command. Not wanting more children, he had gotten a vasectomy a few years back and their 'friends with benefits' relationship had thrived as a result. Lowering himself down, he shoved his hips forward and drove his cock into her already soaked core. They found their fast-paced rhythm together, as they had done countless times before. Following a few more powerful strokes, Emery tightened around his pulsing shaft and was about to explode again. Her fervent moans were all Alex needed to fuel his own climax. With a final thrust, he grunted his release as she came fiercely moments after.

Chapter 3

"Do not be afraid;
our fate cannot be taken from us; it is a gift."
– Dante Alighieri (Inferno)

SIX WEEKS LATER
EMERY

"Mom, according to your checklist, everything's been loaded. You and Dad are good to go." Holding a yellow legal pad in his hand, Randy proudly displayed a check mark after every item. "The only thing left to pack is the cooler."

It had been Alex's idea to involve Randy in the trip preparations. Emery would be away for three and a half months, and they hoped her actual departure wouldn't be such a jolt if Randy saw the events leading up to it gradually unfold.

Emery's eyes scanned her Toyota RAV 4, which was crammed with everything she would need for a semester, including her bicycle, art supplies, and laptop. Pulling Randy into her side, she leaned over him, depositing several kisses on the top of his head.

"I'm gonna miss you, Mom." The boy's arms encircled her waist, and Emery clearly heard the tremor in his voice.

"Not half as much as I'm gonna miss you, sweetie. But don't worry. I happen to know Grandpa has a few surprises planned and Grandma has promised to bake whatever goodies you want, no limit. And the best part is you get to fly to San Francisco every other weekend!"

"And on my weekends with Dad, he promised to help me be ready for my June football tryouts. That'll be cool."

After packing the cooler with several bottles of water, fruit, yogurt, power bars, and an array of sandwiches, Emery and Alex were ready to say their final goodbyes. Numerous hugs, kisses, and more than a few tears later, they were off.

The westbound 10 was a breeze, which was why they decided to travel on a Sunday. It was Emery's goal to drive through Los Angeles, head north on the 101 and stay the night in Santa Barbara. That plan would put them over halfway to their destination, leaving about 350 miles to San Francisco.

Alex nodded his approval as they pulled into the lovely Harbor View Inn. The concierge recommended the hotel's own Eladio's Restaurant, which sounded perfect for the exhausted and ravenous twosome. Although they had shared the driving, Alex had done the majority, with Emery perusing the maps and supervising the iPod musical selections.

Their luxurious room faced west and had a magnificent view of the sunset over the Pacific, hues of bronze and crimson rapidly blending into deep indigo and violet in a matter of minutes. After a quick change of clothes, and a longing gaze at the huge walk-in shower — which Alex promised they would be sure to visit first thing in the morning, together — they found themselves at Eladio's Bar, which overlooked a stunning stone patio and fountain. The gentle sea breezes of early evening captured the essence of the oceanfront, as they waited to be seated for dinner.

Following a splendid meal of steak and various seafood dishes, they strolled along the wharf, eyeing a multitude of sailboats and fishing vessels. They enjoyed live music and a wine-tasting room in one of the charming taverns that overlooked the beach and waterfront. The night air was refreshingly chilly; Emery was glad she had heeded Alex's warning and brought a warm jacket. After a pleasant hour of meandering through the many attention-grabbing side streets, they returned to their hotel room.

At exactly 8:30 a.m., Emery's phone alarm sounded; she wanted to be on the road by 10:15 a.m. at the latest. Alex made good on his promise from the night before, making her scream his name more than once in the shower.

Alex and Emery had learned about sex together, experimenting from the time they were freshmen in high school. They were completely comfortable with each other, and no inhibitions, or topics of conversation were taboo. Every square inch of their bodies was familiar to the other. Emery knew that Alex loved it when she squeezed his balls right before he came, and the secret, ultra-sensitive spot on the underside of his penis which guaranteed a heightened sensation when her teeth and tongue did their magic. Alex, in turn, knew Emery's preferences as well, especially in the shower. She loved leveraging her hands on the tile, and leaning over with her perfect ass in the air as Alex pounded her hard and fast from behind. He had perfected shower sex. His left hand cupped her mound, thumb circling her clit as the middle finger on his right hand plunged in and out of her anus in perfect rhythm with the forceful thrusts of his hips. Occasionally, Emery engaged in a bit of dirty talk; that particular morning was no exception.

"Fuck me, Alex. Get inside me, now. Every hot, sexy, rock-hard inch of you, baby. Oh, my God! Give it to me hard. Faster. Yessss!" Alex bit down on the soft skin of her neck, and then sucked deeply. Emery smirked, knowing that Alex was purposely marking her — exactly like he used to do when they were in high school. It was his symbol of protection, a silent warning that proclaimed, 'Don't fuck with what is mine.'

That evening, after finally arriving at Emery's small, furnished one-bedroom apartment, and helping her move in, Alex glanced at his watch, then attempted to pull Emery into his arms. She resisted, not in the mood.

"Alex, part of the reason I came here was to give you and Randy the time you both need to get close again, like you used to be. I worry he's too dependent on me. I need you to step up in my absence."

"I will, Emery. You have my word." He mentioned a big case was in the works but it would not likely begin for several months. He promised to keep her informed, as well as see Randy as often as possible, then called for a cab to take him to the airport.

"Have fun, work hard in class, learn a lot, and don't worry about us. We'll be fine. Be careful, Emmie. You're in an unfamiliar city, so stay vigilant, okay? And just because this guy appears to have a clean background doesn't mean anything. Promise me you'll —"

"I'll be fine, Alex," she chided while depositing a chaste kiss on his cheek. "*You* are the one who needs to be careful. Take care of our boy and we'll talk soon, okay? Enjoy your flight."

Emery propped her feet up on the small coffee table and poured herself a glass of wine. Taking in her surroundings excitedly, she couldn't wait to embark on the adventure that awaited her. She attempted to rationalize the uneasiness that slowly overtook the pit of her stomach, assuring herself she was only missing Randy. *Alex must keep his promises this time.*

The week was spent becoming familiar with the eclectic neighborhood, which would be Emery's home-away-from-home for a while. SFAI was located in the heart of the city with easy access to the charming, world-famous cable cars, as well as the efficient BART system. Walking was high on her list of preferred methods of transportation, plus she'd brought her bicycle with her. Emery visited the school on Thursday, transporting all her personal art supplies she had brought from home to the spacious classroom and adjoining art studio. Her class was not scheduled to begin until the following Monday, but the rooms were open in order for the students to set up their personal equipment and supplies beforehand. She located the work area that had been assigned to her, and proceeded to store her tools and materials. A few of her future classmates were milling about; some already appeared to be acquainted, the others were busily introducing themselves. Emery joined in enthusiastically; meeting fellow artists was one of her passions. She hoped to meet the professor, but overheard two young girls speculating that he was probably still lecturing somewhere in Europe.

After returning to her cozy apartment, she fixed a quick dinner, took a leisurely bath and then selected the perfect outfit for her evening. There were so many fascinating sights yet unseen; Emery had four months to uncover the City by the Bay's hidden treasures. She couldn't seem to calm the fluttering in her stomach, an odd mix of excitement and trepidation, as she headed out into the brisk night air. *I'm ready. Let's do this.*

Chapter 4

"When I first saw you, I fell in love, and you smiled because you knew."
– Arrigo Boito
(Often attributed to William Shakespeare, this expression is an English translation of a line in the Italian opera Falstaff with a libretto by Arrigo Boito. Falstaff was based primarily on Shakespeare's "Merry Wives of Windsor"; however, the line does not appear in the play.)

TAG

Working his usual weekday evening shift from 7:00 p.m. to 2:00 a.m., Tag Coleman had arrived thirty minutes early. A new bartender had been hired recently and Tag had been showing him around. Brewster McKnight, aka Brew, was a tall, muscular African American who had played for a short time in the NFL. Brew had long dreadlocks and penetrating grey eyes. Tag suspected he might have served in the military at some point in his life, although the man had never volunteered any other personal information. Tag also wanted Brew to help with security. His intimidating demeanor would be a valuable asset as a bouncer.

North Star Bar was not a place where brawls occurred regularly. It was a classy sports bar, but when fans of opposing teams found themselves in the ardent throes of winning and losing, or playoffs and championships, all hell was going to break loose eventually. It was always smart business to have several large, muscular alpha males on display to control the overly enthusiastic rowdies and drunks. They also served as eye-candy for the many women who enjoyed watching sports, or at least pretended that was the reason they frequented sports-oriented establishments. Tag was head bartender and had worked at the North Star for ten years. He loved his job and got along well with the regulars. He was friendly, joked around a lot, and was a fairly good listener. His only fault, if you could call it such, was being a notorious man-whore, although his good buddy, Tyler D'Angelo, was trying his best to rehabilitate him in that area. Tag chuckled to himself; as much as he missed hanging with his best friend, he had to admit he'd never seen him so happy. *Tyler, you old dog. You'd still be whoring it up with me if Robbi hadn't come into your life.*

Tag had done his share of heavy drugs and had abused alcohol, but that was all in the past. His days of living in a booze-fueled, drug-addled purgatory were long gone. Nowadays, he was more interested in a healthy lifestyle, which tied in to his promising new career as a personal trainer. Tag had tremendous will power and self-discipline when he set his mind to a specific goal or task. His only current amnesia-inducing vices were moderate drinking, occasional weed, and uncomplicated sex. Bicep curls and pounding on the heavy bag were healthier coping mechanisms.

Robbi and Tyler had come in earlier and had been chatting up Tag who was laughing boisterously, reminiscing about the couple's first date almost a year ago. Tag was congratulating them on their recent New Year's Eve wedding in Las Vegas.

It was a Thursday, which was usually a slow night, but a basketball game was starting and the bar was beginning to fill up. A pretty girl in her mid-twenties appeared and sat in the chair next to Robbi. She was alone and although she seemed shy, her body language oozed a quiet confidence. She sat stiff and straight with perfect posture, although on the petite side ... perhaps 5'1" or 5'2". Her heart-shaped face was framed by wispy bangs, tapered slightly longer at the sides; her long, shiny, straight brown hair with sunny highlights was pulled up into a high ponytail, which bounced saucily as she sat and looked around. She was casually dressed in skinny jeans, faded and worn out in the right places, a snug-fitting black tank top and red, two-inch platform sandals. It was a cool evening, and her Arizona Cardinals black zip-up hoodie hung loosely on her shoulders. Tag's eyebrows shot up when he noticed the NFL jacket. *Football fan ... cool.* Tag had a volatile love/hate relationship with the sport, and enjoyed debating the virtues of the many college and pro teams with customers.

Her voice was animated and musical, but what made Tag look twice were her eyes — huge chocolate-brown orbs rimmed in amber with tiny golden flecks. They sparkled even when she was not smiling, with lush lashes that fluttered softly against the porcelain skin of her cheeks. She had two Cindy Crawford-like beauty marks on one cheekbone and deep dimples.

Experiencing an unfamiliar shortness of breath, Tag wondered how the brown-eyed beauty had inexplicably sucked all the oxygen out of the room. Shaking his head in bewilderment, he could only ponder, *Shit! Gotta cut down on my weed intake. It's affecting my damn breathing.*

Her eyes scanned the extensive craft beer selection the establishment offered, and a wide smile graced her lips when she spied the one she was looking for. Tag had been watching her since she sat down and could tell she was ready to order.

"May I have an Alaskan Stout, please?" Her voice was soft and melodic, as if she made her living in some sort of performing capacity. Tag did a double take but schooled his features to conceal his reaction to her choice — although his lip had started to curl upward on one side.

"It's a rare woman who can handle a badass stout. I'm quite impressed."

Her shy giggle and sparkling eyes seemed to light up the area around her as if a thousand tiny stars had all decided to twinkle simultaneously. Tag was mesmerized for a moment, soaking in everything he could about this woman. He forced himself to look away, taking in Robbi's raised eyebrows in Tyler's direction. He coughed and looked back at the woman, ignoring his friends' unsubtle smirks.

"My dad makes craft beers and he's partial to the oatier blends. What's not to like?" She took a giant gulp to prove her point, licking her lips in appreciation. "It's like an oatmeal cookie with a caramel kick. Yummy."

Suppressing a goofy grin, Tag pulled his eyes reluctantly from hers once more and went to serve other thirsty patrons. The bar area had suddenly become standing room only.

From the corner of his eye, Tag noticed the woman's phone, which had been lying on the bar, light up with a text message. She excitedly grabbed it and proceeded to spend several minutes typing furiously. It was obvious she was texting someone special; her radiant smile and flashing dimples were a dead giveaway.

I wouldn't mind crawling into one of those dimples and staying there for a while. Whoa! Where did THAT come from? He shook his thoughts clear and couldn't help but wonder who was texting her. His gaze traveled her face, then her neck, where his eyes lingered. *Is that a hickey? Well, fuck me.*

A completely unfamiliar twinge of discomfort invaded his stomach. He shrugged indifferently, as he reached for a bottle of tequila to pour himself a shot, which he downed immediately, foregoing the usual salt and lime ritual. Alcohol was Tag's go-to self-medication whenever uninvited emotions threatened to bubble to the surface of his serene, carefree exterior.

Sighing audibly as she tucked the phone into her purse, the pretty brunette ordered a second drink and pushed a twenty-dollar bill toward Tag. His broad back was turned to her, and her gaze lowered momentarily to his tight-fitting jeans. Her eyes rose just in the nick of time as he faced her, setting the beverage down, declaring, "It isn't every day a beautiful woman orders an Alaskan Stout. Keep your money, brown eyes, it's on me. I'm Tag, by the way." He flashed a devilish wink and a smile — not his usual sexy panty-dropper — a softer, less practiced, more genuine curve of his lips. His tongue snaked out to lick his lip piercing nervously, and as he stared into her startlingly beautiful eyes, a zing of electricity jolted his heart and then seemed to travel downward. He winced as he felt his dick strain against the zipper of his jeans.

She held out her hand, and smiled. "I'm Emery. Emery Lawson. It's nice to meet you, Tag."

Stammering as if his brain and mouth had mysteriously disconnected, Tag managed to mumble, "Um, it's m-my pleasure, Emery. Let me introduce you to Robbi and Tyler." Handshakes ensued as Tag continued, ultimately regaining his confidence. "They're newlyweds ... been married about two months, right? I actually witnessed their first date."

"Well, it wasn't an *official* date at the time," Robbi giggled, clarifying the details to Emery which enabled the guys to converse privately for a moment.

"Ty, can we talk? Outside. Robbi, you mind if I steal your husband for a sec?"

"Of course not. It'll give us girls a chance to become better acquainted." Robbi angled her barstool to face Emery.

"Be back in a minute, baby. Love you." Tyler took her hand and kissed it several times, and then stood up as he placed another loving kiss on the top of her head.

Tag downed a second shot of Patron, and then motioned

for Tyler to follow him. The men walked out of the bar to the parking lot and stood against the brick wall. Tag's usual tanned face paled, reflecting the moonlight eerily. He removed a joint from his shirt pocket and lit it in one smooth motion, inhaling deeply to calm himself.

"Did you tell Robbi anything about my past and all that shit I told you months ago?" Tag hissed, blowing out smoke through trembling lips. "I'm not fuckin' around here, man."

"No. Not one damn word to anybody. Why?"

"I don't know. That girl ... she kinda reminded me of my Randi. It spooked me a bit. That's never happened before. Yeah, I've been seeing her face everywhere for twelve long years, but I've always known it's all up here." Touching his temple with his forefinger, Tag took another long drag on the joint before passing it to Tyler, who indulged in a few casual puffs before handing it back.

"I'm well aware it's wishful thinking, like visions, hallucinations, or whatever," Tag continued, taking a final few deep drags on the joint before pinching it out between his thumb and forefinger and tucking it back into his pocket. "That chick just kinda looks like her. I'm a little freaked out. Her eyes ..." Tag swallowed the lump in his throat, acutely aware that the alcohol pumping through his veins loosened his usual restraint. Over-sharing personal feelings was not his usual behavior, even with his best friend.

Tyler's hand reached out and landed on Tag's shoulder. "Don't over-analyze this shit, buddy. Just go with it. You're obviously attracted to her, and she seems like a nice girl, kinda normal, you know? Robbi's chattin' her up right now and probably gettin' the lowdown. I'll fill you in later, okay, buddy? You just continue to be your adorable, charming self." Wide green eyes glared at Tyler in undisguised astonishment.

"What the fuck are you babbling about? You trying to set

me up? With her?" Pinching the bridge of his nose, Tag simply shook his head.

"And what the hell is wrong with her, Tag? She seems sweet."

A cheerless, sarcastic snicker escaped from Tag's grim lips. "T-man, do you fuckin' know me at all? I don't do sweet, nice, or normal. You know I prefer slutty, crazy, and disposable. Hey, I figure if I'm goin' straight to Hell, then I may as well take the scenic route in the HOV lane. Remember the time we had the epic five-way, when the two of us picked up those three sorority girls? Dude, that was the best fuckin' —"

"Tag, *enough!*" Grunting disgustedly, Tyler sneered, "Yeah, I know all about your love life, or should I say loveless life, because that used to be me. Slutty, crazy, disposable — lather, rinse, repeat. You're the goddamn hat trick of heartbreak, buddy. Been there. Fuck. That."

Tyler affectionately smacked Tag's cheek a few times; the final motion had some power behind it and caused a slight yelp from Tag.

"What the fuck, Ty?" Tag was taken aback by Tyler's semi-aggressive action. Although Ty was a few inches taller, Tag had never felt intimidated by him before.

Tyler's powerful arms caged Tag in against the cold stone wall of the building, then he lowered his head so the two men were nose-to-nose. Pinning Tag with his narrowed eyes, Tyler growled menacingly, the volume of his voice escalating with every utterance.

"That fucking devil who lives up there?" His large forefinger poked Tag's forehead repeatedly. "Inside that thick head of yours — you know, the monster who terrorizes your dreams, eating you alive from the inside out until you rot? You need to face him right the fuck now. Make him your friend, or else. He. Will. End. You." Exasperated, Tag threaded his fingers through his hair, causing the platinum spikes to stand on end.

Tyler inhaled deeply, then blew his breath out slowly, shaking his head in frustration. "Tag, wake the fuck up! Your life is circling the drain. You're thirty-two and going on dead. It's time for a change, buddy. I wasted more years than you have been alive on this Earth, but look at me now. I am living proof it's never too late." An icy chill crept its way down Tag's spine as Tyler's vehement words sunk in.

Tyler has been more of a father to me than my old man ever was. He's never steered me wrong before. Maybe it's time for me to listen.

After a genuine man-hug and a few hearty slaps on the back, the two men returned to find Robbi and Emery chatting comfortably like long-lost sisters. They seemed to be sharing email addresses and cell numbers when Tyler approached Robbi from behind, snaking his arms around her waist while his face nuzzled her neck.

"Baby, we'd better hit the road soon. I have a big day tomorrow," Tyler muttered as he helped her don her jacket.

"And my first-graders are planning our spring garden again. You're going to help like last year, right, babe?"

"Yep. Looking forward to it." He leaned down to kiss her nose softly. Emery looked on, admiring their happiness with a smile that didn't quite reach her shining eyes.

Emery held out her hand to Tyler, who shook it warmly. "It was lovely meeting you both."

"You, too," came their dual response. "Text me anytime," Robbi added. "I can help you settle into your apartment or we can go shopping. And if you are serious about visiting my classroom and teaching an art lesson, let me know when and I'll set it up."

Tag grabbed Tyler in a hurried bro-hug. "Thanks for the chat. I'll see what I can do," he said vaguely, purposely not alluding to what they were actually discussing, as the two men exchanged knowing glances.

Turning to Robbi, Tag was surprised when she wrapped him in a snug embrace. He immediately stiffened at her warm touch, but managed to return the gesture. Tyler smiled and nodded his approval of her actions.

"Nice seeing ya, Tag. Take care of my new BFF Emery here. She's a stranger in town and may need a tour guide." Robbi gave him a mischievous wink and a chaste kiss on the cheek.

Tag nodded and flashed Robbi a sincere smile as the couple walked away. *Alone at last. I've been watchin' Emery since she came in, and if this damn bar ever clears out, maybe I can actually talk to her.*

A small group of men in business attire strolled over, two taking the vacated stools and the others crowding around. They eyed Emery surreptitiously, although the one sitting next to her openly gawked. Rolling his eyes in subtle annoyance, Tag patiently listened to their beverage orders and busily began pouring. The bar regulars had no trouble spotting newcomers, especially beautiful women like Emery. Tag thought he overheard one of the men whisper, "Fresh meat." He couldn't be sure, but made a mental note to stay on high alert. Several law offices and a biotech company were located in the neighborhood, so occasionally attorneys and corporate-type clientele frequented the upscale bar. *These MBA assholes better be on their best goddamn behavior, or I'll show them my MBA — Motherfuckin' Bad Ass.*

About an hour after Robbi and Tyler departed, the game ended and people started dispersing. Tag finally had a chance to engage Emery in conversation.

"Do I detect a slight Texas twang?" he asked inquisitively, making a conscious effort not to revert to his own former speech patterns. Ten years in California and a lot of effort had banished all audible hints of his place of birth.

"You have a good ear." Emery chuckled. "I was born in San Antonio, but my family moved to Phoenix when I was in middle school." Tag sensed a slight hesitation and suspected Emery was not being 100 percent truthful. *Who am I to judge? My whole fucking life is fabricated.*

"I teach art part time at Arizona State University; took a four-month sabbatical so I could study at the San Francisco Art Institute for the spring semester. I'm renting a cute little apartment on Chestnut near Powell Street and just moved in two days ago."

"Welcome to the 'hood. You like SFAI? I hear it's a great school." Tag hung on her every word, tilting his head in rapt interest.

"The few times I visited, I felt very much at home. My class starts on Monday, so I'll know more then."

Turning to pour another stout, Tag was still acutely aware of her presence; a fresh citrusy fragrance was sensually permeating his nostrils. *Randi's scent? No ... hers had been more floral, or ... woodsy? Fuck. I'm losing it.*

A shrill female voice could be heard over the crowd, as Ginger made an appearance out of nowhere. "Hey, Tag! Wanna do something later, baby?" Leaning on the bar right next to Emery, the redhead gave her a quick once-over, dismissing her with a look of obvious disdain.

Tag seethed on the inside, although years of bartending had taught him to maintain control and keep his facial expressions unruffled. *Fuckin' bitch with her ridiculously absurd stripper name. She'd better leave, pronto.* Casually scratching the beginnings of a beard on his face, he shrugged at the redhead.

"Sorry. Already made plans," Tag stated unapologetically, his voice cool with no hint of sentiment whatsoever.

"Humph!" she snorted petulantly, tilting her head toward Emery. "That's not what he said last night." Emery wisely ignored her; she had reached for her phone and was already texting up a storm. "No worries. I know most of the guys in here." Ginger straightened haughtily and strode to the other side of the bar where a group of rowdy drunks welcomed her with open arms. Emery finished her text, placing her phone back on the bar.

"Sorry about that." His heartfelt apology was laced with embarrassment. Emery's grin was devilish as she took a long gulp of her frothy beverage.

"So, Tag, 'fess up. Do you actually have plans tonight?" Her chocolate-brown eyes glistened with amusement.

Pinning her with his trademark emerald-green stare, he leaned over and whispered, "I do. I'm off in about ten minutes and was hoping I could share a quiet drink with a certain beautiful brown-eyed, stout-guzzling, intriguing woman. You up for it, Emery? I also just might quiz you on that hickey, so be prepared." He shot her a playful wink, before turning to serve other customers.

As Tag lay in bed enjoying a light breeze from the ceiling fan, he replayed the evening's events in his mind. Emery's face was ever-present as he recalled their relaxed, but pleasantly intimate, one-on-one conversation. She'd revealed she had a nine-year-old son who had been born shortly after she graduated from high school. She'd never married the child's father, but they were still close friends, and the boy would be visiting her while she was attending SFAI. Tag shared carefully selected tidbits of his life as well; he made sure never to overtly lie, skirting around the more sordid events, and avoided mentioning specific cities in Texas. First, he'd disclosed that he had become disillusioned with the university scene, and decided to strike out on his own. He was proficient at summing up his two-year road trip in a single paragraph; one he had recited scores of times.

"I had a bit of wanderlust, I guess you could say. I roamed up the entire West Coast from San Diego to Alaska, wandering aimlessly, no maps, only a few possessions, clothes, whatever could fit in my truck. I had a shitload of credit cards, but wanted to see if I could survive without that luxury. I slept in my truck most nights, worked in the fields in California ... strawberries, artichokes, and some vineyards. Those experiences were life-changing. I ended up in Alaska, worked the pipeline for almost two years, and then found myself here in San Fran."

Tag chuckled to himself as he reached for the fan's remote control, turning it higher.

Of course, I conveniently left out all the shit about how I'd worn the same filthy clothes day after day until they disintegrated right off my body into rags, or how I'd taken a detour to Vegas. Fuck, what a colossal mistake that was. Sin City — aptly named — a decadent hellhole if there ever was one. I managed to win over a grand at Texas Hold 'Em then blew it on a three-way. You can order whatever you want in Vegas over the fuckin' phone. And it's delivered right to your door ... a three-way, a blow job, or a goddamn pizza. They refused to deliver the whores to my truck, however. Believe me, I tried. I also didn't mention the nights I'd spent in various jail cells, mostly for fighting or mouthing off to cops. Jail wasn't that bad, except for being in a confined space and sharing a toilet with a bunch of creepy degenerates. At least it's warm and you're fed; shit food, but it eases the hunger somewhat. It was more than I deserved at the time.

Sleep overtook him eventually; but as usual, it didn't last. He awoke in a puddle of his own sweat — usually with a raging hard-on — frantically searching for someone who was never there. Tag looked forward to the dreams; they took his pain away, even if only for a few moments.

Often Tag sensed his conscious mind would disconnect from his body, floating miles above although he could still feel himself asleep. He watched as his head turned on his pillow; and still, even after so much time had passed, he couldn't quite remember why Randi's hauntingly beautiful amber eyes were not gazing back into his own. Her presence was still so real. Every detail vivid — the minty taste of her toothpaste on his lips and tongue, her perfume on his pillow, her soft, bare skin pressed against him. Photos of Randi's face were not necessary. The sparse array of freckles, which dotted her cheeks when kissed by the Texas sun, would be right in front of him. Most of all, he recalled the wet heat between her legs. Being inside Randi had always felt like home. A nanosecond later, reality would broadside him as the visions dissipated.

Far too often, Tag wished he'd died in the crash with her. *At least, she would have had my arms wrapped around her so she wouldn't have been afraid.* There was no doubt in his mind she would have been terrified at the final moment. The thought made him ill. He'd never even had the chance to see her beautiful face one last time; it was a closed casket. His mom had said it was probably a blessing under the circumstances.

For over a decade, he had seen Randi's angelic countenance everywhere, in every woman who crossed his path. After she died, he often meditated at night and thought of her, praying she would permeate his dreams. Often she did materialize, but it would always be another horrific dream, one of many endless agonizing sleepless nights when an ethereal, amber-eyed angel would appear; her lips moved, but the message was not always clear.

For years, Tag had blamed God for Randi's tragic accident. He could not fathom how a loving God could be so cruel. He concluded God had a vengeful plan to teach ungrateful humans, like himself, to value life and not take things for granted. Memories of countless times when he had driven drunk haunted him, convincing him Randi's death was a justified punishment for his own sins. *Her death has to be my fault somehow. Randi never hurt a soul, never did an unkind thing, or said a mean word to anyone. She was the unparalleled epitome of an angel on Earth ... loving, compassionate, perfect. Why couldn't I have been taken instead? I would have given my life gladly if it meant saving Randi. I know why ... not a doubt in my mind. God. Does. Not. Exist.*

A sudden, startling reverberation caused Tag to sit up in bed. His internal alarm was on full alert. Earthquake? Break-in? *What the fuck?* An eerie warmth infiltrated the room as the morning sunrise trickled through the partially closed blinds. Randi's lovely countenance emerged, a blurred shadow, indistinct as though gazing through a gauzy, semi-translucent curtain or perhaps thick clouds; it was impossible to see anything clearly. Tag blinked several times as a pair of golden eyes came into brief focus — completely absent of deep brown, only bright amber. A soft voice wafted around him. Her words were serene and peaceful; he felt no fear whatsoever. The message lasted a few seconds ... or was it several hours? He had no way of knowing.

Please, Cole. Live your life, baby. You need to let me go.

Writhing in a pool of his own sweat, Tag was startled awake by the raspy sounds of his own cries. Another torturous, cruel dream had invaded his already agitated mind, but this one had been terrifyingly real. Burrowing back under the sheets, Tag clutched his pillow closely to his bare chest until he eased into a restless half-slumber. A final serene image flitted across his mind, easing the pain a bit. A beautiful brunette who drank Alaskan stout, of all unlikely beverages. A sweet, slightly guarded girl who appeared to be a bit nervous during their conversation. *Emery.* Tag had never heard the name before, and wondered why. It had such a bewitching sound to it and dripped off his lips like honey. *Emery. I need to know more about you.*

Chapter 5

"Beauty awakens the soul to act."
– Dante Alighieri

NORTH STAR BAR

Tag sat at a quiet corner table. It was 5:30, although he was not due to start working the bar until 8 p.m. Emery had agreed to have dinner with him at 6 p.m., but he wanted to have a calming drink prior to her arrival. Their meeting the previous night and subsequent conversation had left Tag in an unfamiliar, yet far from unpleasant, state of bewilderment. Although Randi had invaded his dreams as she usually did, he had thought of nothing but Emery since he awoke in the morning. Even an intense workout at the gym could not erase the anxiety he was experiencing. Tyler's words also stuck with him, searing themselves into his brain: *It's time for a change. Never too late.*

Emery's eyes had lit up when she talked about her young son, sharing a head shot of him on her phone. Tag could easily see the striking resemblance.

He recalled how an unusual warmth had invaded his chest as her sweet, silky voice — although pure and innocent when conversing — became full-on phone-sex husky when she threw back her head and laughed. It was a wake-up call that went straight to his cock; a sensation he had not felt in many long years. A twinge of guilt coursed through him ... betrayal, as if he were cheating on Randi's memory. Tag was a self-described man-whore of the worst kind, but he hadn't gotten a hard-on from just talking to a girl since he was a teenager, with the exception of Randi. Most of the women he met in bars posed no challenge, causing his dick to shrivel up and hide. His body only responded and became aroused from direct contact — a warm, wet pussy, a willing mouth, or a tight fist.

This stunning brunette, however, actually resembled Randi. It was uncanny and unnerved Tag to say the least. Numerous times, he had endeavored to pry his intense gaze off her, but it was difficult, if not impossible.

Checking his cell phone for the tenth time, Tag saw it was 5:55. He was engrossed in wondering if he had gotten any texts from her, always thinking the worst. *Did something come up? Had she changed her mind and cancelled?* He looked up, suddenly noticing she was already sitting opposite him.

"Hey, Tag! How're you doing?"

"Hi, Emery. I was just checkin' to make sure you were still coming." A waitress immediately came over and deposited Emery's preferred beverage in front of her. She smiled at Tag through her long, dark lashes. "Wow. Excellent service. Thanks."

They ate, drank, chatted, and laughed like two old friends might have done. The conversation was easy and comfortable. Tag asked a few questions about her art class, which she answered animatedly. He was enthralled. At one point, he made her laugh so hard, a few drops of her drink trickled down her chin, landing in her cleavage. Tag's eyes widened as they traced the downward path.

Fuck, Valley of the Dolls! Tag swallowed hard, running his tongue along his lower lip while images of licking every drop, sweat included, danced behind his eyelids.

Emery, curious about the immediate neighborhood, asked numerous questions. So far, she had explored several running paths and bike trails; now her main objective seemed to be to locate some good restaurants, movie theaters, and a nearby gym.

"Well, you are in luck, brown eyes. My day job just happens to be personal trainer extraordinaire at a popular fitness center conveniently located a mere four blocks away from your apartment. I could meet you there tomorrow and give you the grand tour as well as an introductory workout." He pulled his wallet from his back jeans pocket and withdrew a business card.

Tag Coleman
Exercise 2 Exorcise
Banish your demons through healthy living!

"Thanks, Tag. Cool slogan. How did you come up with that?" His reaction was pensive, eyes staring downward at the card.

"Nothing gets rid of mental demons like physical pain and a fuckton of sweat." He forced a grin but his eyes were distant.

Emery grinned widely and nodded her approval as she accepted Tag's offer, tucking the card in her purse. His demeanor quickly changed as their eyes met and his smile exuded genuine warmth, but apprehension still resided in the pit of his stomach.

After dinner, Tag recommended they share a slice of the homemade pie du jour for dessert. "Today is apple-rhubarb," he revealed. When she suggested a scoop of ice cream with it, he vehemently shook his head.

"Nope. Don't need it, trust me." The dessert arrived and Emery bounced in her seat in anticipation, shoving a large forkful into her mouth. Tag followed with an even larger bite.

"Some woman in the neighborhood makes it from scratch. Good, huh?" Tag mumbled, chewing at the same time. Emery made an exaggerated orgasm-type face, eyes rolling and eyelashes fluttering.

"Oh. My. God! Absolutely scrumptious. It's hard to find a tasty, home-style pie nowadays." Her pink tongue licked the fork with appreciation, and an image of capturing her luscious lips with his mouth briefly invaded his thoughts. He shifted uncomfortably in his seat.

"Every day is different, depending on her mood and what's in season. Her pumpkin cheesecake pie ..." Tag sighed in appreciation as his voice drifted off. Emery's delightful giggle brought him down to Earth. *Holy fuck, she is cute. Actually, cute doesn't do her justice. She's beautiful.*

Noticing a wayward tendril had escaped her ponytail, Tag reached out to tuck it gently behind her ear. His fingertips lingered on her lobe for a bit longer than necessary. It happened so quickly, so spontaneously, he didn't even have time to think. The inappropriateness of his intimate action didn't dawn on him until he saw the unmistakable look of alarm in her eyes. Her lips parted in surprise, as she rolled her bottom lip between her perfect teeth, biting hard.

Realizing he had caught her off-guard, Tag froze for an instant, then rushed to apologize, mentally kicking himself for touching her, even though it sent an unexpected sizzle through his body.

"I'm so sorry. I just wasn't thinking. I, um, used to do that all the time to my ... baby sister. I guess I just miss her. She's married and lives on the East Coast. Again, I apologize, Emery." The blatant lie rolled off his tongue with ease. He didn't even have a sister; it was simply another falsehood that comprised his fraudulent existence.

"No worries, Tag. It actually felt nice." Her shy gaze was barely visible behind her lush, dark lashes as she peered at him from across the table. Tag felt movement behind the zipper of his jeans again as he squirmed ever so subtly in his seat, placing both fists on the table. *Good thing I wore long sleeves tonight. Don't need to scare her off with all my tattoos. Shit! Too late.*

Emery's eyes immediately fell, scrutinizing his large hands as she read the tattooed message spelled out in an old-fashioned, ornate font on his knuckles: **'ETERNITY'**. More colorful tattoos peeked out of the long-sleeved, snug-fitting black T-shirt, which clearly outlined his substantial chest and arm muscles. Her hands lightly touched his, both forefingers tracing the eight letters that adorned his fingers, just below the knuckle. Her lovely eyes met his as she whispered, "Beautiful work. Is there a story behind the word?"

Nervously chewing on his lip ring, he murmured, "Well, I guess you could say I planned on eternity, but then I lost it." Desperately wanting to change the subject, he quickly interjected, "You have any ink, Emery?"

Her face visibly brightened. "I got one when my son was born, a portrait of his sweet face at about two months old. I'm planning on getting another when he turns ten, then the final one when he's twenty. I want a few more eventually, different designs. I just need to do some research and decide exactly what to get. I'll probably design them myself." She smiled shyly, obviously uncomfortable with self-praise. Unease settled in Tag. Many of his tattoos held great personal significance; each one represented turning points in his life. His love for Randi and her tragic death could be discerned in almost every design.

As if on cue, Emery's phone buzzed and Tag was granted the momentary distraction he desperately needed. Her gentle touch had disoriented him to the extent of light-headedness, which, for once, was not exclusively from alcohol consumption.

"You mind if I answer this, Tag? It's my son. We always exchange a few texts before he goes to sleep."

"No problem. I'll be right back." Tag grabbed their empty

glasses and deposited them on the bar before heading to the men's room. Afterwards, he mentally cursed himself for going commando. *Fuck! I could use the tighty whiteys to keep my damn cock at bay.*

Stopping at the bar to refresh their drinks, he passed Ginger sitting in her usual seat, arms draped around some random glassy-eyed patron, shooting Tag a death-glare, especially after noting his dinner companion. He shrugged and kept walking, not bothering to give her a second thought.

After completing her text conversation, Emery replaced the phone on the table. Tag's natural curiosity took over. "So what kind of interests does he have?"

"Oh, you know, the usual boy stuff. His current obsession is football. Because of the proximity and community involvement of the Arizona Cardinals, we have many after-school programs in and around Metro Phoenix. An acquaintance of Randy's dad is running one in particular for eight to ten-year-olds. Training sessions are starting soon, tryouts to follow. He's determined to kick butt and hopefully make the team."

Tag's heart had skipped a couple of beats when he heard Emery say her son's name. *Randy. Holy shit.*

Tag looked down at the phone Emery was gently pushing in his direction, displaying numerous photos of Randy.

"Alex took him shopping yesterday for football gear. Some of the photos are from his ninth birthday last month." Tag gingerly took the phone in his hand and scrolled through the slide show. Emery dragged her chair next to him, pointing out other people in the photos. The attention Tag paid to every detail brought a wide smile to her face, as he meticulously scrutinized every image, nodding and making relevant comments.

"He has a good grip. See how he's holding the ball here? And the height he gets off the ground on this jump? Shows impressive lower body strength for a nine-year-old. And …" Tag's voice trailed off as he hissed in a sharp breath. "Is that Larry Fitzgerald?"

Emery nodded enthusiastically, eyes shining. "Yeah. My father has a client who's connected to the team. We went to a practice and Randy was able to meet his favorite player … got his autograph on a football, too." She heaved an audible sigh as a faraway look clouded her eyes. Tag laid his hand gently on her forearm, lightly feathering her soft skin with his fingertips. *She feels like silk.*

"You must be missing him bad right about now. When is he coming to visit? I'd love to meet him," Tag murmured, wishing he could brush away the lone tear, which trickled down her cheek. After one inappropriate gesture, his brain was not rushing into a second, no matter what his body might be dictating.

"Next weekend, and every other, or possibly every third weekend depending on what pops up, for the next few months. We'll be racking up the frequent-flier miles big time." Tag was relieved to see the beginning of a smile finally grace her lips.

"Well, I played a lot of football back in high school and college, and I'd be happy to coach your boy, prepare him for tryouts," Tag volunteered.

"That would be awesome. You sure you don't mind?"

"Not at all. I think it'll be fun." A slow smile turned his lips upward as his pierced tongue lightly toyed with his lower lip ring. He couldn't help but notice she was staring at his mouth. "What?" he probed, a mischievous gleam in his eyes.

"So … what's kissing like with those piercings?" Realizing what she said a nanosecond too late, her eyes widened with dismay as a bright blush overtook her neck and cheeks.

Licking the tiny silver ring again, he pinned her with a bright green stare.

"Amazing. Would you like a demonstration?" There was no trace of a grin, although his eyes held a devilish twinkle.

Emery's discomfort was palpable as she swallowed hard. Despite the nervousness, she finally found her voice. "You are so bad, Tag." She coyly gazed at him through her thick lashes. His breathy retort was accompanied by a laugh.

"You started it, brown eyes." Taking a deep inhale, he was hasty to add with a slight chuckle, "I guess that remark was kinda presumptuous of me. My mouth is not always connected to my brain." *They're both on different planets half the time, especially around you!*

She laughed bashfully. "Well, no more than my question was. I guess that makes us even." Ignoring the inner emotions roiling beneath the surface, Tag enjoyed the moment of innocent flirting. It had been a long time since he engaged in sexy, stimulating, conversational banter with such a down-to-earth, intelligent woman. He had gotten used to the easy women who normally gravitated toward him. Throwing a quick glance over his shoulder, his eyes raked over Ginger and two other female barflies. *No 'verbal lubrication', pun intended, needed with those skanks ... just a Benjamin tossed on the bar was always enough to garner their complete attention.* A mollifying warmth immediately replaced his temporary disgust as he turned his attention back to the brown-haired beauty seated beside him.

"So, it's a date, okay? You, me, and Randy next weekend in Golden Gate Park? I'll bring the football. In the meantime, why don't you meet me at my gym tomorrow around noon?"

Lying in bed after another busy night at the bar, Tag found himself restlessly tossing and turning as usual. Jerking off always helped him relax, so he slid his hand down his boxer briefs and began stroking his already throbbing cock. Closing his eyes, the sweet lilt of Emery's giggles filled his ears, causing his hand to tighten and speed up. Grabbing a handful of tissues from the box conveniently placed on the nightstand, he groaned out his release, breathing heavily.

What the fuck am I doing? A date with Emery and her kid. Randy. What are the odds? Unsure he could handle it, he considered cancelling. Reaching to turn off the lamp, his eyes fell upon his blinking phone. He had missed a text.

Emery: I wanted to thank you again for offering to coach Randy. He is gonna be over the moon when I tell him!

Tag: My pleasure. Looking forward to it.

Emery: Thanks for dinner, too. It was fun. Good night.

Tag: 'Night.

Okay, I can do this. And besides, it'll be good to have a football in my hand again.

Chapter 6

"My course is set for an uncharted sea."
– Dante Alighieri (Paradise)

EMERY

Emery woke up to the blaring alarm clock. Her cell phone was blinking, indicating a text message. Smiling, she eagerly hit 'reply'.

EMERY: MORNING, LOVE. MISS U!

RANDY: MISS U 2.

EMERY: GREAT NEWS. MET A GUY WHO PLAYED FOOTBALL AND HE OFFERED TO TRAIN YOU, PREPARE YOU FOR TRYOUTS. BRING YOUR GEAR NEXT WEEKEND.

RANDY: OMG, COOL. THANKS. GOTTA GO, DAD'S WAITING. LOVE U.

EMERY: LOVE U 2!

Emery leaned back on her fluffy pillows and closed her eyes, rewinding selected scenes from the previous night's dinner.

Tag was nothing like she had expected. Although Emery had been subtly brainwashed over the years to despise Cole Taggart, she never could. His agony the day of Randi's funeral still haunted her.

He looks completely different now, the long brown hair and affable, approachable demeanor gone. In his place is Tag's invented persona — short sun-bleached hair, the crazy piercings, all tatted up, and badass. Did he always have that little cleft in his chin? I have no memory of that. I would not have recognized him if I passed him on the street. His eyes, however… those jade-green, transparent pools. Oh. My. God. No mistaking them. Exactly the same as all those years ago. Cole gave me my first kiss from a boy, although technically it didn't count. He was my cousin's boyfriend and it was on my bloody elbow, but I've never forgotten that moment. Thank God, I've changed. There's no way he would recognize me. I'm easily a foot taller, don't have those god-awful braces anymore and that goofy pixie hairdo grew out in high school. My first impression of him was totally off base. He was actually quite charming last night — funny, sweet, definitely sexy. And volunteering to work with Randy? Pretty cool. I need to get close to him and find out what really happened.

Hurriedly donning her workout clothes and sneakers, Emery grabbed her gym bag and headed out the door. The Starbucks line wasn't too bad and shortly she was relaxing at a corner table with her usual dark roast and blueberry scone. After putting her iPod earbuds in, it was time to catch up on email. Several minutes later, a rather large body joined her at the tiny table and she was surprised to see Tag sitting across from her, sporting a giant grin on his face.

"You wouldn't be stalking me now, would you?" Her eyes sparkled with playful humor. Tag's disappointed pout was adorable.

"Damn. And here I thought my badass disguise as your very own personal workout buddy would be sure to fool you." They shared a spontaneous laugh, eyeing each other warily. He yawned then took a few big gulps of his large coffee. Frowning, he stood up, muttering, "Excuse me for a sec. I need a few extra shots of espresso. Be right back." He returned shortly with an explanation, grinning. "Didn't sleep well last night and need the extra buzz."

"So how long have you been working as a personal trainer?" Emery tilted her head, eagerly awaiting his response.

"Oh, I guess it's been four or five years now. I have a dozen or so regular clients and help at the gym sometimes when they're short-handed. It's part-time and I have unlimited use of the entire club and can bring friends to train with me anytime. No charge."

"Thanks. I must be the luckiest new girl in town to have met you!"

No class was being held in the spacious aerobic room when they arrived, so Tag and Emery began by doing a few stretches on the large mat. "Let's get to work. Do you have any specific goals or muscle groups you'd like to focus on? I usually ask new clients to identify their problem areas, but I can clearly see you don't have any." His appreciative eyes scanned her figure head-to-toe.

"Seriously, Tag? If that's true, then I guess I don't need *you*, do I?" she teased, shaking her head, making her ponytail swish back and forth. "Actually I run every day, so I'm not worried about cardio. I think my legs are fine, but I wouldn't mind a bit more muscle mass in my upper body." She reached over her legs, grasping her toes easily as her forehead rested on her knees.

"Great flexibility and I would say your legs are way more than fine. Okay, let's start with shoulders, biceps, and then triceps. Follow me to the free-weight area."

They stood and were ready to leave the room when a young girl approached Tag, purposely ignoring the fact he already had his hand lightly placed on the small of Emery's lower back, in the process of walking her out. Emery had noticed most of the female members were ogling Tag; his intimidating build, good looks, barely-there ripped tank, and colorful body art certainly made for attractive eye-candy.

"Hey, Tag! Think you could show me the trap pull-down machine?" She pursed her bright red lips while fluttering her false eyelashes coyly.

"I'm with a client at the moment, Misty. Maybe some other time, okay? And remember what I told you. Get rid of those long fingernails if you're serious about weight-training," Tag added tersely, ushering Emery out without even a backward glance.

"Sorry about that," he said with a grimace. "Some people have no manners. Besides, I've showed her how to use that fucking machine like ten times already. It's not that complicated. You just have to pull down. Duh." He blew out a frustrated breath.

They worked on upper-body muscle groups for over an hour. Tag was a patient and effective instructor. His emphasis was on good form, and his hands were on Emery the entire time, but always in an appropriate manner. He would demonstrate the exercise first, and then watch closely as she copied his movements. If he needed to make a correction to her form, his touch was consistently gentle yet firm. Her strength was exceptionally misleading for her small frame. He had underestimated her capabilities several times, giving her hand-weights, which were too light. He was spotting her for a particular incline chest-press exercise, when his face came dangerously close to hers; she was momentarily distracted, breathing heavily.

"You okay, Em?" Tag's brows rose in concern. Nodding firmly, Emery grinned at him as she leaned closer to his neck, inhaling deeply through her nose. Mildly taken aback, Tag openly stared at her. "Did you just *sniff* me?" His eyes widened in faux-horror. Giggling, she stammered, "Sorry. You smell like a Christmas tree. I love that scent of pine, kinda woodsy. It's simply yummy." She took several more appreciative sniffs, her nose gently tickling his cheek.

"It's Bath and Body Works fresh balsam shower gel," he exclaimed. "And I'm pretty damn proud of the fact I was able to recall the exact word-for-word name of the product." It was Emery's turn to be stunned and downright speechless. She was doubled over clutching her stomach, shoulders shaking, hands covering her mouth in a vain attempt to stifle her delightful giggles.

Holding back his own amusement, Tag pretended to be offended. "Hey, you girls aren't the only ones who wanna smell nice." Throwing his arm around her neck in a fake chokehold, they both dissolved into near-hysterical laughter. Emery noticed a few of the other employees were staring at Tag intently; mild looks of disbelief crossed their faces. *What the hell was that all about? It's like they've never heard Tag laugh before.*

As they walked back to the aerobics room for some cool-down stretches, Tag reached behind the counter and grabbed two large bottles of water.

"You did great. How do you feel?"

"Good. I'm sure I'll be a little achy tomorrow, but right now, I feel fine. Exhilarated. Thanks, Tag." She licked her lips; the cold, refreshing water soothed her dry throat.

"My pleasure. You have perfect form, by the way." His eyes appreciatively scanned her from head to toe. "Great muscle definition, too."

Heat covered her cheeks as she gazed shyly downward. "Well, I studied anatomy and kinesthesia extensively in college. Knowledge of the body's position in space is essential to an artist."

"I thought so, which is the main reason I skipped the musculature vocabulary portion of my introductory session. Most of the chicks here, their eyes glaze over if I use too many big words. No offense, Emery, present company excepted, of course. So will I ever have an opportunity to see some of your artwork?" Tag seemed genuinely interested in everything she had to say, his eyes rarely leaving hers.

"I can show you my online gallery, and I'll be working on a few projects for class while I'm here in town, so you'll probably see those, too."

"Cool. I look forward to it. So, do you have plans for the rest of the day?" Tag shifted back and forth, awaiting her reply.

"I do, as a matter of fact," Emery purred. "And I think you should join me."

"In art as in love, instinct is enough." – Anatole France

TAG

Emery invited him to accompany her to SFMOMA — the San Francisco Museum of Modern Art. He could not remember the last time he had been inside a museum. It was definitely not his thing but with Emery, it was fascinating. She became his personal tour guide, explaining the history and background of different pieces as well as the artists' lives and the various lovers who inspired them. It was clear to him what a terrific art teacher she was. He imagined what it would be like to be a student in her class; she was simply spellbinding. He unquestioningly followed her from room to room, his hand always lightly pressed to the small of her back, as if guiding her.

Tag recognized that he was way out of his element, so asking numerous questions became his focus. He was happy that Emery seemed to be enjoying the afternoon, leaning into him whenever he touched her. Goose bumps dotted his skin at her proximity and he had to will his cock to behave. His tattoos and piercings, in addition to his physically intimidating bulk, garnered quite a bit of attention. Tag was acutely aware he was the embodiment of the old motto: 'You can't judge a book by its cover.' Chuckling inwardly, his countenance remained serene. *Humph. Who knew art museums were this cool?*

Afterwards, they had dinner at a trendy new restaurant on Lombard Street. Tag had saved a few brochures from the museum and plied Emery with art-related questions throughout the entire meal. He found her enthusiasm with every question she answered disarming. He listened attentively, genuinely interested and not just making idle conversation to impress her. He noticed a few photos on the back of the pamphlet, advertising an upcoming exhibit featuring ancient mosaics.

"Now there is an art form which fascinates me — recycling at its finest. I met a lady who made beautiful mosaics from old broken plates and mirrors. She told me many of her friends and relatives lost priceless sets of antique china in the Los Angeles and San Francisco earthquakes. She used the pieces to recreate trays, picture frames, tables ... anything with a flat surface. She was able to grow it into a profitable business. She has a little store in Santa Cruz. I'll take you down there one day."

"I've done some mosaic work. It's fun, creative, and no pressure to be perfect. It's easier than painting a portrait or carving a profile."

Tag's curiosity was piqued. "Would you consider doing a mosaic for me? There's a flat area in my living room, approximately five feet by eighteen inches. It's a terrible eyesore at the moment and could use a facelift. Interested? I'd pay you, of course."

"I'd love to do it, but the only pay I will accept from you is Alaskan stout, home-made pie, and training sessions at your gym. Take it or leave it. Deal?" Emery tilted her head in expectation, a sexy smile on her lips.

"Deal." Tag nodded thoughtfully. *Cool. I'll get her in my house, and then ... who knows what could happen?*

"So, you wanna work out again tomorrow?" Tag inquired as he pulled up to her apartment building. He surprised himself a bit when he realized what he had blurted out. *What the hell?* He shrugged it off, admitting to himself that she was good company and nothing more.

"I really shouldn't. I need to do a ton of preliminary research for my class Monday. I've been putting it off, so it's now or never. Maybe during the week after I'm more settled?"

"Sure. Text me whenever. So, what class are you taking?"

Emery blew out a prolonged sigh upward, causing her delicate bangs to ruffle and stir on her forehead. "Contemporary Sculpture. The professor is brilliant and known worldwide, but has a reputation for being a hard-ass slave driver. Sculpture has never been my forté, so I'm prepared to get my butt kicked big time."

"I'm sure you'll be fine. If you need any help, I mean, like if you need a model for a sculpture, I would be more than happy to … you know, disrobe for you." His wide, sparkling eyes held a look of pure innocence, but his devilish smirk was anything but.

"Oh, my God, Tag. You are terrible!" A telltale blush crept up her cheeks as she good-naturedly punched his upper arm. His biceps were a brick wall against her feminine fist.

"Well, I've been told more than once my ass resembles Michelangelo's David," he boasted haughtily, sticking his firm jaw forward for emphasis.

"Is that so?" Emery's voice had turned breathy all of a sudden as her lidded eyes met his in a sultry stare. Her moist lips parted; her tongue darted out sensually to lick her forefinger and full bottom lip as her lustful gaze turned to Tag. "Really? Mmm … David is my fantasy guy," she whispered, her head falling back slightly. Slowly she closed her eyes and began to touch herself as one hand delicately caressed her cheek, then moved down to provocatively fondle a nipple through her clothing; the other lightly tugged on her lower lip. Soft moans and gasps — "Oh, David, ooh yes!" — escaped her throat as if a powerful orgasm was seconds away. Tag's mouth dropped open and his eyes almost popped out of his head, as he awkwardly reached down to adjust his crotch. As if a light switch was turned abruptly off, the real Emery returned: arms rigidly crossed across her chest, an irritated scowl on her face and a piercing death-glare aimed directly at Tag.

It only took a nanosecond for Tag to realize he had just been played — and rather expertly, he had to admit. *Holy shit, she totally had me goin'. Damn, that was fuckin' hot!*

Tag threw his head back and laughed. It had been the second time that day and it felt exceptionally gratifying, even liberating. Every morning upon awakening, he said a silent prayer to Randi. *Please, baby. Help me make it through the day.* It was no different in the evening, the identical prayer with the word night replacing day. This lightheartedness was a welcome relief and he couldn't help but smile in appreciation at the gorgeous brunette who, from out of the blue, had become a welcome part of his solitary life.

Emery joined in with uncontrollable giggling; a muffled snort managed to sneak out as well, as she held onto her stomach.

"Did you just snort?" His voice rose at least an octave, faking appalled indignation. He struggled to contain his laughter, but with no success. She wrinkled her nose in response.

"Well played, Emery. I must say, you had me going. If the sculpting thing fails, you may have a career in porn to fall back on." Reaching an arm out for her, she fell into his side, still giggling hysterically. Warmth infused his chest, strangely comforting although he could feel his body grow tense as a muscle tic invaded his jaw. His desire to touch a woman's lips with his own had ceased to exist over a decade ago. He kept those feelings methodically locked away, deeply hidden in the darkest recesses of his mind. He had no need for useless emotions; they only caused pain in the long run. *The lower I sink into the bottomless depths of my own personal Hell, the less actual physical pain I feel.* It had been his mantra for years, his secret to survival. Yet, in two short days, this brown-eyed beauty had somehow gotten under Tag's skin and it terrified him.

"That was fun. You should have seen your face. And, FYI, that was definitely *not* a snort. When I snort, you will be the first to know." Still grinning, Emery grabbed her purse then leaned into Tag again, this time for a swift hug.

"Thanks for dinner. I had a wonderful time."

"And thank you for the museum tour. I really enjoyed it. Good luck with school and I'll text you during the week, okay?"

"Okay. Oh, and Randy will be here next weekend." She nervously bit a fingernail. "Um ... will you still have some time to work with him? He's looking forward to meeting you."

"Absolutely. I can't wait to meet him. I'm free Saturday, so any time after noon is good."

"Great, thanks. It means a lot to me. Good night."

"G'night, brown eyes." Tag leaped from his truck and strode around to open the passenger door for Emery, holding his hand out to assist her to the ground. They both leaned against the side of the vehicle for a moment.

"I was a bit nervous being in a new town by myself, but you have been like a one-man welcoming committee. I just want you to know, I'm extremely grateful."

"Well, to be honest, you're kinda fun to hang out with." Nervously licking his lip piercing, Tag struggled to find something witty to say.

Emery shuffled her feet. "I'd better go. It's late."

Chuckling, Tag ducked his head slightly to meet her penetrating gaze then lifted his chin toward the night sky. "I bet you the big, fat full moon above us would definitely disagree." Emery smiled as her eyes fluttered upward.

"You're probably right," she sighed. His jade-green depths sparkled under the moon's vibrant glow as Emery wrapped her arms snugly around his neck, depositing a chaste kiss on his cheek.

"G'night, Tag. See ya soon." She quickly turned and walked away.

"Text me when you're upstairs and safely inside, okay?" Tag would have preferred to walk her to her apartment door, but there was no open parking space, so he just sat and watched until she was safely inside. A minute later, a second-floor window became illuminated and her face appeared from behind a curtain.

EMERY: SAFE & SOUND!

Waves were exchanged and he took off into the night, humming along to Luke Bryan's tune "I Don't Want This Night to End" on the radio.

Chapter 7

"He stepped down, trying not to look long at her, as if she were the sun, yet he saw her, like the sun, even without looking."
– Leo Tolstoy (Anna Karenina)

EMERY

Emery's first day of class had finally arrived and she was filled with exhilaration and consternation all at once. Sculpture had always been her nemesis, but she was determined to overcome her weakness. It came with its own difficulties that were made worse by intermittent wrist pain and worries about Carpal Tunnel Syndrome, a terribly painful condition, which had plagued a former teacher of hers, who sadly was forced to abandon her fifty-year career as an artist because of the affliction.

Sunday had been spent preparing for the class. Professor Luca Navarro had an extensive online presence and Emery dedicated two hours to combing through his website alone. Additional hours had been devoted to reading his class expectations and numerous guidelines for the two main sculpture projects each student would be responsible for completing by semester's end. The primary focus of the class was human anatomy; no sculptures of inanimate objects, animals, aliens, or any other imaginary beings would be accepted. A brief description of both projects was provided and Emery read each with a mixture of excitement and anxiety. She would need to choose two people and create a sculpture of each.

Project #1 — Someone you have just met or have not known for long. You will learn more about the subject over time, through working on the piece. Your sculpture will reflect any transformations, which may occur during the process.

Project #2 — A person you know well, or think you know well. You will experience how they evolve throughout the sculpting process, and show these changes in your work.

Emery thought about each project for a while before shutting down her laptop. Two people were going to be the focus of her life for the next four months: Randy and Tag. She smiled, knowing she had found her two subjects, but a small frown followed a second later. *This will be a tough assignment.*

Friday finally arrived and Emery had gotten through the week feeling satisfied and extremely reassured. Her professor was fantastic … engaging, talented, understanding, patient, and hot as hell. All the female students, and a few of the males, were already fantasizing about how they could be alone with him in the studio, or would he be posing nude if asked, or a hundred other equally-ridiculous scenarios. Luca Navarro was originally from Barcelona and had swarthy good looks and a confident charm that made the majority of the younger, more impressionable undergraduate students swoon. Emery had been teaching art for three years already, so was a bit older than most of her classmates. *More mature, I hope.*

She went for an hour-long morning run around the neighborhood and was soon cleaning and de-cluttering her apartment in preparation for Randy's arrival. A trip to the grocery store was also on her agenda; her refrigerator was empty, and needed to be fully stocked for her hungry, growing son. Randy's flight was due to land in less than two hours. *Time to put your ass in gear, girl.*

TAG

Because his schedule contained so many sessions with important clients, Tag was extremely conscientious about appointments. He kept a daily calendar in his phone and an extra reminder in the form of a small notebook in his truck. It was perfect for jotting things down as ideas popped into his busy mind while driving. He couldn't help but laugh out loud when he saw his current calendar. Grabbing a pencil, he hurriedly crossed out several words after realizing he had written the reminder numerous times. '***Text Emery.***' With a slight feeling of chagrin, he looked at his reflection in the rearview mirror. *What the fuck, man? You have known her for how many days? Get a grip.*

He had sent a couple of texts during the week, always making sure they were light and casual. As much as he hated to admit it, he missed her company. His feelings unnerved him a bit, but he assured himself she was nothing more than a friend. Emery had responded to every text, sharing her first-week-of-school experiences. She was inundated with classwork and was unavailable for weekday gym workouts until she caught up. Class met Mondays, Wednesdays, and Thursdays; Tuesdays were dedicated to working in the sculpting studio, and Fridays were free. She had already alerted Tag her Friday would be spent preparing for Randy's first weekend in San Francisco. His final text was sent Friday evening, as he was leaning against the alley wall taking his usual ten-minute weed break from the crowded bar.

Tag: How u doing? Hope ur week was good & Randy arrived safe.

Emery: All good. We're getting reacquainted, had a nice dinner at Crepevine, now doing math homework. See ya tmw noon?

Tag: Yep. Looking forward to it.

Emery: We are too.

Attached to the last text was a selfie of the two of them, grinning like fools. Tag chuckled to himself. Randy was a good-looking boy. *I wonder what his dad looks like.*

Tag: Cute.

Snuffing out the joint in his usual manner, Tag stuck the roach in his jeans pocket and went back to work. He was pleasantly surprised to find Tyler seated at the bar.

"There you are. I was picturing you out with your new woman." Tyler's voice was laced with curious innuendo. "Sooo … spill it, dude. What's the latest? Robbi and Emery have been texting back and forth, but girl-code must be stronger than wedding vows, 'cause she won't tell me a fuckin' thing."

Tag shrugged nonchalantly as he poured two shots of tequila. "Not much to tell, man. We grabbed a bite here last Friday before my shift; worked out at my gym Saturday morning, spent the day at the Modern Art Museum, and afterwards had dinner."

"Holy shit! Sounds like you had three dates in under forty-eight hours. You've been a very busy boy, Tag." Tyler's eyebrows waggled suggestively. "Details. Now."

"They weren't real dates and there's nothing to tell. We had fun. You know, good conversation. She's fascinating and super-smart. I'm also gonna help train her son for his football tryouts. She hasn't given me the slightest hint she's interested. We're friends, Ty, which is fine with me. End of story." *Liar!*

"Hey, I'm a big fan of friends. Hell, never thought I'd be sayin' shit like that, but Robbi and I started as friends, and you know something? Looking back on everything now, I wouldn't change a damn thing. Have an open mind; just go with the flow. You never know what life can throw your way. So, you said she has a kid?"

"Yeah, he's nine. She had him right outta high school. Never married the dad but he's still very involved in their lives." With a casual shrug, Tag added with a cynical smirk, "Maybe a little *too* involved, if ya know what I mean." Jealousy laced his words. Tyler nodded in understanding.

"You like this girl," Tyler ventured matter-of-factly; it was not a question. Tag's tongue toyed with his lip ring, deep in thought, and then shrugged as he tilted his head. "Maybe," he pondered while refilling Tyler's beer glass. "Emery has this way of gazing at me so intently. It's a bit unnerving, like she can see everything about me — every dark, dirty secret — and *still* wants to know me. She's able to see the person I used to be, before … you know. When I'm around her, I believe I could be that guy again."

Their conversation was interrupted by a buzz from Tyler's phone. A wide smile graced his lips as he read the text.

"I'm outta here. My beautiful wife misses me and wants me home — and I quote — 'right the fuck now.' Later, dude."

Tag gave him a chin-lift before pouring himself another shot, downing it swiftly. Tyler paused at the door, and turned, calling out, "Remember what I said, buddy. You just never know …" Tag heard the rumble of Ty's Harley as he sped away.

Damn, I miss ridin' my old bike. As soon as I replace the brake pads, I'll be back in the saddle. The remainder of the evening was spent daydreaming about a pair of warm brown eyes, which for the first time in many years were not Randi's. He attempted to drown the uncomfortable pangs of guilt in a few more shots.

Chapter 8

*"Blessed be childhood, which brings down something of
heaven into the midst of our rough earthliness."*
— Henri Frederic Amiel

TAG

As Tag rounded the corner, he spied Emery and Randy immediately. His breathing hitched, causing him to stop in his tracks. From this distance, she could almost be Randi's twin — hair a bit longer with sexy, lightly fringed bangs, breasts a tad fuller, but the illusion was enough to send a twinge to his belly. Pulling in a few calming inhales, he took several steps forward, leisurely tossing the football he was carrying in the air a few times hand-to-hand. Emery had texted him earlier, sharing with him Randy's excitement about training for tryouts. The boy was eagerly craning his neck in anticipation, searching in every direction, a look of enthusiasm on his face. An odd mixture of terror and tenderness filled Tag's gut.

Randy's eyes met Tag's and a huge smile broke out over his face. When Tag had reached a spot about fifteen feet away, he motioned to the boy to ready himself for a catch. Making sure the throw was at a child-appropriate speed, he let the ball fly. Randy caught it easily and then Emery made the introductions.

"Hi, Tag. Thanks for helping me with my tryouts." They shook hands politely.

"Nice to meet you, Randy." A brief auditory flashback from a long-repressed, first-day-of-college, philosophy class introduction threatened to surface. Tag ignored it as best he could.

"You should call me Coach. It's a good habit to have early on, okay?"

The boy nodded earnestly. "Yes, sir. I mean ... yes, Coach." Tag inspected the boy's gear, paying close attention to his helmet. After checking it thoroughly, which included a few hard knuckle taps, Tag nodded his approval.

"Your helmet is the most vital piece of equipment a football player owns. You never go out on the field without it, okay?" Tag's tone was stern, although he playfully ruffled the child's hair before giving him a pat. "Head injuries are common, and you can never be too careful."

"Yes, Coach. Mom always says the same thing."

Emery's attention was elsewhere; she was eyeing the Bath and Body Works shopping bag, which was hanging from Tag's shoulder. "You stop at the mall on your way here, Tag?"

Smacking his forehead with the heel of his hand, Tag sheepishly handed her the impromptu gift. "I bought you a few products with the balsam scent you like. Now your home can smell like a Christmas tree all year."

Emery's radiant smile lit up her face. "Thanks. That was sweet of you. Now you guys chat while I run upstairs and drop this off."

Together, they headed out to Golden Gate Park. Emery tilted her head a bit and peered at Tag's face, eyes narrowed in scrutiny.

"Hey, where's your lip ring, Tag?" she queried. He chuckled, recalling their recent conversation and obviously delighted she'd even noticed.

"Football and any kind of jewelry don't mix, Emery. I would've removed everything but I knew your boy wouldn't be ripping my earrings off, right, Randy?" The child looked up at him with an impish grin.

"Only if you were on the opposing team, Coach." His swift reply caused Tag to burst into approving laughter. When he spied his mother's glare, Randy defended himself immediately.

"Mom. It's *football*, not hide-and-seek. It's rough out there," he huffed, rolling his eyes at her. Tag made a vain attempt to stifle his audible snort, but was unsuccessful. Convulsive laughter ensued with Emery eventually joining in. Inwardly, Tag heaved a huge sigh of relief. *This might actually be fun.*

Arriving at a grassy clearing, Tag squatted down so he and Randy were eye level. His eyes squinted, countenance stern, and voice uncompromising.

"No wandering off, Randy. Make sure your mom or I have eyes on you at all times, okay? This park is safe, but we can't be too careful. Am I clear?" He stood up and threw Emery a subtle wink.

"Yes, Coach!" came Randy's speedy reply.

"So, when exactly are these tryouts of yours? And what position are you thinking about focusing on?"

"Tryouts start middle of June, after school is over. And I'm not exactly sure which position, Coach. Everyone always wants to be quarterback or running back. I'm thinking more about wide receiver."

"Like #11. Larry Fitzgerald is a great player; he's one of my favorites, too. Well, let's see what skills you possess first. Ready?"

Blowing a loud whistle when necessary, Tag ran him through the gamut: a series of different types of throws, passes, and so forth. Running around trying to keep up, Emery snapped as many photos of Randy as she could. After an hour of non-stop drills, they took a much-needed break under a large tree where Emery had been lounging for a few minutes on a spread-out blanket. She took two bottles of water out of her carryall bag and handed them to the sweaty, heavily breathing athletes.

"Your boy certainly has potential; a good sense of spatial relations, timing, and hand-eye coordination." Randy hung on his every word, wide-eyed and grinning proudly. Tag was soon on his feet, motioning for Randy to follow.

"Okay, kid, break's over. Now I'm gonna throw to you and I want you to catch the ball, but not wait for it to reach your grasp. I'd like to see you jump and catch it mid-air. Got it?" Tag ran back to the area where they had been practicing.

"Yes, Coach," came his immediate reply, running to catch up to Tag.

A sudden rain shower appeared, threatening to put a damper on their practice. Randy pouted as he ran for cover, back under the protective boughs of the large maple tree. Tag loudly sounded the whistle, which had been hanging around his neck. "And just where do you think you are going, young man?"

"Um, it's raining, Coach." Tag loved how quickly the child had adopted the moniker from the start. Football was a fun activity, but to be successful required so much more. It was Tag's intention to establish a sense of discipline and structure right from the start.

"This is *not* baseball, son. We don't wuss out for a little rain. This. Is. Football. Rain, snow, mudslide, tsunami, earthquake. We. Don't. Care. Nothing matters except this ball!" Tag's voice was stern, but the underlying tone was teasing and playful as he held the ball aloft. "Now, get ready. I'm aiming for the flagpole over there and you are gonna make an interception. 3 … 2 … 1 … *go!*"

Emery scrambled to her feet and started running as Tag's expertly thrown football floated in a perfect arc through the air. Randy judiciously followed its progress while sprinting at top speed, eventually making a diving catch, arms fully outstretched. After sliding headfirst for a yard or two on the slippery wet grass, he exuberantly leapt to his feet, arms raised victoriously with football in hand. Emery was jumping up and down, wildly waving her cell phone as a relieved expression flooded her face. Randy ran to Tag for a high-five, then proceeded to race toward his mother who wrapped him in a powerful embrace. Tag took his time strolling over to join them, wanting to give them some private time, as Emery attempted to dry the child off with a corner of the blanket.

"So what do you think, Coach? That was a good catch, huh?" Randy looked up at Tag, wide-eyed with anticipation. Tag tapped his chin, pretending to mull over his thoughts.

"Good? I wouldn't say good. That diving catch was awesome. I think you'd make a great wide receiver someday, but you gotta be willing to put in a lot of practice time. I'll work with you whenever I can. You okay with that?"

Randy turned questioning eyes toward his mother. "Mom? I'll be coming up here every other weekend, right?" Emery nodded in agreement, but her eyes held a hint of concern as she glanced in Tag's direction.

"Honey, I'm sure Tag's too busy with—" He politely cut her off.

"Emery, I wouldn't have offered if I didn't want to help. Besides, when he's drafted by the NFL, I'm gonna make sure I go with him as his personal trainer. Deal, kid?" Tag held out his arm toward Randy for a triumphant fist-bump, while shooting Emery a secret wink. As they strolled toward the exit of the park, Randy posed a question. "Hey, Coach? Can I text you sometime if I have a football question?"

"Randy, you don't want to bother—" Again Tag would not allow Emery to finish her admonition. Squatting down so they were eye-to-eye, his tone was determined.

"Sure, Randy. Anytime. Give me your phone and I'll put my number in it right now." Looking up, he gave Emery a warm, reassuring smile. "It's okay. A coach has to be available for his wide receiver at all times." Randy's smile split his face in half as he threw his arms around Tag's neck. An awkward, uncertain half-heartbeat of silence followed as Tag was temporarily rendered immobile. He didn't dislike children; he simply had no prior experience dealing with them. Unfazed, Randy mumbled, "Thanks, Coach Tag. I had fun today."

Tag slowly raised his arms to reciprocate, enfolding the boy in an uneasy hug.

"Me, too, Randy. Remember, football is more than just a game. Sometimes the aches and pains outweigh the fun. Got it?"

Randy nodded in agreement. "Got it, sir."

"Now how about I take my future NFL star and his beautiful mother out to lunch? I know a couple of great places. You feel like burgers or Mexican?"

Exiting the park, Emery whispered, "Thanks," as they each grabbed one of Randy's outstretched hands. Green eyes met golden brown as an unspoken message was exchanged, each grateful for a lovely spring-like day in the park, but perhaps for different reasons.

Randy had opted for Mexican. Tag ordered a little bit of everything on the menu and the threesome shared all the varied dishes. Emery had taken innumerable photos and passed the phone around the table. There was a spectacular shot of Randy's diving catch, perfectly captured in mid-air. To his surprise, there were numerous photos of Tag as well.

"I'm gonna enlarge this and print it when we get home, and then put it in a frame for your bedroom, okay?" Emery's voice exuded with pride.

"Great, Mom. Thanks. Can you take one of Coach and me? I'd like to put it in my room, too."

"Of course. Smile, you two!"

Conversation flowed easily over lunch. Randy talked animatedly about school, classes, and teachers. He also expressed his admiration for Tag's colorful body art, piping up, "Mom said I could get a tattoo when I'm eighteen. I'm gonna design it myself with my initials. Wanna see?"

Randy excitedly borrowed a pencil from Emery and proceeded to make a few sketches of RAZ on a paper napkin. Impressed by the boy's imaginative patterns and configurations involving the three letters, Tag studied each one closely, and then pointed to one in particular.

"I like this design the best. There's a smooth flow to how you connected the individual letters. I see you're an artist like your mom. What other classes do you like?"

Randy had just taken an enormous bite of a fish taco, so Emery interjected, "Honey, why don't you teach Tag the math game you made up?" Emery prodded, her tone brimming with maternal pride.

"Great idea, Mom." The boy beamed, turning to Tag. "So, you remember multiplication tables and division and all that stuff, right?"

Tag nodded solemnly, suppressing a grin while winking at Emery. "I think so, yeah."

"Okay. Here are the rules. I think of a famous athlete, could be NFL, NBA, whatever, and give you a math multiplication or division problem and you guess the name based on his jersey number. Need an example?"

"Sure, buddy. I'm ready when you are." Tag was blown away by the kid's intelligence and ability to communicate.

"Six times three," Randy declared confidently while crossing his arms.

Tag tilted his head a bit, while pondering the clue although his smug grin implied he already knew the answer.

"Peyton Manning." Triumph was obvious in Tag's voice. "You will have to try a lot harder to stump me, kid. Okay, now it's my turn. This is a tough one and there are several right answers.

Ready? Five times ten plus two." He mischievously waggled an eyebrow at Emery as they watched Randy's face scrunch in deep thought; both were enjoying his mental-math computation.

"Thank you," Emery mouthed, bestowing a heart-stopping smile on Tag.

Uproarious laughter resounded as they made their way back toward Emery's apartment. As they passed the AMC Theater, Randy rushed up to the array of posters showcasing the current movie offerings, pointing breathlessly.

"Mom, look. *Star Wars: The Force Awakens* is playing. Can we see it? Please?" He craned his neck to examine the schedule of movie times. "Mommy! The 3-D show starts in fifteen minutes."

Emery faced Tag with a questioning look in her eyes. It was obvious she and Randy were enjoying his company, and did not want the pleasant afternoon to end. The feeling was mutual. He led Emery and a jubilant Randy into the theater. Randy, wanting to sit next to his mother and his coach, ended up in the middle. Tag was not too happy with the situation, sneaking furtive glances at her from the corner of his eye. He had been looking forward to accidentally brushing up against her forearm or casually placing his arm over her shoulder. *Damn little cockblocker! Lucky I like you, kid.*

After the movie, Tag deposited mother and son safely in front of their apartment building. They walked slowly up the walkway toward the front door.

"Thanks for a wonderful day, Tag." Emery released a deep sigh as her eyes opened slowly, long lashes casting shadows in the moonlight as they lifted toward him.

"Yeah, Coach. I had an awesome time," Randy chimed in enthusiastically. Tag squatted down so he could look at the boy directly. "Me, too, buddy. Continue practicing and I'll see you in two weeks, okay?" Randy gave him an enthusiastic hug, which Tag self-consciously returned.

"Maybe see you at the gym, Emery?" Tag enquired casually.

"Definitely. I'll text you." Standing on her tiptoes, Emery softly kissed his cheek, turned, and walked up the steps holding Randy's hand. Tag was immediately compelled to place his fingers where her lips had just been. He could still feel the slight moisture from her lip gloss.

"Okay, good night," Tag mumbled, quickly turning toward his truck as he made a not-so-subtle attempt to readjust the crotch of his jeans, which had become unbearably constricted. A soft sigh escaped his lips. *Fuck me.*

Chapter 9

"The more a thing is perfect, the more if feels pleasure and pain."
– Dante Alighieri (The Divine Comedy)

TAG

An uneventful Sunday had come and gone. Tag found himself back at the gym Monday morning. His 7:00 a.m. client had just finished, and Tag was on the mat, performing a few stretching exercises. Mondays were the most hectic days at fitness centers. Most people partied their asses off over the weekend, eating junk food and drinking to excess then expected to undo all the negative effects with a quick Monday morning workout. Similarly, January was always the busiest month because of New Year's resolutions. The first week or two would be jammed with new, enthusiastic members, all armed with the best of energetic intentions. By February, they all fell by the wayside, back to being their unfit selves, doomed to another year of unhealthy, overweight frustration. Tag saw it all the time. The average human being was weak, in his opinion; each lacked sufficient willpower to make positive changes in his or her life.

Many of his clients at the fitness center were involved in some area of professional sports. Some were athletes, coaches, or television commentators. Others were influential behind the scenes: owners, agents, sports writers, and so forth. Being well liked, highly regarded, and good at his job, Tag was often the recipient of complimentary tickets to different events in the San Francisco area. Reaching into his back pocket, Tag scrutinized the pair of tickets a client had slipped him on his way out. *Sweet. These look like courtside seats. Tyler would KILL for these. Sorry, buddy. Not happening.* Tag reached for his cell phone, and began to tap the screen.

TAG: HOPE SCHOOL IS GOOD. A CLIENT JUST GAVE ME A GENEROUS TIP: 2 TIX FOR GS WARRIORS GAME SATURDAY. WANNA COME? GREAT SEATS.

There was no response; Tag surmised she was in class, so he resumed his usual workout. He spied Misty out of the corner of his eye, but ignored her. The volume on his iPod was turned up to the maximum as he crunched a rapid set of bicep curls in time to the upbeat rock tune. Feeling the scratch of nails on his arm, he abruptly turned to find her posed in front of him, hands on hips. He pushed himself past his usual number of reps just to make her wait.

"I feel like you're ignoring me," she huffed, not-so-subtly pulling her snug tank top lower, exposing more of her ample bought-and-paid-for cleavage. He pulled one earbud out; giving her only half his attention, he hoped she'd take the hint. *Why the hell did I ever fuck this chick? Twice. God, I am a dumbass.*

"I've just been busy, have a lot going on." Taking a quick swig of water, Tag began another set of arm curls. Misty crossed her arms under her breasts, effectively pushing them up even higher.

"You fucking that skinny brunette you had in here the other day? Didn't think *that* was your type." Her voice dripped with jealous sarcasm.

"It's none of your damn business, and how would you know what my type is?" Tag returned the earbud to his ear, and hissed, "Now, if you'll excuse me …" Striding away, he disappeared into the locker room, blood boiling. Leaning over the sink, he turned on the faucet and threw some cold water on his face. *Stupid bitch. Emery ... skinny? Bullshit. Her body is perfection.*

Feeling his phone vibrate, Tag grabbed it quickly, and his frown was immediately replaced by a huge grin. *Finally.*

EMERY: WHO ARE THEY PLAYING?

TAG: DOES IT MATTER?

EMERY: OF COURSE IT MATTERS. I'M NOT GOING IF IT'S A TEAM I HATE, OR IF IT'S LEBRON JAMES.

Tag was laughing his ass off at this point, realizing she was having some fun at his expense.

TAG: COURTSIDE SEATS, PLUS YOU'LL BE WITH ME! WHAT ELSE DO YOU NEED?

EMERY: OK, I'M IN. (POUTY FACE)

TAG: GREAT. YOU, ME, & NY KNICKS.

EMERY: COOL. GOTTA GO. THANKS!

The smile on Tag's countenance lasted for the remainder of his workout and the rest of the day.

Tag had not heard from Emery all week. By Thursday, he decided it was time to make the first move which was not his usual style.

TAG: HEY! WANNA DO DINNER & DRINKS 2NITE? NOTHIN' FANCY, NSB AT 6? (PIE AWAITS.)

EMERY: YESSSSS! UP TO MY EARS IN CLAY. SEE YA 6.

TAG: COOL.

Sitting at his usual table for two in the corner, Tag welcomed Emery with an affectionate hug. They were becoming good friends; conversations were effortless with a good amount of playful teasing back and forth.

"Sorry I've been so out-of-touch this week, Tag. I needed to sketch and finalize the dimensions for my two sculpture projects. I started one this morning and spent four straight hours pounding a giant lump of clay. I'm exhausted!" She drained half the glass of beer that Tag had waiting for her.

"So class is good? Are you learning a lot?" Talking about art intimidated Tag, but he wanted Emery to know he took an interest in it nonetheless. "I checked out your teacher online; impressive resume and damn good-looking too. Has he hit on you yet?" *Fuck me. Did I really just say that?*

"Don't forget his heart-breaker reputation and gigantic ego. And no, he has not blatantly hit on anyone that I know of yet, although a few of my classmates are already infatuated." Emery chuckled, shaking her head. "Anyway, for me personally? A student-teacher relationship is always a no-no, even when both are consenting adults. It can be a dangerous game."

"It sounds like you're speaking from personal experience, Emery." His words were muted, concerned, but not at all accusatory. He placed his hand gently on top of hers. *Did something happen to her in the past?*

"No, but I've seen the aftermath, so I know it can turn ugly." Shaking off the pensive mood, which had pervaded them, she strove to change the subject. Just then Tag's phone buzzed, providing a welcome distraction. Glancing at the screen, a wide grin spread across his face.

"Hey, it's your favorite man." Laughing, Tag held up the screen so she could see her grinning son. Emery scooted her chair next to Tag so they could read the message together.

RANDY: HEY, COACH. HOW ARE U?

TAG: GOOD. HAVING DINNER WITH YOUR MOM.

RANDY: COOL. HAD PRACTICE TODAY AND I DID GREAT. MADE A FEW NICE CATCHES. GRANDPA TOOK PHOTOS. I'LL SEND U NOW.

TAG: OK.

Three photos came through, as Emery oohed and aahed over her son's dexterity and effort. Tag nodded appreciatively, scrutinizing his form including body and hand positions. Emery's head was lightly resting on Tag's shoulder in order to see the screen at a better angle.

TAG: NICE JOB. LOOKS LIKE A ONE-HANDED GRAB ON THE LAST ONE.

RANDY: YEAH. I PRACTICED EVERY DAY. OK, GRANDMA'S CALLING ME TO DINNER. SEE U NEXT WEEK. MISS U, MOM.

TAG: MISS U 2.

RANDY: BYE. I LOVE U!

Placing the phone on the table, Tag glanced toward Emery whose eyes were suddenly awash in tears.

"What's wrong, sweetheart?" The endearment had escaped Tag's lips before his brain fully engaged, thumbs rapidly swiping the droplets from her cheeks as they fell.

Sniffling, Emery whispered, "I just miss him so much." Her face was nuzzled in the crook of Tag's neck; one of his large hands cupped her cheek, while the other tenderly stroked the back of her head.

"Shh, please don't cry, Emery. He'll be back here before you know it. You'll see."

"But I feel like I'm a terrible mother, being away from him like this." Her upturned gaze met his, drops of moisture clinging to her long lashes. He grinned in spite of her dismay.

"Emery, you're a great mom and Randy seemed in good spirits."

During the remainder of the evening, they sat close together, arms and shoulders touching, sharing their entrees, eating off each other's plates, and finally splitting a slab of blueberry pie. To a casual onlooker, Tag was sure they seemed like a couple in love, except for the absence of kissing. His gaze lingered on her full lips more than once during the course of the evening. *We're friends, that's all. Or is that a big, fat fuckin' lie and am I setting myself up for more pain?*

Chapter 10

"Motherhood: All love begins and ends there."
— Robert Browning

TAG

After working with his usual Saturday morning clients, Tag shot Emery a quick text.

TAG: GAME STARTS @7:30. I'LL PICK U UP @ 4. WE SHOULD HAVE ENOUGH TIME TO DRIVE OVER BAY BRIDGE AND GRAB DINNER AT ORACLE ARENA.

EMERY: CAN'T WAIT! SEE U LATER. ☺

Smiling to himself, Tag imagined how her face would light up when she saw the courtside seats. *Hopefully, she likes basketball half as much as football.*

After completing his usual weekend errands, groceries, drug store, and Bev Mo, Tag made a final stop at a nearby florist. It was time to buy Emery some flowers. He opted for a potted plant instead of the typical bouquet with a limited life span. *These flowers remind me of her eyes.*

Upon arriving home, he stretched out on his sofa for an hour and watched ESPN. He had just enough time to catch up on college football scores and drink a beer before jumping into the shower. Grabbing the body wash, Tag proceeded to soap up his chest and abdomen, absentmindedly taking hold of his dick.

Somehow masturbating before a date with a beautiful, desirable woman seemed inappropriate. *What the fuck?* He released his semi, realizing after a few more strokes, it would have been way too late to stop.

EMERY

Her phone buzzed a few minutes early.

TAG: ON MY WAY UP.

EMERY: OK

He arrived with the over-sized plant in his arms: a dozen miniature orchids in unusual amber-brown shades.

"It's a house-warming gift. Hope you like it." His eyes scanned the small kitchen and living room.

"Thanks, Tag. How sweet of you. I don't think I've ever seen orchids in these colors before." She placed the plant on a small table near the kitchen window. Her eyes drank him in, head to toe: black long-sleeve sweater stretched over his massive muscular chest and arms, snug, faded jeans, and black combat boots. *God! Could this man be any hotter? And why is he staring at me so intently? Do I have something stuck in my teeth? Is it my outfit or these sexy boots? Are they too much?*

"You look different, Em. Your bangs …?"

Emery's palm came up to her forehead. "Oh, yeah, I forgot. Once in a while I get in the headband mood, and brush them back." Tag nodded his approval.

"Your apartment smells like Christmas in March. I see you've been using the balsam products I gave you. This scent always reminds me of home. My mom would never allow a fake tree in the house." Tag laughed wistfully, eyes clouding over as if a painful memory had invaded his mind.

"Mine, too, and the bigger the tree the better," Emery chimed in, hugging Tag in greeting.

They chatted a bit more about their families although Tag looked anxious to change the subject. Emery's curiosity got the best of her.

"Are you close to your parents, Tag?"

"I used to be, but I haven't seen them in a few years. Let's just say Dad and I never saw eye to eye. His plans for my future were not what I envisioned for myself. I'm not sure they'd even want to hear from me." He gnawed on his lip and Emery was sure she saw his eyes water. Without a moment's hesitation, she approached him and wrapped her arms around his neck. "What parent wouldn't want to hear from their son, Tag? I don't believe for one second that could be true."

"I don't know, Emery. A lot of terrible shit went down, that ended with me leaving." Emery gently pulled him down so his forehead could rest on hers.

"Now, you listen to me," she began sternly, pinning him with a glare. "I can't comment on your father; but I am a mother, so believe me when I tell you your mom thinks of you every minute of every day. Her first thought each morning is how much she misses you and if you'll call her soon. Every prayer she whispers at night is her hope that you are healthy and safe. Why not call her so she can hear your voice? Please, honey." Emery bit her lip hard, mentally chastising herself for letting the endearment slip past her lips. *Big mistake. Maybe he didn't hear it.*

Tag collapsed into a nearby chair, as his head fell limply into his hands. Emery kneeled in front of him and forced his gaze to meet hers. He tentatively reached a hand to touch her face, but he paused just short of contact. Cupping his cheeks in her hands, she readied a thumb to catch the drop of moisture that threatened to escape from the corner of his eye, while the other caressed the tiny cleft in his chin.

Pressing his lips together, he finally nodded. "Thanks for caring about me. I'll call Mom tomorrow, I promise. And Em?" His eyes desperately sought hers as the beginning of a wan smile graced his lips. "Would you do me a favor? Close your eyes for a moment. Please?" Emery obeyed without hesitation as Tag's palms caressed her face. Exhaling, his warm breath washed over her, causing her heart to accelerate. He then pressed a soft kiss directly in between her eyebrows. Startled by the unexpected touch of his lips, her eyes flew open in surprise.

Tag's lips curled upward even more. "Mom would often kiss me in that exact spot. She said it was where our third eye was located. You know, the one that has the ability to peer deep into someone's heart or soul." His forefinger caressed the spot above the bridge of her nose as he continued. "Of course, it took me years to figure out what she meant. By the way, Mom used to call me honey all the time. I didn't realize how much I missed hearing that. Oh, and I like your forehead bare. It's more accessible." He pressed his warm lips there again as evidence.

Emery could not articulate an appropriate response. Tag had simply stolen the air right out of her lungs. Standing up nervously, she grabbed a jacket then reached for her purse and phone. Tag followed, placed his hand on her lower back, and followed her out of the apartment.

"I figured it'd be easier if we just go straight to Oracle Arena and have dinner there, if that's okay? There's Rosa's Mexican, Ribs and Things, or The Field Irish Pub. "

"They all sound good to me. It's your call."

Emery could not decide which experience she relished more: the proximity of their seats to the court, or the up-close and personal view of famed player and New York Knicks head coach, Phil Jackson. Tag scowled at several men in nearby seats, complaining about their blatant ogling of his date, although they appeared to be with their significant others. Emery playfully feigned innocence, placing the blame on her black leather mini-skirt and platform boots. Tag laughed it off, declaring, "I should be pissed as hell at those assholes, but I know they're all just jealous, 'cause I'm with the most beautiful woman in the entire arena. However, I'm a bit disappointed the kiss-cam didn't find us!" Emery desperately tried to hide her heated blush, but failed. She settled for a subtle eye roll instead.

Emery didn't see Tag the following week. He was given additional responsibilities at the gym due to another trainer coming down with the flu. He had no free time to work out with Emery and sent her more than one apologetic text.

Emery experienced her own time-management challenges. Professor Navarro's expectations were requiring her to spend more time in the studio for hands-on, personal instruction. Thursday evening, it was just the two of them and Emery's unease grew under her teacher's intense stare. She was using her bare hands to mold a portion of the clay that would eventually be one side of Tag's face when Luca — as he insisted his students call him — came closer and placed his hands gently over hers.

"Too much tension in your fingers, Emery. Do not squeeze tight; too much pressure not good for clay. You see?" He softly stroked the cheek area of Emery's sculpture as if it were a beautiful woman.

"Who is this man you sculpt, Emery?" Luca's question seemed professional, but Emery was wary.

"He's my son's new football coach." She shrugged casually.

"I see." Luca's expression was coolly indifferent, as the sensuous brushes of his fingertips fluttered, allowing the subtle shape of a cheekbone to emerge on one side. Emery's gasp was audible.

"Remarkable, Luca! You just brought him to life with a few simple strokes."

He chuckled softly as he took one of her hands in both of his, whispering, "There is nothing simple about the human face, Emery. Please. You must feel." He positioned her clay-stained right hand on his cheek, with her thumb dangerously close to the corner of his full lips. "Do not focus on the skin. Sense what is underneath. Teeth, bones, muscle. Close your eyes. Do you feel it?"

His warm, minty breath fanned her face as he spoke. Temporarily losing her balance, Emery grabbed on to the table with her free hand, feeling somewhat lightheaded. Her eyes slowly opened and his lips were playfully upturned, as he awaited her answer. Yanking her hand from his cheek, she stammered, "Luca, I'm so sorry. I got clay all over your face!"

Laughing heartily, he mischievously pinched her cheek. "It wouldn't be the first time. Paint, clay, hot wax, molten metal, I've been covered in all of it. No worries, my sweet Emery. Let's clean up here, and then I am taking you to the new wine bistro across the street. We must celebrate your progress. Some of the other students will be there, too. I heard them talking."

No other students were there nor did any enter during the two hours they sat at the bar. The bottle of Cava, a sparkling wine produced in the Spanish wine region of Catalonia, was empty by the time Luca had finished giving Emery a history lesson on winemaking in his native land. He was about to order a second bottle when she placed her hand on his arm in protest.

"Not another drop, Luca. My son is arriving tomorrow to spend the weekend with me, and an exhausted, hung-over mother will not be appreciated by an energetic, non-stop, active nine-year-old." Luca nodded and signaled for the waiter to bring the check as Emery's phone buzzed. Thinking it was Randy's customary goodnight text, she opened the message without looking at the sender.

"Excuse me, this is probably Randy right now. I'll only be a moment," Emery murmured apologetically as she examined the screen.

TAG: HEY! JUST WANTED TO CONFIRM IF SAT @ 10 STILL GOOD FOR YOU AND RANDY?

EMERY: YES, PERFECT. LOOKING FORWARD TO IT.

TAG: I ALSO WANTED TO TELL YOU, I CALLED MY MOM. SHE WAS SO THRILLED TO HEAR MY VOICE (SHE SNIFFLED FOR 5 STRAIGHT MINUTES) AND TO KNOW I WAS OK. THANKS FOR CONVINCING ME TO CALL. MOM SAID TO THANK YOU, TOO.

EMERY: SO HAPPY TO HEAR THAT! WE HAVE SOMETHING TO CELEBRATE ON SATURDAY.

TAG: YES WE DO. OK, SEE YOU THEN.

Emery stowed her phone in her backpack and turned to Luca as they exited the bar, heading across the street to where her car was parked.

"Is everything all right with your boy?" Luca queried politely. Emery nodded, pulling out her keys and unlocking the door.

"Yeah, he's great! Excited about practicing for his football tryouts with the coach I found." Luca opened the driver's side door for Emery, and then placed his hand on her arm.

"Ah, I see." He smirked knowingly. "The subject of your sculpture. *He* is the coach you spoke of. Are the two of you *involved?*"

Schooling her features so as not to reveal her annoyance at his invasive question, she kept her tone light. "We're just friends; he's a trainer at the gym I go to."

Luca's eyes lit up and he kissed her goodbye, European style — a peck on each cheek. "So there is hope for me after all, *mia bella*."

Emery tilted her head and peered up at him through her lashes as she hastily sat in her car, feeling uncomfortable at their close contact. "I don't date my students and neither should you." She grinned to show there were no hard feelings. "Have a great weekend, see ya Monday!"

I'd better keep my eye on this guy. Way too flirty but hot as hell. I will not go there.

Chapter 11

"There are two ways of spreading light: to be the candle or the mirror that reflects it."
– Edith Wharton (Vesalius in Zante)

TAG

As they entered Golden Gate Park, Tag was in high spirits, declaring, "I just love it here. It's so peaceful and carefree."

"Me, too. Just smell that freshly cut grass. I like to run on the trails or just sit with my Kindle and read. And look at those fluffy, cotton-candy clouds," Emery gushed excitedly, donning her sunglasses.

"I like your Cardinals cap. It looks cute on you." *I did not mean to say that out loud, although it's true. Fuck me.*

Randy was anxious to start. "Coach Tag! I've been practicing my catches every day. I've gotten a lot better."

"All right, kid. Here's what's gonna happen today. You're gonna start about four or five yards away from me, then we'll gradually work up to about ten yards. I'm gonna throw the ball a yard or two to your right or left, but I'm not tellin' you which, okay? Watch my arm. Anticipate where the ball's gonna go. Watch. My. Eyes. Ready?"

Randy had just made a particularly skilled catch and Tag ran toward him for a high five. A sudden high-pitched squeal could be heard from a nearby clump of bushes, followed by a series of menacing growls. The boy froze in fear. Tag followed his eyes and came face to face — from a distance of ten to fifteen feet — with a snarling coyote. *Fuck.* The animal's teeth were bared and its muzzle appeared to be bloody, although there were no visible injuries. The frightening scene unfolded in front of Emery, who stood motionless, about ten yards away. Tag quickly positioned himself between the animal and the child, shielding him with his large body, as he ordered, "Stay behind me, buddy." He then indicated with his left outstretched palm for Emery to stay where she was, as his right hand cautiously took the football from Randy's trembling hands. Tag confidently stared the coyote down, while stealthily advancing toward the animal. Tag's lightning-fast motion only took a split second. He aimed, threw, and the ball hit the coyote squarely between the eyes. The animal cowered, growled, and skulked off, eventually disappearing into the trees.

Tag sighed in relief, squatting down as the child fell into his arms, hugging him fiercely.

"You okay, kiddo?" Randy nodded just as Emery ran up to them, needing no invitation to join the hug-fest.

"Mom! Did you see Tag's throw? It was dead-on, freakin' perfect. That mean old dog didn't stand a chance."

"That was a coyote, Randy. They're a bit more dangerous than your average dog," Tag explained gravely. He strode in the direction of the football when he heard a sudden faint cry, an anguished yelp of pain. Randy and Emery heard it, too, and rushed over. Cringing under some brush was an injured puppy; a small portion of one ear had been torn off and a hind leg looked bitten, possibly broken.

"Emery, grab the blanket," Tag ordered quickly. "We've gotta take this pup to a vet. Now!"

Luckily, Tag knew the neighborhood quite well. Upon exiting the park, they hailed a cab and were sitting in the waiting room of AES — Animal Emergency Services — within twenty minutes. Tag stroked the trembling puppy's head, while Emery's soothing voice attempted to calm its whimpering. Randy clung to his mother, visibly upset by the puppy's injuries. The dog had no collar or ID tag, was female, and appeared to be a pit bull mix. Her coat was a cinnamon-fawn blend, with a white chest and paws. A spot of bloodied fur sat just above her eyes.

"Will she be okay?" Randy whispered as his hand gently patted her soft fur. It was love at first sight for the child; his rapt attention had been on the puppy from the moment he saw her. Emery's eyes drifted to pamphlets strewn across a table, titled: 'Second Chance Animal Rescue' and 'Humane Society Pet Adoption'. Randy followed her gaze intently and his face lit up with excitement.

"Can we keep her, please? You said I could have a dog someday. Right, Mom?"

A nurse approached them within minutes, and they were ushered into an examining room where the doctor was waiting. Tag carefully placed the still-blanketed puppy on the counter. The fatherly-looking, middle-aged man spoke in a gentle voice as he checked the animal's injuries.

"I'm Doctor Moriarty. So tell me, what happened to this sweet little girl?"

Tag calmly relayed the pertinent facts. Randy, however, raved on and on about Tag's deadly accurate spiral, which saved the puppy from a certain untimely demise.

"Shush, Randy. It was no big deal." Tag blushed modestly, doing his best to deflect the praise. Doctor Moriarty listened carefully during the examination, holding back a chuckle as the animated voices swirled around him.

"You were so brave, Coach. You stared that coyote right in the eyes. He ran away cryin'. You were awesome."

Weak plaintive cries from the puppy brought everyone's attention back to the doctor and his ministrations. He had already applied antibiotics to the animal's wounds, and bandaged her hind leg. Afterwards, stitches were applied to her now-misshapen ear.

"This was one lucky pup. She sustained only three bites from the coyote. The two punctures to her leg were pretty deep, although no major blood vessels were damaged. She'll have some pain and weakness in her leg muscles, but should make a full recovery. This chewed-up ear, unfortunately, will be around forever. So will this tooth." Doctor Moriarty gently put his gloved fingers into the puppy's mouth. Pulling her lip to one side, he displayed a slightly misshapen lower canine that was slightly protruding, lending her a goofy, yet endearing expression. The vet chuckled. "She'd be a definite candidate for a doggie orthodontist, but … you know something? It actually makes her even cuter."

Eyeing the puppy carefully, Emery broached a question. "Are pit bulls good with children? I have to admit, I'd be a little nervous adopting her." The doctor nodded sympathetically. "Sadly, this breed has been misunderstood for a long time. The fault always lies in the owner. This particular dog is a pit bull-beagle mix, and appears to be around four or five months old. Exact age is hard to determine; she seems a bit underweight, which is normal for a stray. From my observation, her temperament displays no aggressive tendencies." He inserted a finger into the puppy's mouth and scratched under her chin with his other hand, while peering curiously in her eyes.

"You're a sweet girl, aren't you? Yes, you are." Gazing up at Emery, he spoke encouraging words. "I don't think she's a biter, although one can never be sure, considering what she's been through."

Emery cautiously scratched the dog behind her intact ear and, even though recently injured, her tail thumped enthusiastically in response. Tag watched as Emery's expression softened; her initial pit bull fear had evaporated. The vet's wide grin sobered as he peered at Tag intently.

"We probably would have had a different outcome if you didn't intervene at that exact moment." The kindly doctor put his hand on Tag's shoulder. "You did save her life, son."

"What happens to her now, Mom?" Randy's arms wrapped around his mother's waist as his forlorn eyes rose to meet hers. Emery stroked Randy's hair, her gaze falling upon Tag. Her head began slowly shaking back and forth in futility.

"Randy, the timing is bad right now. I'm up here for the next few months, and your grandparents can't —"

"I could help take care of her," Tag interrupted, raking his teeth over his lower lip as a look of uncertainty flickered through him. *Wait ... what? Uh oh. I'm thinkin' out loud again.* "At least, until you all decide what you want to do. Any suggestions, Doc?"

"I'd like her to stay here a day or two for observation, and to run some blood tests. That'll give you all time to make a decision. I'm assuming she's a stray; she's not the first puppy to be found in the park. If you plan to adopt her, she'll need shots and so forth. We will also implant her with a microchip ID."

Tag pulled out his wallet and handed a credit card to the vet. "Whatever you need, I'll take care of it. Thanks, Doc."

Doctor Moriarty took a business card out of his breast pocket. "I don't normally do this, but here is my cell number. Text me the minute you come to a decision, and I'll start the paperwork. I'd love to see this pup go to a good, loving home."

After a harrowing day, Emery announced a relaxing, home-cooked meal was in order. They stopped at Trader Joe's on the way home; she shopped for groceries while Tag and Randy picked out a DVD at a nearby Blockbuster.

Later, they prepared dinner while Randy did some homework in the living room.

"Mom? Can you help me for a sec, please?" Smiling at Tag who was meticulously chopping vegetables, she whispered, "Be right back." His emerald eyes followed her as she strode out of the kitchen. He was still staring in the same direction, as if in a trance, when she returned a few minutes later. Turning away from her abruptly, he went to the sink to wash his hands.

"Is Randy okay?" Tag filled a pot with water and placed it on the stove to boil.

"Yeah. He's starting to learn long division." Emery sighed, rolling her eyes at Tag. "At least he knows his times tables." Tag faced her, brushing a few stray hairs out of her eyes.

"He's a helluva kid and you are an incredible mother. If you decide to adopt the dog, I will help take care of her until you are done with school and ready to move back home. Whatever it takes, we'll figure it out. I'm here for you, Emery." *Yep. It's official. I am one of those idiots who's pussy-whipped while gettin' no pussy. Whatever. Emery needs me and it's temporary. No biggie.*

"Thanks, Tag. I appreciate your offer. I need to talk to Randy's dad and my parents first; but if it's okay with them, I'm leaning toward saying yes. I did promise he could have a dog a while back."

Randy, who had apparently been eavesdropping, let out an exuberant screech of delight. "Mommeee!" I love you sooo much! I promise I'll walk her and feed her and teach her tricks and I'll pick up her poop and everything."

"Honey, we need to talk to Daddy and your grandparents first, okay?"

"I'm calling them right now." His footsteps could be heard running down the hall.

"So, I hope you were serious about co-parenting the pup for a few months. I'll reimburse you for whatever —" Tag's finger was on her lips so fast she barely saw it move.

"Not another word, Emery. As that puppy's future godfather, it's the least I can do." They shared a laugh as Randy came bounding back into the kitchen. "Grandma said fine. Dad wasn't home, but I left him a message to call me ASAP. Yesss! Halfway there," he declared victoriously, retreating to the living room. Emery's gaze drifted to Tag and they shared a warm smile.

"Your actions were so remarkable today. You were an angel sent from Heaven, at that precise moment in time, to protect Randy and rescue that puppy. I know you have a brooding, dark side you present to the world, but you don't fool me. You have a kind and gentle heart; both Randy and I saw it today. Don't shroud that part of you in shadows. You need to let it shine like it was meant to do." Cupping his cheek in her soft hand, she got on her tiptoes and kissed him lightly on his lips. Tag froze for a long moment. He couldn't find any words to respond but simply watched dumbfounded as Emery walked to the stove and dumped a box of pasta into the boiling water. *What was that?* He wondered why his heart was palpitating a mile a minute. He hadn't had those feelings for a while. *Is this a premature heart attack? Gotta cut down on the red meat.*

Dinner had been over for a while, as they settled comfortably on the couch. Randy had insisted on keeping the movie he picked out a secret until the perfect moment, which finally had arrived. Tag ceremoniously poured three glasses of red wine — Randy's was tiny, barely a few sips mixed with a bit of grape juice, which Emery allowed on special occasions.

After removing the disk from its case, and inserting it into the DVD player, Randy proceeded to introduce the movie and read the synopsis.

"Tonight's animated movie is called *Bolt*! I chose it specifically for what happened today. **The canine star of a fictional sci-fi/action show, who believes his powers are real, embarks on a cross country trek to save his co-star from a threat he believes is just as real. It stars the voices of John Travolta and Miley Cyrus.** See? It's the perfect movie to celebrate my new puppy."

On the couch, Tag's arm casually draped over Emery's shoulder. He was watching Emery from the corner of his eye, paying little attention to the animated movie. Randy was on the floor, cell phone and DVD remote precariously balanced on his stomach. *This kid is crampin' my style. Shouldn't he be asleep by now?*

Shaking his head as if to banish the distracting thoughts, Tag went to the kitchen to grab a bottle of water. "Anybody want anything?" Hearing no replies, he returned to his seat on the couch, increasing the distance between them while keeping his hands to himself. *Idiot!* He knew Emery wasn't one of those bar sluts. *She's a sweet girl, and she is not interested in me that way. At least, I don't think she is.*

A buzz came from Randy's phone, and he immediately paused the movie. After taking a quick peek, he ran to Emery, shouting, "Mommy, look."

DAD: IF THE DOG'S OK WITH MOM, IT'S OK WITH ME.

Wide, expectant eyes were trained on Emery as she turned to Tag. "You sure you're okay with this?"

"I'm good. It'll only be for a few months." Tag nodded in reassurance as Emery looked back at Randy who was about to burst with jubilation.

"Okay, kiddo, but remember —" Randy was already jumping on the couch, crushing his mother in a bear hug.

"I know, I know. I promise I'll take care of her real good. I already decided on her name, too. Goldie!"

Rolling her eyes at Tag, she murmured, "Wow. I'm impressed. He never notices colors."

Tag was about to contradict her, as if he had already figured out Randy's thought process — and it had nothing to do with the color of the puppy's fur.

"No, Mom. I picked Goldie 'cause we found her in Golden Gate Park." Tag tilted his head and chuckled. *Well, I could have told you that.*

Tag grabbed his cell phone and the vet's business card from the coffee table. Staring at the card, his eyes narrowed and he turned to Emery as a concerned expression marred his features.

"Emery, is this a dog-friendly building?" As much as Tag was willing to share puppy walking and feeding duties, having an animal live in his home full-time was not going to work.

"Yeah, there are several pooches in the building, don't worry." Her sweet smile was reassuring.

Looking from Emery to Randy, then back again, he queried, "So, are we doing this or what?" Emery nodded definitively, much to the delight of her son, who began shrieking at the top of his lungs, "YESSSS! I'm *finally* gettin' a puppy."

There was no immediate response from Doctor Moriarty, so they resumed watching *Bolt*. As the final credits were rolling, Tag noticed he had received a text. Quietly reading the message, he attempted to be subtle, but Randy was already on high alert. The child was on his knees in between Tag and Emery, eyes huge in expectation.

"We can get Goldie Monday afternoon," he announced as Randy launched himself at a mildly dazed Tag.

"Thanks, Tag. Thanks for saving Goldie's life. Now we need to go to the pet store and buy a bunch of stuff and …" Randy's face abruptly crumpled as he turned to his mother, huge tears beginning to form in his dark eyes. "Monday? I won't be here, Mom. I'll be back in Phoenix. I wanna be here to pick up Goldie."

"You have school, sweetie. I don't think it's a good idea to miss a day of school," Emery countered.

"We have a half-day Monday, teachers' meeting or something. Please, Mom? I wouldn't miss much." Randy was extremely good at bargaining, but Tag knew from observation that Emery was no pushover.

"Suppose I email Ms. Kaplan. If she assures me you will not

miss much work, I'll consider it. I will also ask her to email your homework, so you don't fall behind."

The boy looked somewhat disconsolate. The last word he heard was homework, completely overlooking there was a good chance he would be allowed to stay. "I hate when you're so strict, Mom," Randy pouted.

"Hey, buddy," Tag interjected, seeing Emery's crestfallen expression. "Part of being a good parent, a successful coach, and a responsible pet owner is setting rules and making sure they're followed. You're going to learn that the hard way if you don't set strict rules for Goldie." Randy sat back down on his mother's lap, eyes glued to Tag's piercing glare.

"Suppose you have established a whole list of rules for Goldie to follow, but because she is so damn cute — oops, sorry, Em — so darn cute, you become soft-hearted and let her do whatever she wants." Tag could clearly see he had Randy's undivided attention, so he quickly went in for the kill. "Imagine this: you come home from a hard day at school to find pee and poop all over your room, even on your bed. Picture it, Randy. Doggie poop. On. Your. Pillow." Randy's face morphed into an amalgam of revulsion and dismay. *I'm just gettin' started, kid.* "And then you see your Larry Fitzgerald jersey and autographed football chewed to shreds." Gaping in pure horror, Randy buried his head in Emery's neck. Tag unsuccessfully attempted to stifle a grin, winking at Emery, who flashed him an appreciative thumbs-up.

"I'm sorry, Mom. I understand. I'll do anything you say, I promise. Just please let me stay an extra day, *please?*" Randy kissed his mother on both cheeks.

"Let's see what Ms. Kaplan says." Grabbing her cell phone, Emery shot off a quick email. Randy continued to stare at his mother, awaiting an answer.

"Sweetheart, she may not answer tonight. She could be out or already asleep. In the meantime, why don't you get ready for bed?" Randy usually fought bedtime, but Emery pinned him with an authoritative glare. A pensive expression clouded the child's eyes for a brief moment.

"Okay, Mom. I love you." Randy climbed off the couch and headed to the bedroom.

"I love you, too, baby. Don't forget to brush your teeth," Emery called out after him.

Tag and Emery exchanged furtive glances, and then burst into laughter while trying unsuccessfully to control the volume of their voices.

"Can you believe him?" Emery giggled, covering her mouth with her hands.

"He's a remarkable kid. You should have seen me when I was his age. I'm sure my mother has stories which would curl your hair." He playfully twirled a strand of her perfectly straight, silky locks. "Even *this* hair," he added with a chuckle.

"I'd love to hear your mom's stories sometime." Emery's smile was genuine, but Tag was reluctant to respond, nor did he volunteer any further information on the topic. It had taken Tag years to develop his persona. He was an enigma, a Rubik's Cube of sorts: complex, secretive, mysterious. Sensing his reticence, she deftly changed the subject.

"I have school Monday morning. If Randy stays, is there any way you could watch him? I know this is asking a lot, but ..."

"No problem. I'll take him to Petco and we'll buy everything Goldie will need."

"Thank you so much, you're a life saver." After a brief hug, she quickly rose and strode over to the corner desk. Tag uncomfortably rearranged his crotch area. *Down, boy. Didn't you get the memo?*

"I'm gonna change Randy's flight to Monday evening. I'm not waiting to hear from his teacher. I'd like him to be there when we pick Goldie up." Emery opened her laptop and began typing away.

Randy emerged from the bedroom and quietly approached his mother, but audibly gasped when he spied the Southwest Airlines page open on her laptop.

"Mom, what are you doing?" A hopeful question hovered in the air. Emery's wide grin, as she turned to face him, said it all.

"You're letting me stay? Ms. Kaplan said it was okay?" His arms hesitated a fraction of a second before encircling her neck.

"Sweetie, I made the decision myself. It's vital that you are the first person Goldie sees. That way she will always know she belongs to you, the one who loves her and fought to keep her."

"Thanks, Mom. You're the best. I'll take *super* good care of her — just like you take care of me. I promise."

Tag was now standing next to Randy, his large hand on the boy's shoulder. Emery finished the online transaction, and after printing Randy's new boarding pass, closed the laptop.

"Randy, you need to thank Tag. If he wasn't willing to babysit you Monday morning while I'm in class, none of this would be happening."

Randy looked up at Tag, idolization filling his innocent eyes as he hugged Tag around the waist.

"Thanks, Tag." Shifting on his feet uncomfortably, Tag was quick to recover. He put his fists on his hips, and assumed his best drill-sergeant voice.

"Let's make one thing crystal clear. There will be no *babysitting* involved. We men will be doing some serious shopping Monday morning. Purchasing proper supplies for a new pet is important business, right, buddy?" Tag smiled at the boy affectionately, ruffling his hair.

"Yes, sir! Only the best for my Goldie. Right, Mom?" Tag watched with envy as Emery's countenance relaxed whenever she gazed at the child. Mother and son exchanged a heartfelt look; a glance so replete with unconditional love, Tag felt a twinge behind his ribcage, as if his heart was being squeezed. The physical pain was so potent he was compelled to look away as he fought to regain his breath. Thinking about his own mother caused unwelcome emotions to wash over him like a twenty-foot Pacific swell. A few deep breaths later, the ache dissipated and his breathing calmed. He glanced down to find Emery's soft hand resting on his forearm; her warmth permeated his every cell and when she stepped away, he felt somewhat bereft.

Emery finally heard from Ms. Kaplan and Randy was officially cleared to ditch school Monday. He was happy to learn his only assignment was to read the next chapter in *The Lion, the Witch, and the Wardrobe*. He enjoyed the book so much, he was already way ahead of the rest of the class, and the plane ride back to Phoenix would surely mean he would be starting the next book shortly.

Since their football practice time ended so abruptly, Randy asked Tag if they could possibly arrange for some extra time Sunday. Unfortunately, Tag had back-to-back clients at the gym all day and was subbing for Brew at the bar in the evening.

"Sorry, buddy. Next time you're up here, I'll make sure to save you some extra practice time, okay? I promise."

"It's okay. Mommy and I can go to the Walt Disney Museum tomorrow." Although disappointment showed clearly on his face, Randy still had a smile for his coach.

Squatting down at eye-level, Tag gave the boy a hug. "I'll see you Monday morning, bright and early, all right?"

"Okay. Thanks again for saving Goldie's life."

Emery walked him to the door, where they embraced as Tag whispered in her ear. "Sorry I'm not available tomorrow. I hate disappointing him."

"After everything you did today? It's all right, and besides, I can't have you hogging up all his time," she teased, kissing his cheek.

"See ya Monday, Em." Tag planted a soft kiss on her forehead and left.

Tag's pensive reflection in the bathroom mirror glared back at him as he brushed his teeth. *Be careful; don't get in over your head with this girl. You enjoy her company and hangin' with the kid is fun. That's all it is … fun. Innocent. Keep it casual.*

He climbed into bed, naked as usual, and took a deep breath as his hand reached for his cock, stroking it — his nightly ritual — in a futile attempt to relax and avoid the dreams, which never seemed to abandon his subconscious mind. Substituting Randi's face with Emery's was relatively easy. Their features were eerily similar, but the idea of her was a bit more alarming. Dreaming about Randi was comfortably safe, although painful. Emery, on the other hand, represented the real possibility of experiencing love again. The thought was exhilarating as well as completely terrifying; jumping out of a plane without a parachute was the only comparison Tag's confused mind could fathom, as an aching nausea permeated his every cell.

Chapter 12

*"Animals are such agreeable friends —
they ask no questions, they pass no criticisms."*
— George Eliot

TAG

Tag showed up at Emery's apartment Monday morning to pick up Randy; Emery would be returning from class around 3:30 p.m. Doctor Moriarty had said Goldie would be ready any time after 2 p.m.

Prior to visiting Petco, Tag decided to take Randy to his gym for an hour. An introduction to weight training was in order, especially with football tryouts happening in a few months. Showing great patience and care, Tag methodically demonstrated several different types of exercises Randy could do to strengthen and tone his upper body. Watching Tag easily lift 100-pound dumbbells made the boy's eyes pop.

"It took me years of hard work, lots of blood, sweat, and tears, kid. You gotta start light; try these five-pounders. See how they feel. Maybe the tens would be better. Let's see." Copying Tag's motions, Randy completed several sets of exercises under Tag's watchful eye.

"Slow and easy, buddy. Good job. Don't overdo it. That's when injuries happen, and we don't want that, okay?"

"Okay, Coach," came Randy's enthusiastic assent. *This kid is every coach's dream.* A fifteen-minute workout followed on a mini-trampoline. If Randy was to be a successful wide receiver, jumping ability was paramount. Tag had learned children did not respond well to lower-body machines; it was grueling and a tad boring. Their shorter legs were an additional disadvantage.

"Coach, this is soooo fun!" Randy exclaimed after five straight minutes of jumping. "Maybe Mom can buy one of these things so I can train at home in the backyard." Tag never took his eyes off Randy, always holding at least one of his hands in his own strong grip. Trampolines were deceptively dangerous; hours of seemingly innocent entertainment wrapped in a potentially lethal package. Even when a pretty girl approached him to ask a question, his attention never wavered from the bouncing child.

"Not. Now. I'm workin' here." His curt reply brought a scowl to her face and she strode off, rolling her eyes in frustrated annoyance. Any bystander could tell she was not used to being ignored, especially when her competition was a mere child. Tag blew out an annoyed breath in frustration. *Why are some chicks so fuckin' clueless?*

⊗

They were the first customers to enter Petco. Randy had made a list the night before, and had done extensive online research in the morning, so the pair simply went up and down every aisle, loading a shopping cart. Tag gave him free rein to choose items himself, only intervening if he deemed it necessary. Having had a few dogs growing up, Tag felt his opinions and insight would be valuable.

"She'll need a high-protein dog food to repair her injuries and increase lean muscle mass. It's the same with athletes like us. More lean meat, chicken, fish, and veggies; less soda, candy, and cookies, right? Your tryouts will be here before you know it." Randy nodded enthusiastically. Emery had mentioned that healthy eating habits were instilled in the child since birth. After leaving the pet food aisle, Tag commandeered the cart; he had one more key item on his mental checklist to purchase.

"Randy, because Goldie is young, she will need to spend some time in a crate, until she is house-broken and trained. I suggest a sturdy, plastic one. It will be easier to carry when it comes time to transport her home to Arizona. Let's go pick one out."

The sales clerk was ringing up the items, looking everything over carefully, as Tag handed him his Visa card.

"Is this your son's first dog?" he queried, attempting a friendly conversation as he waited for credit approval.

"Yes, it is, but he's not —"

"Tag's not my dad; he's my football coach!" Randy interrupted proudly.

A hard lump formed in Tag's throat as unfamiliar emotions surged through his chest. Shaking it off, he grabbed the larger bundles, and motioned for Randy to carry the rest. They loaded the truck and headed back to Emery's apartment.

"Okay, buddy. We'd better set up everything before your mom gets home."

When Emery arrived, the apartment had been transformed into a well-equipped, new-puppy haven. Her eyes widened, taking everything in, then settled on the largest object in the room: the sturdy plastic crate, which would be Goldie's home until she was fully trained. A leash, ID tag, collar, several chew toys, and a blanket were neatly arranged on the couch. Bags and cans of dog food were stacked in a kitchen corner, along with assorted bowls and treats. A stack of newspapers, indoor potty pads, a pooper-scooper, a can of flea and tick spray, and puppy shampoo, as well as stain-removal products sat on the kitchen counter.

"Wow! I see my two favorite men have had a busy morning. I am impressed." Rushing up to greet his mother, Randy was bubbling over with ideas.

"So, me and Tag —" Emery interrupted him with a subtle glare, eyebrows raised.

"Sorry, Mom. So, Tag and *I* were just discussing housebreaking and training and stuff. I wanna help figure out a schedule, for when I'm not here, to keep track of walking and feeding Goldie." Randy smiled wanly, but it did not reach his eyes. Emery bent down to wrap the boy in her arms, smothering him in kisses.

"Honey, I know you'd rather be here to help, but we will Skype every evening and Goldie will see you and hear your voice. She's not going to forget you, if that's what you're worried about. Now, let's go get her."

It was time for Tag to leave for his evening shift at the bar. Emery and Randy had already gone to San Francisco International Airport, leaving Tag to puppy-sit a while longer. The youngster had become rather attached to Goldie in such a short time; there were kisses, sorrowful goodbyes, and a few plaintive yelps from Goldie as they departed.

The puppy had been picked up and transported back to the apartment without incident. Tag showed Randy how much food and water to give her, had taken her out for two walks around the block and crammed in the basics rules of crate training. Goldie was now snugly wrapped in her blanket, sitting on Tag's lap watching *Scooby Doo* cartoons on TV. As he looked down at the helpless animal, his heart swelled with pride and gratification; he was solely responsible for saving this one, small, seemingly insignificant life. Pulling the blanket further up on his chest, he allowed Goldie to snuggle against his neck.

Soon she was happily licking his face and he found himself laughing aloud at her antics. After giving her a few more playful scratches on the top of her head, he carefully placed her back in the crate, making sure it was securely latched. Taking one last look to make sure everything was secure, he departed, leaving the TV on at low volume to keep the puppy company. Tag chuckled to himself as he locked the apartment door, using the extra key Emery had given him. *I bet Goldie will enjoy watching* Bolt*!*

EMERY

Back from the airport, Emery breathed a sigh of relief as she flopped down onto the couch. After a busy day, it felt great just to relax. She looked happily at the new addition to the family. Goldie seemed quite comfortable and content in her luxury-sized crate. Tag had left a note advising her that the pup would probably be ready for a walk around 10:00 p.m. After checking the dried food and water bowls, Emery snuggled on the couch, and grabbed the TV remote.

9:10 p.m. Time to catch up on my DVR shows.

Emery was in the process of scrolling through her recordings when her cell phone buzzed. Her lips curled up in a wide smile when she saw the name. She was gradually beginning to comprehend what a good friend Tag had become, refusing to let her pay him back for all the doggie supplies he had purchased.

TAG: BACK FROM THE AIRPORT?

EMERY: YEP. RANDY'S PROBABLY HALFWAY HOME BY NOW. THANKS FOR EVERYTHING YOU DID TODAY.

TAG: HOW'S GOLDIE?

EMERY: GREAT. CHEWING AWAY ON ONE OF HER MANY TOYS. OMG WAS THERE ANYTHING LEFT AT PETCO

AFTER YOU TWO STORMED THRU?

TAG: NOT MUCH. LOL. SO, IT'S DEAD HERE AND BREW SAID I COULD TAKE OFF AT 10. WHY DON'T I STOP BY AND SEE MY 2 FAVE GIRLS.

EMERY: HMMM. ARE YOU USING ME TO GET CLOSE TO GOLDIE?

TAG: DAMN RIGHT! SEE YA 10:20-ISH. DON'T WALK HER ALONE. WAIT FOR ME.

EMERY: OK.

Using his key to enter the apartment, Tag found Emery on the couch with a languid Goldie on her lap. The puppy appeared to be sleeping, lying on her back, four legs splayed out.

Emery's fingers were softly stroking her fur — up and down, back and forth — rubbing her limbs gingerly. Tag sat next to her, a questioning look on his face.

"It's puppy massage. Robbi sent me a video on Facebook. It's supposed to be calming and relaxing."

"Well, I think it's working. In fact, I wouldn't mind a massage myself." Tag chuckled a little too loudly as he sat next to her, wiggling his eyebrows suggestively. Hearing his robust voice, Goldie immediately emerged from her massage-induced stupor and leaped onto Tag's chest, licking his face enthusiastically.

"How's my good girl?" he crooned into the puppy's ear, kissing her snout affectionately, as Emery's mouth curved downward in feigned jealousy.

"I knew you were using me to get to her."

"It's actually the other way around, Em." Tag sighed, kissing her lightly on the tip of her nose as he stood up. "Now, you grab her leash and I'll bring the scooper and poop-baggies. She needs to go out."

It was a beautiful moonlit night as they leisurely strolled around the neighborhood. Several people, mostly young women, stopped to admire Goldie and ask curious questions about her bandages and wobbly gait. As they approached the apartment, Emery linked her arm through Tag's and shook her head, laughing heartily.

"Wow. Goldie is a total chick-magnet! No wonder you want to hang out with her."

Giving her a playful scowl, Tag retorted, "Well, I have to admit she is cute, but you are the better conversationalist." He leaned toward her, gently kissing her temple. "Look! Another pee and a pretty nice poop," he declared proudly, leaning down to scoop up the waste. "I think our Goldie is well on her way to being house-broken. This is a very promising start."

An hour had passed and Goldie was snoring lightly in her crate, as Tag and Emery relaxed on the couch watching TV, a half-empty bottle of red wine on the coffee table. Emery was resting against Tag's chest, his arm casually draped over her shoulder.

"I intend to pay you back for what you spent on Goldie today," Emery declared emphatically as she refilled their wineglasses. He stubbornly shook his head.

"No, Em, I wanted to do it for you and Randy. Besides, you agreed to do that mosaics project in my house. We'll be even then, okay?"

"I guess so," she conceded resolutely, turning to face him. "When would you like me to start on that?"

"I'm still working on my bathroom and the place is a mess right now, so I guess in a couple of weeks, okay?"

"That's perfect. I need to focus on my two sculpture assignments. They're kicking my ass at the moment."

"Well, my offer still stands. I'm available for nude modeling anytime." Tag's expression was dead serious, although his tone was mischievous.

"I just might take you up on your offer, but you won't have to be naked. I would just need your face."

"Well, where's the fun in that?" He chuckled. "Wait ... what? You really want me to pose for you?" His eyebrows shot up in disbelief.

Emery chewed on her bottom lip. "Yes, I would. One of my sculptures is of Randy, and the other one is ... you." Her voice was timid, almost a whisper.

"Seriously, Emery?" Tag swallowed hard, licking his lips. "Wow. I'm flattered, I think." He suppressed a smile.

"Well, I've barely started it, and it's proving to be a bit difficult. I'll let you know."

Tag gently took her face in his hands, and proceeded to stare deeply into her eyes. She could clearly see his inner emotions as if she was gazing into a mirror; the exact sensations were fluttering in her ribcage. *Oh, my God. Is he going to kiss me?*

Soft canine whimpers could be heard in the stillness of the room. Goldie was awake and in apparent distress, as two pairs of concerned eyes flew in the direction of the crate. Tag was the first to move toward her, removing his T-shirt in a flash. *What the hell?*

"Em, grab that blanket." Reaching into the crate, he gingerly lifted up a trembling Goldie, who appeared to be groggy, and placed her on his bare chest as he lay back down on the sofa. "Now, put the blanket over her. I'm just gonna hold her for a while. She'll be able to feel my warmth and hear my heartbeat. I saw my father do this once. You'll see. It'll calm her right down.

Emery's mouth was agape, her eyes as huge as saucers. Watching Tag in full-on rescue mode was quite an impressive sight to behold. It was, however, the glorious sight of a shirtless Tag, which had her stomach doing somersaults, not to mention her lady-parts. Her efforts to avoid gawking at his well-defined, muscular chest and colorful tattoos failed miserably. *Oh. My. Freakin'. God. Move over, Goldie.*

A life-like pair of caramel eyes inked right over his heart caused her breath to hitch in her throat. *Randi.* Averting her eyes was difficult; the tattoo, along with an inked quote, was mesmerizing.

Emery sat next to Tag and placed her hand on top of his while her forefinger lightly rubbed the puppy's snout. Her concerned eyes met Tag's; words were unnecessary as each seemed able to read the other's thoughts.

"The doctor warned me this was a possibility. Post-traumatic stress. She was in that coyote's mouth, Emery. His teeth pierced and tore into her body."

Horror filled Emery's eyes as she buried her face into the crook of his neck. "How will she ever be able to forget that?" Concern laced Emery's words as her chestnut eyes searched Tag's for reassurance.

"We give her a safe environment and tons of love. Doc said she should be fine as she becomes accustomed to us and her new surroundings." Tag turned and deposited a kiss on the top of her head.

"I'm glad you were here, Tag. I probably would have freaked out, but at least now, I know what to do if it happens again. I'll move the crate into the bedroom, so I can …"

"Emery, I have a much better solution. Why don't I just stay over? I'll sleep on the couch, of course, so you won't be disturbed. I can't have you falling asleep in class and ruining your sculpture of me, right? And besides, if she needs to be walked in the middle of the night, I certainly don't want you to be out there alone."

"I can take care of myself. And in case you have forgotten, Goldie is part pit bull: a ferocious beast that will protect me from any and all threats." She giggled, delivering a playful punch to his shoulder.

"She'll be a good watch-dog one day, but it won't be for a

while. I don't mind, Emery, honestly. I'm staying, end of discussion. Even if you throw me out, I have my own key, so it won't do you any good. Now, go put on your pajamas ... or not, whatever, and I'm gonna get comfortable on this couch." He stood, tossed the blanket back on the sofa, and then gingerly carried a peacefully snoozing Goldie back to her crate. She was barely able to resist the urge to run her fingers down his chiseled pecs, past the lickable eight-pack, ending at the V pointing toward ... *Holy shit! He's staying over.*

Emery quickly escaped to the privacy of her bedroom, shaking the tension out of her wrists and fingers. After washing her face and brushing her teeth, she hastily put on her favorite Cardinals tank top and matching flannel shorts. She also put two clean towels on the counter along with a brand new, still-in-the-plastic toothbrush for Tag. Before entering the living room, Emery stopped at the linen closet and removed an extra blanket and pillow.

"Tag, are you decent?" she called and waited for a response. She heard his amused chuckle.

"Decent? Hmmm, that's debatable, Emery. If you're asking me if I'm naked, then the answer is no, unless you want me to be." His tone was naughty with a touch of good-natured teasing.

"You are incorrigible, Tag." Upon entering the living room, she found him on the sofa wearing snug Lycra running shorts, feet up on the coffee table, texting. His jeans had been neatly folded and placed on a nearby chair. Emery tossed him the blanket, and then aimed the pillow directly at his head. "Hey! Is that how you treat guests?" He pouted.

"I am the perfect hostess. Clean towels and a toothbrush are in the bathroom."

"Well, I'll only need the toothbrush if you plan on kissing me, Emery." He smirked, shooting her a sexy wink. Her eyebrows shot to the ceiling as she delivered an exaggerated eye roll.

"Mister, you will need that toothbrush if you plan on even breathing in my vicinity," she declared haughtily, while collapsing next to him on the couch in a fit of laughter.

His arm instantaneously enfolded her shoulders and held her close. Kissing the crown of her head, he whispered, "Don't worry, babe. I'll be a perfect gentleman. I promise."

Well, damn, Tag.

TAG

Tag may have told Emery he would behave, but his dick made no such promises. He found it necessary to keep either the blanket or pillow on his lap most of the time. *So fucking embarrassing. I don't want her thinkin' I'm some kind of sex maniac. Well ... not yet, anyway.*

They snuggled on the couch, watching the acclaimed indie movie *Boyhood,* which was Emery's choice. She explained how the director and film crew made the drama over a period of twelve years, beginning the process when the star was eight years old, and documenting his coming of age as he experienced adolescence.

"That was pretty cool, watching the real-life changes over time."

"Yeah. It makes me want to take videos of Randy every day for the next fifteen years." Her breathless laugh made Tag's heart swell.

"Well, that might not be possible. What you could do, however, is videotape him playing football. You know, running, throwing and catching. Narrow your scope — focus on one specific aspect of his life. As he ages, his skill level will increase exponentially and the tapes will also provide feedback for him to analyze his mistakes and improve his performance."

"That's a brilliant idea! I'll start the next time he's here." Emery squealed excitedly, clapping her hands like a kid on Christmas morning. Tag grinned at her innocent exuberance. The unexpected commotion caused Goldie to stir in her crate.

Two pairs of concerned eyes were immediately directed toward the puppy. Emery's guilt-ridden face flushed as her hands flew to her mouth. The puppy yawned and turned over, kicking out her injured leg, then stilled. Emery sighed in relief as she leaned into Tag's side.

"No worries. She's stronger than she looks. I'm pretty sure she will sleep through the night. Maybe you should turn in, too. You look exhausted."

"Okay. If you need anything, help yourself." Waving her hand toward the kitchen, she rose off the sofa, turning back to Tag for a moment. "Thanks for staying. It means a lot to me." She leaned down, cupped his face with her hand, and placed a soft kiss on his cheek. She started to walk away but he grabbed her wrist, causing her to freeze. Their eyes met for a long moment as Tag inhaled deeply.

"I have clients all morning and early afternoon, but I'm free after 3:00 p.m. Wanna meet me for a workout, grab dinner, then maybe squeeze in a movie?" His sea-green eyes bore into her; he held his breath, awaiting her response.

"Um … actually that'd be great. It will give me some extra time to work in the studio."

Tag beamed, eyes sparkling. "Cool. See ya then. I'll be in the aerobics room."

"Okay. Good night."

"Sleep tight, Em."

After he heard her bedroom door softly close, he went into the kitchen and grabbed a bottle of water, a fistful of paper towels and a small plastic bottle of hand lotion, which was on the counter. Taking deep cleansing breaths, Tag stretched out on the couch then turned the television off. The only sound, besides his own breathing, was Goldie's light snoring. There was a small night-light in the corner, so he was able to discern clearly the layout of the room.

Tag had a nightly ritual; one that helped him release the usual tension of the day as well as ease the constant aching in his groin. Being so close to Emery was pure torture; he had so much pent-up sexual frustration, he felt close to exploding. Every glimpse of her pouty lips instantly filled his mind with erotic images.

Instinctively, his hand slid into the front of his shorts, palming his semi-hard cock. Sliding his shorts down a bit, his dick sprang free with a thump, hitting his taut stomach. His semi was now a full-blown — *pun intended?* — erection, throbbing painfully. Grabbing the plastic bottle, he squirted some lotion into his hand, and massaged it up and down his length. Moaning softly in pleasure, he fisted himself, stroking roughly, imagining Emery's strong hands on his cock.

God, Em, you feel so fuckin' good. Harder, baby. Please. Yes, just like that, Emery.

He closed his eyes and simply let the sensations overwhelm his entire being — the building of pressure deep within, followed by a tingling radiating outward like bolts of electricity shooting through his lower body. His orgasm was powerful, bursting in short but potent spurts that were consumed in the mass of paper towels. After his breathing stilled, he methodically cleaned himself off, disposed of the mess, and strode to the bathroom to take a piss. Looking at his reflection in the mirror, he scoffed to himself. *Is this what my life has become? Jerking off while a beautiful, desirable woman sleeps in the next room ... alone.*

EMERY

Tag was already gone when Emery woke up. She noticed the towels and toothbrush she had set out for him had been used. A slow smile emerged as she washed her face. *He must have been super quiet. I didn't hear a thing.* A note from Tag sat on the kitchen table.

Good morning, Em. Goldie's been walked and fed. I'll be back around noon to give her lunch and another walk. You'll take care of her before the gym, OK? Then we can discuss her evening schedule. Have a great day! Later, Tag

There were several other students in the art studio also taking advantage of the free day to work on their sculptures. Professor Navarro was there as well, walking around — praising, commenting, making suggestions, demonstrating helpful techniques. He had a warm, approachable demeanor although Emery felt a bit unnerved whenever he gazed at her. He was a stunning man, imposing, authoritative and downright sexy as sin.

"You are making good progress, Emery. Are these your two subjects?" He pointed to the array of photographs she was using as inspiration.

She gave him a wide smile. "This is my son, Randy; he just turned nine. And this is his football coach."

Nodding approvingly, he leaned in a bit closer, murmuring, "Would you like to get together for dinner later? I know a place that makes fantástica paella." Luca's smile was beguiling, showing his perfect white teeth.

Emery's slight grimace was apologetic. "Sorry, Luca, I already have dinner plans tonight. And besides, you know my policy regarding teacher/student involvement."

"Of course, Emery. Enjoy your evening." Luca's smile was polite, but there was an intensity in his eyes that was noticeable as he moved on to the next student — a pretty, petite blonde who had been trying to capture his attention for a while. *Well, that was awkward. He seemed annoyed. I'll bet he doesn't get turned down often.* Emery breathed a small sigh as she turned back to the large lump of clay that she hoped would eventually become Tag's likeness. It was faceless at the moment, although the substructure — skull, forehead, and cheekbones — was apparent.

After Emery cleaned up her area, she gathered her things and headed out the door, waving to the remaining students. The petite blonde's singsong voice could easily be heard. "Oh, I simply *love* paella, Professor!" Emery chuckled under her breath.

◇

She found Tag in the aerobics room, already doing a few stretches on the mat. Emery couldn't help but notice how his ample biceps filled his snug T-shirt. *Stop staring. He doesn't deserve to be eye-fucked like a piece of meat! But he is terribly delectable looking.*

"So, how's my sculpture coming along?" He handed her a bottle of water.

"It's great, except my hands always suffer. They constantly ache and the damn clay takes a toll on my nails."

Taking her hands immediately into his massive, strong grip, Tag massaged them in forceful, kneading waves. As his thumbs dug deeply into her palms in small circular motions, Emery's low, husky moans escaped her throat in short bursts.

"Oh, that feels sooo good. Harder, please." Her head had fallen back and her eyes were closed in obvious ecstasy because of his ministrations.

"Well, it wouldn't be the first time I heard that request from a satisfied woman. Your wish is my command, Emery," he chuckled seductively. Her eyes flew open and she glared at him in feigned indignation; it didn't last long, however. His touch was warmly electrifying as her aches and pains rapidly disappeared. Tag continued to apply the perfect amount of pressure to each finger joint, alternately squeezing and caressing every spot.

"I've always had an obsession with hands — not a fetish, per se — more of a fascination. Football is all about the hands

... throwing, catching, dexterity, flexibility, strength, and speed. Often the ball is moving so fast it can barely be seen, but I can always feel it. My fingertips caressing the laces, palm sensing the texture of the leather ..." His eyes fluttered closed, as if drifting into a wonderful, yet painful, reminiscence. A few seconds later, his dark green eyes reappeared, as a warm smile returned to his lips.

"You have tremendous strength in your hands, Emery, yet your skin is extremely soft."

Emery beamed, warmth creeping up her neck and cheeks. Electric sparks danced along her skin from his touch.

"I give myself a hot wax spa treatment on a regular basis." Seeing Tag's bewilderment, she proceeded to expound. "You dip your hands in hot, melted paraffin several times, let the warm layers build up, then sit back and chillax. When the wax cools, you peel it off and your hands are refreshed and rejuvenated, not to mention as soft as a newborn baby's butt. Sometimes I do my feet, too. It's freakin' heaven."

After an invigorating two-hour workout, they grabbed some quick sushi, and headed to the Embarcadero Center Cinema. Tag had read a recent review of an indie movie that he was anxious to see. *Whiplash* — the story of a promising young drummer who enrolls at a cutthroat music conservatory. Tag had taken drum lessons as a child, but he gave them up when he discovered football. Emery, having seen the movie's star, Miles Teller, in several other films, was a devoted fan.

The theater was not crowded, so they had their choice of seats, which featured retractable armrests. Tag quickly dispensed with the armrest that separated them and pulled Emery into his side, announcing, "I am not quite finished with your hands yet."

He took one hand in his and held it for a while, close to his chest. As the film's plot became more involved, they seemed to lose themselves in the intense drama. Tag began pressing their palms together, sliding up and down in a sensual slow-dance of skin barely touching. His fingertips ran along both sides of her hand, tickling her palm one minute and the back of her knuckles the next. Then he rubbed tiny circles in the center of her palm ... hard, soft, then hard again. At one point, he gently placed soft featherlight kisses across her wrist. Emery could barely focus on the screen; her breathing became ragged, and her hand felt like it was having a mini-manual orgasm all on its own. When she thought she was about to hyperventilate, Tag brought their joined hands to rest on his thigh where they remained until the end of the film. *Holy shit! That felt beyond amazing.* They held hands all the way home and enjoyed an animated, non-stop discussion of the film and its stars' performances.

Tag stayed over two more nights to make sure Goldie was adjusting to her new home and surroundings. Emery tried to dissuade him, insisting it was not necessary, but secretly felt thrilled, although filled with nervous trepidation. Tuesday night Goldie woke up once, whimpered briefly, then went back to sleep after being held by Tag for about ten minutes. On Wednesday, they had personal activities and responsibilities to attend to, but managed to have dinner together, with Tag bringing take-out Chinese food home.

Goldie was responding beautifully to crate-training and house-breaking — only having three minor accidents, both which happened inside the crate or on the spread-out newspapers in the kitchen and not on any carpets or furniture. After dinner, Randy called and requested an extensive Skype session with Goldie. The boy was determined to teach her to bark on command. After almost an hour, the lesson was mildly successful — a 'ruff' or two were elicited from the puppy, who was being prompted by Tag, who 'woofed' in her ear more than once. Emery put on a happy face for Randy's benefit, but her eyes brimmed with tears as she longed to hold her son close.

There were kisses all around as Randy signed off Skype, and a few more from Tag — although quite chaste — were placed on Emery's forehead and nose before she retired to her room.

A startling noise awoke Emery from a deep sleep. She padded into the living room, expecting to see Goldie awake, but a more upsetting sight greeted her: Tag sitting on the couch, head in his hands, breathing heavily and mumbling to himself.

"Tag! Are you okay? I thought I heard a noise." Emery kneeled on the floor facing him, hands softly cupping his cheeks. Shaking his head, he yanked her hands down.

"I'm fine. It was just a dream. More like a nightmare. I get them sometimes." Raking his fingers through his hair, he avoided her eyes. "I'm okay now, gonna go back to sleep. Thanks for checking on me." Laying back on the couch, Tag squirmed a bit, then covered himself with the blanket, as Emery leaned over and tenderly pressed her lips to his forehead.

"You can talk to me anytime. I'm here for you. Always." Nodding, Tag turned quickly away from her to face the back of the couch. She longed to lie down beside him and hold him until he fell asleep in her arms. "Good night," she whispered, softly caressing the back of his head. Silence was the only answer. *He's not ready. He may never be. He hasn't even mentioned Randi yet.*

TAG

Spending the weekend with Emery and Randy, then additional days and nights alone with her had proved to be a highly emotional week for Tag. He had not felt like part of a loving family in over a decade. He arrived home feeling exhausted from a whirlwind combination of emotions. Terror, confusion, exhilaration, depression, and to top it all off, he was unbelievably horny. Being around Emery was becoming increasingly torturous. The erotic handholding and massages, not to mention sleeping under the same roof, had him feeling on edge and out of control. In the past, he would simply find a willing female at the gym or the bar and get sucked off in his truck. The idea no longer seemed tempting.

After peeling off his clothes, Tag jumped in the shower, and turned the water on full blast; the intense heat and steam always seemed to clear his head. Dousing his hand with a squirt of shampoo, he leaned back against the tile and let the scent fill the air.

He rubbed his palm up and down his growing length, speeding up a bit when the familiar tingling sensations overwhelmed his lower body. Jerking off in the shower had become second nature; part of his daily routine, an uncomplicated way to release pent-up sexual frustration. It certainly was a lot simpler than hooking up with random chicks all over town. Using his thumb softly on the underside of the head, Tag's other hand settled into a stroking rhythm and soon his hips were taking over the sharp, thrusting movements. He began to moan softly as the familiar, delirious pressure followed, building and falling, increasing and decreasing, approaching closer and closer … finally propelling him across the threshold. *God. Ahhh!* Groaning his release loudly, he gritted his teeth as spurts of cum hit the shower door for what seemed like a full minute. Sliding down the tile wall, his head slumped into his hands. He would need Emery to invade his dreams; help him survive another possible sleepless night.

Emery. What an asshole I was last night. She came out to comfort me and what did I do? Turned my back on her like the gutless coward I am. I hated myself for it, but I just couldn't let her see my tears.

The relentless nightmares began soon after Tag's head hit the pillow. Flames, smoke, a hand desperately reaching toward him, but he could not save her in time.

The flowing quicksand engulfs me, its darkness dragging me under. I stare into nothingness, as a hand appears from above. I reach for her, but she always slips away.

Chapter 13

*"You must live in the present, launch yourself on every wave,
find your eternity in each moment."*
– Henry David Thoreau

TAG

Tag expressed interest in going to another museum, so after their usual Saturday morning workout, they set off to the Asian Art Museum. Emery suggested Tag be on the lookout for designs, which might work for the mosaic project. There were Japanese ceramics and Buddhist sculptures, as well as an abundance of varying genres of paintings and tapestries. Tag admired the simple lines and curves of Asian characters, and decided they would be ideal for his home. He found a calligraphy book in the gift shop and bought it immediately. It was the perfect day in early spring, as they strolled stepping-stone paths bordered by serene koi ponds and a stunning Zen garden. Trees laden with cherry blossoms were mid-bloom, filling the air with their sweet, intoxicating fragrance. Afterwards they visited the Japanese Tea Garden, the oldest public Japanese garden in the United States, which was located inside Golden Gate Park. They sat in a charming stone pagoda, flipping through the book's pages hoping to find the perfect symbols to adorn whatever surface Tag had in mind.

"I would like you to pose for me at the studio, perhaps Tuesday?" Emery's voice was barely audible, her manner shy and reserved. "I don't think it will take too long. Maybe two or three hours? I'll treat you to dinner afterwards. You pick the place."

Pulling his phone out, Tag opened up his calendar. "Hmmm ... let's see. I have a few free hours before I start my shift at the bar. Let's do it."

"Great. Thanks. I need you to promise you will not look at my work until it is completely finished. Do I have your word?" Her raised eyebrows got no argument from Tag; he realized she was dead serious.

"Of course, Em. Cross my heart. I'm well aware of how temperamental you artists can be," he teased. Simultaneous buzzing could be heard as both their phones went off to indicate incoming texts. Tyler's communication finished first — he was a man of few words, succinct when relaying information. Tag had already sent another text and received an answer by the time Emery was done.

"Tyler invited us to join him and Robbi at the Red Devil Club tonight. Ty's friends' band is playin' and they kick serious ass. Brew said he'd sub for me." Emery giggled as she held up her phone showing Robbi's identical text invitation. "Cool. I love hangin' out with them," Emery gushed. "They are the perfect couple."

Tag winced although he covered it up with a wide, although forced smile. "Yes, they certainly are." His throat constricted as he murmured the words, while his reflections aimlessly wandered to the countless times he and Tyler had shared women in the not-so-recent past. It had been a common occurrence, usually after a night of heavy drinking. A willing woman or two, an empty parking lot or the back seat of a truck ... it was a hazy blur in Tag's mind. The emotions he presently had concerning his best friend were conflicted; intense jealousy of Tyler's happiness and a burning contempt for his obvious love and devotion to his wife. *He is too damn old to be such a pussy-whipped fool!* Painful memories of Randi invaded his thoughts, but he shoved them back into the darkness.

Emery

Tuesday afternoon found Emery working diligently in the art studio getting ready for Tag's arrival. Her stomach fluttered in anticipation; working with a live model was not an everyday occurrence, made even more nerve-wracking by the presence of Professor Navarro and several students. Her eyes flitted around the room. Spying an empty chair in the corner, Emery quickly dragged it over and placed it in front of her work area.

Both of Emery's sculpting projects were progressing better than she had expected. Professor Navarro, although inappropriately flirtatious at times, taught some distinctive techniques, which helped Emery overcome her innate aversion for the art form. She had chosen Randy's diving catch from the first practice with Tag as inspiration for her bronze-cast piece, which was coming along nicely. Her clay sculpture of Tag was proving to be more challenging, which was the reason she had asked him to pose.

It was not going to be a traditional bust; only the head and neck would be shown, and there would be two distinct faces staring in opposite directions. Emery had observed one hundred eighty-degree opposing personalities displayed during the time they spent together: positive versus negative, joyful versus melancholy. Slowly but surely, Tag's smiling, upbeat countenance began to outweigh his despondent persona. She hoped to capture that fascinating dichotomy in her clay piece. Reluctant to ask Tag to model a second time, she planned to get as much accomplished as possible during their session. Her back-up plan was to capture a few close-up photos of him as well. She also could rely on her surreptitiously taken photographs of him during practices with

Randy. Feeling her phone vibrate in her pocket, she gave it a quick glance and saw his text.

TAG: I'M OUTSIDE.
EMERY: COME ON IN! I'M ALL SET UP IN THE BACK, NEAR THE SINKS.

Tag seemed a bit out of his element, so Emery casually made a few introductions before she instructed him regarding what she envisioned for the session. She planned to suggest a series of visual images and requested that he think deeply about them for several minutes.

Tag chuckled apprehensively. "So this is kinda like seeing a shrink. You want me to conjure up some emotions you can capture in clay, right?"

Emery offered Tag a warm smile. "I guess you could say that. The difference is, you don't have to say a word if you don't want to. You can just let your mind wander and think about whatever pops into your head. Ready?" Tag nodded anxiously, as she reminded him of his promise. "Don't forget, no peeking." Emery grabbed a large pad and made a few preliminary sketches. Several photos were also taken from various angles.

Tag's bravado about posing aside, Emery was keenly aware of his discomfort; his neck muscles strained against his snug T-shirt and she could discern the subtle grinding of his teeth. As she began a casual series of lighthearted, yet probing, questions — each designed to elicit specific reactions and emotions — Tag's shoulders visibly relaxed and soon both artist and model were chatting spiritedly.

Three hours later, they sat at their usual table in North Star Bar. Tag was plying Emery with provocative questions about his future as an artist's model.

"I was pretty good, right, Em? I mean, you were working that clay hard. Imagine if you had let me take my shirt off like I suggested."

Emery swatted his arm following an exaggerated eye roll. "Be serious! You are exceptionally photogenic; your face can be quite expressive when you let your guard down. I hope my questions weren't too intrusive, especially about your childhood memories."

Shrugging, Tag frowned. "I had a relatively happy childhood, so I didn't mind sharing that at all. Dad and I never saw eye-to-eye on my choice of a career in football. I'll admit he was a strict disciplinarian and was heavy-handed at times, but his wanting me to be a partner in his construction business? We settled that years ago when I turned eighteen. I told him it was never going to happen. End of fucking story." Emery digested his words, tilting her head in thought. *Hmmm ... not sure I should do this, but he needs to let his guard down and be honest with me. No more hiding the truth.*

"What was your father's relationship with your sister like? Was it as strained?" Tag blinked rapidly, glanced around the room as if searching for an escape route, then rubbed his chin. "My sister? Um, I ..." Beads of sweat were forming on his forehead; he drew in a deep breath, exhaling slowly.

"I have a confession to make. I don't have a sister. If you recall, I had just touched you inappropriately and it was the only explanation I could think of that wouldn't be embarrassing and somewhat lecherous. I mean, we had just met the day before. I apologize."

Emery reached out and stroked his arm as she attempted to put him at ease. "I'll accept your apology *if* you 'fess up the *real* reason you touched me so 'inappropriately'." He grinned at her casual use of air quotes.

"Okay, deal. I wanted to touch you ... *needed* to touch you at that moment." He reached out to her. Although her hair was perfectly in place, he dislodged a long strand, curled it around his index finger — never taking his eyes off hers — then tucked it gently behind her ear.

"So, tell me, Emery,"—Tag took a long pull from his beer, then drilled her with a heated glare, which caused her lady-parts to liquefy—"what's goin' on between you and that professor of yours?" His voice was a low growl.

Completely taken off-guard by his tone and the out-of-the-blue question, Emery was momentarily speechless. Purposefully using a few extra moments to chew her mouthful of pecan pie provided ample time to formulate an appropriate reply.

"Nothing's going on. I mean, he flirts occasionally, but he's like that with all the students, even the guys. You're not jealous, are you, Tag?" Emery teased, tilting her head provocatively as she twirled the stray tendril around her finger.

Tag scoffed, "Of course not. I'm just lookin' out for you. I caught him ogling you more than once, and I swear he was giving me the evil death-stare." Emery chuckled and shook her head, but Tag maintained eye contact. "Be honest, Emery. Has he hit on you, asked you out?"

Emery heaved a sigh. "Not that it's any of your business, but yes, he did. And I turned him down. I already told you how I feel about relationships between teachers and students." Emery chewed on her lower lip as her face flushed with warmth, recalling her impromptu sharing of drinks at the wine bistro with Luca. Although it had not been an official date, she still had pangs of guilt nonetheless.

Tag snorted, but managed to appear contrite. "You're right, it's none of my business, but he seems like a player to me and probably uses his professor role to intimidate the younger, more naïve students."

"I'm a big girl, and trust me ... I can spot a player a mile away." Her giggle was meant to lighten the situation, but Tag bristled at her remark. Sitting stiffly back in his chair, he closed his eyes, dejectedly scrubbing a hand down his face. The abrupt silence between them was uncomfortably palpable. Emery was baffled by his reaction to her seemingly innocent words.

Taking a deep inhale, Tag gradually opened his eyes and leaned toward Emery, piercing her with the steadiness of his gaze. She noticed a visible tic in his jaw muscles.

"I know my reputation is shit, and I don't know what Robbi has told you about me, but I swear I am trying so fuckin' hard *not* to be that guy anymore."

Taken aback, Emery reached for his hand, covering it with her own. "I wasn't referring to you when I said that. I'm somewhat aware of your so-called reputation, but I prefer to judge people by the way they treat me. And you have been my best friend since I moved here."

Nodding resolutely, Tag flipped his hand over so they were palm-to-palm, and entwined their fingers. "Thanks. I didn't mean to pass judgement on your love life. I just feel the need to protect you, keep you safe. And yeah, maybe I do feel a tiny bit jealous." Chuckling while shaking his head, he sheepishly added, "And I probably shoulda kept that last part to myself."

Chapter 14

*"If thou remember'st not the slightest folly
That ever love did make thee run into,
Thou hast not loved."*
– William Shakespeare (As You Like It)

TAG

Unbeknownst to Emery, whenever Tag had a bit of free time, he'd been making clandestine trips to her apartment while she was in class. His regular visits certainly weren't secret; he had carte blanche and his own key to come and go as he pleased. They had agreed to share feeding and walking duties, but Tag had another mission in mind. He was determined to train Goldie, and had already been working diligently with her. Simple commands such as 'sit' and 'stay' were coming along nicely. The puppy also immediately seemed to recognize the word 'walk,' always whining excitedly and shuffling her paws when Tag or Emery held up her leash. After some online research and a discussion with Brew, his coworker — a self-proclaimed doggie-discipline expert — he was ready to teach her a valuable new command: 'attack'. Brew suggested a one-syllable code, short and to the point. Tag settled on 'tack'.

Goldie was a fast learner, attentive, intelligent, and responsive. The puppy had survived in Golden Gate Park before the coyote attack. Who knew what hardships she endured during that time? Tag wore a heavy protective glove that covered his entire arm during the training sessions, and was pleased at the progress she was making. *Goldie's gonna make one helluva guard dog someday.*

Tag always allowed her some playtime afterwards; the two of them would roll around on the floor in a writhing heap, limbs akimbo. It was difficult to discern who was having more fun: man or man's best friend?

After walking the energetic pup around the block a few times, Tag returned to the apartment and prepared to lie on the couch for a brief nap. He had experienced a restless night, due to another disturbing dream. Goldie appeared a bit fatigued as well, and Tag placed her on his chest, where she snuggled comfortably. He dozed off as a familiar presence infiltrated his subconscious mind.

Randi's voice sounds like it's on the far side of a distant, long-forgotten, discarded memory. She haunts my days, my nights, my dreams; I follow her voice through grey shadows. I need to find her, save her.

Tag gasped and awoke with a start, jostling Goldie in the process. Glancing at the clock, he saw only forty-five minutes had gone by. As if sensing his agitated breathing, the puppy inched closer to his face and rested her cold nose on his cheek, coaxing Tag to pet her. She licked him affectionately, her buoyant spirit refusing to let him wallow in his gloom. Somehow, Goldie discerned what he needed. Tag scratched behind her ears, being careful not to touch the injury, which had almost completely healed.

"You're a beautiful girl, Goldie," he cooed as she slobbered wet kisses all over him. "Yes, you are." She rolled over in his arms, squirming ecstatically as he scratched and tickled her tummy.

Hearing the key turn in the lock, Goldie tried to escape his hold in a vain attempt to greet Emery as she came into the apartment. Normally the puppy was in her crate, never allowed free rein of the apartment while no one was there. This was the first time Tag had stayed, hoping to spend some time with Emery since his 1 p.m. client had cancelled. Realizing too late he should have texted her, he called out quickly to alert her of his presence.

"I'm here, Em! Me and my favorite girl are makin' out on the couch." He waited until Emery had securely shut the apartment door before allowing Goldie to run free. The pup immediately darted toward her, scampering exuberantly around her feet. Looking over at Tag, Emery's eyes sparkled.

"What's up? Am I disturbing you two lovebirds?" She giggled, joining him on the couch as the puppy followed her, climbing back onto Tag's chest. Goldie bestowed an additional sloppy lick on his cheek before settling down, panting contentedly, with her pink tongue comically hanging out to one side, exposing her oddly shaped lower tooth. Emery's face broke out in a wide grin as she gazed at the pair.

"Oh, my Lord. You two are beyond freakin' adorable. Hold still while I shoot a few photos to send Randy." Emery grabbed her phone and busily snapped away as Tag proceeded to answer her question.

"I trained her for a bit then we shared a nice nap together. So, what time does Randy's flight land? Wanna hit the gym first?"

Emery glanced at the time. "He should be heading to the airport now, ETA in a few hours. We have plenty of time to work out."

After getting Randy, they all went to North Star for a quick dinner. Tag had to work the evening shift, so it was the most efficient way for the three of them to spend quality time together. After catching up, Randy shared that he wanted to work on specific footwork drills, which his after-school coach had suggested.

"Great idea, buddy. We'll incorporate footwork with changing directions as you run on the field. Your coach seems like a smart guy."

"Bob Tomlinson is actually part of the Cardinals' organization. He volunteers his time with the kids during the NFL off-season," Emery chimed in.

Tag nodded thoughtfully as Randy slid his phone in Tag's direction, displaying a recent video of football practice. *Hmm ... that's a familiar name.* He scrutinized the video and got a quick look at the man in question. A swift flash of recognition flickered in his eyes. *Bob was our equipment coordinator at UT. Small fucking world.*

○○

Goldie accompanied them to Golden Gate Park on Saturday. Tag suggested they go to a completely different area to practice and kept a close eye on the pup the entire time, hoping no residual memories of the coyote attack would surface. She seemed nervous at first, sniffing the area every few minutes, but Emery kept her on a short leash or cuddled her closely on her lap as she watched Tag and Randy practice their usual drills.

After a couple of hours, Tag and Randy collapsed on the blanket, high-fiving and laughing boisterously. Emery rewarded them with protein bars and bottles of water.

"Mom, Tag says I have speedy feet! I think playin' soccer with Dad has helped my foot coordination." Randy's arm shot in Tag's direction for a celebratory fist-bump.

Tag nodded in agreement. "Football and soccer are not so different; players are attempting to move a ball down the field to a desired location in order to score. Any sport improves hand-eye-foot coordination. If you continue workin' this hard, you're gonna ace your tryouts."

Emery held an arm out, which quickly wrapped around Randy's shoulder in a warm embrace. "I'm proud of you, sweetie." Randy pulled Tag toward him, yelling, "Come on, Tag! It's time for a group grope!" They huddled together, with Goldie somewhere in the middle, yelping excitedly.

"A group what?" Tag's eyebrows raised in question as Emery giggled, "That's something Alex made up. Don't ask."

Emery

After walking Goldie through the neighborhood, they had stopped at a local pizzeria to pick up a few pies for an early dinner. Everyone was comfortably sprawled out on the floor, surrounding the coffee table, which was laden with pizza boxes, warm garlic bread, and beverages. As usual, Goldie was the center of attention until she wandered into her crate in search of her own dinner, after which she nestled amongst her plush toys for a nap.

Emery busied herself in the kitchen, cleaning up and wrapping the leftovers in foil, then stowing everything in the fridge. Upon returning to the living room, she was mildly taken aback at the heart-warming vision that met her eyes. Tag was wedged into the corner of the couch with Randy sitting on his lap. Arms firmly circled around the child, there was a large sketchpad opened in front of them. Tag's strong hand gripped a marker as he drew swift lines, Xs, and circles across the page. The vocabulary was all football, but not a single utterance registered in Emery's mind. They looked more like father and son than coach and player, and certainly, the short length of time since they met belied the close bond that was already forged. Nervously crossing her arms, Emery had to school her features, hiding the rush of warmth that threatened to give away her emotions. She couldn't help but wonder what kind of father Tag would be or if he ever contemplated having children. She had vague remembrances of Randi fantasizing about their future family.

"Mom, Tag and I are making up different plays. He used to be a quarterback, you know, and the quarterback's the one who decides what's gonna happen on the field, so the more I know, the better I'll be for tryouts. I'll be ready for anything, right, Tag?"

Tag nodded vigorously. "As long as you're always keepin' your eye on his throwing arm, anticipating which direction he's gonna aim the football, you'll have plenty of time to get there."

Beaming at them, Emery couldn't keep her gratitude and pride effectively under wraps. Plopping down on the couch, she embraced them both, planting kisses on cheeks and foreheads. "Randy's self-confidence and skills have really skyrocketed. We are so thankful. Randy's father is a great athlete, but he just doesn't know the ins and outs of football like you do."

"And lately Dad doesn't have that much free time to spend with me like he used to. He said he's gonna be busy with a big case coming up soon." Disappointment clouded Randy's eyes for a moment, but Tag ruffled his hair lightheartedly.

"Don't you worry, buddy. Between your coach and me, we got you covered. You're gonna kick some serious butt!"

Randy turned to face Tag and threw his arms around him. "Thanks for helping me. You're the best!" Noticing that Goldie was stirring and had emerged from her crate, Randy leaped from the couch and scooped the puppy in his arms. Emery grabbed her tablet off the desk and sat next to Tag.

"I'd like to show you a few designs I've made for your mosaics project. Let me know if any of them work." Emery opened a folder and proceeded to display an array of colorful images. Randy sat on the floor, Goldie in his lap, as he peered upward curiously observing the slide show. "Hey, Mom? Maybe Tag can come with us tomorrow."

Tag's eyes rose to meet Randy's inquisitive gaze. "What's happenin' tomorrow, kiddo?" Excitement flooding his face, Randy placed Goldie carefully on the couch, and then raced to the desk where he grabbed a piece of paper.

"We're going to the Exploratorium. It's like a museum, but not really, 'cause you're allowed to touch stuff and interact with most of the exhibits. I printed this from their website. It sounds so cool!" Randy began to read excitedly.

"It's an eye-opening, playful place to explore how the world works, through creative, thought-provoking exhibits, experiences, tools, and projects that ignite curiosity, encourage exploration, and lead to profound learning."

Visibly impressed by the boy's articulation and expression, Tag blurted, "Whoa, what grade are you in, Randy? You read like a high-school kid."

A proud grin graced Emery's lips. "He'll be going into fourth in the fall, although he reads on a sixth grade level," she boasted. Randy's head bobbed up and down in agreement. "He's read it to me several times already. I suspect he's got it memorized," Emery chuckled.

"Grandma and Grandpa have been reading to me since *forever*, and Mommy read to me when I was still in her tummy!" Tag's mouth opened in surprise, eyes blinking rapidly, and he appeared for a brief moment to gasp for air.

"R-really?" came Tag's shaky response, after swallowing hard. He took the paper out of Randy's hand to peruse it himself. The boy's eyes were wide in excited expectation.

"So, can ya come, Tag? It would be so fun if you were with us.

Right, Mom?" Emery had been studying Tag's body language from the corner of her eye, and she sensed his hesitation. *Why is he stalling? What the hell just happened? He is as white as a ghost.*

"Sweetie, you know Tag has a lot of clients at the gym. We've had him all day, so be grateful for that."

Randy audibly sighed, but managed a forced smile. "I know, Mom. Thanks, Coach, for today. It was fun and I learned a lot." Randy's arms snaked around Tag's waist. Tag ruffled the boy's hair and murmured, "If my schedule clears up tomorrow, I'll let you know, okay?"

They spent a few more hours watching basketball on television, playing with Goldie, and making ice cream sundaes. Emery sensed something was bothering Tag, but did not feel comfortable prying him for information. The sudden shift in his mood had been evident, and there was an uneasy, awkward distance between them that she did not like.

After one last walk around the block, Tag made sure Goldie was settled in her crate for the night, before heading home.

"I'll see you in two weeks, kiddo. Practice every day, no exceptions. Don't give those muscles of yours time to forget what they learned." Tag's voice was stern although his lips curved upward in a warm smile. "You be good for your mom, too, okay?"

Emery held her arms out for a quick hug. "Thanks, Tag. I appreciate your time working with Randy." Tag reciprocated stiffly, and mumbled a hasty, "I'll call you tomorrow if my schedule changes."

TAG

Thirty minutes later, Tag sat in his driveway, head forlornly resting on the truck's padded steering wheel. *What the fuck is wrong with me? I feel out of control, but why?*

Grabbing his phone, he found Emery's number.

Tag: Sorry for acting weird. I just feel ... I'm having a tough time ...

Tag's fist came in contact with the dashboard after quickly pressing the 'delete' button. Resting his head back, he struggled to make sense of what had just happened, mentally hitting 'replay' on the visions he had perceived. For a split second, the image of a very pregnant Emery had appeared in his mind's eye. He had seen her sparkling eyes, his hand covering the soft curve of her rounded belly, as his arms protectively encircled her. *What. The. Fuck?* Scrolling through his contacts, he located the one he wanted and started typing furiously.

Tag: Hey, Ginger! Long time no see. Whatcha doin', baby?

Chapter 15

"The greatest happiness of life is the conviction that we are loved; loved for ourselves, or rather, loved in spite of ourselves."
– Victor Hugo

EMERY

The weekend was quickly approaching and Emery had been so immersed in her sculpting class that Tag's mysterious MIA routine did not hurt as much as she expected. When he failed to give her a heads-up about not joining the Exploratorium outing, she knew something was wrong. Goldie was still being walked and fed on schedule, and there was always a short note from him left on the couch — just the facts, no silly anecdote. *Cold.* Her spirits were lifted when Friday morning arrived.

Emery had been looking forward to visiting Robbi's first grade class ever since the women had met at North Star. After texting Robbi she was five minutes away, Emery arrived at the Blanchard School for Special Children, and as Robbi had promised, her TA was waiting to greet her. Toby, Tyler's nephew, was a mini-Tyler: younger, leaner, slightly shorter, but just as striking looking. He approached her car, waving animatedly.

"Welcome, Emery. Let me help you with your stuff." He grabbed her ArtBin Tote Express, which was perfect for carrying art supplies anywhere at a moment's notice. Toby led her through a side entrance.

"So, the kids are still at lunch, which will give you a bit of time to set up. They return to the classroom at 1:05. We have twelve students and they'll be sitting at a large round table. They're super-excited to meet you."

"Well, I'm excited, too, although a bit nervous," Emery was quick to confess. "I usually teach at the university level, so this is a big change, but I have a nine-year-old son, so I'm not totally unfamiliar with this age group. Randy loved bringing his friends over to do art projects during summer vacations."

After Toby introduced the other assistant, Mia — who also happened to be his wife — Emery and Robbi shared a warm hug. The foursome arranged the art supplies in the center of the large round table, which had already been covered in newspaper. Emery planned two activities, both involving lots of paint. Teamwork and organization averted any potential disasters and the day was a resounding success. Thankfully, Emery did not have a spare moment to dwell on Tag and his standoffish behavior, although she did plan on asking Robbi's opinion on the matter eventually.

Afterwards, Robbi and Emery went out for an early dinner at North Star. Tag's shift started at 6:15 and Tyler had mentioned that he might drop by as well to watch a game. The two women had become close in the relatively short time they had known each other, and comfortably chatted about anything and everything. Robbi recounted how she and Tyler had met and eventually married. The topic of Daisy, Toby's sister, also came up; her accident, subsequent death and the miraculous location of her donated heart as well as the incredible family who came with it. Emery was flabbergasted when Robbi related the details of how the family in Los Angeles had located Toby, and all the strange events that had occurred as a result.

"Mia's pregnancy was not planned. They loved each other and knew they wanted to be married someday, but Mia was scared to death about what Toby's reaction would be when he learned she was pregnant. Well, when she finally gathered the courage to tell him, he was thrilled. Over the freakin' moon! Toby was convinced it was a sign from God, or possibly from Daisy herself. Violette, the little girl who has Daisy's heart beating in her chest, was Toby and Mia's flower girl. Toby firmly believes his sister's spirit lives within her." Robbi grasped Emery's hand when she saw her eyes fill with unexpected tears. "I've heard of unusual events surrounding organ transplants, but that is a true miracle," Emery whispered.

Robbi insisted on hearing more about Emery's life as a mother and university art professor. She also was curious about Randy and Alex, and then eventually the conversation wound its way around to Tag.

"He is an enigma, a mystery, a closed book, Robbi. I can't figure him out. He's a good friend one minute, then he disappears with barely a word or a text, and the next minute he's sleeping over so he can—"

"Whoa, girl! What did you just say?" Robbi leaned in, mouth agape.

"Oh, don't get too excited. It was when we first brought Goldie home. He insisted on staying over for a few nights so he could watch her, and take her outside at night. He slept on the couch and was a perfect gentleman." Emery pouted a bit and Robbi couldn't stifle her laughter for another moment.

"And you didn't want him to be a gentleman, did you? Oh, my God, Emery. You like him. I mean, *really* like him."

Shaking her head resolutely, Emery sighed. "I know I shouldn't. There's a darkness in him, a profound sadness that scares me a bit. He and Tyler are pretty close, right?"

Robbi's pensive expression became more serious as she

chewed on the corner of her mouth. "They've known each other for almost a decade, but were acquaintances. They drank together, partied, and probably fucked the same women, you know … male slut behavior, whatever. Something changed between them, however. It happened around the time I met Tyler. I've asked him about it several times, but he won't tell me a thing. Ty used to bad-mouth Tag before, called him hateful names, but no more. He's done a complete one-eighty. They're extremely close now, like brothers." Robbi took a breath and her eyes began to shine with moisture. "Ty's older brother died last year. Rocky wasn't the best brother and sometimes I think Tyler is attempting to be the strong, big brother to Tag that Rocky never was to him. I suspect Tag confided some of his deep, dark secret shit and Tyler could relate somehow."

A pair of large hands appeared from nowhere and settled softly on Robbi's shoulders from behind. Strong fingers massaged her neck as Tyler leaned over and gave her a hard, possessive kiss.

"Missed you, sweetheart. Hey, Emery! How'd your lesson go? I hope the munchkins behaved themselves." He wrapped Robbi's hand in his own, pressing a few open-mouthed kisses on her palm. A twinge of envy pinched deep in Emery's chest.

"So, lovely ladies, I'll be at the bar hangin' with my boy. Come join us whenever you're ready." After depositing a kiss on Robbi's temple, Tyler headed to join Tag, who already had his favorite beer in a tall, chilled glass.

TAG

Ty and Tag greeted each other with their usual fist-bump ritual. Tyler's attention turned immediately to the TV where a game was already in progress. It didn't take long before he noticed Tag's attention was elsewhere. Following his gaze, Tyler was met with a meaningful glare from Robbi, winking as she blew him a kiss. Grinning at her, he returned his eyes to Tag who was busy pouring ingredients and ice into a blender. A sudden hand on his bicep momentarily startled him; he turned and was surprised to see Ginger.

"Hey, handsome," she purred, stroking his arm. "The wife let you out for a few hours?"

Reluctant to spar verbally with the feisty redhead, Ty merely shrugged and returned his focus to the television.

"Nah. Robbi's having dinner here with a friend of hers." Tyler nonchalantly lifted his chin in their direction without taking his attention from the game. Ginger's eyes narrowed to slits as she noticed the women peering at a cell phone screen, giggling contentedly.

"What can I get you, Ginger? It's on me, by the way. Sorry about the other night." Tag avoided her heated glare as he spoke. "Something came up last minute and my phone, um ... died on me. It won't happen again."

Ginger huffed, rolling her eyes. "Damn-fuckin'-straight it won't happen again," she gritted out through clenched teeth. "Suck *yourself* off from now on, asshole." She stomped off, her sky-high heels clicking against the tile floor. Tag's shoulders sagged as he released a sigh.

"Whoa, what the hell did you do?" Tyler's wide eyes followed the woman as she haughtily strode to the other side of the bar.

Tag lowered his gaze, sheepishly muttering, "Guess you could say it was what I *didn't* do. I told her I'd meet her here one night last week and then didn't show up."

Tyler's ice blue eyes pinned Tag with a steely glare. "Are you insane?" Judging by Tag's resolute nod, Tyler knew he had struck a nerve. "Spill it, Tag."

Noticing Emery and Robbi were getting up from their table, Tag lowered his voice and hastily spit out a few rushed words. "I hung out with Emery and her boy all day Saturday, then they invited me to spend Sunday with them and I guess I freaked out, felt trapped, whatever. I told her I was busy all day which was kind of —"

"A big, fat, fuckin' lie." Tyler cut in, shaking his head in disbelief. "Did you enjoy their company? Is the kid a pain in the ass?"

"Just the opposite. Randy is a great fuckin' kid, a natural athlete in the making. I just don't want him to get too close, ya know? I mean, they live in another state, for Christ's sake! When her class is over, she'll be outta here. Gone. What's the point?"

Tyler frowned, eyebrows knit in suspicion. "Is there more you're not telling me?"

Tag huffed out a voluble breath. "Her resemblance to Randi freaks me out, like I am attracted to her for all the wrong reasons. I just think we're better off staying friends."

"I get that," Ty agreed. "Just don't rule out the other possibility. Do you know who said 'You miss one hundred percent of the shots you never take'? I'll give you a hint. It was a famous athlete, one of the greats."

A slight upturn was beginning to form on Tag's lips. He had been the unwilling recipient of Tyler's many fatherly lectures, but he loved him for it. "Well, it sure as hell wasn't a quarterback 'cause he woulda said 'throws'."

After smacking Tag on his cheek a few times, Tyler confided, "It was Wayne Gretzky, buddy. And if he was standing at this bar right now, he'd tell you himself. Take the goddamn shot."

Chapter 16

"Remember tonight ... for it is the beginning of always."
—Dante Alighieri

TAG

After a strenuous Saturday afternoon workout, Emery expressed interest in seeing the exact location of the mosaic project Tag had requested. He was not one to ever bring women to his home, but the circumstances with Emery were different. They had known each other for over six weeks, and had become close friends. Tempted by his offer to cook her a full-blown Italian dinner, she had followed him in her own car and parked behind his truck in the narrow driveway. Her hand was locked firmly in his as Tag carefully led her up the narrow walkway and around a curve to behold a small stone house tucked away in the hills, overlooking the Golden Gate Bridge. Emery appreciatively oohed and aahed as he gave her the grand tour — inside and out.

The home was purchased with a hefty down payment, thanks to the money Tag's paternal grandfather left him fifteen years prior, so his mortgage was low, which enabled him to add a few amenities. The stone structure was not large, less than eight hundred square feet inside, but the outside yard was a showplace: a two-person Jacuzzi, fire pit, BBQ area, several flowering trees, and a small cactus garden. Tag watched her expressions closely as Emery inquisitively eyed the Jacuzzi. "This yard is completely private, so anytime you'd like to get naked in my hot tub, just holler." He shot her a devilish wink.

"Oh, my God, Tag. This place is gorgeous," Emery gushed enthusiastically, kicking off her shoes after they stepped back inside. "Did you have a decorator? It's stunning." Tag flushed with pride, following her gaze as she took in the high-beamed ceiling.

"Nah, I did it myself. It's the perfect man-cave, right?" The furnishings were rustic and masculine, with a lot of stone, wood, and earthy tones. A chocolate-brown leather sofa and matching loveseat were artfully placed in the center of the living room, a few wrought iron chairs, a coffee table, and a massive stone fireplace complemented the décor. On the floor was a huge fluffy sheepskin rug in a soft beige hue, which matched several throw pillows adorning the sofa and loveseat. Emery walked over to admire the fireplace, after stopping for a few seconds to rub her bare feet and wiggle her toes in the rug's thick fur. Running her palm over the surface of the mantelpiece, her eyes followed, noticing the charred, uneven wood splotched with wax from countless forgotten candles allowed to burn. Her gaze fell to the rug again as her eyebrows furrowed.

Tag's expression immediately softened as he came to her side and took her hand in his. "The answer to your question is zero, babe."

Staring at him as if he had lost his mind, she queried, "What are you talking about, Tag? I was about to ask if this was where you wanted me to do the mosaic design. This mantel desperately needs something to cover these unsightly old wax stains."

"Oh … um, sorry. Yeah, that's the exact spot I had in mind." He was stammering, a flush of mortification creeping slowly up his neck. "I've been meaning to do something about that for a year. I actually have a shitload of leftover tile, granite, marble, and grout from when I renovated the kitchen and bathroom. Maybe you could use some of that."

"Great idea." Emery's artistic eye was already scanning the room for ideas. "Maybe something with Asian characters, or how about a scene from Dante's Inferno?" Her gaze drifted to his tattooed arm as she walked up to him, looking deep into his bright green eyes. "Oh … and Tag? I *was* trying to figure out how many women you have fucked on that rug. Good answer, by the way." She planted a soft kiss on his cheek, and then walked saucily to the couch, plopping down comfortably and grabbing the TV remote. "So, what time's dinner? I'm starving!"

Working side by side, the pan of spinach lasagna with Italian sausages was soon in the oven, and they were busily munching on the arugula salad Emery had prepared. A bottle of red wine was already almost depleted.

The oven timer dinged and Tag went to retrieve the pasta, setting it on the coffee table along with a small loaf of warm garlic bread. They ate in relative silence watching the end of the evening news.

"So how long have you lived here?"

"About six years. An elderly lady lived here and it was put on the market soon after she passed away. It was in pretty bad shape especially the yard, so I was able to buy it at a good price. I worked on it for over a year; did most of the renovations myself with Tyler's help."

"It's just beautiful, like Hansel and Gretel's cozy little fairytale cottage." Emery sighed, grinning over at him.

"Oh, *hell* no!" he bellowed, eyes sparkling with mischief. "There are no fairies here. This is my castle and I am its king."

Emery rose and gave him a mock-curtsy. "Yes, your majesty. I'll just be cleaning up this mess and fetching you another bottle of wine, sir." She flounced off but not before Tag gave her a playful swat on her perky ass. *Damn her, she drives me crazy. I'm still not sure if she wants me or prefers to be friends. Fuck!*

The *Country Music Awards* were on, so they got comfortable on the couch, each holding a wineglass, and munching on a bowl of nuts and dried fruits. Tag gently placed his arm around her shoulders; the subtle warmth of her body in such close proximity made his skin tingle. Realizing his decision to go commando while wearing low-riding sweatpants wasn't so prudent, he rearranged his position on the couch, pulling Emery even closer.

Emery

Tag enjoyed country music but admitted he wasn't exceptionally knowledgeable on the names of the many artists, so Emery was attempting to give him the lowdown on each star. Blake Shelton and Miranda Lambert were introduced, and Emery explained that they used to be married and had written some songs together. The opening chords of "Over You" began and Emery gasped; it was too late to change the channel and if she said anything, Tag might become suspicious. She had no choice but to sit, listen, and pray he did not lose it. Emery was all too familiar with the emotional ballad. The singing duo co-wrote the song in memory of Blake's older brother who had died many years before. The poignant lyrics always affected Emery and made her think of Randi every time she heard it. She rested her head on Tag's chest and entwined her fingers with his. Looking up at him, she whispered, "I love this song but it always makes me cry."

Halfway through the acoustic duet, panic invaded her and she felt Tag's body stiffen as his breathing became ragged. Visibly upset, he pushed Emery away and changed the channel abruptly, then threw the remote on the couch. He stood up, ran a hand through his hair, and made a beeline to the kitchen.

Emery heard a few cupboard doors open and close roughly. Peeking into the kitchen, she spied Tag standing in front of the sink, hands resting on either side with his head lowered, breathing heavily. She heard faint muttering, "Fuck! I can't do this anymore."

Walking softly behind him, she whispered, "Tag. It's okay," as she slipped her arms around his waist, resting her head against his back. More words of reassurance stuck in her throat as his fists pounded the tile counter.

"Leave me alone for just a minute," he gritted out. Emery withdrew her arms as if she had been burned, scurrying back into the living room as tears stung behind her eyelids. She stood there for a moment or two, reining in her emotions, then began gathering her purse and jacket, preparing to leave. Tag eventually returned clutching another bottle of wine, but froze when he saw Emery slip her shoes back on.

"You're leaving?" Hurt and disappointment colored his voice as he placed the bottle on the coffee table.

Emery nodded, confusion written all over her face. "Well, you just told me to leave you alone; so yes, I am. I ... I actually have an early day tomorrow," she stammered uncomfortably.

Tag heaved a sigh, moisture glistening in his eyes. "You don't need to lie to me. I'm so sorry. I didn't mean what I said. That song ... the lyrics really hit home, made me realize I need to stop pushing you away. Don't go, Emery. Please don't leave me."

She calmly laid her belongings on the coffee table and turned to face him directly. A breathy exhale whooshed upwards from her lips, causing her bangs to ripple.

"Be honest with me. Why do you want me to stay? Is it because you're afraid to be alone? Or because you really want to be with me? Tell me the truth, Tag. I need to know." Her tone was not confrontational, but rather passionately determined.

"Emery, I've never been afraid to be alone." A despondent groan escaped his lips. "Being alone is what I do best. I've become used to loneliness. I'm comfortable with it, excel at it. It's who I am. It's how I have lived for the past twelve years. What scares me is for the first time in over a decade, I don't want to be alone anymore." Stepping closer to him, her warm caramel eyes softened as she cupped his cheek in her hand. His day-old stubble felt rough against her palm but it was his reaction, which melted her heart. He closed his eyes and leaned his head into her hand. His warm lips softly brushed the inside of her wrist and it made her wonder who was the last woman to touch him in this way and how long it had been.

"Tag, don't you realize I can see the terrible pain you're in? You have a dark secret that you are desperately clinging to, and it's destroying you from the inside out. I'm not saying to deny the sorrow you feel. Often there is beauty in pain and you must search for it relentlessly; embrace and utilize it to give you the strength to face your demons head-on. You don't have to reveal all your secrets to me. I just need to know that you want me here with you; that you desire to know me and you are willing to let me know you in return." Her hand dropped to her side and his eyes followed its path as if he missed its gentle warmth.

"I do want that, Em. Very much." Tag held his hand out to her and she placed her soft hand in his. He pulled her gently back to the couch, where they sat facing each other. He apprehensively held her hand up to his lips, kissing it softly. Pulling her lower lip between her teeth, Emery took a deep, uncertain breath.

"I'd like to stay with you tonight — no expectations, no explanations, no strings. I just want to hold you in my arms. All night. Will you let me? I promise, tonight you will not be lonely. I won't allow it."

TAG

Tag's eyes clouded over; a raging storm brewed in his gaze. "Why, Emery? Why would you want to do that for me?"

"Because I know it's what you need at this moment." Emery's statement took him by surprise; it had no hint of opinion nor judgment, no ulterior motive. A simple, straightforward fact. Tag searched the depths of her shining upturned eyes, half-expecting duplicity or — even worse — pity. He saw only compassion and empathy. Honesty and truth.

"Tag?" She said his name even though he was already gazing raptly into her eyes. "And because we're friends. I care about you."

"Is that all we are … just friends?"

"At this moment in time? Yes." Her eyes were smiling even though she was nervously chewing on her bottom lip.

"Do you think it's possible for us to be more?" He sensed more questions hung in the space between them, but they would remain unasked for the time being.

Emery's voice was barely a whisper as she tightly grasped his cold, shivering hands in her own. "We can be whatever we want to be, Tag. But, in the meantime, this secret of yours, whatever it is — you're letting it define you, control you. It has you imprisoned; it's become your warden. Why do you choose to hide your light from the world? I've seen blinding flashes of it — you are as radiant as the sun, but you only allow your soul to be observed in tiny, microscopic bits — one bright spark at a time. I want to see more, Tag. Please give me more of you."

Overcome by her honest eloquence, Tag could only hang his head as he struggled to calm his breathing. Emery tenderly enfolded him in her arms, stroking the back of his head while threading her fingers through his hair. He eventually lifted his head and touched his forehead to hers.

Tag had grown accustomed to burying his emotions. Being engulfed in oppressive darkness for so many years had consequences. He longed to accept the flicker of hope Emery offered, knowing it would require his full surrender and trust. *I want some of what she has; the light in her eyes, the kindness in her heart, her warmth that surrounds me. Emery takes me to a place where I feel safe and protected. I'm ready.*

"I'll give you the short version, Emery. I lost the love of my life twelve years ago. Her name was Miranda, by the way. Randi. Weird coincidence, huh?" Emery nodded in agreement, her lips nervously pressed into a tight line.

"I did not directly cause her death, but some irresponsible actions on my part led up to it and I have blamed myself ever since. Guilt has eaten me up inside for years, like a monster squeezing my heart and soul. I have been paralyzed with grief, immobile — encased in a block of ice that eventually melted somewhat. Now it's as if I'm walking through thick, heavy mud … just slogging along, struggling through life. I have wounds inside me that will not heal. I feel like I don't deserve to be alive, and I certainly do not merit happiness." Emery's gentle brown pools reflected the sadness in his eyes.

"Survivor's guilt, Tag. I understand completely. I lost someone years ago, too. We feel undeserving of happiness, but nothing could be further from the truth. I deserve to know you and have you in my life. My son deserves to learn from you and you deserve his love and respect, which you have already earned. You and I both deserve to share this friendship and maybe save each other in the process. People you have yet to meet — whose lives you might one day change for the better — they deserve to know the man I see right here in front of me."

Pressing his lips to her forehead, Tag held her in his arms for a few long moments before pulling her tightly into his chest. "Thank you for recognizing the good in me, even when I can't quite see it myself." After smoothing her hair, he gave her a weak smile and kissed her nose. *God … she is so beautiful. I can't let her leave. Please don't leave me, Emery.*

"So, were you serious? About staying over and holding me all night?" Tag chewed on his lip ring until she nodded. "I can hold you, too, if I want, right?" He attempted to give her a confident smile and added a persuasive wink. Her head tilted a bit as she pondered his question.

"Maybe … we'll see. I need a minute to text my neighbor who walks Goldie occasionally. Mrs. Drozdov owns the building and has a key. She has two dogs and doesn't mind walking one more."

"Tell her to leave some extra snacks for Goldie, too. I'm sure she would enjoy an evening treat. Oh, and tell her to make sure my girl has her favorite chew toy, because —"

Emery cut him off with a soft fingertip on his lips. "Don't worry, Godfather Tag, your girl will be just fine."

Emery

Things were awkward at first; they had shyly undressed in separate rooms. Tag stayed in his bedroom, while Emery retreated to the bathroom. He had pointed out a drawer full of his T-shirts and suggested she pick one to sleep in. He also gave her an extra toothbrush and showed her where the bath products were located. Tag hastily burrowed under the sheets as Emery emerged from the bathroom wearing his UT Longhorn T-shirt, which barely covered her ass. Her bra and thong almost stayed on, but she decided against it, leaving her underwear neatly folded on the bathroom counter. His eyes widened when he saw her, and the expressions which clouded his countenance were mixed — wonder, annoyance, and eventually melancholy. Emery mentally chastised herself. *I hope this wasn't a bad choice.*

She self-consciously tugged on the shirt's hem, not wanting to expose too much bare flesh. His frown quickly dissolved into the hint of a Cheshire Cat-like grin. Tag's eyes roamed her body, head-to-toe, as he swallowed hard.

"I ... kinda like you in my shirt, but feel free to join me in my nakedness at any time."

Emery propped herself up against the headboard in Tag's massive king-sized bed, resting on a mound of soft pillows. As promised, he was snuggled in her arms while she massaged his neck and played with his hair. After a few hours of TV, they had finished the third bottle of wine and she was feeling sleepily tipsy. Emery continued to cuddle him in much the same way she would cozy up to Randy when tucking him into bed at night. His head rested on her chest; her fingers gently stroked the skin on his back and arms, lips softly planting kisses on his forehead. Tag's breathing was calmly regular, with intermittent soft pleasurable moans punctuating the silence. Emery could hear his pounding heartbeats; they echoed against the walls of his room, matching the rhythm of her own. *Is it wrong to want him to kiss me? What do those piercings feel like?*

She carefully began to trace his facial features with the tip of her index finger; his eyebrows, his aquiline nose, followed by his strong cheekbones, and finally his lips. He tilted his head and watched as she shifted her gaze to his. Tag's pierced tongue snaked out and sucked her finger sensually as he grabbed her hand and held it in his own. He began to kiss and lick her entire palm, completely laving every single finger in the process. To Emery, it felt as though his warm, wet mouth was making love to her hand, strangely sensual and surprisingly erotic. Paying special attention with his tongue to the soft, sensitive uncalloused skin in between each finger gave her goose bumps. It was even more sensual than when he had fondled her hand in the movie theater. His fingertips were lightly caressing each sensitive area of her palm … tracing every rough spot or scar and kissing each softly. *If I had panties on right now, they would be drenched.*

"I'm sculpting with bronze casting and clay molding. It's awfully rough on the hands, unfortunately," she offered in explanation.

"You have beautiful hands, strong artist's hands," Tag whispered as he laced his fingers with hers, kissing her knuckles tenderly. "I love that you don't have those god-awful, freakishly long, fake nails." Both were breathing heavily at this point; Tag raised his pleading eyes to meet hers.

"I think it's my turn to hold you now, right?" Her breathless response came immediately.

"Okay." She slid down off the pillows and scooted underneath him as he held her, slowly flipping her around so her body covered his.

"This is nice," he murmured softly, breathing her in as she buried her face in the crook of his neck. "God, you smell so good."

Emery propped her arms on his chest and gazed directly at him. He was smiling up at her and she couldn't help but return his grin.

"What's so funny?" he queried, eyebrows furrowed in consternation.

"You have a magnificent smile. You need to reveal it more often."

"It's all you, Em. You're responsible for putting this smile on my lips." A sudden warmth bloomed in her chest. *I love when he calls me Em. Randi called me that sometimes. When will I have the courage to tell him the truth?*

"And thanks for staying with me tonight. I … I need you."

Tag's expression grew more serious as he stared at her lush mouth, which was dangerously close to his. She felt his strong hand grasp the back of her head as he pulled her closer, fingers deftly tugging the elastic from her ponytail. Her silky hair fell free, loosely blanketing them both in a soft, fragrant curtain. They were nose-to-nose, lost in the depths of each other's eyes.

"What are you thinking about, Tag?" Emery's teeth raked her lower lip warily.

"Kissing you, but I can't decide whether to come in hard and fast, or take it soft and slow. What should I do, my beautiful girl?" Tag's husky words trailed off as his mouth captured hers in a gentle, yet passionate kiss. Emery half-expected Tag's mouth to crush hers with unbridled, out-of-control lust; however, his actions were completely the opposite. His lips were soft as they tenderly pressed against her mouth, caressing but not demanding, gently coaxing at first until she parted her lips slightly, inviting him in. Soon he was kissing her as if his life depended on the next brush of their lips, the next soft, warm contact of their tongues. Because of his tongue piercing, he explored her mouth slowly, carefully; Emery reciprocated, sucking gingerly on his lower lip, while the tip of her tongue stroked his lip piercing. Her kisses became more fervent as the taste of him overpowered her senses, sending a spine-tingling surge of heat down her spine. There was no mistaking Tag's arousal as she felt his cock prod her lower abdomen. A growing need and desire permeated her; she was drowning in him, in the sensations his touch brought rushing through her body. She stiffened slightly. *Uh oh. Am I ready for this?*

Tag reluctantly broke the kiss. He gently rested his forehead against hers and smiled, affectionately brushing their noses together, as he gave her his best nonchalant smirk.

"Sorry about that. He has a mind of his own; I guess it's been a while." He shrugged casually, tucking stray tendrils of her luxurious hair behind her ear.

"Really, Tag? You? I see how the chicks at the gym are constantly all over you. How can that be true?" Emery was incredulous, but secretly hoped his admission was sincere.

"I won't lie to you, Emery. I've banged some of them plenty, the bar chicks, too. I'm no saint; I've done some things

I'm not proud of, but my partners were always willing. There was even a time in my life when I thought I was a bona-fide sex addict. To be honest, I've kinda tapered off recently. Watching Tyler meet Robbi, fall madly in love, and ultimately get married, completely opened my eyes. I guess whoring around just got old after a while, or maybe I'm gettin' old. I don't know. After Randi, all I wanted was mind-numbing, meaningless hook-ups. Night after night. Year after fucking endless year. Lather, rinse, repeat. Now I feel like what's the point?"

Emery's face lowered and she kissed the tip of his nose. "You didn't do anything wrong, Tag. You did what you had to do to survive … to stay sane."

"I know. I've been lucky, always used a condom, got tested regularly, and never caught anything. I had a test two weeks ago and it's all good."

Emery nodded, whispering, "Me, too. And I get the Depo shot."

Tag grasped her face in his hands, eyes piercing hers with intensity. "The way we kissed a few moments ago? I have not experienced that since … since my Randi. She was the only woman I have ever made love to. Everyone since has just been a quick, random, whoever-was-available, easy fuck." Unable to continue, Tag simply closed his eyes, as a single tear rolled down his cheek. Emery's lips brushed it away as she proceeded to kiss him softly, the saltiness of his teardrop still on her tongue.

His eyes opened languidly as he turned to face her. "Em, that song? What's the story behind it? Was it written specifically for someone?" She nodded solemnly.

"When Blake Shelton was fourteen, his older brother was killed in a car crash along with his girlfriend and her little boy. Blake and Miranda co-wrote the song in his memory. I love that song so much; it's difficult to listen to, but cathartic at the same time." Her cheek rested against his.

"Randi died in a car accident as well. Someday maybe you'll play that song again for me and we can listen together." Several more tears threatened to spill, as her fingertips gently caressed every inch of his face, comforting him as best she could. He fought to maintain his composure, but a soft sob escaped his lips.

"Shh, it's okay. I'm here. Know that every tear you shed honors her memory." Her murmurs and soft, gentle touches continued until she sensed his breathing had calmed.

"You know, I dream about her almost every night. I talk to her, ask for her forgiveness; it comforts me somehow."

"Why do you feel you're to blame?" Emery probed gently, desperate for answers.

His head dropped to his chest. "I was videotaped in a ... very compromising position, and someone made sure Randi saw it. I was drunk, but I suspect someone drugged me because I have no memory of it whatsoever. I tried to explain, but she wouldn't ..." Tag shook his head in desolation, as Emery stroked his hair.

"Are there things you'd like to say to her? You could share your feelings with me; imagine I'm Randi and just say whatever comes to mind. Perhaps you'll be able to sleep more restfully."

Nodding hesitantly, he murmured, "Okay, Em. I ... I'd like that. Please forgive me if I say anything inappropriate." They exchanged positions so she cradled him in her arms once more. Their combined breathing and the gentle hum of the ceiling fan were the only sounds in the room. Emery silently stroked the back of his head delicately, not wanting to intrude on his reflections. When Tag finally began to speak, his voice was calm and quietly serene; Emery was not 100 percent certain if he was awake or asleep. Perhaps he was hovering somewhere in between.

"For years I've waited for you to come back for me. I've been ready all this time to join you, but you'd never let me. I'm beginning to understand why. Your presence has always been so strong, but recently I feel like you are slowly dissolving ... fading. I know you're telling me it's time to move on with my life. Maybe it means I'm starting to forgive myself, just like you have always begged me to do. I'll never absolve myself completely, nor will I ever let you go entirely, but I sense you want me to move on. When you left me, my heart and soul were shattered and every single piece went with you, leaving nothing for me. I've been dead inside for so long. But now, I'm coming to life again — little by little, one single heartbeat at a time."

His words stunned her with their clarity and eloquence, as if he had rehearsed this farewell speech a thousand times. Emery's body was frozen in place, although a hand was woven into his hair while the other softly stroked his arm. His body shifted slightly, molding himself closer to hers.

"I will always experience the beauty of this world through your eyes. Sadness has been a constant in my life, a strange consolation in a way, but now I've had a small taste of happiness again and I want more. People always say to 'follow your heart' and that's exactly what I've done. I have followed you and only you from the day we met. But when that path comes to an unexpected end, we need to find a new one or life is over. I know you would want me to find my new path, but will that mean I'll never see you in my dreams again? I couldn't bear it. If you're going to leave me for eternity, then I need to feel you, hold your hand, kiss your lips. Please, baby. I need to crawl into your soul one final time before I let you go." Tag's words became muffled as he buried his face in Emery's neck. He slowly began to press his body even closer.

Presently, Emery became aware of a light snore emanating from Tag's throat; he had miraculously fallen asleep. So much heat radiated from his body, Emery eventually peeled off the football jersey. The sensation of his heated skin on her bare breasts felt like heaven. Eventually, she drifted off to sleep, thoughts of her beloved cousin foremost in her mind.

Startled, Emery's eyes abruptly flew open. Tag was still asleep but his body had convulsed unexpectedly for a few seconds, shaking her out of a deep slumber. The whirr of the fan was still the only audible sound. For a split second, she thought it could have been an earthquake, which, in California, was almost a regular occurrence. Noticing the wineglasses were undisturbed on the nightstand, her eyes fell upon Tag. He was partially lying on his side, with one arm draped across her waist, but his expression was troubled. He was talking in his sleep, eyes barely open; voice breathily mumbling, yet coherent. Pain seemed to emanate from his soul, permeating every cell, every word he struggled to utter.

"Please say you forgive me. I can't let you go until I know you don't blame me for what happened." Images of Emery's childhood flooded her mind as she subconsciously willed Randi's essence to infiltrate her. *I can't pretend to be her. It's not right.* Tag's movements had stilled; his forehead rested on Emery's as a hoarse whisper escaped her throat.

"Tag, it's me. Emery. I'm sure Randi never blamed you, because it wasn't your fault. There's nothing to forgive." Memories plagued her, as a few tears began to fall.

"I'm begging you. I need to hear you say the words. I will never rest, never be able to live or love again, until I know for sure …" His pleas were becoming more urgent.

Emery took a huge breath; she knew what she had to do. Her whispers were barely audible, as her mouth found his ear.

"Randi will always love you and watch over you. I know she would want you to live your life, be happy, and find your bliss. She forgives you, Tag."

Tag began to ease himself on top of her, face tucked in the curve of her neck. Emery instinctively spread her legs wide so he could nestle in between them comfortably; it felt as if he had always belonged there. As he inched up a bit higher, Emery could feel his arousal; he was huge and hard as a rock. *Oh, my God. This is actually happening, right now. Without a condom, but I don't care. I want him. Every empty place within me longs to be filled by this man.*

Her palms roamed down his massive back, ending on his ass cheeks, which she grasped firmly. She could feel him at her entrance and was grateful for the moisture that had pooled between her thighs. Emery allowed her knees to fall apart, opening her legs wider and brought them up to wrap around his waist, hooking her ankles for better leverage. There was barely time for her to take a breath when he had thrust himself into her fully, stretching, and filling her slick, tight channel completely. It was the perfect, indescribable blend — a twinge of pain mixed with an abundance of exquisite pleasure. Emery had not been with many sexual partners, but Tag seemed to be remarkably well endowed. He appeared to be on autopilot — pounding her hard, fast, and deep. Emery had not anticipated such strong, intensely emotional feelings flooding her chest. Although his movements were forceful, a gentle tenderness and passion was unmistakable; so much love poured out of him that it was excruciatingly easy for Emery to forget that his emotions, in truth, were not meant for her.

Tag's eyes were lidded as they peered down at her; barely open with a faraway, disoriented look as if unable to focus effectively. Grateful for the utter blackness of the room, Emery's lips hungrily captured his as she gripped his ass firmly, attempting to angle him even deeper. The powerful desire to absorb his pain with her body outweighed the enormity of the deception she had knowingly allowed to transpire. His hips gyrated in a slow, torturous dance, which was driving her insane. At the same time, it finally dawned on her something unusually hard — as in metallic-hard — was internally hitting her in all the right places. *Oh, my God. His dick is pierced!*

Tag's breathing was erratic as his moans became more guttural. His release was imminent; Emery sensed she, too, was on the edge, although her own orgasm was unimportant at that moment. Under normal circumstances, she required extensive foreplay and oral stimulation. This situation was anything but normal; his pierced cock had certainly kicked things up a notch. Tensing her core muscles, she attempted to hold her climax at bay even though the sensations were overwhelming.

His thrusts were frantic; he clung to her desperately as his release rushed over him, his cries reverberating throughout the room. Emery felt his cock throb deep inside one final time before his hot sperm flooded her core, mixing with her own arousal. Their eyes connected and held in a timeless whirl of unspoken emotions — a rare, unforgettable sharing of souls. Collapsing onto Emery's chest in exhaustion, Tag continued to breathe heavily while his hand softly stroked her breasts.

Thoroughly exhausted, he was asleep almost immediately. His upper body glistened with sweat and a puddle of sticky fluids was oozing between her thighs, but she didn't care. He was incredibly beautiful as he slept, his countenance so peaceful and angelic; the only sensation filling her heart was contentment. Emery knew the possible ramifications of what had transpired might forever haunt her, but easing his torment and suffering far outweighed any negative consequences.

Tag stirred a bit, snuggling deeper into the space between her neck and shoulder. After peppering his forehead with soothing kisses, she attempted to calm her racing heart and close her eyes. *Will he think Randi appeared in a dream, or wake up with no memory at all? He also might remember it was me and be okay with it. Or not.*

Sleep eluded her for a long time, even though a peaceful

tranquility had returned to her body. Tag was nestled so securely in her arms; his breathing had calmed but Emery continued to caress his back lightly with her fingertips. *Damn. I gotta pee … and clean up.*

Emery gingerly scooted out from underneath Tag's dead weight, and tiptoed to the bathroom. It wasn't until she placed her hand between her thighs when reality hit.

What have I done?

Chapter 17

"Love is a spirit all compact of fire."
– William Shakespeare (Venus and Adonis)

TAG

The clock read 4:35 a.m. in the semi-darkened room, a faint glow emanating from a bathroom night-light. Surprised to feel something tickling his cheek, Tag found Emery still asleep, her tousled head sharing his over-sized pillow. In fact, he lay somewhat tangled in the glorious mess that was her silky brown mane. One of her legs was intertwined between his. Unexpectedly taken aback by her serene beauty and self-assurance even in slumber, Tag couldn't escape the uncertainty that settled deep in his ribcage. It had been twelve excruciating years since he had experienced such a powerful connection with a woman. The rational part of his brain sought to attribute it to the strong resemblance she bore to Randi, but his heart knew better. It was more. So. Much. More. *I don't deserve her. I will fuck it up and hurt her in the process.*

Tag's breathing accelerated as random thoughts and indistinct images replayed in his mind. He recalled taking a sleeping pill, which had been helpful in the past with his chronic insomnia, and drinking an exorbitant amount of wine. Pressing his eyelids tightly shut, a cold sweat began to creep up his spine. *At first, it was Randi in my dream, but when I opened my eyes, it was Emery. Our connection was intense and very real. We kissed for a long time; it was beyond passionate. I recall wanting more, needing much more. My body was covering hers, and I remember … Holy shit, I had sex with Emery. Mind-blowing. Passionate. Intense. Unprotected. Sex.*

Carefully extricating himself from her embrace, Tag hastily grabbed a pair of shorts and exited the bedroom, quietly closing the door behind him. For a fleeting moment, he wished they were at Emery's. A brisk walk around the block with Goldie would have cleared his muddled brain. After grabbing a bottle of water, he paced around the living room, frantically running his fingers through his hair. *I don't think I can do this. I'm not ready. This could destroy our friendship. Or, maybe lead to more. Is that what I want?*

Grabbing an old football and clutching it to his chest, Tag sprawled out on the loveseat. He appeared to be asleep, but his fingers deliberately tracing the ball's stitching indicated the opposite. The longest hour of his existence passed, floating in limbo — a foggy, half-asleep state — as the brilliant sunrise began to peek through the curtains. After hearing his bedroom door open, Tag sensed Emery's soft approach, and lazily opened his eyes. The sight of her wearing his old jersey stole all the breath from his lungs. Again. She padded to the loveseat and crouched at his feet, gently placing her hands on his knees. He offered her a pensive, bittersweet smile and covered one of her hands with his as he put the football aside. He lifted her chin with his other hand and leaned toward her. Fear and insecurity filled her eyes and the guilt at having caused her undue pain tore at him.

"I'm sorry I left you alone in my bed, Em. That was the last thing I wanted to do, but when I awoke and remembered everything, I … I guess I was a little freaked out." His eyes clouded over in confusion, forehead lined with concern.

"Only a little?" Emery offered, in an attempt to lighten the ominous mood.

"Well, extremely at first, and my gut instinct was screaming that I could *not* do this." Emery drew in a startled breath and Tag was quick to alleviate her anxiety with a gentle brush of his fingertips along her cheekbone as his expression softened.

"I've had some time to think. I mean, I was talking to Randi in an apparent dream and then became aware of your voice. I remember being on top of you, inside you, and it felt so fucking incredible, but at the same time, completely terrified me." Emery started to say something, but he quickly put a finger on her lips.

"I need to get it all out, Em. Please let me. You have to understand something. I have been alone for so long. Since I lost my girl, every woman I have fucked was always faceless to me. I didn't want to know their names, and never once looked into their eyes. I believed that I was destined to lead a loveless life and I had accepted it. The possibility of feeling happiness again always felt like a betrayal to Randi's memory, but when you said those words of forgiveness last night it hit me fucking hard. Your words reached my *soul*." Tag leaned closer and pressed his forehead to hers. The silence was deafening as they searched each other's eyes for comfort and validation. It was vital for him to articulate honestly the myriad of thoughts that bombarded his mind. "When I was inside you, it was *your* beautiful face I saw. *Your* eyes staring into mine. Only you, Emery." Tag blew out a relieved breath, then lowered his mouth and captured her lips in a hesitant, yet tender kiss as his hand stroked the back of her head.

"There's so much more I need to share with you, but the bottom line is we experienced an intense connection; and although my brain is scared shitless and wants to run like hell, the rest of me is staying right here. With you. That is … if you'll give me a chance. Since you've come into my life, I feel different, like something deep inside me is changing. I'm a better person when I'm with you. I only ask that you be patient with me. I might need some time to wrap my head around you and me. Us." Tag's eyes shone with hope, need and desire.

"I want that, too, but you ... um, we didn't use a condom." Her lower lip trembled but a firm kiss from Tag soothed her fears.

"I know, sweetheart. *That* I recall clearly. I was half-asleep and you didn't want to wake me, right? Don't worry. I'm sure it will be all right."

The worry lines that had been creasing Emery's forehead dissolved, and her eyes shimmered. Standing in front of him, she threaded her fingers snugly with his, whispering, "Let's go back to bed. We have all the time in the world to talk. I can see you're exhausted, and I need you in my arms for a few more hours. Okay, honey?"

Tag opened his eyes around noon, grateful his usual early morning clients had been out of town all week. He reached to turn off the fan out of habit, but changed his mind as a wave of exquisite warmth unexpectedly rolled over him. One side of his chest, as well as the space between his thighs, was being seared by a pleasurable heat emanating from the skin-on-skin contact with Emery's body. Shifting slightly, she rolled off him, exposing her bare back. Soft, regular breathing indicated that she was still asleep, although he could not see her face. Scooting down a few inches, Tag pressed his cheek against the silky skin of her back, placing gentle kisses everywhere. Unfamiliar feelings washed over him; he felt a calm peacefulness that had been missing for years. His body felt oddly disoriented; it had been a long time since he'd woken up and felt something other than a painful ache in his chest. Basking in the sensation, his eyes fluttered closed as he simply inhaled her essence.

"Mmmm …" Emery's soft moan broke the silence, as she stirred beside him. Hastily scooting back up, Tag waited until she turned in his direction, eyes still closed. Propping his head on an elbow, he stared at her face intently; their naked bodies were still mostly covered by the rumpled bed sheets, although Tag's massive torso was exposed. *Damn, she is gorgeous. Just like Randi, a natural beauty, no makeup or artificial enhancements needed.*

Noticing a corner of her mouth turn up, Tag realized she sensed his gaze on her even before her eyes dreamily flickered open. Leaning into her, he placed a soft kiss on her lips. "Good morning, my beautiful sunrise girl. You sleep okay?" His smile was wide as he momentarily lost himself in her caramel eyes; he found it impossible to look away. *She has Randi's eyes. Those amber flecks … mesmerizing.*

"I slept pretty well, once I brought you back to bed. So, should we talk now or have some breakfast first?"

Tag lightly ran his finger down the bridge of her nose. "Have I told you this is the cutest, most perfectly shaped nose in the history of nasal appendages?" His lips descended on the tip of the object under discussion. "And don't get me started on these beauty marks."

Emery giggled for a brief moment, but soon her expression grew serious. "Don't change the subject, Tag. We're in this together, now. You can tell me anything." Nodding determinedly, he laid back on the pillow as Emery's fingertips stroked his cheek. Tag heaved a deep sigh. *I trust Emery, so I think it's time to share everything.*

"I took an Ambien last night. They can cause side effects like sleepwalking and vivid nightmares, and those bottles of wine certainly didn't help. I've told you Randi often appears in my dreams. It's been occurring for years. Right after she died, the dreams were relentless — every fucking night. I would see the flames of the crash, smell the gas fumes, I could hear her screams, her wails of agony …" His eyes squeezed shut as he inhaled deeply.

"As the years passed, the dreams were less recurrent — a few times a month. They were also less graphic, but still so fucking real ... like the time I woke up with the sensation of her hair curled around my finger. Often I would hear her voice, we would be having a conversation. I'd plead with her to let me join her. I couldn't live without her, how much I missed her and still loved her and so on. I would also beg her to forgive me. Her responses were consistent: 'Live your life, baby. You need to let me go.' I just wanted her forgiveness, but she would never say the words. Then last night, when you said Randi forgave me, I sensed her spirit was guiding you. I felt at peace."

He sighed in resignation, shaking his head back and forth. "I sound insane, don't I?" Her sympathetic expression coaxed him to resume his train of thought.

"The strange thing is I don't feel overwhelmed with sadness. I feel inexplicably free, like I can finally breathe, as if a two-ton weight has been removed from my heart. It's as if she gave me permission to live again. I need you to understand something. When I was talking to you, imagining you were Randi, I said —"

"Tag, there's no need to explain anything."

Pulling Emery into his arms, Tag kissed her forehead. His voice quivered as he whispered, "Yes, there is. Randi has always been in my head and in my heart — that fact will never change. But here you are in my bed, in my arms — real, warm, breathing, heart beating in sync with mine. Emery, with your lovely brown eyes and perfect nose. I need you to know what I said last night, about feeling alive again ... I meant every word. Some of last night is still a bit hazy in my mind, but I recall those words exactly. In the past, if I woke up and my heart was not in agonizing pain, I felt like I was okay because that was my 'normal.' I know now that is not good enough. I want to wake up every morning feeling content and looking forward to what the day has in store for me. Like today, which I will be spending with my sunrise girl." Tag enthusiastically peppered her forehead with soft kisses and finally smiled; Emery's heart was bursting with exhilaration and relief.

"I truly believe that life is a screenplay. Every day we can make a conscious decision to live a brand new scene, one that we have freely written. If yesterday was a shitty day, we simply rip that page out and rewrite ourselves a better, more fulfilling scene with a happier ending."

Pondering her words, Tag's eyes met Emery's as she scanned his torso appreciatively. She lightly caressed the striking tattoos adorning his body: numerous tribal designs in addition to two well-known quotes.

"What is it about tattoos that make them so enthralling?" Emery mused, her fingertips continuing their exploratory journey across his muscular chest.

"Well, the physical pain of the needle can be a cathartic release, kind of like listening to the heart-wrenching lyrics of a song. Plus, the designs are usually quite revealing; most people wear their painful secrets as constant reminders of events or loved ones who shouldn't be forgotten. Some people use tattoos to hide behind, like a disguise." Remorse painted his words.

"I like how you have taken Shakespeare's quote and made it your own." Her voice was thoughtful as she traced the meaningful words with a fingertip.

'Your eyes are the windows to my soul' was inked close to his heart, just below a beautiful pair of amber-tinted brown eyes. The second quote, **'The path to Paradise begins in Hell'**, spanned his left upper arm. After reading the words silently, she laid her cheek against Tag's chest.

"*Dante's Inferno*, right? Have you found the way to your Paradise yet?" Emery queried, eyes turned up to his. He turned away abruptly, unable to hold her sympathetic gaze. Eventually the beginning of a wan smile could be seen. "There's a weird story that goes with that tattoo. Would you like to hear it?" As Emery nodded, the constriction around his heart loosened.

"When I was workin' in Alaska, there was this old dude, a member of the Inuit Tribe, who was an incredible tattoo artist. He also had quite a reputation as a psychic, and was revered throughout the neighboring towns. Anyway, I went to his home and told him exactly what I wanted: 'The path to Hell begins in Paradise'. I was astounded when he corrected me, insisting that was *not* what Dante had said in his Inferno. I attempted to explain that I was making a statement about my life. I had already experienced Paradise and was now doomed to live in Hell for eternity. Well, you should have heard the howl of laughter that came out of him! He scoffed, 'What would a wet-behind-the-ears kid know about eternity? You might think this is Hell now, but your Paradise could be just around the corner.'"

Emery's lips parted as she edged closer, waiting expectantly to discover how Tag had lost the debate. "Don't tell me, he pretended to go along with your version, and then he—"

"Yep. I had my earbuds in and kinda dozed off while he was inking me, so you can imagine how fucking *pissed* I was when I first saw it. He looked straight in my eyes and said, 'Son, you *will* get your Paradise. Trust me, I've seen it. It'll take some years, but don't ever give up hope.' He had this faraway look in his eyes, like he could foresee the future. *My* future. I was mad as hell, but there was something about him … magical, maybe even spiritual. I could sense his aura and an eerie calm swept over me. When I offered to pay him anyway, he adamantly refused to take my money, although I slipped a few Benjamins in his wife's apron pocket on my way out. We made good money workin' on the pipeline back then."

Emery sighed, brushing her lips over the word 'Paradise'.

"You okay, sweetheart?" Tag tilted her chin upward; he needed eye contact. When she smiled weakly and nodded, he took a deep breath and pulled her closer, kissing the top of her head as his hands threaded through her silky hair.

"Emery, I think we should talk more about what happened last night." She held her breath, murmuring, "Um ... okay. You first."

Tag took another full inhale then let his breath out slowly. "I don't want anything to be awkward between us and the last thing I would ever want is to lose your friendship. You and Randy mean the world to me." He leaned in and kissed her forehead softly, then placed an even gentler kiss on her lips. "We crossed a line last night that can't be undone."

Emery swallowed hard before speaking. "Do you regret kissing me? That's what started it, which then led to … what followed. Would you undo it, if you could?"

"Absolutely not. In fact, I can't wait to do it all again, especially the kissing part." Tag's puppy-dog eyes and heartfelt words sent Emery into giggles. She raised her lips to his, a ready and willing approval of his statement. Tag sucked and nibbled on her lower lip hungrily, before invading her warm mouth with his tongue. Abruptly, one of two cells phones that were resting on the nightstand began to buzz incessantly. Emery gasped for breath as they reluctantly separated.

"That's probably Randy. He likes to touch base on Sunday mornings." Emery propped herself up on a few pillows, self-consciously covering her naked breasts with the sheet. Tag was mischievously eyeing the sheet, pretending to sneak a peek underneath. Playfully batting his hand away, she gave him her most convincing death-glare. "Stop! No distractions. We have not yet finished our conversation."

Emery read the message, but a frown emerged as she scrolled through several sentences. Her head was sadly shaking back and forth as she typed her lengthy reply. Tag lightly stroked her forearm as he waited for her to finish.

"Damn. Alex blew him off this morning. They were supposed to run laps together at the park and then go to lunch. Randy said his father's been doing that a lot lately, saying he has to work. Randy suspects he has a new girlfriend, someone he met once and didn't like very much. Something's up, probably work-related. Alex has always been a devoted father."

"I'm sorry, Em. What's Randy gonna do today?"

"Oh, no worries. My parents are always available. Grandpa will think of something fun. I'm gonna need to have a chat with Alex, sooner rather than later."

"I wish Randy was here with us. I love hangin' with your boy. He's a great kid. Do you think he's gonna be okay with this?" Tag waved his hand, pointing to the two of them. "With us? You know, being together?" Emery was quick to smile, brushing her lips against his.

"Oh, I wouldn't worry about him. He already asked me if we were dating and when I said we weren't, he immediately demanded to know why not. My nine-year-old son made it perfectly clear he knew more about my love life than I did." Emery made a snorting sound, putting a hand on one hip. "Do you want to know what he said to me?" Tag's eyes widened in rapt anticipation as Emery continued. "He said, and I quote: 'Mom! You're not getting any younger. Tag's perfect for you. And I like him, so you'd better make it happen.' Can you freakin' believe him? He's apparently watching *way* too much of that reality TV shit."

Doubling over in laughter, Tag could barely contain the thunderous guffaws, which were rumbling from his throat. He laughed so hard, he could barely catch his breath.

"Just another reason why I like your boy so much. You've done a helluva job with him."

"Thanks. So, what were we talking about?"

"Hmmm … kissing, I think." Tag sported a giant shit-eating grin. "I had stated that I did not regret kissing you. Are you sorry you kissed me back?"

"No. Not at all. I guess it's time for us to DTR," Emery suggested timidly.

Tag was perplexed. "Uh … DTR? Is that like OMG or WTF?" Emery chuckled, nodding while tracing his jawline with her finger.

"Define the relationship. Just another modern-day acronym to utilize while texting, I suppose." Emery tilted her head as their eyes met in an intense stare.

Tag sighed, his shoulders visibly sagging as he relaxed. "Everything nowadays is so complicated. Randi and I met; we became friends then fell in love. It was simple and straightforward. There was no over-analyzing. It happened organically."

"It was similar for Alex and me, too. We were in seventh grade, although he was a year older. He was struggling in English class. Spanish was his first language and there was no one at home who could help him, except his older sister, but she was busy with her own life. Our teacher suggested I tutor him after school. It was a bit awkward at first; his soccer buddies gave him endless shit, but we eventually became friends. Things changed in high school and the rest is history, as they say."

"So, has Randy ever met this perceptive teacher? You know … the one who is responsible for his existence?"

Emery giggled, nodding enthusiastically. "Many times. She's the principal of the school he now attends. How's *that* for a small world?"

Tag wholeheartedly nodded in agreement. "Well, he is such

a good kid, I doubt he's had many run-ins with her." He kissed her forehead a few times before continuing.

"Seriously, Emery, I'll be the first to admit I'm clueless here. I've been out of the dating scene for so long; I don't know what the rules are anymore. All I know is this: we have been friends for a month and a half, and I like you a lot. I think you're beautiful, talented, funny, and an awesome kisser. And — most importantly — your son approves. I love spending time with you, and if that's called dating, then I suppose that's what it is."

"I love being with you, too. Whatever this is, it's ours." Tag nodded then placed his forehead on Emery's. Peace settled in his chest as he looked into her eyes.

"So, I believe it's about time I took you out on an official date. Would you do me the honor of accompanying me to Tyler's restaurant tonight? We've been invited to attend a special dinner party. Sorry, I can't remember what the occasion is."

"Oh, right. I recollect Robbi mentioning it's her mother-in-law's birthday. Cool. Do we have time to hit the gym?"

"Of course. But first, I'm planning to kiss you senseless. Now lose this sheet, brown eyes."

Emery

Extreme shyness, not to mention modesty, won out in the long run — the offending sheet did not budge, but Tag didn't seem to mind all that much, as they passionately kissed for a while. Emery was not a prude — far from it. She had great confidence in her lean, toned body, although a desire for a few additional inches in height as well as one bra-cup size bigger had always been on her wish list. *My bouncy Cs have never gotten complaints before, but I see how guys ogle the double Ds.*

Realizing it was daylight, and she would be naked in front of Tag, gave her pause. She had, after all, been fighting her attraction to him for over a month. *He's already seen me naked, but it was pitch black in the room, not to mention he was half-asleep in a wine and sleeping pill-induced fog at the time.*

"It's only me, Em," he whispered, kissing down her neck on his way to the top of her breasts.

"That's just it, Tag. It *is* you, my friend and recently acquired partner in the adventures of dating. You are not some random guy that I picked up in a bar. Well … forget the bar part; you know what I mean. It's more difficult baring my body to you than some nameless stranger. I know it sounds silly, but …"

Tag's mouth descending on hers was a welcome interruption. "Emery, I totally understand. I don't want to do anything that you are not 100 percent comfortable with. I sincerely mean that, although if you have relegated me to the dreaded friend zone, well,"—he scowled, eyebrows slanting menacingly—"we *will* be having a serious difference of opinion."

Emery scoffed, rolling her eyes. "You in the friend zone? With all this hotness going on? I don't think so." Her hand waved up and down his body, stopping to point in the general direction of his still-hidden groin. "And whatever is happening down there? I am almost afraid to find out, although, I must say, I'm kinda curious." Emery could feel the rosy color flood her cheeks, as she bashfully covered her face with her hands.

"So, I take it you caught a glimpse of Prince Albert?" His expression was mischievous, eyebrows raised inquisitively.

"Well, last night when you were thrashing around, you kinda threw off the sheets, but it was dark so I didn't get a close look. However, it *felt* amazing. Incredible." She groped for adequate words, having a difficult time meeting his intense stare.

"I can tell you're curious about it, Emery. Most people find extreme piercings repulsive, likening it to self-mutilation. I did some research on the topic in college, and there's one consistent theory. Extreme physical torture can be effectively utilized to replace emotional pain, often erasing it completely or making it more bearable. Some people need to feel extreme pain to remind them they're still among the living. The ways and means are endless: piercings, tattoos, cutting, whipping, S & M, and bondage, to name a few."

Tag's warm smile put her at ease as he rubbed his thumb softly over her bottom lip, successfully dislodging it from between her teeth.

"It's okay, baby. I'll make the up-close-and-personal introductions soon. He's not as terrifying as he looks. Now, can we please go back to me kissing you stupid?"

Tag made good on his promise; their make-out session was epic and would have lasted longer except for the sudden interruption of extreme hunger pangs accompanied by the voluble growls of two empty stomachs. He hastily threw on a pair of running shorts and she donned her camisole and panties, which she had left in the bathroom the night before. Watching him putter around the kitchen half naked caused a rush of heat to travel straight to her core. She was especially distracted by his low-slung shorts, which seemed to be clinging onto his hips for dear life.

Tag made a sumptuous breakfast and served it to Emery outside next to the rustic stone fire pit. The sun's glorious shades of crimson and bronze seemed to splash the mountains with shimmery gold dust. She gazed at the beauty of his property, which included several dwarf fruit trees, one of which held a large, ornately decorated, glass bird feeder. Emery turned her curious gaze toward Tag, a question formulating on her lips.

"Watch what happens when I fill it, Em." Reaching behind his chair, he grasped a gallon container filled with a bright pink liquid and proceeded to fill the cylindrical feeder. Within a few moments, hummingbirds appeared, drawn to the sweet scent. There was a mad frenzy as the speedy creatures fought each other for the nectar. Emery scampered about, excitedly attempting to snap a few photos with her cell phone.

"Do you know what a group of hummingbirds is called or how fast they flap their wings?" Tag queried, watching her every move.

"Hmmm…" Emery pondered, pretending to count the frantic, fluttering movements. They appeared like sparkling gems in the morning glow of the sun, suspended in a colorful blur. "I would say somewhere around seventy-five times per second. I also know, for your information, they do not merely flap their wings; they rotate them in a figure eight, which makes hummingbirds even more remarkable. This unique capability enables them to go backwards and hover in one spot."

"Okay, smarty-pants, you are correct, but my question had two parts."

"Oh, right. What do you call a group of hummingbirds? Hmm … let's see. A hummer?"

The most raucous guffaw escaped Tag's lips as he doubled over in laughter at her retort. "As much as I *love* your answer, you would still be wrong. The correct term is a charm of hummingbirds."

Emery's nose crinkled in disbelief. "That is a ridiculous term. I'll stick with hummer."

They ate the remainder of breakfast in comfortable silence, then Tag kissed the top of her head and began gathering up the plates and utensils.

"Emery, go get ready for the gym and I'll load the dishwasher."

"Okay. Oh, and I need to borrow a comb. Someone swiped my ponytail elastic last night, and I suspect my hair looks like a wild bird's nest." Tag's smile was wide and a tad guilty as he looked up from the dishwasher.

"Sorry, babe. My bad, but rolling around in your gorgeous nest was well worth it. I gotta warn you, however. I might be replaying that sexy move regularly. When your silky smooth hair fell all around me, I … wow!" Shooting her a playful wink, he added, "Top shelf in the bathroom cabinet — all the hair products you might need are in there. Help yourself. I'll join you in a sec."

Emery tugged at the ends of her hair which were hopelessly snarled. Catching Tag's eyes in the mirror, she was momentarily startled to see him leaning against the doorframe. Her cheeks blushed shyly, as she whispered, "How long have you been watching me?"

"Not nearly long enough." Tag stepped behind her, taking the wide-tooth comb and gently detangled her long, chocolate brown tresses in soft, even strokes. Emery's head fell back as a breathy sigh escaped her throat. "Damn, that feels so good." Locking eyes with him, Emery giggled as she reached back to run her fingers through his spikey blond locks.

"I hate you, Tag. You get to wake up looking sexy as sin, with this adorably hotter-than-hell bed-head thing you got goin' on, and I look like something out of a —" His mouth crashing on hers drowned out whatever words she was about to utter.

"Something out of a sexy, heavenly wet dream. You take my breath away and you aren't even aware of the effect you have on me." He then gathered her hair gently in his hands and moved it to one side over her shoulder, to give himself better access. Their eyes locked onto each other's in the reflection; Tag softly kissed her bared neck, then licked and nibbled her shoulder — never breaking eye contact. A brightness in her eyes appeared to be reflected in his own. Resting the comb on the counter top, he snaked his arms around her waist.

"You and me, this is the point of no return, right, Emery? There's no going back." His bashful smile was dazzling. "You good with all this?" The simple question hung in his bright eyes, the shadows no longer lurking in their depths.

Emery's smile was equally radiant. "Yeah. Maybe a little scared, but I'm good." His mouth hovered near her ear as he murmured, "Me, too, Em." She turned in his arms, and her lips sought his in a blistering kiss. As he held her in a tight embrace, her eyes clouded over with a hint of worry. *I never planned on this. I'm falling for him.*

TAG

After sending Emery a quick text that he was on his way up, Tag strode to her door as it opened. His eyes bulged when he gazed at her outfit: denim mini-dress, topped off with a cropped, black lace jacket, and black leather knee-high boots. Her hair was not in its usual ponytail, instead flowing softly around her shoulders. He was staring, mouth hanging open. Emery appeared chagrinned.

"What? Too casual? I can change, Tag. It'll only take me a minute." She took a step to turn away, but he grabbed her wrist. The heated desire in his eyes was unmistakable as his gaze roamed her body. "Emery, you look sexy as fuck. No need to change, baby. You're perfect."

After stopping at a florist to purchase a bouquet for Mrs. D'Angelo, they chatted during the drive to Rocco's Italian Restaurant, when Tag inquired with a half-chuckle, "So, what's the proper protocol when two people are newly dating? Do we make a formal announcement?" *Calm down. Nothing to be nervous about.*

"No announcement should be necessary, Tag. If we demonstrate appropriate dating behavior, everyone will know right away. The dating couple — which would be us — can hold hands whenever and wherever we choose." *Huh? She's fuckin' with me, right?*

"We may call each other any or all of the following endearments: honey, sweetie, baby, darling, love bug, or pumpkin. We can touch, pat, rub, fondle, or caress *almost* any body part on each other, depending on the age and gender of the person, or persons, who are witnessing the act. We also can kiss each other publicly from now on in any location. The amount of tongue used would be contingent on the discretion of the kisser." She finished with an exaggerated eye roll and a sexy air-kiss aimed in Tag's direction. *Well-played, Emery.*

"Fuck, baby, I am so turned on right now, I may have to pull the truck over." As if on cue, the traffic light changed from yellow to red right in front of them. Taking full advantage, Tag leaned sideways and captured Emery's lips in a powerful kiss. It might have lasted longer, but a multitude of car horns disrupted their romantic moment. After driving a couple more blocks, Tag turned into a large parking lot and cut the motor. Unbuckling his seat belt in a flash, he lunged at Emery, taking her by surprise as his hungry mouth claimed hers in a searing kiss, tongue demanding immediate entry as he threaded his fingers roughly in her hair. Emery was gasping for breath by the time Tag released his secure hold on her body.

"Baby, it's downright dangerous talking to me like that when I'm driving. I can't control myself. Do I have to remind you what Albert Einstein once said?" There was an evil twinkle in Tag's bright green eyes. Emery eyebrows knitted together, deep in thought.

"Ummm … E equals M C squared?" Her faux-sweet, overly innocent expression and response caused him to convulse in unruly laughter.

"No, Emery. Einstein is known for something even more significant than relativity, in my opinion. It's actually quite a romantic quote."

"Really? Well, as usual, you and your mind-melding lips have kissed me stupid again."

"He said, 'Any man who can drive safely while kissing a pretty girl is simply not giving the kiss the attention it deserves.' Swoon-worthy, right?"

"Very, but right now I am more impressed by your use of 'swoon-worthy'." Emery beamed as her lips quickly found his, licking and sucking on his full lower lip, tongue gently circling his piercing. Abruptly pulling away, Emery appeared deep in thought, nose scrunched. "I seem to remember another Einstein quote and it's way more romantic than yours." Eyebrows furrowed, her mouth moved soundlessly, struggling to recall the phrase. "Give me a moment. I want to find the exact words." After typing a few phrases into her phone, Emery squealed, "I found it! 'When you trip over love, it is easy to get up. But when you fall in love, it is impossible to stand again.' Lovely, huh?"

Tag had no response after the eloquently delivered quote. His lips parted but could not form words, although his heart was virtually bursting with emotion. He simply stared into her soft brown irises as their gazes met. *Those magnificent eyes have held me for ransom since that first night.*

※

Rocco's was filled to capacity when they arrived. Tyler's parents were known to everyone as nonno and nonna, which meant grandfather and grandmother in Italian. Nonna Gina was everyone's favorite, from her relatives and extended family to the restaurant's fiercely loyal customers. BASH was belting out a rock tune as Tag ushered Emery around, making casual introductions as they went. It wasn't long before Robbi accosted them, linking arms with Emery and leading her off to meet the guest of honor and Nonno Rocco. Tag was left with Tyler as they meandered up to the stage, enjoying the band appreciatively. Tyler's large hand patted Tag's shoulder, a know-it-all smirk playing on his face.

"Tag, my old friend." He paused for dramatic effect, nodding as his eyes leisurely followed the two women. "Sooo, what's new, buddy?"

Shuffling his feet, Tag was reluctant to meet Tyler's piercing stare. After a nonchalant shrug, he muttered, "Well, I guess you could say Emery and I are on our first official date." Seeing Tyler's head tilt slightly accompanied by a wry eye-squint, Tag hastened to add, "As a couple."

Sporting a wide grin, Tyler good-naturedly slapped Tag's cheek. "My boy is growing up. I'm proud of you, Tag. You two look real good together, but I was kinda hoping you'd have waited another month. Robbi and I had a bet goin', and I fucking lost!"

Tag was about to ask for further clarification when his eyes drifted to Emery and Robbi, who were standing off to the side of the stage. Emery was peering at her cell phone, a concerned expression marring her lovely features.

"Something's wrong," Tag exclaimed and quickly walked toward the women, Tyler following closely behind. Emery was about to put the phone in her purse when the men approached.

"Is everything okay, Em? Is it Randy?" Tag's arm snaked around Emery's waist as she leaned into him, displaying the phone's screen.

ALEX: WANTED TO LET YOU KNOW I WILL BE OFF THE GRID FOR A WHILE, BIG CASE, DEEP COVER. THIS CELL # IS GOING DARK. IN CASE OF EMERGENCY, CONTACT CAPTAIN JACOVO (YOU HAVE HIS CELL #). I'LL CONTACT YOU WHEN I CAN. MY LOVE TO YOU & RANDY.

"This has happened before. It's the dangerous part of his job, but he thrives on it. He'd be gone for months at a time, one of the many reasons marriage wouldn't have worked for us. It'll be tough on Randy, but my dad will step up. He's a devoted grandfather, and his connections to the Cardinals certainly don't hurt." Her smile was forced, and it didn't quite reach her eyes.

Tag wrapped his arms around Emery in comfort, stroking her back. "Anything you or Randy need while Alex is gone, just ask. I'm here for you both."

Worrisome thoughts plagued Tag for the remainder of the evening, which prevented him from fully relaxing and enjoying the party. He harbored suspicions that Emery was holding something back. *Maybe she's still in love with Alex.*

Chapter 18

"We love life, not because we are used to living but because we are used to loving."
– *Friedrich Nietzsche*

TAG

Randy was a bit despondent; his dad was back undercover and wouldn't be available for several weeks, perhaps longer. It was Emery's habit not to focus on the dangerous aspect of his father's work when talking to Randy. Tag often found himself worrying about what would happen if … *Don't even go there, not my responsibility!*

After football practice, the threesome grabbed a late lunch then drove to the Aviation Museum in Oakland. It was a remarkable place for both children and adults. Two replica aircraft allowed children to experience sitting at the controls in a real plane. They also spent twenty minutes in the tower, listening to air traffic controllers in real-time. There were also many aircraft engines, including one from a jet fighter, on display.

Tag enjoyed interacting with Randy. He'd never had any interest in children before, but Randy was different. He was a good kid, respectful, well-behaved, smart as a whip, and fun.

After arriving home and walking Goldie around the block a

few times, Tag and Randy relaxed on the couch engrossed in all things football, while Emery puttered around in the kitchen preparing a few snacks for an On Demand movie marathon she had planned for the evening.

"So, Coach, do you like my mom?" Randy whispered with the pure, straightforward innocence of a child. They were lounging on the couch, casually tossing a football back and forth.

"Of course, I do, buddy." *Hmm ... what's this about?* Exasperated at Tag's feigned cluelessness, Randy huffed. "I mean do you *really* like her? Are you guys dating? Is she your girlfriend? I don't mean to be nosy, I'm just checkin'. Dad says it's my job to look out for Mom. You know, protect her when he's not around." Emery entered the room at that moment. Placing the snacks on the coffee table, she faced the couch, hands on her hips.

"What are my two favorite men up to? Trouble, I presume?" Emery's eyebrows waggled in lighthearted curiosity.

"I was just asking Tag if you were dating, like boyfriend and girlfriend, stuff like that."

"Well, Randy, umm ..." Emery stammered self-consciously, eyes nervously seeking Tag's.

Bloody hell! I'd better jump in here.

"I'm actually relieved, Em. I thought he was going to ask me what my intentions were with regard to his mother." Tag rose, and casually draped his arm over her shoulder, then led her to the couch where they joined Randy.

"And what exactly are your intentions, Tag?" Emery inquired, eyes sparkling with an exaggerated, contrived sweetness that let Tag know she was teasing him. Tag happily took the bait, leaning closer and whispering in her ear, "Wanna be my girlfriend?"

Batting her eyelashes furiously, Emery whispered back, "Yes, please." Randy observed the exchange wide-eyed. Finally, Tag made the declaration.

"Your mother and I are pleased to announce that we are

officially a couple. I will now kiss my beautiful sunrise girl. Close your eyes, kid. This might be X-rated."

"That is *so* not happening," Randy stated matter-of-factly as he waited patiently for their semi-chaste kiss to end before yelling, "Finally!" He hugged his mother first, but managed to high-five Tag simultaneously, ending with a double thumbs-up.

As Emery turned on the TV, Tag couldn't help but notice that Randy's exuberant expression had quickly morphed into one of pending gloom.

"What's up, RAZ, my man?" Tag knew exactly how to lift the boy's spirits. Randy sighed deeply, and then looked directly into his mother's eyes.

"What happens when your class is over, Mom, and you're back home for good? Will we ever see Tag again?" Randy's dark eyes began to brim with tears. Tag's reaction was instantaneous and he pulled the child into his side for a warm embrace. Although Randy's emotions unnerved him to some extent, Tag realized strong feelings had been growing for both Emery and her son. *Please. No tears, kid.*

"Randy, listen to me. No matter what happens between your mother and me, you are always gonna be an important part of my life. Remember, Phoenix is only a two-hour flight from here. Both of you can come up to visit me anytime and hopefully, I'll be coming to see some of your games." Tag's chest tightened as he reassured Randy. It hadn't taken long for the boy to weave his way into Tag's heart, and the thought of not being a part of his life pushed emotions to the surface he'd never expected to feel, especially toward a boy not of his own blood. But it didn't matter. Tag loved him. It was as simple as that.

"So you'll be kinda like my extra dad? You know, a substitute when my real dad's not around?" The boy's eyes became huge, expectantly awaiting Tag's response.

"Absolutely," Tag whispered softly as Emery squeezed his hand.

Later they were flipping through the TV channels, looking for a movie to watch. The *Divergent* trailer popped on the screen and Randy expressed interest. Emery had to remind him it was PG-13. Randy pouted for a moment, then turned to Tag, who was sprawled shirtless on the couch, Goldie in his lap. Randy studied his many colorful tattoos.

"You coulda starred in that movie, too. All the actors had tons of cool tats."

"Well, I'm probably a bit too old, kiddo. Most of those guys are teenagers." Emery scoffed at Tag's words, looking up and down appreciatively at his muscular torso.

"Oh, puhlease! The character Four? He's supposed to be eighteen in the movie, but Theo James, the actor, is actually over thirty."

"Is that so?" Tag countered, as a mischievous glint appeared in his eyes. "And how would you know that obscure tidbit of celebrity trivia, Emery?" Tag guffawed loudly as she stammered her response.

"I … I'm a big fan."

Tag continued his mocking laughter, while subtly flexing his biceps. "So do you like guys in their thirties, Em? And I know it's not polite to ask a woman how old she is, but—"

"Mom's twenty-six and Dad's a year older!" Randy piped up proudly as Goldie climbed happily onto the child's lap. "How 'bout you, Coach? I bet you're over thirty," Randy declared, furrowing his brows as he stared at Tag's forehead. "You're not losing any hair yet, so I'm guessing you're nowhere near forty, right?"

"Randy, mind your manners!" Emery chided, shaking her head in Tag's direction. "Grandpa's got a ton of hair and he's in his fifties." Randy pondered her statement, and then added, "If Grandpa ever does go bald, he can use the extra hair in his eyebrows for a transplant!" Randy howled at his own joke as Emery and Tag joined in.

As the boisterous laughter died down, all eyes turned to Tag. Even Goldie appeared to raise her snout expectantly in his direction.

"I'll be thirty-three on September ... whoa, girl!" Goldie's paws scratched at the hair on Tag's chest as she furiously initiated a sloppy face licking. "I think she needs to take a stroll outside. Who's coming with us?" Tag chuckled, eager to change the subject.

"Mom and I will both go so we can discuss your birthday party at Alice Cooperstown! It's such a cool place, Tag. It's right down the street from the US Airways Center where the Suns play, and I heard that the Cardinals sometimes —"

Emery interrupted the excited child. "Sweetie, Tag's birthday is months away. Right now, you need to focus on school, your football tryouts, and someone who needs to go outside before she has an accident, which *you* will be responsible for cleaning up."

Randy resolutely reached for Goldie's leash as they all headed for the door. Although Emery smiled when Tag reached for her hand, entwining their fingers, he caught a fleeting glimpse of worry flicker in her eyes as he brought the back of her hand to his lips. As her soft skin brushed against his mouth, he looked into her eyes knowing Emery had the power to heal his heart or smash it into a million pieces. He had no idea which it would be. *What secrets are you hiding behind those big brown eyes?*

Chapter 19

*"See how she leans her cheek upon her hand.
O that I were a glove upon that hand,
That I might touch that cheek."*
– William Shakespeare (Romeo and Juliet)

TAG

It had been a week jam-packed with numerous activities. Spring was in the air, and Tag's inconsistent — aka flaky — clients were now demanding more sessions in a vain attempt to get into 'bikini and speedo shape' in a ridiculously short amount of time. Although thankful that the majority of his regulars were dedicated, all it took were a few to fuck up his perfect schedule. His workouts with Emery unfortunately were curtailed, but coincidentally, her required sculpting time in the studio increased, so the outcome was acceptable. Tag made sure his weekends remained mostly free, especially when Randy was in town.

It had been two long weeks since Emery had stayed over, and Tag craved more of her. He was able to change shifts with another bartender Friday night in order to free up his entire weekend to spend with Emery at his house. She arrived with a high-spirited Goldie in tow. It was the puppy's first visit to Tag's home and he was ready, purchasing a few necessary items for the weekend. A small, chain-link enclosure had also been constructed in the backyard so Goldie would have a safe area to run and play.

After making a salad, Tag barbequed two steaks and some chicken tenders with roasted corn on the cob, which he served Emery outside on the patio. It was the perfect evening; the fire pit was roaring and a silvery crescent moon hovered overhead as the brilliant sun was beginning its descent.

They were cuddling on the oversized chaise lounge while Goldie, whose long leash was anchored to an iron stake, chewed contentedly on what was left of the delicious steaks. Emery lay on top of him, her back to his chest. His arms were wrapped around her waist, her head tucked under his chin. *She is the perfect fit for me. I need to nibble on that beautiful neck for a while.*

Sweeping her long ponytail to the side, he lowered his mouth and nipped playfully on her soft skin, just below her ear. Emery's soft moans confirmed what he already knew; it was her favorite spot. His tongue swirled around the shell of her ear and ended at the lobe, which he gently pulled into his mouth. He suddenly became aware of Goldie's front paws on his forearm.

"I think she wants to snuggle," Tag briefly murmured in Emery's ear as he scooped Goldie up, and then placed the squirming pup next to him, where she settled down for a nap. Emery's right hand scratched the pup's head while her left arm reached back, attempting to snake around Tag's neck. Her eyes were still closed as she searched for his mouth. Their lips collided in a blistering kiss, tongues dueling for control as they delved deeper into each other's hungry mouths.

"You have no idea how much I love kissing you. I can't get enough of your sweet mouth." He sucked on her lush bottom lip, running his tongue piercing gently over the soft flesh, careful not to forcefully hit any of her teeth. His piercings had chipped a girl's tooth once … well, twice actually, but since it was the same girl *and* the same tooth, Tag only counted it once.

"Em, did you bring your bathing suit for the Jacuzzi? Although you don't need it, babe. Nobody can see back here. That's why I planted those trees."

"I brought it." She glanced demurely over her shoulder at him. "Wanna go in now?"

"Yep," Tag declared, pulling his tank top off, now clad in only cutoffs. "I'm ready." Rolling her eyes, Emery headed for her overnight bag, which she had deposited in Tag's bedroom.

When she emerged through the sliding glass doors, wearing a revealing burnt orange and gold bikini, it appeared as if a radiant sun was approaching as Tag shaded his eyes to capture a clearer view. The blazing colors from the fire pit and the western sky's sunset reflected off the glass, startling him for a brief moment … *a flaming inferno, smoke, screams.* Shoving the panicky feeling away, he gingerly took Emery's hand and guided her into the Jacuzzi where she sat on his lap.

"What were you just thinking of, honey?" Emery gently probed. "You can tell me. No more secrets, remember?"

"Once in a while, with certain colors — like a sunset or the fire pit — I get a flashback and imagine the crash, for the millionth time. I try my damnedest not to go there, but …" His voice trailed off as he heaved a deep sigh. "I'm sorry."

"No apology necessary, but can I share something with you? When someone we truly loved is no longer here with us on Earth, I believe they not only watch over and protect us, but they are able to share our emotions and see people and events through our eyes as well. Do you think that's possible?"

Tag's gaze lowered as he struggled to fill the aching void in his chest with a few deep breaths. Emery remained quiet, pressing her forehead to his, until he began to speak softly.

"I do. And if it *is* true, I have caused Randi a fuckton of sadness, worry, and pain. That ends today. I promise you, Emery." He tenderly kissed her forehead then unhurriedly explored her eyelids, nose, and cheeks with his mouth. He nipped her lower lip, then began to kiss her more fervently. She opened, inviting his tongue into her warm mouth. Desire radiated from every cell of his body, and he held on to her with a desperation that both excited and terrified him.

The intense heat of the day had finally dissipated, leaving a cool, fragrant breeze, which rustled through the citrus trees. The steamy, bubbling water was working wonders as they submerged their bodies in the relaxing heat. Goldie's leash allowed her to frolic nearby, but not fall into the hot water, although she tried her best to jump in. Tag had just spent a good ten minutes brushing her fur, and was now scratching her belly playfully. It was as if Goldie sensed she owed her life to him. When he was around, the animal simply could not get enough of his affectionate roughhousing.

Tag's other arm was wrapped snugly just underneath Emery's breasts; her upper back pressed to his chest, her lower body floating near the water's surface. Tag's face was nestled in the crook of her neck, as Emery's head languidly rested on his shoulder, face skyward.

"I need to see more of your beautiful body, Em." While one hand distracted her with tickles up her back, the other deftly unhooked her bikini top, allowing it to float away. Snaking his arms around, he lavished his attention on her lush breasts bobbing in the Jacuzzi's rippling waves. Every tweak and pinch on her nipples elicited a sexy moan or sigh. Aware that his dick was misbehaving badly, Tag was grateful for the few centimeters of distance between their lower bodies. Emery scooted backward and sat on his throbbing cock, and began naughtily grinding her backside into him. Tag let out a low groan.

"You are gonna kill me, woman. As I'm sure you remember,

our first time together was a bit unconventional, so I've been planning something romantic to make up for it. However, if you want me right here, right now, I'm more than happy to oblige." Emery laid her head back on his shoulder and their eyes met.

"Tell me your plan," she whispered after gently biting his earlobe.

"Slow, soft, sweet, and in my bed. Now."

Since the momentous night they slept together, Tag had thought of nothing else but sharing his bed with Emery again. Her essence had permeated every dream, what she would taste like on his tongue, how it would feel to slide inside her again, but this time 100 percent awake and sober. Tag was aware that this would not be some random, one-night fuck, and the thought unraveled him, which was the main reason he allowed so many days to pass. *What the hell? I've had sex hundreds — and if you count jerkin' off — thousands of times, so why the fuck would I be nervous?* Smiling peacefully to himself, the answer was obvious. Emery meant more to him than any other woman he had been with, since Randi. *She's become a vital part of my life, and I feel as though I've been welcomed into a new family. Goldie and me, both of us … lost, alone, hurt. Saved. Maybe even loved.*

Emery

Tucked under the freshly laundered sheets and cozy comforter, Emery snuggled in Tag's arms. Both were completely naked — not to mention sober — and the room was dark except for an array of brightly lit candles on the dresser. His limbs were intimately tangled up in hers, arms protectively encasing her upper torso. She was the willing insect, trapped in a magical, silken web. The warmth from his bare skin seeped into her bones, enveloping her in a thick velvet comforter. She found refuge in the crook of his neck where her head fit so perfectly, and reveled in the softness of his skin that was stretched taut over thick, corded muscles. The rhythmic sounds of his heartbeat and steady breathing were music to her ears, but the secret she was keeping ate away at her conscience. *Am I waiting for the right time, hoping it will never come?*

Tag's fingers sifted through Emery's long tresses, while his other palm traced circles on her back. She pushed herself up on her forearms so she could stare directly into his eyes.

"Could you do me a favor?" she murmured as her gaze fell to his lips, running her tongue lightly along the seam of his mouth while avoiding his lip ring.

"Anything for you, sweetheart. Just give me a minute." He carefully removed both his lip and tongue piercing, as Emery's eyes widened in astonishment.

"Oh, my God, Tag. Now you're a mind reader?" she queried in amazement.

"Well, I knew you were holding back a little whenever you would kiss me, and there will be none of that tonight. But, I'm warning you, Em. Later on? When I am tasting that sweet pussy of yours? You are gonna be thankin' me for the tongue ball, baby!" His devilish wink and eyebrow waggle sent her into convulsive giggles as she blushed furiously, hiding her face in her hands.

After placing the jewelry on the nightstand, Tag gently flipped Emery on her back, covering her body with his. Her legs opened, allowing his lower torso to nestle comfortably in between. His gaze heated as he took Emery's face in his hands, one thumb softly caressing her mouth.

"You have no idea how bad I want you right now, but I need to tell you something first." *Shit. Here it comes.* Worry clouded her features as Tag rushed to put her at ease.

"Emery. My beautiful brown-eyed girl, I've been suppressing my feelings since that night we met. Hell, I've had twelve long years of trying not to feel anything, except fear, regret, and guilt. Did I say fear?" He continued to trace her lips as he returned to his reflections.

"You bear an uncanny physical resemblance to Randi — especially your eyes — and I admit it unnerved me at the beginning. But now? For every one thing that is similar to her, there are a hundred astonishing, incredible things about you that are unique and distinctively you. I swear, Emery. You are the only one I see."

Tag wrapped his hand around her neck and brought their lips together in a soft but searing kiss that rapidly increased in fervor. Taking control with his tongue, no fear of chipping a tooth to rein him in, he sought hers and began a torturous dance of mutual need. Emery's body pressed into his, not wanting a millimeter of space between them. Sensing his engorged cock was close to her entrance, she gripped his ass firmly, nails scratching lightly, and then digging in.

"Baby," Tag breathed in her ear. "We have all the time in the world for slow and sweet. You're makin' me crazy, so this is gonna be hard and fast. You okay with that?" Reaching for a condom from the nightstand drawer, he opened the foil with his teeth and quickly sheathed himself as Emery nodded her assent.

She smiled as his hand caressed her breast, swirling his tongue around the hard peak. He palmed her mound with the other, gratified when he found a pool of moisture between her thighs. Bringing his fingers to his mouth, he greedily licked each finger clean.

"I love how drenched you are for me. Tell me what you want, baby." Pinning her with a scorching gaze, he placed their palms together, interlocking fingers and raised her arms over her head.

"Please, Tag. I need you inside me. Now." Arching her back, she thrust her hips upward, grinding into him to increase the friction she craved on her aching clit. He sank into her warmth, and a primal groan escaped his lips as he pistoned in and out of her slick channel, slowly at first, then gradually increasing his speed. Emery's soft gasps and moans of pleasure brought a smile to his lips, her soft brown eyes never looking away from his. She was hyper-aware of every subtle movement his cock made, with its large piercing on the head, as he moved in a circular rhythm, stretching and filling her ... hard, fast, and powerful. Releasing one of her hands, Tag extended his arm down between them, and circled her swollen clit with his thumb. As he pulled out slightly, she felt the metal ring of his piercing drag along her inner wall. Angling his hips, he plunged back in and her cries of ecstasy echoed throughout the room. *Oh, my God. There really is a G-spot!*

He continued his relentless assault until her breathing became short, frantic bursts. A tidal wave of sparks exploded behind her eyelids as his cock throbbed unremittingly inside her. Emery attempted to silence the screams that burst from her throat, but her traitorous body had other ideas. "Ooh, I'm so close. Please. Don't stop. Taaag!" Emery cried out as a powerful orgasm rippled through her, causing the bed to creak.

Her pussy convulsed and clenched around him, drawing him deeper into her body. Their eyes glistened in the candlelight, still locked onto one another. Groaning, Tag plunged in deep one last time, then stilled. His face found the curve of Emery's shoulder as he collapsed on top of her, muffling his groaned release. He continued to gently rock into her and his body's shudders calmed as Emery pressed soft kisses onto his sweat-covered forehead.

Tag had just finished gently cleaning between Emery's thighs with a warm washcloth, and languidly kissed his way from her navel up to her lips and everything in between. As his face hovered over hers, his penetrating gaze never wavered, not once blinking. His large hands cradled her face, as his expression grew progressively more contemplative. Emery pulled back slightly and grasped his wrists, still maintaining eye contact. The pace of her breathing increased, eyelashes fluttering apprehensively, as Tag sought to soothe her with feather-soft kisses to her nose and cheeks.

"Emery, sweetheart, there's something I need to ask you." Taking a deep breath, the strain on Tag's countenance betrayed his inner struggle to maintain composure. "Two weeks ago, when we were in bed, you encouraged me to talk to you as if you were Randi, and I did. She even followed me into my dreams. But the moment you whispered, 'It's me, Emery,' I *knew* I was making love to you. Did you know for sure I had heard you? Did you imagine for a moment I still thought you were Randi? You could have stopped me at that point, but you didn't."

Their foreheads pressed together, eyes peering into the depths of each other's soul. A solitary tear escaped Emery's eye and her voice shook as her explanation poured out. "I can't quite explain what I was feeling at that precise moment. I wasn't sure you had heard me; you could have been in a semi-conscious state. I won't lie and say I didn't want you. I did. You were having a terrible nightmare, sobbing and begging to be with her one last time. At that moment, when I welcomed you inside me, I felt it was what Randi would have wanted — what she knew you needed — her forgiveness. I wanted to ease your pain, and I somehow allowed myself to absorb every memory you shared with me of Randi. I sensed her take possession of me in that fleeting moment, and she felt so real. It was her final gift of pure love to you and I couldn't bear to wrench it away. I'm sorry, maybe I shouldn't have—"

"Shh, baby. You didn't do anything wrong." Tag held her close as his fingers gently combed through her silky hair. His arms were clinging to her for dear life, mouth claiming her possessively, swallowing her cries. Kissing a path to her ear, he soothed, "It's all good, I promise you. Everything's clear to me now. Randi was giving me her blessing to finally let her go after all these years so I could find you."

Emery became immersed in two bottomless pools, which had lightened to a pale jade hue. What she noticed made her heartbeat race. She had seen that look in Cole's eyes many years ago, the intensity seared into her memory. As a teen, she had fantasized one day a man would look at her the way Cole had gazed with adoration at Randi. She was experiencing a silent argument in her mind. *Is he hallucinating, imagining I am Randi again? No, he is wide-awake. He is looking right at me. Could it be ... could he ...?* Lightly fingering the faint, jagged scar on her elbow where Cole had kissed her all those years ago transported her back to reality. Tag's countenance had become a roadmap of raw emotions breaking free, no longer buried under years of guilt and denial.

They spent the rest of the night with limbs entwined, leisurely exploring each other's bodies, Tag with a gentle reverence that took her breath away. He did not leave a square centimeter of her soft skin unkissed, as his tongue explored every crevice. When they eventually made love again, it was at an unhurried, languid pace. They moved as one, rocking rhythmically to the beat of their hearts. Emery wrapped her legs around his waist, and lifted her pelvis causing him to sink even deeper, welcoming him home. Pools of sweat engulfed them, but Tag simply smiled and reached for the fan's remote control. A deep slumber eventually overtook them, and they remained in each other's arms until beams of morning sunlight streamed through the partially opened curtains.

∞

Saturday afternoon rolled around and Emery's mosaic project was underway. Goldie had spent the greater part of the day outside in the enclosed play area Tag had built for her. Because of the tile shards, toxic adhesive and messy grout, the living room was off-limits; Emery had just given her a bath the previous morning.

Emery and Tag had been working on the fireplace mantel for hours. Tag eagerly tackled the initial prepping of the surface, which involved sanding away old candle wax build-up and any other bumpy imperfections. Emery had laid out the pattern stencils she had drawn for the seven Japanese characters that would make up the main design: fire, earth, air, water, eternity, strength, and love. The symbols would be made from black marble; the background formed by contrasting earth-toned tiles. Deep in thought, Emery had a habit of leaning her cheek on her left hand, while cementing the various pieces to the mantel. Tag was watching basketball on TV while he worked, but Emery could sense him casting furtive glances in her direction.

Sneaking up behind her, he buried his face in the crook of her neck, licking hungrily before covering her skin with open-mouthed kisses.

"Tag! I'm all sweaty and probably covered with toxic grout, silly!" she admonished with a peal of laughter. "You are, too." She wiped a smudge of dirt from the fireplace off his cheek.

"I don't care. You always taste sweet to me, and I'm especially looking forward to tasting my soon-to-be favorite spot right between your —"

"Ugh! I am super sweaty and gross there, babe!" Faux-horror was etched on her startled face, rolling her eyes for emphasis.

"Not. Possible. I love your body any way I can get it. I'm serious, Em. I do love your body; it's perfect in every way. Perfect for me." He wrapped her ponytail around his hand, pulling her mouth to his hard and fast; his tongue demanded entrance as it battled hers for control. Coming up for a breath, his bright green eyes penetrated her.

"Emery, you have thirty minutes to finish whatever you are working on and not one second more. Then I will be carrying you to the shower where I will make sure that every drop of sweat and each minute particle of grout is removed from this delicious body of yours. Now get busy while I feed and walk Goldie."

Tag's sensual words travelled straight to Emery's core, lighting a fire only his talented tongue and cock could extinguish. It was not necessary to cajole him into the shower when she presented herself to him — wrapped only in a fluffy bath towel — seven minutes before his proclaimed deadline. Scooping her up in his arms, he strode directly into the bathroom, and turned on the jets. It wasn't until they were under the spray, when Tag realized he was still wearing his cut-offs. He stepped out of them quickly, laughing while tossing them on the tiled floor. He seemed so carefree and happy; Emery had worried perhaps the realization he had finally relinquished Randi's hold on his heart would have negative repercussions. Following twelve long years in mourning, banishing the memory of the love of your life would take more than a new romance to extinguish. She prayed his apparent contentment was real, and not short-lived.

Tag

The shower's warm water was cascading down, surrounding them in an intimate shroud, like gentle spring rain. They were seeing each other's naked bodies — completely, in full, bright light — for the first time, but it was not frenzied like the typical romance novel or porn movie. Tag held her in his arms reverently, kissed her face and neck then lapped the water droplets flowing down her glorious cleavage. An innocence existed between them; friends unhurriedly and cautiously becoming lovers, curious to touch, feel, and learn about each other. His hard-on was obvious, but her demeanor was so shyly fragile and vulnerable that fast and furious sex was not foremost in his mind. Cupping a breast in his hand, he marveled,

"You are so perfect, so beautiful," as he kissed her deeply while his thumb and forefinger pinched her nipple, teasing it until it peaked. She moaned into his mouth, pressing her breasts against him.

Tag grabbed the shower gel, and proceeded to cleanse her body worshipfully from head to toe with a giant sponge, taking extra time to press soft kisses down the length of her damp back. Emery reciprocated soon after. Shampoo followed as they washed each other's hair. This was a first-time experience for Tag; feeling his fingers in her soapy tresses was almost as erotic as watching the bubbles slide over her breasts and impeccable, heart-shaped ass.

As Tag reached to turn off the jets after rinsing, Emery's strong hands gripped his cock from behind. One hand gently massaged his balls while the other stroked up and down his hard length. Tag let his head fall back, groaning in pleasure. Emery's thumb softly caressed the head of his penis, probing the large metal ring delicately. A primal growl escaped his throat.

"Baby, don't touch me like that unless you want me to fuck you senseless. Right now."

"That's exactly what I want," she purred as he whirled to face her, pressing her back against the cold, hard tile. "Then I'm gonna need that condom I stashed on the top shelf. Give me a second, babe."

Tag lifted one long leg and wrapped it around his waist, his throbbing erection poised at her entrance. Grasping his backside with her hands, Emery pulled him toward her with such force that he was almost balls deep in one thrust. His mouth sought her neck, biting gently, savoring the heat of her as he pulled out slightly, then plunged back in fully as she welcomed him with a voluble sigh of unabashed ecstasy. He began to move his hips rhythmically, striving to achieve the precise angle that he knew would caress that oh-so elusive spot deep inside.

"Oh, my God, Tag. That's it. Right. There. Ooh, don't stop." He smothered her mouth with his own, swallowing her cries. As her body shuddered in his arms, Tag felt his own powerful release hit him. They held onto each other for several minutes as their breathing stilled. Emery was the first to speak, murmuring something from the crook of Tag's neck. Her lips vibrating against his damp skin sent shivers across his shoulder.

"What did you say, baby?" he queried while nibbling on her earlobe.

"Amazing shower sex, honey, but I'm freezing. Look! I'm all goose bumpy."

"No worries, love." Chuckling, he disposed of the condom, and then grabbed two oversized towels from the counter. They took turns drying each other off before he swooped her up and carried her to his bed.

They never left the bedroom except for Tag's mad dash to the door for the Chinese takeout he had ordered. Afternoon merged seamlessly into early evening as their bond deepened and became so much more. Laughing uproariously one minute, kissing passionately the next, the time passed. Several loud barks unexpectedly disrupted their reverie, causing both to gasp simultaneously, "Goldie!"

After walking and feeding the forlorn pup, Tag guiltily brought her to join them in bed. Goldie was quite content to cavort between them while Tag rambunctiously wrestled with her, donning the thick protective glove he used during her training sessions.

"Watch this, Em!" Tag commanded, while engaging the animal in play, which quickly morphed into a growl-fest. Goldie's teeth were clenched around her favorite rubber bone while Tag was attempting to yank it away. Although the dog's jaws had it in a death-grip, Tag managed to pull it free and flung it into a far corner, bellowing, "TACK!" Goldie sprung from the bed and leaped on the bone, mauling it while growling ferociously.

"Tag, what the …?" Emery's mouth hung open as Tag grinned proudly.

"Goldie, come." The pup's demeanor immediately became docile as she jumped on Tag's lap, licking his face as her tail wagged vigorously. "I've been training her. She'll soon be the ultimate watchdog you wanted. Cool, huh?"

The DVR was finally turned off and Emery was getting comfortable in Tag's arms when he suddenly turned from her and reached for something on the nightstand. His back was deliberately turned toward her, as if hiding his actions. Emery glared at his shit-eating grin until Tag stuck out his tongue, and displayed his piercing, although it appeared a tad larger than the previous ball. Emery's excited smile was enhanced by the deep blush that crept up her neck and cheeks.

"Are you ready, sweetheart? After I make love to you with my mouth, you will never want another man's tongue on you again. *Ever.*"

Tag crawled toward her on his hands and knees, a hungry predator ready to feast on his prey. Emery opened her legs wide as he snuggled in between. The delicious scent of her arousal mixed with the shower products had his cock aching for relief, but he had another plan in mind. Starting at her navel, he trailed slow, wet kisses downward until he reached her smooth, bare mound. His tongue took over, licking a path from her entrance to her clit, then around the outer edges and back again, purposely avoiding her sensitive bundle of nerves. Needing more of her sweet taste, he rolled his tongue and drove in and out, tongue-fucking her as her hips rose to meet each thrust.

Emery, gasping for breath, moaned in pleasure, "More, Tag. Please." Smiling as he rubbed his facial stubble against her soft skin, Tag hummed his agreement, knowing the vibrations would set her off. She bucked her pelvis again, and sighed. Using his thumbs gently to spread her soft folds wide for his exploration, he skated his tongue slowly along her slit. Flattening his tongue and alternating between long, languid strokes and feather-light flicks had her writhing within seconds. Simultaneously, he inserted two fingers into her channel, pumping them rapidly. Her walls clenched around him and he knew she was close to the edge. One arm was flung behind her, with the headboard in a death-grip; the other hand was buried in Tag's hair, tugging insistently.

His gaze moved upward to watch her for a split second. Emery was breathtaking: mouth open in ecstasy, head rocking from side to side as deep, guttural moans of pleasure emanated from her throat. A profound revelation hit him. Making love with Randi had always been gentle and sweet; they were young, innocently exploring all that sex had to offer. *This is something else: primal, wild, out-of-control; I will never get enough of this woman. My Emery.*

Exposing her clitoris even more with his fingers, and lightly pulling back the hood, he began his final assault armed with the metal ball designed for the ultimate in pleasure. Applying varying amounts of pressure, he swiped his tongue directly on and around the tiny throbbing nub. It didn't take long before Emery's thighs tightened alongside his head and she shattered as the sensations of his tongue piercing on her over-stimulated clit caused her to explode.

"Give me all you got, baby. I *love* it when you scream my name," Tag murmured, as he slipped his palms under her ass and lifted her closer, coaxing an additional aftershock from her body with his mouth. His gaze wandered over her as she stilled, chest rising and falling in short, shallow breaths. Inching upward, he laid his head on her abdomen, fingering a nipple tenderly.

"I love how responsive you are, baby, and I have never seen anyone as beautiful as you, especially after I've made you come." As Emery's breathing quieted, she playfully tugged on Tag's hair.

"Holy shit, Tag! That was *unreal*. The most mind-blowing orgasm of my life. How did you learn … I mean, who taught you all that? Oh. My. Fucking. God!"

Chuckling, Tag nestled his head in between her gorgeous breasts, kissing and delicately licking each pert nipple in turn. Emery gazed at his tongue piercing with appreciative eyes. "Every guy should get one of those, by the way," she whispered seductively. "It feels … *wow*!"

"If I share my 'sex education' story, will you judge me?" Tag's grin held its usual captivating charm.

"Probably not, but will it be necessary for me to send someone a 'Thank You' note?"

Unable to hold in his laughter, Tag wondered if he dared tell her about a twenty-two year old student teacher who had unexpectedly — and quite illegally — changed his sex life at age fifteen. He rolled over on his back, taking Emery with him. She crossed her arms on his chest, propping her chin on top. "Tell me everything, Tag. Every sordid, sex-filled, juicy, orgasmic detail!" Her smile was adorable.

Emery and I promised to have no secrets, but this will be the one exception.

"Let's just say an older woman made me an offer I couldn't refuse. She had a fantasy and requested my assistance to make it a reality. End of story."

"Well, I certainly appreciate her attention to the elusive female orgasm. Did her lessons include anal instruction, too?" Emery ventured, gnawing on a fingernail. Tag's mouth fell open, eyes bulging. His cock twitched, poking her abdomen. *Holy shit! Did she say what I think she said? Should I mention that 'end zone' has a double meaning to a football jock? Hmmm … maybe later.*

"No, they did not. Is that something you'd enjoy?" His grin was devilish as he played with a long tendril, curling it around his finger.

Emery smiled coyly. "Alex and I used to play around a bit. Nothing hard-core or painful, an occasional toy or two."

Although the idea of playing around with Emery's luscious ass made him instantly harder, the vivid image of Alex doing the playing was like being doused with an ice-cold shower. Tag scowled and Emery hastily changed the subject before his eyes darkened any further.

"So, if you're not planning to divulge any dirty details, you are just gonna have to *show* me, Tag. Again. Now!" Emery commanded in between soft kisses.

"Your wish is my command, beautiful, but after dinner I plan on formally introducing you to Prince Albert — up close and *very* personal. Oh, and before I forget. You need to show me those 'toys' you referred to. Soon. Promise?"

Emery

Emery had just finished putting the dinner plates and utensils in the dishwasher and upon entering Tag's room, found him already in bed, leaning on a few pillows. Emery snuggled alongside, shyly peering up at him through her dark lashes.

"Come here, brown eyes. I crave your lips." After pulling her on his lap, Tag placed his hand on Emery's nape, brought her toward him and their lips met in a heated kiss. His tongue demanded entrance and she opened to him, as they savored each other's warmth. One hand caressed her face, his thumb sliding over her cheekbone, while the other buried itself in her luxurious hair, fingers threading themselves desperately around the strands. Emery leaned in closer, her palms on his chest, as he devoured her mouth hungrily. His cock was throbbing between them; she knew exactly what he wanted.

Moaning into her mouth, he breathed, "Baby, I need your hands on me. Please." Emery nodded, as her hand reached down, wrapping around his length. Gently stroking the smooth skin with her palm, her thumb moved to the tip and felt the hard, cool metal of Tag's cock ring. Emery's other hand gripped the base of his shaft while her thumb and fingertips continued their tentative exploration of the head and its piercing. Tag began to moan in pleasure at her ministrations and broke their kiss to take a much-needed breath. Glancing down briefly, she noticed the glistening drops of pre-cum, and rubbed her fingers through the moisture, then brought them to her mouth. Tag's eyes widened as she licked her fingers clean, before scooting down to nestle herself between his legs.

Okay, I can do this. Tag said it's just like an earring, and … oh my! A lot bigger than an earring.

Emery began by stroking his muscular thighs and kissing the soft skin inside, inching her way upward, deliberately avoiding his cock at first, which stood at attention. She glanced up to find his lidded eyes locked onto hers.

"Em, you can't hurt me, but there's always the possibility of a chipped tooth if I lose control, so when I'm close I'm gonna pull out. Okay?"

Holding the base of his cock in one hand, Emery nodded her assent, while the other hand stroked him from root to tip. When she finally enclosed her mouth over him, Tag moaned and ran his hands through her hair, tugging her closer.

"God, baby, your mouth feels so good on me, so fuckin' hot." Encouraged by his reaction, Emery relaxed and darted her tongue out in timid exploration, feeling the coolness of the metal ring in contrast to the warmth of his silky smooth skin. Circling the head, then teasing his slit with the tip of her tongue, had him fisting the bedsheets and thrusting his hips deeper as her mouth wrapped around him, licking and sucking forcefully. His spicy scent was intoxicating and when Emery felt the metal hit the back of her throat, a surge of power ran through her, causing her mouth and tongue to go into overdrive. Tag's ab muscles pulled taut; he gasped and let out a low groan, "Emery, I need to be inside you. Now, baby."

Tag

The powerful orgasms Tag experienced with Emery were unlike any he had ever experienced … even with Randi. He found himself reaching for something, not just the usual physical release, but something more elusive, almost spiritual. Feeling her warmth pulse and clench around him, hearing her child-like giggle at something he said, watching her dazzling smile light up a dreary room as well as his aching heart — it was all too much to fully internalize. She both thrilled and terrified him as he fought with himself to comprehend what had transpired since they met. His mind raced with possible explanations.

I'm a lot older, no meaningful relationships for over a decade. Emery is special … unique. She's lightning behind my eyes, thunder booming in my ribcage, warm sunshine on my face. I am losing myself in her, and that scares the shit out of me.

Chapter 20

"In that book which is my memory,
On the first page of the chapter that is the day when I first met you,
appear the words, 'Here begins a new life'."
– Dante Alighieri (Vita Nuova)

TAG

May had arrived bringing warmer weather and glorious sun-filled days. Tag had arranged for the following Saturday's football practice to take place at a local high school where a client of his worked as a P.E. teacher. Randy needed to become accustomed to the size and dimensions of a real football field. Tag's buddy, Curt, brought his two sons along for fun. The three boys had a blast cavorting around the field, while attempting to follow the loudly yelled plays called by Curt or Tag, who were acting as coach, referee, or player as needed. Lenny and Jeff were a few years older than Randy and had a lot more football experience and finesse, but after seeing the younger boy's skills and fearless play, they didn't hold back. After several hours of exertion, the group went to California Pizza Kitchen for an early dinner, where Curt's wife, Dana, joined them. The laughter and conversation flowed easily. Tag found himself grinning more than usual, especially when Emery affectionately reached for his hand or Randy leaned into him for a hug or a high-five. His gaze wandered to the family sitting across from him and his chest tightened, causing him to lose his breath for a moment. Half-expecting the usual dread to overcome him, he was caught off-guard as a warm wave of contentment invaded his chest instead. *This is what happy families do. This is how normal people feel … secure, appreciated, valued, and loved.*

After much discussion, a decision was reached. Sunday afternoon would be spent at the nearby Marine Mammal Center. Randy was studying mammals and their environment in life science, so it seemed like the perfect choice. The highlight of the tour was the animal care facility, where sick and injured seal pups were being rehabilitated.

Randy chattered non-stop during the drive home about what he had learned. "Mom, can we adopt one of the little seal pups or maybe a baby otter? They're so cute and we've done such a good job with Goldie. She'd love having a playmate even though they're different species. You know how Goldie is, she loves everybody!"

Tag interjected, with a sympathetic shake of his head. "Sorry, buddy. Those guys need an ocean to swim in and Arizona … well, it simply wouldn't work. If you'd like, we can make a donation to help take care of their injuries, okay?"

The boy's face fell, nodding in reluctant agreement. "I could donate part of the money I was saving up for Christmas presents. Right, Mom?"

Emery's response was a fierce hug and a barrage of kisses on her son's blushing cheeks. She beamed proudly in Tag's direction as she threw him an appreciative wink. As they rounded the corner, Randy craned his neck out the passenger's window and sucked in a startled breath.

"Mom, look. It's Daddy! What's he doing here?" The child's eyes widened in amazement. As soon as Tag pulled into the closest parking space, Randy burst from the car and ran toward the black-clad figure who was now leaning against the front gate of Emery's building, arms folded across his chest.

Emery's brows drew together as she turned toward Tag. "Something's wrong. I had no clue he was coming. Oh, God, my parents—" She hastily fled out the open door leaving Tag to gather their belongings and lock the vehicle, which he did as unhurriedly as he could to give them some private, family time.

Tag half-expected to see signs of distress but the opposite scene presented itself as he drew closer. Randy's father was holding the child tightly and ruffling his hair affectionately in between random scattered kisses. A relieved look flooded Emery's countenance as Alex teased, "Sorry to scare you, Emmie. I don't need a reason to come see my family, do I? I just missed you both so much." Jealousy churned in Tag's gut as he watched the trio. Alex's devotion to his family was obvious in his shining gaze, as Emery leaned against his chest. The carefree grin quickly morphed into a scowl as Tag approached, striding briskly, hand outstretched.

"I'm Tag. It's great to finally meet you." They shook hands, each man striving for the more powerful grip, but both seemed equally matched.

"I'm Alex. It's good to meet you too. Thanks for workin' with my boy. I haven't had much free time lately so I really appreciate it." Tag felt the man's eyes bore into him, sizing him up, and Emery appeared uncomfortable, so he decided to give them some space.

"Hey, Emery, I'm gonna go up and get Goldie. She's probably overdue for a walk. Okay?" Tag bounded up the steps without waiting for a response and disappeared, closing the door behind him. Goldie greeted him with enthusiastic yelping as he entered the apartment, and after removing the pup from her crate, they snuggled on the couch while Tag scratched her belly with one hand and checked his phone with the other. He was consciously stalling, not wanting to intrude on personal family matters. Knowing that Randy's flight back home was scheduled to leave in a few hours, he had planned to stick around until then.

Tag was in the middle of answering a few emails when Goldie made it abundantly clear that going outside was an urgent priority. He rose from the couch at the same moment Emery and Randy came through the door. Randy squatted down and Goldie immediately started licking his face.

"Me and Dad are gonna go walk her. He says we need a man-to-man. See ya in a few!" the boy yelled as he grabbed Goldie's leash and left.

Emery rubbed the back of her neck as she sank into the couch next to Tag. He gently lifted her chin so their eyes met.

"What's wrong, sweetheart? Everything okay back home?" Emery nodded but her wan smile did not reach her eyes.

"Alex always gets like this when he's about to go off the grid. He makes sure that ... you know, everything is in order. It's part of the job, but he seems a bit more anxious this time. If all goes well, he could be in line for a huge promotion. Oh, and by the way, Alex flew here and he will be flying back with Randy. He was able to get a seat on the same flight, so we don't have to take Randy to the airport after all."

An hour had passed and Goldie was nestled languidly on Tag's bare chest, when footsteps hit the stairs. Expecting Emery had returned from saying her goodbyes, Tag was quite startled at the heavy slam of the door. Astonishment overtook him as Alex's large frame loomed over the couch.

"Can we talk for a moment?" he demanded as his hands deliberately balled into tight fists. Remaining outwardly unperturbed, although his stomach was roiling, Tag calmly stood, holding a squirming Goldie in his arms.

"Of course. Let me put her down first." After depositing the pup in her crate and kissing her snout, Tag rose to his full height, turned, and then calmly strode up to Alex. The men were almost nose-to-nose, about two feet apart. The air was thick with testosterone and alpha-male posturing.

"What's on your mind, Alex?" Tag's rippling muscled torso and intimidating tattoos were on full display.

"I know more about you than you may think, but that doesn't concern me at the moment. I am a police detective first and foremost, and protecting *my* family has always been my top priority. Although I have my doubts, Emery believes in you and I trust her judgement. She and my son both speak highly of you, and whether I like it or not, you've become a part of their lives. I don't know what's going on between you and Emmie; that's not my business. My *only* business is the wellbeing of the two people who are *my entire world*. I want your solemn promise to protect them if, for any reason, I can't. Do I have your word on that?"

Nodding gravely, Tag whispered, "You have my word, Alex." They shook hands, but Alex did not let go immediately, increasing the pressure of his grasp until Tag began to wince. Alex's face had suddenly taken on a purple tinge, eyes ink-black.

"I warn you. If you fuck her over or hurt her in any way, you *will* regret it. Emmie and my son have always been who I live for, the two reasons I do what I do." His words were hushed, yet urgently menacing. "You got me?"

Although initially taken aback by Alex's intimidating tirade, Tag comprehended the motives behind it. His response was curt as he nodded. "Loud and clear." *What the fuck did he mean by he knows* me?

Turning toward the door, Alex came to an abrupt halt and turned to face Tag again. Lifting his chin toward Goldie's crate, he muttered as an afterthought, "By the way, Goldie's a beautiful animal. I heard about what you did, how you saved her and my boy, too. I'm forever grateful."

⊗

Emery

Days turned into weeks as the month of May slipped away. Emery's sculpture class continued to be the highlight of her day; she had made tremendous progress and no longer looked at the medium as her nemesis. Luca was a brilliant instructor and played a significant role in boosting her confidence. Although his persistent desire for Emery was apparent — asking her out a few more times — she maintained her professional distance.

Tag and Emery's lives became increasingly intertwined: gym workouts, dinners with Robbi and Tyler, exploring the landmarks of San Francisco, and intimate weekends at each other's homes. If Emery sensed Tag was feeling 'closed-in,' she would give him space, spending extra time in the art studio or going out with SFAI friends. During these times, he would often text 'miss u' or 'u OK?' and no longer disappeared for days without checking in.

Emery noticed that Tag's innate reticence about his past seemed to disappear around her. She strived to be a patient, empathetic listener, never judging him or speaking in a negative manner. He related some childhood and teenage experiences, but refrained from over-sharing too many painful memories of Randi.

Emery was constantly tormented by guilt, aware of the dangerous game she was playing, but manufactured excuses why the time was never right to tell Tag her identity. She considered breaking the news before the weekend, but was unsure. Not wanting Randy to bear the possible repercussions of her admission, she determined after the long Memorial Day weekend, Randy's final visit to San Francisco, might be better. *If he loves me, he will have to forgive me.*

⊗

Randy was due to arrive in two days for the holiday weekend. Emery needed to get both sculptures finished by Thursday's class at the latest. They were basically done, although a few final touches were required: sanding, buffing, polishing, and attaching the title for each piece. After weeks of deliberation, Emery had decided upon *The Catch* for Randy's piece, but was still uncertain about Tag's double-faced bust. Something far more life changing had been weighing heavily on her mind as she recalled her spontaneous lunch date with Robbi the day before. They had met for sushi, a favorite of both women, but Emery didn't have much of an appetite.

"I think I'll just have miso soup. Does the fish smell bad to you today? It's kinda making me nauseous." Emery laughed but Robbi's expression was of mild horror. She reached for Emery's hand as her eyes widened.

"Could you be … is it possible you're pregnant, Emery?"

Raising her palms while vigorously shaking her head, Emery snorted. "No way. I've *been* pregnant and I think I would know if …" Her jaw abruptly snapped shut as her hands flew to her breasts. After a few tentative squeezes followed by a grimace, Emery buried her face in her hands. Robbi pulled her chair next to Emery and folded her into a comforting embrace.

"When was your last period?"

"I think … hmmm. It's been a while. I've always been so damn irregular, I'm not sure of the exact date."

In a soft voice, Robbi suggested, "Let's go get you a pregnancy test right now, okay? Then you'll know for sure."

Two different tests — including the Clearblue Digital Pregnancy Test with Weeks Indicator — and two positive results later, they sat in Robbi's kitchen, sipping chamomile tea. Emery had already shed a multitude of tears and was now contemplating her options. Robbi was empathetic, stating, "I won't bombard you with questions, sweetie. I'm here to listen and support you in any way I can."

Emery sighed in defeat. "Alex had a vasectomy years ago. The baby is Tag's. The first time we had sex, we didn't use protection for reasons I cannot go into now. I'm on birth control, of course, but I know damn well it's never 100 percent. I'm not sure how I feel about all this yet. I need time to think."

"I'll give you my OB/GYN's number. You should get a blood test to make sure and you can talk to her about how you want to proceed. I'll call her right now if you'd like. Perhaps she can see you tomorrow." Emery noticeably brightened as Robbi went into unflappable-teacher mode, grabbing her phone. Following a terse conversation, Robbi shook her head in frustration. "Doctor Gill's going out of town for the holiday weekend. The first available appointment is Tuesday, 9:30 a.m." Emery nodded resolutely. *There is no way I can tell him my identity now. I need to deal with this first.*

After four straight hours of work in the art studio, Emery finally had put the finishing touches on both sculptures. Luca approached looking extremely pleased with the results.

"Beautiful work, Emery! I am proud of your progress and effort. Would you like to go out and celebrate this evening?" His smile was as captivating as ever, but Emery barely noticed.

"I'm sorry, Luca. I have an urgent family matter I need to take care of tonight. Have a lovely weekend." She was out the door before he had a chance to respond.

Plans had been made earlier in the week to spend Thursday evening at Tag's house. He was excited about making chicken enchiladas and had been boasting all week about his search for the many necessary ingredients. Emery knew the moment she strode through the door that she would be unable to hide her dismay. Tears filled her eyes as she collapsed in his arms.

"What's wrong, sweetheart? Is Randy okay? Are your parents …?" Tag's concerns were mounting; Emery was hyperventilating, unable to formulate coherent words.

"Tag, I'm … my fault. So sorry. Fucked up. Please don't hate me." They sat on the couch and he continued to comfort her, wiping away her tears. Eventually her breathing calmed and he lifted her chin to look at him directly.

"Em, you are the strongest person I know. We will get through this, whatever it is. Together. I promise you."

"I'm pregnant," she breathed, burying her face in his chest. "Five to six weeks, which means it happened that first night we slept together."

TAG

There were no discernable sounds in the room other than Emery's heart-wrenching sobs. Tag consoled her as best he could, stroking her hair, kissing her forehead and offering soft endearments occasionally. "Shh, baby, I'm here. I got you, always will. I'm not angry, just shocked. Please talk to me."

"I was so afraid to tell you. I thought you'd be upset, and maybe want me to …" Her face fell as both hands caressed her belly protectively.

Tag's mouth hung open, at a loss for words. "I would never ask you to end this baby's life. If that's what you want, I'll support you, but"—he shook his head back and forth in despair—"surely there are other options."

Sniffling, Emery resolutely nodded. "I can't think straight at the moment and honestly, I'm feeling a bit dizzy so I probably should —" Scooping her up in his arms, Tag strode in the direction of his bedroom. At his insistence, there was to be no further discussion until after they had dinner. He ordered Emery to relax in his bed, propped up on several fluffy pillows. She wore only his UT jersey and a pair of lace panties; he was clad in running shorts. They ate almost picnic style: a large tablecloth was spread out on the bed and over-sized trays were used to transport all the necessities from kitchen to bedroom. Plenty of bottled water was on hand with no wine or beer in sight. "You shouldn't be drinking, and as long as you can't, I won't either," he offered in explanation. "Oh, and I've already made a note to get you the best pre-natal vitamins on the market." Emery smiled wanly at his words as the color returned to her cheeks.

Tag was upbeat as he explained the art of preparing enchiladas and the exotic spices they contained. He noted that she attempted to relax and was able to eat a fair amount of food without discomfort.

"That was really good. I am stuffed," Emery sighed, swallowing a few gulps of cool water while she rubbed her stomach in contentment. Tag's eyes immediately followed her hand, staring at her belly. As their eyes locked, he saw tears start to form. Immediately, he cradled her face, using his thumbs to brush away the moisture. His lips skimmed hers softly, then moved to her cheeks, and finally rested on her forehead as he held her close.

"Sweetheart, whatever decision you make, I'll support you. I'm not going anywhere." Her chin trembled and as he pulled back, her eyes widened in disbelief and gratitude.

"Thank you, Tag. We just need to get through this weekend. Randy's been so excited about all the Memorial Day plans, and I don't want to ruin that for him. I have a doctor's appointment Tuesday morning to have a blood test and to discuss my ... um, I mean *our* options. Can you come with me?"

"Absolutely, Em. I told you. We're in this together. You, me, and"—he gazed down at her belly in awe and smiled—"this baby that we made."

Chapter 21

"This love will undo us all."
– William Shakespeare (Troilus and Cressida)

TAG

Memorial Day weekend had finally arrived. It would be Randy's final visit to San Francisco and Emery wanted to make the three-day weekend extra special. Tag had extended an invitation for Emery, Randy, and Goldie to stay at his house in the hills for the entire weekend, and had gone to great lengths and preparation to plan a few surprises for both mother and son. He was determined to put the gravity of Emery's pregnancy on hold in his own mind. The thoughts of fatherhood terrified him in ways he could not fathom. In the distant past, Randi had always been the other half of the parent scenario. After her death, the possibility of having a child never entered his mind. He had convinced himself it would never happen; he didn't want children and felt undeserving of them.

Early Saturday morning, they stopped by AES for Goldie's final checkup. Recognizing her savior, Goldie galloped up to Doctor Moriarty who squatted down, allowing the excited animal to slobber his face with grateful kisses. After giving her a thorough once-over, he was thrilled at how well the happy dog was doing.

"She is obviously thriving under your care. Her weight is ideal and that hind leg looks as good as new — no permanent damage."

Their next stop was a two-hour practice at the same high school field followed by a visit to the Tech Museum of Innovation in San Jose. The highlight of the day was Tag's preparation of dinner: barbequed hamburgers and hot-dogs, served with a variety of side dishes and an endless array of ice cream treats for dessert. While Tag was outside manning the grill, Emery and Randy were working on his *The Lion, the Witch, and the Wardrobe* book report, which was due Tuesday.

A beach outing was planned for Sunday; Emery had been working out the details for a while. Robbi and Tyler were in charge of the guest list, which included friends and several family members. Toby arrived with his father-in-law and Mia's four brothers in tow: fifteen-year-old Shane and the younger triplets. Grateful for a foursome-free day, Mia stayed home with her mother and one-month-old Daisy Regina.

Tyler took great pleasure in recounting the events surrounding the baby's birth, throwing in embellishments here and there. Mia's hospital bag had been already packed, and it came with her everywhere at Toby's insistence. After hearing Mia's father's horror stories of the night his triplets were born two months early, Toby wasn't taking any chances. He doted on his wife hand and foot; Mia constantly protested his over-attentive ministrations but secretly adored the pampering. Randy and the triplets, Aiden, Brendan, and Colin, were actually the same age and bonded instantly. Shane was autistic — extremely high functioning but not as active and boisterous as the three younger hellions. He immediately gravitated toward Goldie, the two becoming inseparable rather quickly.

Toby, Ty, and Tag — aka TNTNT — supervised the various activities. Tag had toted two surfboards, one long and the other short, on the roof of his truck. He and Tyler frolicked in the water for hours, patiently teaching the boys how to surf. There weren't many large waves, which made the lessons a lot more fun. None of the boys had ever stood on a surfboard. The only newbie with any success was, not surprisingly, Goldie. She seemed to take to the water like a fish, making Emery and Tag even more curious as to what might have happened to her prior to ending up in Golden Gate Park. Randy laid stomach-down on the long board with Goldie in front of him, his head on the puppy's rump. Goldie's head swung back and forth, her tongue lolling out with what appeared to be a huge grin on her face. Although Randy had been to a few beaches in Galveston, Texas, and learned to swim as a child in local swimming pools, it was his first time in the Pacific Ocean. He displayed a bit of trepidation for a few seconds, but when Goldie fearlessly bounded into the waves, Randy was right behind her.

Land's End Beach was dog friendly and boasted an off-leash area that was unfenced. The day was glorious, bright sunshine and warm sand, with numerous seagulls squawking overhead. Randy was thrilled that the Golden Gate Bridge could be seen in the distance. He proceeded to relate the saga of 'Goldie and Tag versus the coyote' to a rapt audience. The triplets, who had never been allowed pets other than the occasional benign, low-maintenance fish or turtle, could not get enough of Goldie. They were either running around along the nearby hiking trails or splashing in the surf with the exuberant puppy always at their heels.

Emery

Tag paid special attention to Randy all day, much to the admiration of Emery. Her heart swelled with pride and love when her gaze fell upon the two. They behaved as father and son; their opposite hair and eye color were the only things that indicated otherwise. She was determined not to obsess over her dilemma, preferring to compartmentalize her emotions, but watching Tag with her son filled her heart with equal parts of elation and fear of what the future held for her and her baby. Unconsciously, her hands came to rest on her belly, one rubbing absentmindedly. Tag was by her side in a nanosecond, his eyes probing hers as his arm wove snugly around her shoulders.

"You all right, sweetheart? Can I get you anything? Water or maybe a sandwich?" He kissed her temple. "Maybe you should sit. I'll move one of the chairs to a shady spot, okay?"

Laughing uproariously, Emery stroked his cheek. "Calm down, honey. I'm fine!"

Randy was having too much fun to dwell on the fact that it was his final weekend in San Francisco. It was perhaps the last time he would be enjoying Tag's company, who in a very short time, had become Randy's temporary stand-in father. Although Tag was planning to fly to Arizona in mid-June for Randy's tryouts, Emery knew in the recesses of her mind, that anything could happen in the next few weeks. Her heart became wedged in a powerful vise whenever she thought of what loomed ahead of her — the fate of her unborn child, and the truth.

Afterwards the entire group went to Rocco's for an extravagant family-style dinner. Toby had disappeared for a while, but eventually returned with Mia, her mom, and his new baby daughter, who immediately became the center of attention. Emery had shared with Tag the details of Toby's sister's heartbreaking accident and subsequent life-saving heart transplant donation. Emery, who was immediately drawn to tiny blue-eyed, black-haired Daisy, asked to hold her for a moment, while Tag looked on. The baby's eyes met Emery's then flitted up to Tag's, where they settled. Then Daisy smiled.

He was mesmerized, staring in disbelief, until his body unexpectedly stiffened. Leaning down, he breathed into Emery's ear, "I'll be right back." Emery's stomach plummeted. *He's freaking out.*

⊗

Emery's parents had planned a huge barbeque, complete with a fireworks display, for family and friends, which was scheduled for Monday afternoon. Randy, not wanting to miss the festivities and seeing his cousins, opted for an early Monday morning flight back to Phoenix. Tag and Emery were actually grateful for the time alone. A critical discussion was approaching, one which would change their lives forever.

As they walked through the door of Tag's house, Emery exhaled a weary breath, so he took her hand, and led her to the loveseat. Emery gulped, and bit her lip to keep it from trembling.

"I'm gonna bring you some water, and then we can talk." Depositing a quick kiss on the top of Emery's head, he left the room. By the time he returned, she was close to hyperventilating, as her mind played out different scenarios — all of which featured her as a single mother. Again. Returning with two open bottles, he placed one in her hand.

"Honey, you don't have to—" His fingers flew to cover her lips, whispering, "Me first."

Taking a long pull from the water, Tag licked his lips and stated, "After seeing you holding that precious life in your arms yesterday, the decision is crystal clear. Did you see the way Daisy smiled at me? It was like she could see into my heart, assuring me I could do this." Encouraging her to sit on his lap, Tag tenderly caressed her stomach with his palms making gentle soothing motions.

"I'm not sure how everything will work, but I want to try. Our baby deserves that."

Their eyes met and communicated in silence. Tag blew out a series of short breaths, then stared at her belly in apprehension.

"I don't know the first thing about being a father, Em. I'm probably gonna fuck it up big time." He shook his head despondently. Emery's gaze softened as she smoothed his unruly hair.

"Tag, since the first moment you met Randy, your every word and action has been that of a caring, loving father. You're a natural; you instinctively know what to do without even thinking about it. Trust me. You will be amazing."

After an hour of quiet discussion accompanied by lots of snuggling and feeding each other an array of sumptuous leftovers from Rocco's, they had been relaxing naked in the Jacuzzi for a while. Tag had just returned from walking and feeding Goldie, and had grabbed a small cooler of bottled water and iced herbal tea, which he placed within arm's reach. Before he jumped back into the bubbling, steamy water, he dimmed the backyard lights so only the faintest glow remained. At that precise moment, Emery happened to glance upward.

"Whoa! Look at all those stars, Tag." Her radiant smile sparkled as her eyes caught Tag's, but he was not looking toward the sky. Puzzled at his intense stare, she queried, "What?"

"I have my own stars right here in front of me, swimming in a sky of chocolaty-caramel yumminess." Emery smirked as she pretended to shake non-existent water out of her ear.

"Did I just hear you say yumminess, Tag?" There was no mistaking the teasing snicker in Emery's voice as her eyebrows impishly arched upward.

"Ahh ... maybe? And no, I did not just grow a vagina," came his adamant reply.

"Are you sure?" Her expression was mischievous, but heat

and desire glowed in the depths of her lidded eyes. Perhaps it would only serve as a brief escape from the tumultuous event that had recently overturned their lives; but at this moment, she wanted nothing more than to show Tag how much she was committed to the decision they had made.

"I could show you, Em. Right here. Right. Now."

Tag was already hard as a rock. Emery had been sitting sideways on his lap and it didn't take much for him to become fully aroused. "I want to be inside you so bad, Em. I've missed you these past few days. You're sure it's okay?" Tag sought Emery's eyes for reassurance. Her smile was wide as she nodded. *I almost forgot how horny I get when I'm pregnant!*

Emery turned to face Tag, straddling him, capturing his mouth as she sucked on his bottom lip. Her nails scraped lightly across his chest as her tongue traveled the length of his neck, then teased his nipples with delicate flicks. He squeezed her rounded ass-cheeks which fit perfectly in the curve of his palms. No condoms were mentioned, the untimely pregnancy having at least one immediate benefit.

"I need you, baby." Tag's voice was husky, his breath warm as he licked the shell of her ear. Emery opened her thighs wider, wrapping her legs around his waist. They were surrounded by the pulsating jets of the hot tub, which were sending stimulating bursts of forceful bubbles in their direction. She could sense his need as his thick shaft was poised at attention, ready to penetrate her. Emery's thumb and forefinger encircled the head as she rubbed it against her clit, loving his metal piercing and the sensations it sent straight to her core.

"Put your hands on my shoulders, babe. I got you." Grasping her hips tightly, Tag lifted her up, guiding her into the perfect position, and then gently lowered her onto his aching cock. His head fell back and he moaned, drawing his lower lip into his mouth.

Emery's hands cupped his cheeks as she covered his face with kisses, ending with her lips by his ear.

"Open your eyes. Look at me, honey."

He complied, a dreamy, lust-filled glow in his eyes, which had deepened to forest green. His breathing became ragged as the movement of her hips quickened to match his thrusts. Emery loved this dominant position and was ready to take control, as she caressed every inch of his cock. Threading her hands roughly through his hair, her eyes sought his and the commanding growl in her voice caused them to widen.

"I'm gonna ride you now, and I want you to fuck me hard. And your beautiful eyes need to be on mine the entire time. Watch me make love to you."

God, how I love being on top watching his responsiveness to me. Just when he thinks I'm pulling away, when only the tip of him is still inside me, I clench hard and slam back down. After a few times, I can sense he's close. He's buried so deep inside me, I swear to God he's hitting places I never realized existed. My thanks to Prince Albert.

"Emery, you feel incredible. So. Fucking. Tight. God, I'm so close. Come with me, baby. Let yourself go for me." Tag grunted between gasps for air. His eyes still locked on hers, which he could barely discern through her thick lashes. Two pairs of eyes shone with unspoken words, which hung heavily in the space between them. Emery rubbed her thumb over Tag's bottom lip before sliding her hand in between their lower bodies. Quickly finding her clit, she massaged it firmly using a quick circular motion. Tag's eyes followed her hand and seemed mesmerized as he gazed intently through the swirling water at their intimate joining. A few more vigorous thrusts, and waves of pleasure overwhelmed them as they watched each other come apart while the outside world melted into nothingness. Collapsing on top of him, Emery's mouth needed more as their tongues desperately tangled, licking and sucking frantically until their heartbeats and breathing stilled. Tag's hands stroked her cheeks as his forehead came to rest on hers.

"That was mind-blowing. After so many years of being numb, I'm alive again. Resurrected. Human. When I'm with you, my heart's not broken anymore. You took the shattered bits in your hands and — like the gifted artist you are — you pieced it back together. Hell, you super-glued it, brown eyes." Tag's fingers laced with Emery's and he peppered her hands with soft kisses.

"And just now, when I was deep inside you? I swear I felt like I could see right into your soul. I fought it at first, feeling those emotions again frightened me, but I'm done fighting. I want to be with you, Emery. I'm all in. You. Our baby. Everything." Tag's heartfelt words sent a shivering vibration down to her toes.

"I have two more weeks of class, and then I ..." Emery clung to him desperately; she willed herself not to cry, but a soft sob escaped her throat. He stroked her hair comfortingly, while nibbling gently on her earlobe.

"Shh, sweetheart. We'll figure something out. Don't worry, there's plenty of time to talk about it. Right now, we both need a shower." Emery nervously chewed on her bottom lip. She knew differently. *No. I'm almost out of time.*

TAG

Their shower might have broken endurance records had the hot water not been depleted after an hour. Tag lost all self-control, taking her twice, but Emery was not complaining. First, with her back pressed against the cold tile, legs encircling his waist, hard and fast, she screamed her release into the crook of his neck as the warm water cascaded around them. Ten minutes later, Emery was bent over with Tag fucking her from behind, her feet spread wide, allowing room for him to stand in between. Emery's breasts were mesmerizing as they bounced with every thrust, nipples erect from the now-freezing cold water. His teeth grazed her neck, hands firmly grasping her hips as he plunged in and out.

"More, baby, please. I need more," Emery panted breathlessly. "Now." This was her pre-arranged signal for Tag to grab the sex toy she had brought with her: the sleek black, silicone, waterproof, vibrating butt plug. Tag had been on the giving end of anal sex numerous times, but not since getting his genital piercing. *Sex toys in the shower. What's next?*

While endeavoring to stay seated inside her, Tag reached up, and carefully grasped the item, which Emery had pre-lubed and placed on a washcloth. Gently inserting the tip, he gingerly moved it past a ring of resistance, but at Emery's begging, thrust it fully inside and turned the vibrator on low. Upon hearing her ecstatic moans, he found himself holding back his own orgasm as he focused on working the plug in and out. The view of her gorgeous ass cheeks with his cock sliding in and out of her soaked pussy was almost too pleasurable to bear.

And this thing is pumping inside her ass. So fucking hot!

Emery's moans were increasing in volume. "Tag, I'm so close." He increased the speed of his thrusts, while altering his angle of penetration to massage her clit. *Now we turn this bad boy on high.* Emery screamed, then exploded around his cock and Tag had never experienced anything that equaled the intense sensations. The vibrations sent electric sparks up his spine where every nerve ending detonated, one by delirious one, and he sensed a loss of consciousness at one point. Moaning in ecstasy, Emery shuddered and Tag soon followed, grunting out his own release before they collapsed into each other's arms.

⚭

Tag had cleared his morning schedule at the gym so he could accompany Emery to the doctor, but had risen a bit early to take care of Goldie, and prepare breakfast. After doing a quick Google search on 'healthy eating while pregnant,' he had gazed longingly at the coffee beans and grinder before stashing them in a bottom cabinet. He was determined to support her 100 percent when they were together, but at work, all bets were off. He heard the alarm ring shrilly as he carried the tray of oatmeal, fruit, yogurt, and hot tea into the bedroom.

"Good morning, sunrise girl. Room service has arrived unless you'd prefer breakfast on the patio." He placed the tray on the nightstand and kissed her forehead.

"Here is fine. Could you help me sit up, Tag? I feel a little light-headed." He propped a few large pillows behind her back, then turned to grab the breakfast tray.

"Wait, honey. I really need to pee first, and … oh. Oww!" she gasped. "Cramps. Shit, that hurt like hell." Clutching one side of her abdomen, she flung the covers off and was ready to swing her legs onto the floor when Tag reached to lift her into his arms. His face paled, eyes widening in terror. Emery's gaze followed his and stared at the bright red stain marring the bedsheets for a moment before she fainted.

Tag was able to revive Emery almost immediately with a cold compress. After coaxing her into a T-shirt and yoga pants, he swiftly carried her to his truck while on the phone with the OB/GYN who — after asking a few very pointed questions — advised he bring her directly to the office, which luckily was only two miles away. The doctor also explained that her office was part of a larger clinic and should any emergency surgery be necessary, Emery would get immediate attention. *Surgery? Fuck.*

Arriving in record time, red lights and stop signs

notwithstanding, a waiting gurney whisked Emery inside. By this time, she was fully conscious and Tag held her hand the entire distance, soothing her. "Doctor Gill said it's just a precaution, sweetheart. You need to remain still, no unnecessary exertion. I got you, okay? Don't worry." He squeezed her hand in reassurance.

Emery managed a wan smile, bringing his hand to her lips. "Please don't leave me," she pleaded.

"Never, sweetheart."

Doctor Gill began the examination immediately. Tag kept his eyes locked on Emery's face the entire time, whispering to her, stroking her hair, and trying his best to keep her calm and relaxed.

When the exam was over, Tag assisted Emery into a chair in front of the doctor's desk. He sat in an adjacent chair, and took her hands in his. Doctor Gill took a deep breath, her voice sympathetic.

"This was an ectopic pregnancy, which occurs when the fertilized egg attaches someplace other than the uterus, most often in the fallopian tube — which is what happened here. There is no way to save an ectopic pregnancy. If the egg had continued to grow, your fallopian tube could have ruptured with deadly consequences. The vaginal ultrasound showed your tube appears to be intact which is fortunate, and the egg was most likely dispelled. I will need to monitor you for the next few days, check your hormone levels regularly, and perhaps prescribe medication to ensure the pregnancy has been terminated. I am very sorry. I'll leave you two alone. Take as much time as you need."

The ride home was awkward; they were in shock, neither one willing to be the first to bare their emotions. Tag kept his eyes on the road while sneaking concerned glances her way, but

Emery could only lean her head against the window, staring at the passing scenery as it sped by.

Tag did not want Emery to see the bloody bedsheets, so he insisted she lie down on the couch. His jaw clenched as he ran his hands through his hair. *She lost the baby. Our baby. What do I say to make it better?*

"Will you be okay? I'm gonna check on Goldie, then fix you another breakfast." He paced a bit before turning toward the kitchen. "Tag, please talk …" she begged, but the sounds of food preparation drowned out her pleas.

The second breakfast was identical to the first with the addition of an English muffin, but there were two portions of everything and Tag's large mug now held steaming black coffee.

"Honey …" Emery began hesitantly, not wanting him to withdraw any more than he had already. "Considering the circumstances, this is probably for the best. A co-worker of mine almost died from an ectopic pregnancy that ruptured, destroying one of her tubes. She was eventually able to have a child, but it was difficult and took a few years." Tag nodded, busying himself with buttering her English muffin and placing it in her hand.

"You need to get your strength back. Please eat something." His words were soft but without emotion. Cold.

"I won't eat a bite until you talk to me. I mean it, Tag. Do *not* disappear on me. I need you." Her face crumpled and the tears she had been holding at bay cascaded down her cheeks. Tag's arms enfolded her, lips pressed to her forehead.

"The thought of losing you …" His head shook back and forth, as he tightened his hold on her. "I thought it was my fault at first; maybe the rough sex had hurt you somehow. I understand this baby was never meant to be, but I started to accept it, maybe even looked forward to …" Unable to complete his thought, Tag fought desperately to squelch the ache in his chest.

"Tag, honey, listen to me. There was no hope for our baby, but if this pregnancy had continued, I could have died. You *saved* me." Emery's hand cupped his cheek, and although he responded to the warmth of her touch, the words did not register.

I don't deserve to be a father.

Chapter 22

*"I'm not upset that you lied to me,
I'm upset that from now on I can't believe you."*
— *Friedrich Nietzsche*

EMERY

Emery went to the clinic every morning for blood tests to monitor her hormone levels. Doctor Gill determined she was no longer pregnant and the medication was unnecessary. While she was relieved, her relationship with Tag had become strained; even though he said all the right things, a chilly distance was between them. *He blames himself, but I'm not sure why.*

Discussions with Robbi — who had experienced a short pregnancy before opting for an abortion when she was in her twenties — did little to mitigate her apprehension. She longed to share her identity with Robbi but innately knew that would jeopardize everything. *If Tag doesn't want to continue our relationship, then he never has to know who I am. But I can't keep Randi's journal from him. He deserves the truth.*

By the time the weekend arrived, Tag seemed like his old self: back to morning clients at the gym and working a few nights at North Street. Emery was puzzled at his change of heart until Doctor Gill called to share some information.

Unbeknownst to Emery, Tag had made an appointment with the physician to discuss the pregnancy in more detail. Charts were referred to as well as several medical websites, which explained ectopic pregnancies in great detail, including some extreme worst-case scenarios that ended in the death of the mother. The doctor assured her that he left the clinic with a deeper understanding of what had transpired and how fortunate they were, considering the alternatives.

Emery's final week of school was approaching. All her assignments were complete, except for a written final assessment, then studio clean up. She would return to Arizona the following weekend. Tag wanted to make the trip with her, but needed to clear it with the gym and North Star first.

Early Friday morning, Emery remembered she had left several art tools at Tag's house when the mosaic project was being completed. Hopes of seeing him before he left for the gym were for naught; the driveway was empty. Sliding the spare key out from under a planter, she stealthily let herself in. Even though she knew he was not there, it was slightly unnerving to be in someone's home without their knowledge. After entering the small storage closet, her box of tools was easily located a few feet from a powder-blue shopping bag that was tucked in a corner. Upon reading the store name, a sudden wooziness overtook her and she collapsed to the floor, breathing heavily. **Babies "R" Us**.

Pulling out the various bundles of tissue-paper enclosed items, Emery's tears became uncontrollable as each precious gift was revealed. A baby-sized nerf football, a fluffy pink bunny, colorful sets of plastic links, numerous bath squeeze toys, a few rattle balls, and a stack of children's picture books. At the bottom of the bag sat an unwrapped cardboard box, which Emery lifted out with trembling hands. Inside were two tiny onesies. The blue one boasted "Daddy's Little Quarterback," and the pink one stated "Daddy's Little Princess". Emery sat surrounded by the items for a long time, numb and unable to move. While Tag had been shocked at her unexpected pregnancy and pledged his support, she never would have predicted this level of commitment and acceptance. *I know he loves me. This proves it. I'm still scared to tell him the truth, but now I'm sure it will be okay.*

A folded note slipped out from between two books. Barely recognizing her own voice, Emery read it aloud, her throat raw and clogged with tears.

"*I will strive to be the best father I can be. My plan is simple: I will follow your lead, the most amazing, caring, loving mother on this planet.*"

Sunday afternoon found them lounging in the living room, limbs entwined as usual, drinking wine, and watching a movie. The sex has been life changing, but a persistent gnawing lodged in the pit of Emery's stomach that no amount of alcohol would erase. She had dropped Goldie off at Mrs. Drozdov's as a precaution, in case her confession did not go as she hoped.

The heat of his body is so comforting and I feel cherished. Safe. I never need a blanket when he lies next to me. I want to kiss him a million times, so I can memorize his lips ... what they feel like on my own. Just in case I never see him again, I'll be able to relive his kiss for the rest of my life. It is now or never.

Without warning, silent tears sprung from her eyes. She had already lost a baby. Now she wept for the man she loved and could possibly lose.

Hearing her soft sobs, Tag's body tensed beside her. "What's wrong, sweetheart? Are you in pain? Can I get you anything?"

Emery shook her head, but no coherent words came forth. After a few deep breaths, she whispered, "Tag, what's your greatest fear?"

He swept her bangs to the side and tenderly kissed her forehead. "My greatest fear would be failing you, Em. What if I can't be all the things you need?"

"That could never happen. I know you see yourself as broken, honey, but you are wrong. Every one of us on this planet is damaged in some small way, but you are the most amazing man I have ever known. You're strong, compassionate, and full of pure, unconditional love. When I look at you with Randy, I can't begin to tell you how it makes me feel. The time and affection you have freely given him will last his entire lifetime. He is a better person with a kinder heart and a more forgiving soul — all because of you. Honey, I have been concealing a huge secret from you and *my* greatest fear is you won't be able to forgive me." Emery's chin dropped to her chest, but Tag cupped her cheek, forcing her eyes up to meet his.

"What are you talking about, Emery? What secret?" His serious tone turned her blood to ice.

"I need to show you something. It's in my car. I'll be right back."

After throwing on her T-shirt and yoga pants, Emery headed outside, returning with a large, intricately carved wooden box, which she placed on the coffee table. As they sat on the couch, Tag stared at it absentmindedly, not recognizing it at first.

"I should have told you the truth way back when we first met, but it never seemed like the right time. We became friends, then lovers. I kept putting it off because I was terrified of your reaction, then I got pregnant and now I'm leaving soon and …" Tears brimmed in her eyes again and proceeded to cascade down her cheeks. Tag immediately took her face in his hands, kissing her cheeks in a vain attempt to stop the flow.

"Em, you're scaring me." Tag's eyes were wide, pupils dilated and glassy. Beads of sweat formed on his brow.

"Tag, what if there was a way Randi could communicate

with you. Would you do it? Would you take that chance if it meant finding out what she was thinking those last days of her life?" Huge chocolate-brown eyes were waiting for his response.

"Baby, what do you mean? A séance ... the Long Island Medium? Some crazy-ass fuckin' ghost whisperer?"

Emery shook her head, as pure, unadulterated fear invaded her stomach. She turned toward the box and carefully opened the lid. Reaching inside, she pulled out a suede-covered journal and reverently placed it into his hands.

Tag

Tag was vaguely aware of a persistent tickle in the depths of his chest, a subtle itch that simply could not be scratched. It haunted the dark recesses of his mind — ancient memories fluttered — or were they recent? Childhood? A previous life? His eyes flitted to the journal, as the smile vanished from his lips.

Emery took a deep, fortifying breath. "This was Randi's journal. Her parents found it in this box filled with her mementos and keepsakes. They gave it to me, but it all belongs to you. I'm Emma Marie, Randi's cousin."

His breathing became strained, almost painful as if every drop of moisture in the room's atmosphere had frozen solid — tearing into his lungs like microscopic needles. An inexplicable hollowness sliced his chest, an insatiable abyss threatening to suck every bit of warmth from his body. Emery's admission unleashed the devil lurking inside his soul ... raw, ugly, vile. His demons lashed out — the painful past and all the guilt that came with it overpowered him. His eyes darkened; the usual vivid green had vanished.

Tag felt his brain and belly spinning, but at different speeds and in opposite directions. Tangled cobwebs spun around his memory … wispy, fragmented, strangling him. In a blinding flash, without warning, the puzzle pieces clicked into place: Randi's memorial service, the cemetery, the young girl crying hysterically, whose eyes had searched for his through the dismal rain. One pair of anguish-filled amber eyes had connected with his that horrific day — eyes that did not look at him in an accusatory manner; no hatred nor blame like everyone else in the crowd, only empathy and compassion. Randi's young cousin, Emma Marie.

Tag had already pulled back from her, and she shivered as he stared intently at her eyes, lips, then body, as if searching the recesses of his mind for a lost memory. A flash of recognition caused his eyes to widen as they settled on her right forearm. "You remember, don't you?" she whispered, tracing the outline of her scar with trembling fingertips.

This can't be happening. Randi's cousin? I'm going to need a fuckin' drink for this.

⊗

Emery

He gently replaced the journal in the box and closed the lid, stood and walked toward the kitchen, taking his warmth with him, leaving chilly, dank air behind. Emery collapsed on the couch as all the oxygen was sucked from her lungs. Deep, gut-wrenching sobs threatened to wrack her body, but she stoically reined them in, calling after him, "Tag! *Please* let me explain." She could hear footsteps in the kitchen, then the clink of glasses. He returned with a bottle of Jack Daniels and two large shot glasses, which he filled to the brim. Sitting stiffly on the couch a few feet away from her, Tag quickly downed his first shot, then poured another.

"I'm listening, Emery." The coldness in his tone caused her optimism to disintegrate. Tag's arms crossed over his chest as he turned toward her. Beads of sweat inched down the back of her neck as she drew in a fortifying breath.

"Tag, it was never my intention to deceive you. After reading Randi's journal, especially the last few entries she made"—Emery paused to grab a tissue from her pocket—"I just knew I had to find you. Alex used the APD database to locate you. SFAI was one of three art schools I was considering for my spring semester, so when I discovered you were here, I enrolled and found an apartment close to where you worked."

"So, you stalked me, got close to me. For what purpose?" Tag gripped his glass so tightly Emery thought it would break under the pressure. She downed her own shot, hoping the liquid courage would give her strength to continue. He mechanically refilled the glass.

"Do you remember that horrific day and the hateful faces in the crowd? Everyone despised you; their expressions teeming with reproach, blame, condemnation. You must remember — every single fucking face except mine. My heart ached for you. I shared every tear with you, sensed your heartbreak because my heart was shattered too. Since I first read the journal, I have thought about nothing else. Finding you was my ultimate goal. I was desperate to give you Randi's diary and make sure you finally learned the truth. I could see what kind of life you had made for yourself here … alone, keeping your heart protected, not wanting to ever experience pain and loss again. I guess I wanted to save you, and—"

"*Save* me?" Tag screeched, eyes wildly out of focus. "You can't save me. Nobody can," he scoffed bitterly.

"It was a fourteen-year-old girl's fantasy, Tag. You would eventually realize the truth, forgive yourself, and then you'd —"

"And then I'd what? *What*, Emery? Fall in love with you? Was that your plan from the start?" His voice had precipitously dropped in volume, chillingly controlled, yet full of contempt, as his face contorted and flushed with rage.

"That was never my intention, Tag. I needed to see for myself the person I believed you to be — *not* the image people had of you after the accident. My only desire was for you to forgive yourself and live again. Have a full, happy life in the real world."

Tag continued his incensed rant, unable to suppress his emotions. "I lost the only person who ever saw me for *me.* Randi's fire was extinguished from my life only to become a distant memory ... so fleeting, like running my fingers through a rushing stream. I can see her, feel her presence, but I can't hold her in my arms. Guilt consumes me and I've cut myself off from everyone, only to be swallowed up by complete and utter darkness. Don't you dare preach to me about living in the real world. You don't know all the shit I've been through."

Shaking her head vehemently, Emery was inconsolable. "I only know what you have shared with me, but I've learned so much about you these past few months. I understand why you hide your heart behind the carefully self-constructed emotional wall you've built, but I can see through all that. Do you think you're alone in all this, Tag? That you are the only one who has suffered? What about her parents? Aunt Morgan was hospitalized after bouts of depression and an attempted suicide. Uncle Victor coped in a different way. He opted to drown his sorrows between the thighs of his secretary, almost ending their marriage. Cousin Marshall got out of the house as soon as he could. He was accepted into law school at Newcastle University in London and he still lives there. And then there was me, the forgotten younger cousin." Emery took a deep breath and wiped her eyes, then continued in a calmer, steadier voice.

"Randi has inhabited my subconscious for twelve long years. At first, the heartache was unbearable, every minute of every day. I filled up countless journals of my own, with my never-ending emotions, writing down every word. My grief was ever-present, an oppressive shadow on a sunny, summer day. As the years passed, the torment and agony waned, but never completely disappeared. I'd be in class or riding my bike — you know, happily living my la-dee-dah, carefree life — when I'd feel a twinge of discomfort, a pang of uncertainty in the pit of my stomach. I'd say to myself, 'What the fuck? What is this feeling? My life is perfect at the moment.' Then the floodgates would open and *bam*! The realization that Randi was no longer on this Earth would return to taunt me all over again. I understand better than anyone the excruciating anguish you've endured, but you have *never* been alone in your pain. Not. Once. Every person who ever loved Randi has been there with you, every single day. You were not the only one who loved her, Tag. I named my baby boy in her honor — a tribute to her memory. Every time I speak his name, I am reminded of her. He is her legacy." Grabbing another wad of tissues, Emery dabbed at her eyes. Tag made a small movement toward her, but her arm jutted in his direction, palm out, halting him.

"I admit I had a teenage crush on you, but I never, *ever* imagined I would fall for you; actually fall deeply, head-over-heels in love. I'm sure that's way too much information for you to handle at the moment, but it's the truth. I am so sorry, Tag. I always meant to tell you everything; but as we got to know each other more intimately, I was terrified I would lose you. You became Tag Coleman to me. Your real name didn't matter anymore. *You* are the man I love. The person you are now, the man you have become. Complete with your pain, guilt, and fear — all the god-awful shit that has made you this incredible person — the one right here in front of me. The man I will never let go of. *Never.* I don't give a shit if you hate me at this moment. I will not lose you, Tag. Not. Happening. I'll fight for you if I have to." Emery looked deep into his eyes, searching for the connection that had been there, but the man she loved was shattered, lost, gone. *I won't give up.*

"I don't expect you to say the words, but I know — down deep in my soul — how you feel about me. I sense it in your kiss, in your kindhearted eyes when you gaze at me, and I feel it every time we make love. Yeah, you heard me correctly. We do not *fuck*, Tag. We. Make. Love. Don't you think I realize how scared shitless you are of the future? We all are, honey! Every soul on planet Earth is terrified of what lies ahead. We wouldn't be human otherwise. No one knows that better than the two of us. Every wondrous person or precious thing in our lives could be randomly ripped away at a moment's notice, in the blink of an eye. Will any of those fears stop me from loving you? No. Living, breathing, and loving you are all the same to me. One does not exist without the other two. I know you use your guilt as a barricade to protect yourself from the outside world. I get that. But you're forcing me out, as well as all the other people who love you. If I could un-break your heart, bring Randi back, don't you think I would do it in a heartbeat? I know you're still in love with her, but can I be honest with you? I don't mind being your second choice. All you've been doing these past twelve years is surviving. Please, let me teach you how to live again, how to *love* again." *I know you love me, Tag. But if I'm wrong, I promise — I will love you enough for both of us.*

Tag slowly brought his tightly balled fists up to chest level. If Emery hadn't recognized the stance as an unconscious boxing reflex, she might have been afraid. Her eyes followed the movement and rested on his knuckle tattoos, displaying **'ETERNITY'.** Taking a small, wary step toward him, she cradled his fists in her hands, and tenderly kissed the letters.

"You said your eternity was lost, but you were wrong." She gently pressed a palm on his chest. "It's been right here, all these years. In your heart. Please, honey, promise me you'll read her journal."

Tag

A growing panic caused Tag's throat to constrict; breathing was becoming almost impossible. The only audible sound was the rush of blood, pumping through his pounding head. His soul seemed to splinter like shards of a mirror being flung against a brick wall. The air surrounding him was thick; every breath became a struggle. He needed to be alone … to think. Yanking his hands away, he took a step backwards. His rough, guttural growl splintered the silence between them and his eyes glowed with ferocity.

"Don't you get it, Emery? Can't you see the ugly truth? I am *poison*," he seethed. "Terrible things happen to people who love me. Randi, our baby …" His voice cracked, eyes lowering to the floor. "I didn't deserve Randi or you, and I sure as hell wasn't worthy of being your baby's father. Please, Emery. You need to go. I'm sorry, but I can't look at you right now. It hurts too much."

One lone tear threatened to escape from the corner of Tag's eye, but he forcibly blinked it away. The future he dared to envision, after catching an all-too-brief glimpse, was slipping away, dissolving before it ever fully took shape. Emery reached a tentative hand out to cup his cheek softly. Tag's eyes fluttered closed as his lips pressed into a grim line. He was on the razor's edge of losing control as he slowly brought his hand up to join hers. For a brief moment, he leaned into her soothing touch, brushing her warm palm with his lips — wanting to commit to memory the taste of her soft skin as if for the last time — before grabbing her wrist and shoving her hand away.

"I need you to leave. Now." His measured words lacked emotion as he took a tentative step back. The surrounding space was dead quiet, devoid of every sound including their breathing. Emery's clear, forceful words finally shattered the awkward silence.

"I have one question for you, Tag. If you had the ability to go back in time, knowing what you know now, but powerless to change the outcome — and you saw Randi for the very first time — would you turn your back on her and walk away in order to save yourself from this heartache?"

The surrounding air was inexplicably thick and heavy, as every breath became a struggle. Tag's eyes clouded over, unseeing, unable to focus, as he felt himself disconnect from reality. He found himself viewing a dramatic performance in a silent, darkened theater; the scene unfolding was painful to watch, but he was powerless to get up and leave. Staring at the floor, he simply turned his back on her and walked toward the couch without uttering a word, his throat clogged with tears.

Emery

The temperature in the room plummeted as an ice-cold fear crept up her spine. Whatever breath Emery tried to inhale was immediately sucked from her lungs, a brutal punch delivered straight to the gut. As if in a trance, she stood, gathered her belongings, and then wordlessly walked toward the door. She sensed his gaze boring a hole in the center of her back, and although Emery longed to glance over her shoulder one last time, she resisted as her fragile heart broke even more. *Breathe in. Breathe out. Inhale. Exhale. He'll forgive me eventually. He has to. Please, Randi, guide him. Help him understand.*

Tag's gut-wrenching sobs could be heard through the half-opened window as she stumbled down the driveway. She was not able to drive away immediately … her eyes could not focus through the tears and her breathing had become sporadic. Bile rose in the back of her throat as she dry-heaved into the small garbage bag she kept in her car. Grabbing a few tissues, Emery made a futile attempt to wipe her eyes and mouth. *He's broken … again, and it's my fault.*

TAG

Emery's straightforward words pierced Tag's soul, causing him to cry out in sorrow. That moment didn't require remembering. It was seared into his retinas for the rest of time; nothing could erase the memory of Randi's beauty — the light in her eyes, the sheer radiance of her smile. *Walk away from Randi? Never. Two years of sheer bliss, even though it came with a lifetime of pain and loneliness? No contest. I would choose Randi. Every. Single. Time.*

When he failed to hear the rev of Emery's car engine, Tag suspected she was still parked in his driveway. Straining to hear the faintest of sounds, his ears were met only by the familiar chorus of crickets from his backyard. He fought the temptation to race after her; his heart longed for her, but his mind was reeling, his body immobile. Breathing was becoming more labored as he drained his drink, then grabbed Emery's glass and downed its contents as well. Gripping both glasses, he furiously hurled them across the room where they smashed into the fireplace. Shards of crystal flew in all directions. A monumental weight had descended on his chest, which threatened to crush his ribcage and the heart that had barricaded itself within. An attempt to inhale deeply failed, as if the same oxygen his lungs craved was trying to smother him. A drowning sensation overwhelmed him and he sank to the floor. *What the fuck is happening to my life? Jesus. Fucking. Christ. Randi's cousin. Emma Marie.*

Tag dozed off on the couch for an hour or two. A laughing, brown-eyed beauty had filled his dreams, cavorting in an endless field of flowers, swinging a fair-haired toddler in her arms. He was screaming, but the wind blew his cries in the opposite direction. "Emery. *Emery!*" His throat was raw; a foreign-sounding voice assailed his ears, hoarse as if he had been howling for hours. *How many times have I said her name in the past few months? Hundreds? Thousands. Her beautiful name has become a prayer to me, my mantra. I love her name and the way it feels on my lips. Emery … musical, it calms me. Holy shit, I remember now. That's why they look so much alike … their mothers are twins. Fuck! How the hell did I not see it?*

He continued to drink for the rest of the evening. Not bothering with another glass or even to read the labels, Tag simply grabbed whatever bottle was easily accessible and drank directly from it.

His living room was pitch dark, the only light was emanating from the muted TV. At one point, he had opened the box and lightly fingered the journal. He spied some of the mementoes and shook his head. *I can't do it, I'm not ready. I may never be.*

Confusion and grief continued to churn inside him, like ocean tides ebbing and flowing, until he was drowning in his own emotions. The fact he was intoxicated did not help the situation. Feeling nauseous, Tag got up several times to vomit, barely making it to the bathroom as he stumbled through the house. Unexpected sharp pains caused him to glance at his bare feet, where streaks of blood covered the tiled floor. He had inadvertently walked through the slivers of glass in front of the fireplace.

Fuck. Me. More pain. But, hey, I'm used to it. Bring it on.

Finally making it to his bedroom, sleep eventually crashed over him in sporadic waves, providing the cruel evidence of just how empty his life would be without her. He was alone in his giant king size bed — devoid of the warmth that was Emery. His dreams were replete with sounds and images from his past and present alike, overlapping, entwining, incoherent.

Randi … Emma Marie.
I'll fight for you. We don't fuck. We make love.
I know how you feel about me.
I love you, Tag. I won't lose you.

When Tag managed to open his eyes, a pounding headache preoccupied him for a moment as he reached out for Emery, but only empty space could be found. There was a short span of a few seconds before Tag remembered what had transpired the night before. His bed was cold and the soft object his arms had been clutching so urgently was nothing more than his over-sized pillow. He missed her desperately; every part of his body ached with emptiness. In the past, he had craved loneliness, thrived on it; now the feeling was eating him alive from the inside out.

Tag attempted to go about his day as usual, but it was nearly impossible; Emery's impassioned words were on a constant loop in his subconscious. One heated declaration stood out: *"I don't give a shit if you hate me at this moment."*

Tag shook his head despondently at the memory — the sheer absurdity of her statement. He should have taken her in his arms and demonstrated exactly what he was feeling at that precise moment. *Hate you, Emery? It's not possible to hate someone who has taken up permanent residence in my soul. My heart is in a million shattered pieces, and you, Emery, reside in each and every one.*

Chapter 23

*"When you depart from me sorrow abides,
and happiness takes his leave."*
– William Shakespeare (Much Ado About Nothing)

EMERY

Her body had entered some kind of unconscious survival mode. Class, eat, sleep, repeat, for three excruciating days. Numbness had invaded every cell of her being. She found herself just gazing off into the distance, searching for his face. Emery saw him everywhere, but nowhere. There were no calls, no texts, complete silence. *I have lost him forever.*

An intimate get-together had been planned by Luca for Wednesday evening since Thursday was the final day of class. He had been flirtatious with her throughout the four months of class, but Emery did not take his attentions seriously. She had made it clear to him; while she was his student, nothing would happen.

There had been no contact with Tag since that terrible night. Her stomach had been in knots — nauseous and queasy — zero appetite. Some people overate when they were sad or upset; Emery was the opposite. A female coworker of hers referred to it as the broken heart diet, scoffing, 'I don't recommend it, but it's remarkably effective.'

She had planned to attend the class dinner party, but found herself heading in a different direction. Pulling into the North Star Bar's parking lot, Emery felt like a crazed stalker; a nervous energy pulsed through her body and her heart rate sped up as an eerie excitement overwhelmed her senses. No clever, calculated plan had formulated in her mind; her decision to see Tag was a subconscious one, driven by the fact she missed him terribly. Not wanting to be seen and still unsure of what she was going to do, Emery simply sat in her car and waited in the dark.

Fuck! What the hell am I doing here? This is so unlike me. But knowing he is so close is strangely comforting. If I could just see his face, make sure he's okay. Does he miss me?

Suddenly, the back door swung open and Tag stumbled out, an equally drunk redhead hot on his heels. He strode a few paces, and then leaned with his back against his truck as the redhead stood in front of him. She pressed her breasts into him, then dropped to her knees.

Needles of sharp pain shot through Emery's chest as she gasped for air that couldn't come fast enough. Her stomach churned and bile rose up the back of her throat as the moonlight illuminated his face for a few seconds. His head was thrown back, lips pressed together in a tight grimace, while glistening moisture streaked his face. *Is he sweating? Or … crying?* Eventually he looked downward, said a few angry words, and after furtively looking around the parking lot, returned to the bar. Ginger slowly stood and came into view; she wiped her mouth with the back of her hand, got into a beat-up old Volkswagen, and tore out of the parking lot.

What the hell just happened? The fastest blow job on record, or … whatever. Fuck.

After a few minutes of quiet crying, Emery decided to go to the dinner party after all. The get-together was being held at an upscale Spanish restaurant Luca had suggested. It was in the same general vicinity as North Star; she arrived fifteen minutes later. After touching up her makeup, Emery decided to forego the ponytail she had worn every day of class. Yanking the elastic out, she checked her reflection in the rearview mirror. Smoothing her hair with her fingers, she practiced a seductive smile, licking her lips. *Luca. Class is a done deal.*

Last to arrive, Emery's classmates greeted her with hugs and smiles all around. She had easily become the most popular student; already an established teacher with a genuine desire to assist anyone in need had endeared her to every student. She had also become the teacher's 'pet' of sorts, an off-the-record assistant and Luca had come to rely on her willingness to lend a hand when necessary. Projects had been completed and all grades were recorded in the school's computer system. Emery was elated — she had received an A.

Luca had saved her the seat next to him. Greeting her with a chaste kiss on each cheek, Luca told her how beautiful she looked, how he loved her hair, and proceeded to refill her wineglass non-stop throughout the evening. His arm was constantly brushing hers and she welcomed the overt attention, fluttering her eyelashes shamelessly and giggling at everything he said, no matter how inane. Luca Navarro could be egotistical, pompous, and thoroughly irritating at times. He was also an amazingly talented, internationally known artist and hot as hell. Emery was on a mission; she needed to create a memory large enough to blot out the sickening image now forever engraved in her psyche. *Tag's beautiful cock in that slut's mouth.*

People started to leave, promising to save their long drawn-out farewells for the next morning, when everyone would be showing up one last time to gather their projects, supplies, and leftover clay, wood, bronze, and other materials, which had not been depleted.

"So, Emery, class is officially over, and grades are finalized. Ready to come to my place?" His hand inched up her short skirt, dangerously close.

"*Ay Dios mío, perfecta*!" he growled as his forefinger pushed her panties aside, eyes flashing with lust.

"How big is your backseat, Luca?" Her tongue snaked out gliding over her full bottom lip. *Oh, God! What the hell am I saying? I am so drunk, feel weird. My brain … fuzzy.*

"Big enough, baby, and you can call me Luc." Yanking her up roughly, he led her out the door toward his shiny black Range Rover, which was unobtrusively parked in a shadowy corner spot. He hastily opened the door and climbed in, assisting a stumbling Emery as she followed.

"Whoa, Luc. You weren't kidding. It's sooo roomy back here!" Emery squealed, feeling the effects of the potent wine hitting her unexpectedly.

"It's the full-size luxury SUV, designed for transporting large sculptures *and* fucking beautiful women." He was already lying lengthwise on the seat, hands frantically unbuckling his black leather belt. Emery knelt in between his legs and reached for his zipper. He hissed through his teeth as she pulled it down, releasing his cock. Tugging his jeans lower, she fisted his enormous erection, stroking its length.

"So, Emery, I'm curious. What changed your mind?" Luc's breathing was ragged, lips compressed, eyes glued to her hand.

"I'm trying to forget someone," she murmured, the truth spilling from her lips, squeezing his shaft as if it were Tag's neck. *I know he expects me to blow him, but that is not going to happen.*

"Glad to help, baby." Reaching under her camisole, he grabbed and caressed her breasts, while Emery clumsily pulled the material up, giving him free access. Surprised at her unusually wanton behavior, she mentally disengaged from reality; the windows were darkly tinted and she would never see

Luc again after tomorrow. The painful image of Tag's head thrown back in apparent ecstasy while being royally sucked off made tears spring to her eyes.

Luc grabbed a fistful of her long hair and pulled her down to him, taking a nipple into his mouth — sucking, licking, biting, while his thumb and forefinger fondled her other taut peak until it pebbled. Luc was groaning loudly; Emery's hand continued to stroke his dick, which was twitching in anticipation, moisture beading on the tip. His mouth began to travel upward, kissing and licking her neck. He was inches from her mouth, but she pulled away.

"No kissing," Emery commanded in a shaky whisper.

Luca shrugged. "Whatever, baby."

He shoved Emery's skirt up exposing her thighs as she straddled him. Gazing down at Luc through her long lashes, lower lip pulled in between her teeth, Emery subconsciously channeled her inner porn star. Salacious seduction did not come naturally to her, but the turmoil caused by Tag's actions had pushed her over the edge. Luc's fingers were inching toward her entrance, as Emery's fist tightened around his dick. He groaned lustily at the pressure.

"I'll bet you're still fucking tight, baby, even though you've had a kid." Luca hissed as his thumb circled her clit.

Emery gasped, every muscle of her body stiffening as his tactless words sunk in. *What the fuck?* A shameful wave of self-reproach rushed over her and an apparition of beautiful emerald eyes was all she could see. *What am I doing? This is wrong on so many levels.* Both hands pushed against Luca's chest as she disengaged herself from his grasp.

"I can't do this, Luca. Sorry, I'm outta here," she spat as she pulled her camisole down, grabbed her belongings, and hastily exited the vehicle. *Asshole.*

Tears blurred Emery's vision as she exited the parking lot.

The startling screech of skidding tires pierced her clouded mind and resulted in her slamming both feet on the brakes. Sensing the rapid approach of blinding headlights, her arms instinctively flew up to cover her head. Emery braced herself for the imminent impact.

TAG

On autopilot, Tag dragged himself through the evening, smiling and acting like the perfect, cordial bartender when in reality, he had a vacuous, gaping hole where his heart should've been. As he followed Ginger out to the parking lot, he already knew it was a colossal mistake. *What the fuck is wrong with me? Why would I let that bitch suck me off? I am pathetic.* It felt good for a second, when she wrapped her palm around him, but then he buried his fingers in her hair and it hit him. Rough, stiff hair. Not silky smooth. *Not my Emery.*

Tag was instantly jolted out of his semi-drunken stupor as he pushed Ginger's head away, snarling, "Get the fuck off me!" She lost her balance and fell backwards on her ass. His dick had already deflated as he quickly pulled his jeans back up. After making sure Ginger was unhurt, except for her pride, Tag scanned the parking lot — *holy fucking hell* — and purposefully strode back into the bar, head tucked into his chest.

That was Emery. FUCK. What have I done?

Tag returned to his station behind the bar and met a pair of cold, dark blue, penetrating eyes giving him the dreaded death-glare. *Tyler fucking D'Angelo.* His worst nightmare, his conscience, his occasional therapist, and his best friend.

"Well, you weren't out there long, stud. Can't get it up for that skank anymore? I thought you and Emery had something solid going on, something good. What the fuck happened, Tag?"

Tag leaned over the bar menacingly; he was nose-to-nose with Tyler.

"Emery was sittin' out in the parking lot just now, and I think she saw that disgusting shit go down. And you wanna know what happened with us? She lied to me from day one. Emery is the fucking cousin of my dead girlfriend. I met her a few times when she was a kid. She came to San Francisco specifically to find me, to give me Randi's journal and some other stuff. Remember how I thought Emery resembled Randi? Well, their mothers are twins. She played me, Ty. And stupid me, I fell for it." Tag's face began to crumple as his eyes lost focus. He turned his back to Tyler and faced the cash register, pressing buttons in a transparent ruse to compose himself. After a full two minutes, he turned around wearing a perfect mask of serenity and self-control, and he politely asked, "What can I get you, T-man?"

Tyler sat until the last customer had departed and the doors were locked. The two men talked for almost an hour. At first Tag did most of the talking, relating what had transpired in as much detail as possible. Tyler was a good listener, and had several questions, but Tag eventually answered most of them as he spoke.

"She adamantly denied purposely deceiving me and swore she didn't play me for a fool. She stated every time she was about to confess the truth, she got scared because she felt herself falling in love with me. Believe me, I get that. Something huge happened between us that's too painful to go into, but I know that delayed her from telling me the whole truth sooner. I don't know what the fuck to think, Ty. Obviously, I have major trust issues. All I *do* know is Emery has tilted my whole fucking world off its axis. Forever." Tag pinched the bridge of his nose — a pounding headache was beginning to form at the back of his skull. Tyler took a deep breath, then drained his beer.

"Tag, every once in a while, you gotta take a leap of faith even if it scares the fucking shit out of you. It seems to me

Emery took a huge leap when she risked everything to bring you Randi's journal. So, tell me, what did it say?" Tag shrugged, shaking his head forlornly. *The journal. Randi's thoughts. Her final words to me.*

"I don't know, Ty. It's been under my pillow since Emery gave it to me. The closest I've gotten is to run my fingers over the cover. I can't even bring myself to open it, let alone read it. Seeing her words, her handwriting, and knowing she touched those pages, which are probably stained with her teardrops, I just can't fucking do it. Emery also gave me a carved wooden box Randi's parents found in her dorm room. It's filled with all kinds of personal stuff including every gift I ever gave her: jewelry, love letters, dried flowers, silly trinkets, beach glass, and photos of the two of us. I briefly peeked inside, but couldn't bring myself to touch anything."

His head dropped into his hands. Tyler draped an arm around his shoulders in comfort, letting Tag get all his pent-up emotions out in the open. *Tyler's one of the lucky ones; when he hit rock bottom, he had his parents to cling to. He's the closest thing to a father I've had these past few years.*

"Okay, let's analyze this situation. Did she tell you blatant, malicious falsehoods, or were they all just lies of omission?" Tyler probed gently.

"Does it matter? A lie is a fucking lie!" Tag sneered, downing a quick shot of tequila.

Tyler remained unperturbed, his voice calm.

"I disagree, buddy. How many times have the two of us watched UT Longhorn games while you never once divulged you were their star quarterback for two fucking years? Tag, you are the damn *king* of lies of omission, but would I call you a liar? No, I would not. Your intent was never to hurt anyone. You did what you felt was necessary to protect yourself. Forget the fact she withheld the truth. If you love her, just tell her how you feel. My gut tells me Emery's heart was in the right place, and I think you owe her the benefit of the doubt." Tag nodded in silent agreement, while he gnawed contemplatively on his lower lip. Tag's fury and bravado were beginning to dissipate, as Tyler continued his fatherly lecture.

"Do you recollect way back when I fucked up with Robbi? Who set me straight? Who kicked my ass and told me exactly what I had to do? The brilliant advice you gave me back then is what I would say to you now. No more looking back with regret. It's time for your life to move forward. Bury the past; put all that shit to bed. Make room in your heart for the future. You are one of the lucky ones. You've been given the precious gift of a *good* woman — for the second, and perhaps the last, time. Some of the answers you seek are obviously in Randi's journal. You gotta read it, buddy. You have no choice in the matter. Either Robbi or I could be there if you don't want to do it alone. I know she wouldn't mind. She cares about you too."

Walking out to the parking lot, they exchanged a shoulder-bump and a brief, but sincere, man-hug.

"You're a good friend, Tyler. Thanks for having my back."

"Anytime. I'm always a phone call or a text away."

As an afterthought, Tag's hand shot out and grabbed Tyler's shoulder, forcing him to turn around.

"For the record? The second I felt Ginger's hands on me, I pushed her away. The thought of it made me gag." Tag let out a burst of hollow, mirthless laughter. Tyler chuckled right along with him. "I guess this means I'm in love, huh? Or my dick's broken. Well … Fuck. Me."

Grinning, Tyler affectionately, but quite firmly, smacked Tag's cheek several times. Well aware Tyler's signature 'love taps' were coming, Tag had pulled back but not far enough and certainly not quick enough.

"Don't worry, kid. It's not fatal." Tyler smirked as he walked away, chuckling under his breath.

Tag arrived home feeling inundated with self-recrimination. He spiraled between his past and present, unsure of his purpose in life. He longed to be with the only person who could anchor him, and prevent the darkness from sweeping him away, but he had told her to leave, threw her away just like Randi. *I'm a worthless asshole ... always have been, always will be. I deserve every shitty thing that has ever happened in my life.*

Emery

Waking up slumped over the steering wheel, disoriented, nauseous, with the worst cotton mouth of her life, seemed to be the least of the problems facing a bewildered Emery as she took in her surroundings. Her car was parked on a side street a few yards from the restaurant's parking lot. *Thank God I stopped when I did.* Sights and sounds raced through her muddled brain: bright headlights, tires screeching, a crash? *No crash. No drunk driving.* After giving her clothes and limbs a perfunctory glance, a whoosh of air escaped her lungs. *No blood. I'm okay.* An unanticipated rush of grateful tears flooded her eyes. *I am either dead or the luckiest hungover woman on the planet.* The blinding sunrise did nothing to alleviate her aching head, as she reached under the passenger seat to find one of her emergency bottles of water. Vague recollections of the previous evening fast-forwarded: drinking, more drinking, Luca, backseat, Luca's cock. *My hand was on that cock. His hand was ... oh, God.* The memory brought a flush of humiliation to her cheeks. *He touched me but that was as far as it went. This behavior is not me. I'm so ashamed.* Wiping her eyes, she headed home.

After stopping by her apartment for a quick shower, a change of clothes, and two large mugs of black coffee, the remainder of Emery's last morning at SFAI was predictable and uneventful. Projects were loaded into cars, classmates said their goodbyes, and email addresses were exchanged. She could barely look at Luca after their impromptu backseat encounter. He slipped his business card into her hand as they air-kissed in farewell. She inwardly cringed at the contact, but a few of her classmates were watching them closely. Although he was an influential contact in the art world, she tossed his card in the trash as she exited the building. There existed one singular goal in her mind … leave San Francisco immediately and never look back. *If Tag doesn't want me, then there's nothing here for me.*

TAG

On Thursday afternoon, after staring at the wooden box and Randi's journal for several hours, Tag reached his decision. He needed to see her, to talk and clear the air. Tentative plans had been made the week before; he had offered to accompany Emery on her road trip to Arizona so she would not have to make the long trip alone. They were scheduled to leave early Saturday morning and arrive in Phoenix Sunday evening. Tag would stay over one or two nights, then fly back home.

Tag headed to Emery's apartment after numerous calls that went straight to voicemail. A last minute decision to take his Harley, even though the box of new brake pads was still unopened, would ensure maximum speed and easy parking. A chill of foreboding slithered down his spine as he ascended the stairs of her apartment building. Knocking unsuccessfully for a few minutes, he tried his key in the door. It no longer worked; the locks had been changed. Emery was gone.

Tag's back hit the wall with a thud and moments later, his body collapsed to the floor. Propping his elbows on his knees, his head fell into his hands. The anger that had consumed him for days had disappeared. Emery was gone, and it was entirely his fault. He missed her so terribly it made him physically ill. Every cell of his body ached and the void in his chest was excruciating, making breathing almost impossible.

I love Emery. I need to forgive her for hiding the truth, but I'll have to forgive myself first ... for being a dick, a thoughtless asshole, and a fool.

A bright ray of sunlight beamed through the hall window; it warmed his face, banishing the chill, which had settled into his bones.

Resolutely, he got to his feet and looked at the apartment one last time. Pressing his ear against the door, he quietly listened for several minutes as he took a few deep breaths, imagining her lingering scent.

Hearing a noise, Tag whirled around and found himself face to face with Emery's elderly, but quite feisty neighbor, Mrs. Drozdov, who was in the process of taking her two Chihuahuas out for their afternoon stroll. Noticing Tag so close to the door, she stepped toward him and got right in his face with an accusatory glare.

"What happened with Emery? She packed up everything and left this morning, so suddenly. She was crying when she dropped off her key, but she refused to tell me anything. Is she all right?" The dogs picked up on the woman's distraught tone, yapping shrilly. "Her dog seemed a tad distressed, too."

"I'm sure she's okay. I'm gonna call her right now. Thanks."

Tag frantically ran down the stairs taking two steps at a time, running his fingers absentmindedly through his spikey hair. *Fuck. Fuck. Fuck.*

Grabbing his phone, he hit her name in his contact list. As he expected, it went straight to voicemail. He hung up without leaving a message. *She's on the road. I need to give her some time. I'll wait 'til tomorrow.*

After sitting on his bike for a few more moments, staring miserably at the phone, he stowed it in his jacket pocket and sped away. Rounding a corner too fast, the bike got away from him as he swerved to avoid another motorcycle.

TYLER

Tyler was concerned. Two days had passed without a word from Tag. A recent call from Brew, informing him Tag had not shown up for his Saturday evening shift, had him even more worried. After several unanswered calls and texts, Tyler drove to his home. He pulled up to the darkened house and immediately spied two days' worth of newspapers and magazines by the door. He peered through the small garage windows and could see Tag's truck and Harley. After locating the correct key on his keychain, he knocked a few times before turning the lock. The door creaked open and a foul odor immediately assailed Tyler's nostrils … alcohol, probably stale beer, vomit, and spoiled food.

"What the hell …" he muttered as his fingers found the hall light switch.

The living room was a disaster. Countless empty beer and liquor bottles were scattered about; plates of half-eaten takeout littered the floor, along with a bowl of leftover dog food, much to the delight of a bevy of ants and a hungry cockroach or two.

Despite the mess, Tyler chuckled at what he spotted in the middle of the floor. A shirtless, snoring Tag — clad only in gym shorts — half-wrapped up in the sheepskin rug. His expression darkened when Tag suddenly stirred. One leg protruded from under the fluffy material, the knee and calf badly scraped and covered in dried blood.

"Wake the fuck up, Tag!" Greeted with a loud snore, Tyler not-so-gently prodded Tag's foot with the toe of his heavy boot.

A gravelly voice could be heard, slightly muffled by the thick sheepskin. "Go. Away. Now. Let me die in peace."

Tyler's shoulders shook with mirth as he strode to the fridge, grabbing two bottles of water and a roll of paper towels. Squatting down near Tag's head, he removed the cap from one bottle and began to pour a small amount in the general vicinity of Tag's half-opened mouth. Sputtering noises filled the room as Tag awoke fully, revealing bloodshot eyes and a slight bruise under his chin.

Tyler's voice was sympathetic. "You got some hydrogen peroxide or antiseptic? We need to clean up your leg a bit. Your knee's pretty banged up. Can you move it?"

Snatching the open water from Ty's grasp, Tag gulped down half of it in a few swallows. "What day is it?" he croaked, rubbing a large hand over his head.

"Saturday," came Tyler's patient response. "Nine-thirty p.m. to be exact. Brew called from the bar, said you were MIA. Glad to see you're okay, for the most part, anyway." Tyler's gaze roamed the scrapes and bruises. "Looks like you got up-close-and-personal with a rough patch of cement. Coulda been much worse."

Resolutely nodding his head, Tag conceded. "Yeah. I know." Propping his upper body on an elbow, he gingerly flexed his injured leg a few times. "Nothing seems to be broken." He exhaled heavily, relief flooding his weary eyes.

"You got lucky, kid. This time. Let's get you cleaned up, then you and I are gonna have a serious talk." After much exasperated grumbling from Tag, Tyler was able to hoist him to a standing position. As they ambled toward the bathroom, there was a derisive snort from Tyler.

"Shit. Is that dried *puke* in your hair?"

Tag

The brilliant midday sun streamed through the curtains when Tag finally awoke Sunday. He was on the couch, still clad in the same shorts; the only difference appeared to be his knee and calf both were swathed in clean bandages. On the coffee table was a bottle of water and two Tylenols with a yellow stickie note.

Take these immediately with the entire bottle of water. Doctor's orders!

Smiling for the first time in days, Tag reached for his phone, which blinked incessantly. Scanning the screen hastily, he saw a few texts from North Star and one from Tyler. Crestfallen, he heaved a sigh. *Nothing from Emery.* He knew in his heart there would be no messages until he made things right. *I said hateful things. I need to tell her how sorry I am.*

Vague snippets of the previous night's mostly one-sided conversation with Tyler replayed in his mind. His best friend had held nothing back.

"I know why you're so fuckin' out-of-control, Tag. You. Love. Emery. Admit it. Are you willing to change in order to be with her? To possibly have a future with her? What will it take, kid?"

Swiping the phone's screen, Tag opened the cryptic text.

TYLER: WELCOME BACK TO THE LIVING! ROBBI WILL BE THERE AFTER DINNER. IT'S TIME. (AND CALL YOUR CLEANING SERVICE ASAP.)

Pinching the bridge of his nose, Tag took a deep, cleansing breath and began to type. It required all his focus to keep his hands from shaking.

TAG: I FUCKED UP BIG TIME. I WAS A STUBBORN IDIOT, A FOOL. I'M SO SORRY FOR THE THINGS I SAID, EM. I DIDN'T MEAN ANY OF IT. I WAS SHOCKED, HURT, AND CONFUSED AT FIRST.

Tag: Not angry anymore, except u drove to AZ without me. Losing my mind picturing u on the freeway alone, without me to help drive.

Tag: The only feeling I have now is profound loss. I am empty without u. I miss u so much it's making me crazy. I haven't been able to breathe since u left my house.

Tag: FUCK! Sorry, phone limits characters. Robbi's coming later to be here when I read the journal. I'll text u after. Miss u sweetheart.

Robbi came to Tag's house, as promised, that evening. She assured him her presence was for support and a sympathetic ear — not to comment nor pass judgment of any kind, promising that her friendship with Emery would not influence her in any way. Tag had given Tyler permission to share his true identity as well as the backstory: what led up to Randi's fatal accident.

The wooden box and suede-bound journal had been placed on the living room coffee table. There was also a tray of healthy snacks laid out, along with a bottle of red wine and two crystal glasses. Robbi glanced at the refreshments and gave Tag a comforting hug. He apprehensively reciprocated the gesture, then filled the wineglasses and handed her one.

"Thanks, Tag. First, do you mind showing me the mosaic piece Emery created for you?"

Tag's face lit up with pride as he led Robbi to the fireplace. Smoothing his hand over the granite and marble designs, he beamed. "It's pretty spectacular, huh?"

Robbi nodded, smiling warmly in agreement. "Magnificent. I recognize the four elements: fire, earth, air, and water. What do the other symbols represent?"

Tag sighed, taking a couple of ragged breaths. "Eternity, strength, and love. I could use those last two right about now."

Robbi cupped his face with her hand and gave him a few

motherly taps on his cheek. "These smacks are from Tyler, by the way." She chuckled, but her tone grew somber immediately. "Tag, you already possess strength and love. Now, you must utilize both to move forward with your life." Sitting on the couch, they touched their glasses together and Tag echoed her words, "To moving forward."

Robbi caught his eyes as he began to gulp the Merlot. "One rule, Tag. This will be the only bottle you open this evening. Promise?" He nodded solemnly. "I promise. Thanks, Robbi."

It took over two hours for Tag to get through everything, including numerous photos. He talked a lot and Robbi listened attentively. They took turns reading excerpts from the journal. Robbi shared the day she lost her parents. They both wept, shared happy anecdotes, reminisced, shed a few more tears, laughed, drank, and eased each other's sorrow.

The final few pages described the events that led up to the accident. Reading together silently, combined with what Tag had previously revealed, the tragic story unfolded.

The second to last entry appeared to have been made the day after the gangbang video went public. Cole had called Randi a few times to explain, but she had refused to talk to him. She left the dorm to stay with a friend off-campus.

Jake had approached her the next day and admitted Clark Campbell, the fraternity president, had drugged Cole, then set Jake up with the intent to blackmail him. Clark had incriminating evidence proving Jake had stolen answers to an exam, so Clark coerced him into taking the video and then leaking it to the on-campus TV station. Campbell's motivation appeared to have been his younger brother, who was being pursued by UT Longhorn scouts, and coveted the quarterback position. If Cole was out of the way, the kid's chances increased exponentially. Jake regretted his involvement and wanted a chance to explain and apologize to Randi. That opportunity would never happen. They were heading out to a local restaurant when a drunk truck driver hit them and both were killed instantly.

The final entry in the journal had been scripted directly to Cole. Robbi scanned it, and then asked Tag if he'd like her to read it aloud. He nodded, lips compressed into a tight line as he mentally prepared himself. Robbi took one of his hands in hers and held it tightly.

His tears fell silently as Robbi read. Halfway through, she draped an arm around his shoulders and he leaned heavily into her. His eyes were cast downward toward the journal, but his vision was mercifully blurred. He planned to read Randi's words himself at a later date. Simply leaning her head on his, Robbi held him quietly.

"It will get better, Tag. I promise you. My parents have been gone eighteen years. The first few years were excruciating. I thought about them every minute of every day. You get so used to the pain, you think it's normal, but it isn't. Every memory I had was intertwined with Mom and Dad. Then gradually it was every other memory, then all the joyful recollections steadily became an intrinsic part of who I am and the grief lessened somewhat. It is not a betrayal to Randi if you find happiness somewhere along the way." Tag listened attentively. Finally, after scrubbing his hands down his face, he turned to Robbi.

"I know we can't change the past, but I keep thinking if only I had …" Robbi immediately put her finger to his lips.

"Do *not* allow your mind to go there. I wish memories were like texts and email; simply hit 'delete' and poof! Gone. Forgotten. I did the destructive, self-blame shit for years after my parents were killed. If only I had called Mom that afternoon, they would have left the house ten minutes later. Or what if I had invited them to dinner? They would've been at my house and not on the road. Or suppose Dad and I had watched the basketball game together? Then he would have been safe at home. Those 'what ifs' accomplish nothing and do not move us forward. Don't let your grief paralyze you. Think about this instead. What can you do today, tomorrow, and every day for the rest of your life that will honor Randi's memory? Think of ways you can pay tribute to the unconditional love she gave you. I know her love is bottled up inside your heart, so take a portion of it and bestow it on someone else. Remember Randi's final act of forgiveness she gave you? Offer that same gift to a person in your life who needs and deserves it."

Tag sat quietly, clasping the journal with both hands. "Thanks, Robbi. Tyler's a fortunate man to have you in his life. I'm gonna make things right with Emery, I promise you. I'm guessing you already know what happened between us."

Robbi nodded, as Tag ran his hands anxiously through his hair, causing it to stand straight up.

"She left town Thursday without even saying goodbye. I had planned to make that road trip with her. I've been kinda freaking out imagining her on the freeways all alone. Damn. I sent her a fuckton of texts apologizing." Tag grabbed his phone expectantly, but his expression turned from hopeful to despondent in a flash. Still no messages.

"She'll contact you when she's ready. Emery understands why you were so furious with her."

"I'm not anymore. I'm just scared I've lost her. She has hovered on the edge of every waking thought I've had for the past week. I love her, Robbi. I know that now and I just miss her so damn much."

Robbi emptied the bottle of wine into their glasses and raised hers, as Tag met it midair with his own. He had made good on his promise; no additional wine had been necessary.

"To what lies ahead for all of us," Robbi announced, smiling sincerely. Draining her glass, she kissed Tag on the crown of his head, enquiring, "You gonna be okay?"

His smile was weak, but genuine. "Yep. Thanks again, Robbi. I'm so grateful. Give my best to Ty."

"Will do, sweetie." After a few additional gentle pats on his cheek, she was gone.

As Tag cleared off the coffee table, something shifted inside him; the constant pressure weighing on his chest had noticeably lessened. He felt considerably lighter in body as well as spirit. Running his hand over the smooth suede of Randi's journal, he kissed it reverently before placing it back in the wooden box, atop his old UT jerseys. "Good night, baby. Miss you." He then strode over to his laptop and fired it up.

Clark Campbell. Let's see what Google has on you, motherfucker. Maybe I'll pay you a little visit, you fucking bastard. After typing a few key words into the search engine, several headlines popped up from Texas media sites and newspapers.

'Prominent Texas Businessman, Clark Campbell, Fatally Shot in Domestic Dispute.
Wife and Sons Questioned, Released, Will Not be Charged.
Rumors of years of infidelity, physical and emotional abuse at the hands of ...'

Tag did not need to continue reading and abruptly shut his laptop. *Karma can be a nasty bitch, Clark. I hope you bled out real fucking slow, and went straight to Hell.*

An eerie sense of calm settled over Tag as his gaze fell upon his phone. After staring at the screen for a full minute, he began typing furiously.

Tag: I finally read everything. Took me a while, kept the journal under my pillow all week. Robbi helped me get through it.

Tag: I will NEVER abandon u and Randy. Still coming for his tryouts, day before to practice.

I WANT U BOTH IN MY LIFE.

TAG: I WAS SCARED WHEN U TOLD ME THE TRUTH, WHAT IT ALL MEANT, AND HOW I FELT ABOUT US. STILL SCARED, TERRIFIED, BUT I CAN'T LOSE U.

Tag scrubbed a hand haphazardly down his face, scratching at his overgrown stubble, which had been ignored for days.

TAG: I APOLOGIZE FOR WHAT YOU SAW IN NSB LOT. I LOST IT FOR A MOMENT. THE SECOND SHE TOUCHED ME, I PUSHED HER AWAY. I ONLY WANT U, SWEETHEART.

TAG: MY WORLD IS BLACK & WHITE WITHOUT U. I MISS MY BROWN-EYED, SUNRISE GIRL. PLEASE TEXT ASAP AND CALL WHEN U CAN. XX

Chapter 24

"What is done out of love always takes place beyond good and evil."
– Friedrich Nietzsche

TAG

Tag was due to tend bar Monday evening. There was still no word from Emery. She had mentioned the possibility of staying a night in Burbank, California with a friend from college, before driving home to Phoenix, but for all he knew, she could have been anywhere.

The bar was packed; any night during baseball season was always jammed and Tag was swamped. Every so often, he would check his phone. His heart almost leaped out of his chest when he saw a text.

EMERY: I'M STILL AT SUZY'S, LEAVING EARLY TMW. ALL IS WELL, GOLDIE'S GOOD TOO. I KNOW UR BUSY AT NSB, SO CALL WHEN U HAVE A BREAK. I'LL WAIT UP. MISS U 2.

TAG: I WAS SO WORRIED. CRAZY BUSY HERE. I'LL CALL SOON. MISS U MORE.

Thank fucking God. He wondered when the last time was that he'd uttered those words. *Um ... never?* He didn't believe in that shit. *I don't do the whole 'blind faith praying to God' routine. So why do I feel like all my prayers have just been answered?*

Emery

It was close to midnight. Suzy had gone to bed, leaving Emery on the pullout couch in the small living room. Lying back with Goldie snuggled on her chest, she was deep in thought, mentally composing the words she wanted to convey to Tag. Her phone, set to vibrate, was in one hand, while her other was buried in Goldie's neck fur. Judging by her soft yelps of pleasure, the pup was enjoying the brisk massage. After the terrible night when she told Tag who she was, Emery found it unbearably painful and lonely to sleep in her bed. Subsequently, she had spent the ensuing nights on the couch with Goldie's crate close by. Goldie was exceptionally intuitive, seeming to sense Emery's unease. Tag had been stopping by daily to care for the dog, so Emery was sure they both were suffering from separation anxiety.

"Tag's calling soon, girl. Aren't you excited? I know I am. I miss him so much, Goldie. You miss him too, don't you, girl? I know you do." Goldie's head perked up instantaneously when vibrations emanated from the phone. Emery's reaction was similar; her heart almost stopped beating.

"Hi, Tag!" Her voice came out breathy; she felt strangely uneasy and her anxious mind became a complete and utter blank as the sound of his deep, sexy voice sent a jolt of heat through her body.

"Emery, before you say anything, I need you to know. What you said to me that night — you were right about everything. Every fucking word you said was the truth. I didn't want to hear it. I was afraid to face it and what it all meant. But no more looking back, I only want to move forward … with you, if you still want me. Please, Emery. Please say you still want me. I want you in my life so bad, baby."

Goldie must have heard Tag's voice because her excited squeals were impatiently out of control.

"I still want you very much, honey, but your other girl cannot wait another second to talk to you. Can you hear her? She's going crazy, Tag. I'm gonna put you on speaker phone."

"Hi, Goldie girl!" Exuberant yapping resounded around the room. "You takin' good care of your mama for me?" Two excited barks were aimed at the phone. "That's my good girl. I'll see you soon, Goldie." A few more woofs were followed by one final yelp, then Goldie contentedly returned to her favorite chew toy.

"She sounds great, Em. Was she okay in the car? Did she behave? Was she carsick?"

"She was fine, Tag. I threaded the seatbelt through the slats of the crate so she'd be safe and wouldn't jostle around." They shared a laugh at her ingenuity.

He apologized profusely for every hurtful word he had expressed, in addition to his selfishness regarding Randi's parents and asked if they were all right. Emery filled him in on their adopted twins and the way their lives as a family had changed for the better with the addition of the two orphaned girls. Emery had not yet told her parents Tag's true identity; she briefly considered not divulging the secret at all, but innately realized that would not be an option. She would reveal the whole story prior to Tag's Arizona visit. Although Tag's appearance had changed radically, Aunt Morgan and Uncle Victor would surely recognize him. Luckily, they were scheduled to be out of town the weekend of Randy's tryouts.

Plans were finalized for later in the week. Tag would fly to Arizona Thursday afternoon, practice with Randy Friday, then attend tryouts on Saturday and return to San Francisco Sunday night. Emery would reserve a room at a nearby five-star hotel through Alex's sister, who worked in the hotel industry and was usually able to procure a luxury suite at a hefty discount. They chatted for a while longer before Tag had to return to the bar.

Goldie's soft snores lulled Emery but her heart was still racing as her mind replayed their conversation. Tag's heartfelt apology and promises for their future filled her with a blissful sense of peace and contentment that she had longed for.

He didn't say the words, but I know he loves me.

TAG

Since his conversation with Emery, random ideas and plans had been bouncing around Tag's mind, as a mental list started to formulate. *So much to do and so little time.*

Tag and Brew were hunched over a corner table with their heads together, in the midst of a heated discussion. They had closed the bar for the night and were having a quick chat at Tag's request. Brew's eyebrows were raised in concern.

"Have you thought this through, Tag? I mean, it's a bit sudden, eh?" Worry laced his tone as he took a long pull from his beer. Tag absentmindedly picked at his beer bottle's label.

"I'll be gone three or four days max and depending on how everything goes, I'll figure out the details when I get back. Tyler said he wouldn't mind bartending, if you need him." The two men locked eyes in understanding and tapped their bottles together.

"Good luck, Tag. Keep me posted. Now, how 'bout helpin' me swab the bar so we can get the fuck out of here?" Brew stood, heading back to the bar area as Tag lagged behind, adding, "Do you still have contacts with the Forty-Niners' organization?" Brew nodded and Tag flashed him a thumbs-up.

"Cool. We'll discuss that next week. Give me ten minutes, Brew. I gotta make a quick call first."

After several rings, Tag was about to hang up when a male

voice answered curtly, "Yeah?" After a deep inhale to steady his breathing, Tag gathered his confidence and stated, "Coach Tomlinson, this is Cole Taggart. I was hoping you'd remember me." Tag's shoulders visibly relaxed as a small grin stole across his countenance. "Yeah, Coach, it *has* been a while."

Chapter 25

*"Forgiveness is the fragrance that the violet
sheds on the heel that has crushed it."*
– Mark Twain

Tag

His hungry eyes finally located Emery, an angel amid the faceless throng, and in that microscopic moment — before she spied him, when time froze in a vacuum — he studied her face. Although nothing had changed physically, she had become exponentially more beautiful. She was a beacon illuminating the darkness as he made his way toward her. His life of suppressed emotions flashed before his eyes; he barely had been existing, simply going through the robotic motions, every single forgettable day. Sleep, eat, work, drink, fuck. It was all just a well-rehearsed façade for anyone who cared enough to watch. A searing pain burned in his chest; he deserved it, as he recalled the angry words he had directed at her just two short weeks ago. *It hurts to look at you. Leave. Now.* He had accused her of stalking him, lying to him.

The pain in his heart when Emery first told him who she was had been excruciating, threatening to rip his chest wide open. It was nothing compared to the endless ache, which had invaded his soul following her return to Arizona without him.

After reading Randi's journal, Tag had finally come to his senses, acknowledging that the universe had given him an unexpected, miraculous second chance.

Emery finally spotted him; he was carrying a large bouquet of long-stem red roses. She did not move a muscle, waiting for him to approach her. Tag blinked apprehensively as he stared deeply into her shining eyes, searching, and ultimately finding forgiveness. Gathering her into his arms, he held her gently at first, then frantically as if these were their last moments on Earth. Every nerve ending ached for physical contact. He could not seem to get close enough, breathing her essence in. As a child he had never found himself lost for hours in a shopping mall, but imagined this was how it felt to be reunited with the missing loved one — secure, cherished, home. His lips gradually moved to her forehead, where he planted numerous soft kisses; her hands were gripping the back of his neck and in his hair. Tag had missed the strength of her fingers more than he realized. It was the first real breath he'd taken since she'd left. *I will never let her go again.*

A desperate need to swallow his guilt overwhelmed him as he began the exquisite journey toward her lush mouth. Emery lifted her chin slightly, meeting him halfway. Their lips ultimately connected after an agonizing pause; silent communication between two pairs of eyes attuned to each other in unfathomable ways. *She still loves me. Perhaps God exists after all.*

Tag could taste the salt of her tears when he captured her mouth in a blistering kiss. Parting her lips, he thrust his tongue inside her warmth, savoring the taste he had missed for much too long. He devoured her, wanting to absorb any residual pain he had caused. Tag reluctantly pulled away after several blissful moments, cradling her cheeks in his hands.

"I am so sorry!" they blurted out simultaneously.

"I wish I could un-say every hurtful word."

"I should have told you sooner, Tag."

"I ached for you, babe."

"I missed you so much."

"I was pissed you left without me."

His ravenous mouth scorched over hers again, nibbling her bottom lip.

"I apologize for what you saw in the parking lot. I pushed her away before anything actually happened."

"And I'm sorry ... for what I did after I saw you that night," Emery whispered, eyes turned upward, almost afraid to meet his emerald greens head-on. Anxiously biting her lip, she abruptly dropped her chin to her chest. Tag held her closer, pressing his lips to her forehead. Lightly stroking her hair, his mouth slowly lowered to her ear.

"Luca?" Tag's breath on her neck caused shivers throughout her body. Emery nodded but still could not look at Tag directly. "I had way too much wine and we fooled around in his car a bit, but I did *not* have sex with him because all I could think about was you. Please forgive me, Tag." He could hear sniffling through the curtain of her silky brown hair. Gently lifting her chin, he placed a feather-soft kiss on her lips.

"There's nothing to forgive, sweetheart. After the way I spoke to you, I probably deserve that and much worse. You know, when I went to the florist I originally wanted sunflowers, 'cause I know you love them, but when the salesgirl asked me how colossal my fuck-up was on a scale of one to ten — and I said a *thousand* — she recommended the roses." Emery's mouth turned upward and Tag began to breathe a bit easier.

"I don't wanna think about any past shit. From this day forward, it's you and me. We. Us. That includes Randy, of course. A fresh start, okay? I got a brief glimpse of my life without you and I realized I couldn't live that life anymore. I won't. I don't know how to live in a world that doesn't include you. You know, I still haven't changed my bedsheets. I couldn't bear the thought of washing away your scent. I cannot lose you, Emery. I … I just found you."

EMERY

When their eyes connected again, Emery's heart eased as she scanned his appearance. Tag's content grin transformed his face from hard planes to pure, tender adoration. He had not lightened his medium-brown hair since she had last seen him, and had a carefree shaggy appearance, which was enhanced by his week-old stubble. He smelled woodsy, like pine needles. *Christmas trees in June. Damn him. He smells as good as he looks.*

"You're not gonna lose me, Tag. I already told you, remember? Not. Happening." Tag was travelling light; he only brought a carry-on, so they immediately exited the airport and headed for Emery's car, walking hand-in-hand. Tag's eyes were sparkling as he gazed sidelong at her profile.

"So, I got you a suite at the Four Seasons. Are you hungry? Wanna grab dinner somewhere? Would you rather go straight to the hotel and relax?" *We haven't been together in a while. Is that why I'm babbling so nervously?*

"Two questions first, Em. You got *me* a suite, or us? And if it's for us, I assume they have room service?" Noticing her RAV 4, Tag pulled her into his arms and roughly walked her backwards until her body was pressed against the vehicle's side door. He yanked the flowers from her hand and hastily deposited them on the roof of the car as his mouth sought to devour hers, tongue teasing at first, then demanding entrance past her lips, possessing her in every way. One of his large hands cupped her ass while the other was firmly threaded in the hair at the nape of her neck. He moaned deep in his throat as his hips ground into her. Tag's greedy mouth had moved to her neck, licking, biting, and sucking the soft, sensitive skin below her ear. His erection pressed against her and familiar wetness invaded her panties, an aching need begging for immediate release.

"God, Emery, I want you so bad. You have no idea how much I missed you, baby." He thrust his pelvis into her again, a bit forcefully; the car rocked slightly and then the piercing alarm shattered the quiet of the parking structure.

"Oh, shit! Let me get that." Grabbing her keys from her pocket, Emery frantically pressed the alarm button a few times but nothing happened; the auditory assault was threatening to wake the dead. As Emery peered into the front seat, the reality of the situation finally hit her.

"Tag! This isn't my car. Oops, my bad. I think I'm one floor up." They frantically raced back toward the elevator laughing hysterically. "You gotta go back. My flowers!" Her giggle was infectious; his hoots and hollers resounded through the parking structure as he rescued Emery's bouquet.

The ground floor, spacious one-bedroom suite was magnificently furnished in rich, earthy shades and hardwood floors. There was a lovely private patio area, complete with a small, heated plunge pool and a chiminea fireplace. Fantastic views of Camelback Mountain could be seen in the distance.

"Wow. This room is amazing. I'll reimburse you; just let me know what the cost was."

"Not necessary. Alex's sister owed me a big favor. She's an executive with this hotel chain; it was practically free, don't worry about it." After tossing their bags on a nearby chair, Tag turned his heated gaze toward Emery, grasping her hands in his.

"No more talking, brown eyes," Tag instructed tersely, picking her up and carrying her to the king-size bed. "Screaming my name, however, is encouraged and will be rewarded."

There was no sensual, languid undressing of each other. They simply tore their clothes off at the speed of light and dove under the duvet, lips crashing, tongues whirling amid heavy panting. Tag came up for air long enough to whisper, "As much as I'd love to take my time with you, slowly savor you, and make you come apart for me, I can't. I know it hasn't been that long, but it seems like I've waited a lifetime to be inside you again."

Tag trailed wet kisses all the way down her jawline, neck and through the valley between her breasts. He tenderly encircled a taut nipple, teasing it with his tongue as Emery gasped. His nibbles were gentle at first, followed by one firm bite, sending a fiery path of heat straight to her already-liquefied core, causing her thighs to clench together. Several moans escaped her throat from the brief pain, followed by intense pleasure coursing through her veins. The throbbing between her legs was becoming magnified, and her clit desperately craved a special kind of friction. She reached between their bodies and found his rock-hard cock already thick with arousal. Tag was poised and ready, coating the head of his cock with her essence, waiting for her to take control. Grabbing his shaft forcefully, Emery rubbed his piercing around her sensitive bundle of nerves, alternating the smooth skin of his penis with the heavy, metal ring at just the right amount of pressure and intensity. Delicious torture combined with out-of-this-world ecstasy; after so many days of numbness, Tag had brought her back to feeling alive.

"Now, baby. Please, I need you," Emery breathed, wrapping her legs around his hips, effectively imprisoning him between her thighs. Grabbing his ass and pulling him toward her forcefully, he entered her in one swift, explosive thrust making her cry out in half-pleasure, half-pain. Stretching her inner walls with each exquisite stroke, Tag arched and leaned back slightly, his pierced cock caressing that most sensitive place inside that only he knew how to locate. Locking his eyes onto Emery's, his thumb found her aching clit and began a tender assault that took her breath away. Waves of heat washed over her as her vision blurred. *Melting. Floating. Drifting. Soaring.* Her body shuddered uncontrollably as he moved his hips in a grinding motion. Her fingers found his hair and she simply held on for dear life as if she couldn't get him deep enough inside her. The bed creaked then shook in response to his forceful pounding as an earth-shattering orgasm ripped through her.

Riding the intensity for what seemed like forever, Tag pumped out his own release and groaned, collapsing on her chest. Immediately nestling his face in the space between her shoulder and neck, he managed to murmur, "Fuck, babe. Perfect. You are perfection. I missed being inside you. This connection we have, it's like we're one. We share the same heart, the same soul. I was so afraid I would never feel this again. Being here with you, inside you, is where I belong." Emery nodded as she scattered tender kisses across his forehead, while endeavoring to catch her breath. Emery's skin still burned from his touch and she felt more alive than ever.

Snuggling for a while, her back to his chest, he reached around her waist, lacing their fingers together, planting wet kisses on her neck and shoulder.

"God, Emery, I've missed your hands." Placing one of her palms on the side of his face, Tag leaned into it, brushing his lips against her wrist. "I never want to live another day without your hands on me somewhere, anywhere," he murmured as he gently nibbled on each finger. "And your mouth, your lips, your smile. I've missed all of you. The world is in full-blown Technicolor again. My sunrise girl is home." He kissed the top of her head and sighed deeply, as the vibrant sunset began to peek through the curtains, casting bright beams of light across their bare limbs, tangled up in each other. Time ceased to exist.

"So, no more keeping secrets, Em. Promise?" Tag waited for her nod before he continued. "All I know is that wherever you are, that is where I want to be, too. From this day forward, there is no more you and me. There is only us."

Tag's roaming eyes came to rest on a large gift basket atop the coffee table. Following his gaze, Emery was quick to explain.

"That's from my parents, to thank you for working with Randy. Dad seems to think he is a shoe-in for first-string wide receiver." Tag nodded absentmindedly and forced a smile, but it did not reach his eyes.

"Em, I'm a bit nervous about meeting your parents. I mean, there's no chance they would *ever* recognize me. It's been twelve years and I look completely different, but …"

"I already told Mom and Dad everything," Emery blurted out as she turned to face him, caressing his cheek. "Except for the baby, they know the whole truth, so there's no need to worry. They're looking forward to seeing you again. Randi's parents are out of town for the weekend, so you can discuss with Mom and Dad how you'd like to handle that reunion. They will tell Randy *after* his tryouts. The short, simplified version. He knows the basic facts about his namesake, but none of the details." Noticing his creased forehead, Emery sought to alleviate Tag's apprehension.

"Honey, my parents will handle it. Trust me; they're on your side. *Our* side. Now let's open this lovely bottle of wine and celebrate your arrival."

TAG

Although he was uneasy, Friday's meeting with Emery's parents went better than expected considering the circumstances and the number of years that had passed. Both had witnessed Randy's significant improvement in football skills, and they were indebted to Tag for his commitment and obvious adoration for the child. While Randy gathered his practice gear, Tag happened upon Emery's impressive sculpture capturing that famous diving catch the child made in Golden Gate Park. Lightly running his fingertips along the bronze figure entitled *The Catch*, Tag's countenance relaxed, becoming introspective.

"This is magnificent work, Emery. You have exceptional talent." He beamed with pride, but his eyes held a question. Emery's understanding expression revealed she knew what was on his mind.

"Would you like to see yours, Tag? It's in my room. Come." Not waiting for his response, she took his hand and led the way down the long hall.

The double-faced bust, which bore the title *Lost and Found*, was prominently displayed on top of a tall dresser. Tag's face paled when he read the title, emotions playing havoc with his self-control. The 'lost' face revealed desolation, despair, and agony while the other exhibited joy, elation, and contentment. His eyes shone with admiration as his gaze connected with hers.

"The title is beautiful. *Before and After* might have worked too. My life — before and after you. How were you able to capture my emotions so perfectly?"

Emery's laugh was music to his ears. "You were in that lump of clay before I began. I just had to remove all the negativity and self-doubt you were hiding behind."

Randy's tryouts on Saturday went extremely well; he was by far the most competent and self-assured athlete on the field. Tag heard Emery's dad boisterously stating, more than once, "See the boy kickin' ass out there? That's my grandson!" Goldie, who had joined the family's outing, barked enthusiastically whenever Randy was on the field.

Tag's heart swelled as the youngster executed every catch perfectly. He noted Coach Tomlinson nodding approvingly several times and afterwards approached him for a chat. Tag spied Emery watching them from afar, and felt a pang of guilt. *Part of our conversation has to remain a secret … for now.*

Emery's parents had dinner plans with friends, so they scurried off to the restaurant in their own car. Randy grabbed Emery's hand as they, with Goldie in tow, walked to Emery's vehicle. Tag stowed the football gear in the trunk.

"Mom, Coach Bob says I need new cleats. I've outgrown mine. Can we stop at Big 5 before we go home?"

They had just parked when the unimaginable happened. It was like a scene from a B-movie on fast-forward speed. A beat-up, black van with tinted windows screeched to a halt right in front of the parking lot. Simultaneously, the door slid open and two masked males emerged, one brandishing a gun, the other a switchblade. A strained male voice from somewhere inside the van screeched, "Emmie, *run!*" It was ear shattering, piercing the quiet street, only a few yards from the sporting goods store.

Emery reacted in a nanosecond, screaming loudly while pulling Randy toward her, away from the grasp of the man wielding the blade.

"*El niño, rápido!*" the gun-wielding thug growled in a low gravelly voice. Tag's subconscious internal quarterback took over: analyzing threats, predicting opponents' movements, deciding on a course of action. His mind's eye surveyed the scene in a millisecond. *Randy. Goldie. Knife. Emery. Gun.*

"TACK!" Tag commanded as he instinctively dove toward the armed assailant who was heading in Emery's direction. Goldie snarled as she lunged for the other man who had a rough hold on Randy, sinking her teeth into his wrist, forcing him to let go of the child and drop the knife, but not before the blade sliced the boy's forearm. Tag tackled the man, attempting to shield Emery from the gun. He managed a left hook to the guy's jaw, before wrestling the thug for the weapon as they both fell to the pavement. Several passersby had been observing dumbfounded; two were frantically on their phones and a teenager was shooting what appeared to be a video. The raucous screams and chaos came to an abrupt halt as two rapid-fire gunshots rang out. By this time, Goldie had released the man's wrist but her mouth was dripping with blood and a bit of torn flesh.

"*Pendejo! Vámonos!*" The gun skittered along the cement, but it was hastily picked up by its owner. Both men jumped into the van and it tore down the street, sideswiping several cars along the way. A middle-aged woman approached cautiously, assuring Emery the police had been notified.

Tag lay on his back, both hands on his upper left chest; blood seeped through his fingers. Still clinging to Goldie's leash, Randy darted to Emery as she kneeled by Tag's shoulder. She removed her fleece jacket and pressed it to the gunshot wound, gently putting Tag's hands on top. Covering his hands with one of her own, she applied pressure, encouraging Randy to follow her lead as the boy knelt beside him. Tag's eyes were open. When his gaze met Emery's, he attempted to focus, mouthing, "You okay?"

"We're fine. Goldie, too. Help is on the way. You hold on, Tag. You hear me? I just got you back. I am *not* losing you again, do you understand? I'm right here. Stay with me, honey. Please." Emery's free hand cupped his cheek and her lips were softly on his mouth, as if it were possible to breathe life into him. Her face was only a hair's breadth from his, their eyes locked onto each other's, her silky hair grazing his cheeks as her teardrops fell. Tag recognized the horrific fear in her eyes and the profound sadness that followed, as a frisson of pure terror slithered down his spine.

My chest ... on fire. Burning. Hard to breathe. Can't leave her.

His mouth moved sluggishly as she strained to hear his feeble whispers.

"I'm okay, Em. No pain. You're so beautiful, baby. I …" His wheezing breaths were barely audible as a single tear escaped from the corner of his eye. Randy clung to his mother, sobbing softly as Goldie whimpered in the background.

"Don't you dare leave me, Tag," she desperately breathed into his ear. Her tear-streaked face was the final image he perceived before his vision faded to black.

"I … love you …" Tag's voice cracked, weakening as he choked out a muffled cough. His head fell back onto something cottony-soft and he caught a glimpse of somber grey clouds drifting overhead. His strength was deteriorating quickly. Without warning, a familiar face came into view, startling him out of his daze.

"Randi? Why are you … where am I?"

Shh, baby. Don't try to talk. I've got you, Cole. He felt something brush his cheek, but there was no discernable hand he could see. Randi's serene countenance was barely perceptible, as if hidden behind a shimmering translucent screen. Her arms enfolded him in what felt like a petal-soft blanket, shrouding the two of them in complete darkness. Randi's cheek laid on his, as her breathy voice murmured in his ear.

I have always been by your side, Cole. I knew you were aware of my presence, even though I tried to keep my distance. He felt soft kisses pressed to his forehead.

You can't stay here. Too many people need you now. They're counting on you, and she loves you so much. We'll see each other again someday. Trust me, Cole. My love lives inside you. Go. She's waiting for you.

<hr>

Emery

A few onlookers had called 911 when the assault took place. The ambulance and a police car arrived quickly. Emery's initial terror had been replaced by an overwhelming helplessness. There was nothing more she could do except offer comforting words to Randy. Two paramedics immediately began tending Tag's wound and he was soon hoisted on a gurney, then wheeled toward the waiting vehicle. After making sure Randy was in the care of a policewoman, Emery accompanied the gurney as far as she could, her fingertips lightly skimming Tag's hand as he was lifted into the vehicle. Gazing at his face one last time, memorizing every beloved feature, she withdrew her hand. The doors slammed shut and the ambulance screeched away. Heartbeat racing, her hands flew to her mouth as she stifled a muffled cry.

Please, God. Don't let him die.

Randy's wound was superficial; one of the paramedics was able to clean it, and wrapped a quick bandage around his arm assuring Emery stitches would not be required. Goldie was in the care of another officer, who was swabbing the animal's mouth and teeth for the assailant's DNA. The police guaranteed after a few preliminary questions, they would be escorted to the hospital as soon as possible.

Emery, Randy and Goldie were finally in the back of the police squad car, en route to Phoenix General Hospital. Outwardly, she attempted to remain calm for her son's sake, but her insides were churning furiously and her heart was disintegrating minute by agonizing minute. *Tag shot, Alex a captive? I could lose them both.*

"Mom, someone was tied up in the back of the van. He was blindfolded, but I saw who it was. It was Dad. He was the one who screamed for you to run," Randy revealed to his mother in hushed tones.

"I know, sweetie. Daddy saved us. Because he's undercover, we can't mention this to anyone but the police. Not even Grandma and Gramps, okay?"

Randy nodded, and panic rose as Emery struggled to process the information. Alex had been in deep cover for almost two months. She knew it was a dangerous assignment; the drug wars between rival cartels in Mexico were a constant threat. Reaching for her phone, she sent a text to Captain Jacovo, Alex's supervisor.

Emery: Alex in trouble. Randy almost kidnapped. My boyfriend shot. Heading to PGH.

Captain Jacovo: Got details from officers at the scene. Squad car headed to hospital. They will meet you. Call me when you arrive. I notified your parents.

Emery and Randy, with Goldie in his arms, entered PGH Trauma Center and immediately saw a police officer. Giving him a quick nod, she hit Captain Jacovo's number, then relayed the events, which had just transpired along with what she and Randy had seen and heard. Emery corroborated Randy's story; she had also recognized the voice in the van as Alex. Captain Jacovo promised to keep her informed, adding he would arrive at the hospital soon.

Mother, son, and Goldie the Super Pup, which Randy was now calling her, found comfortable seats in the waiting area. After reading a text from her parents, who were on their way to the hospital, Emery approached the desk, attempting to get some information on Tag's condition. She was numb, drained of all emotion, operating on zombie-like cruise control. Her heart was in pieces, fragmented and weeping on the inside while her stoic, outer persona — mother to a terrified nine-year-old who had come face-to-face with gun violence — was now in charge. No observable tears, face unemotional, fiercely brave under pressure.

Her phone rang again and seeing the captain's name appear, she walked a few feet away from Randy so she could speak freely. His voice was somber and controlled.

"Listen carefully, Emery. The undercover operation has been compromised. I need both of you to stay with the officer until I get there, and do not let Randy out of your sight. Am I clear?" His tone immediately caused goose bumps to rise on her arms.

"Yes, sir. My parents texted to say they're on their way to take Randy home, but I'm staying until I can find out how my friend is doing." Captain Jacovo's grave tone was causing panic to flood her chest. Her world was falling apart, but she needed to keep her demeanor controlled and remain strong for her son.

"Just don't let anyone leave. I must speak to all your family members. I'm five minutes away." The call ended as Emery went back to her chair, pulling Randy tightly into her side. Shaking uncontrollably, she attempted to channel her nervous energy into stroking Goldie's fur.

A few moments had passed when Olivia and Sam arrived, rushing to embrace their daughter and grandson.

"I was worried sick, sweetie." Olivia wept as she smoothed Emery's hair. Sam had scooped Randy into his strong arms, as Goldie jumped up happily against his legs.

"Goldie saved me, Gramps. She bit the bad guy. And Tag saved Mommy, but … but he got shot." Randy started to cry, as Emery and Olivia came to Sam's side.

"Baby, you know better than anyone, Tag's incredibly strong. He's gonna be okay, you'll see." Blinking back her tears, Emery turned toward her parents.

"Captain Jacovo is on his way over. He needs to speak with all of us, so why don't we sit and wait for him. He should be arriving soon."

The family had just gotten comfortable when Captain Jacovo burst through the doors accompanied by two more uniformed officers. He was a tall, larger-than-life figure. He had salt and pepper hair with a pleasant face and gregarious manner, although his tough, ball-busting reputation was renown throughout the precinct. Emery's father and Joe Jacovo had known each other since college, and they were quick to embrace.

"May I introduce Officers Melendez and O'Hara. Officer Melendez is our tech expert; he's going to take a look at your phone, Emery, and your son's as well. We have reason to believe these men knew your whereabouts and you were specifically targeted." Emery paled as she handed her phone to Officer Melendez, who then took Randy by the hand and led him and Goldie out to the squad car, which was parked in front. A somber Captain Jacovo then turned to the family.

"I can't give you any specific details, but here are the facts as of twenty minutes ago. Detective Zamora has been undercover for close to two months. He was to infiltrate a known gang with the assistance of a CI — a confidential informant. He befriended this CI, a female by the name of Claudia Barrios, and unfortunately, they became involved. It's still unknown exactly how it happened, but his cover was blown. We suspect the CI was a gang plant all along and betrayed him. The gang coerced Detective Zamora into giving up information regarding Randy and exploited that intel in an attempt to abduct him — and perhaps you too, Emery — to use as leverage. They might have been successful had it not been for your friend Mr. Coleman. Eyewitnesses stated he took a bullet for you. I'm looking forward to meeting him. One witness said he was bigger than those two perps put together. They certainly got more than they bargained for, and your feisty little pit bull obtained the DNA we needed. Both men have been identified, thanks to a young eyewitness's video. They are low-level thugs in the narco gang. We're close to taking down this entire operation, but until it happens, I want all of you to have round-the-clock police protection."

Alarm crossed their faces, as Emery's head fell onto her father's chest. Olivia's hand had flown to her mouth and was muttering,

"Dear Lord," repeatedly in disbelief.

"I have my best detectives on top of this situation. Officer O'Hara will remain here with you, Emery. Officer Melendez will accompany your parents and son home. I have another officer waiting upstairs to safeguard your friend, Mr. Coleman."

Emery was close to tears. "Captain …" Her usual eloquence had disappeared. "Alex is in danger, isn't he?"

"I'm afraid so, honey. We're gonna try our best to extract him, but it doesn't look good." The conversation came to an abrupt halt when Randy and Officer Melendez reappeared.

"Captain, I found a tracking app on Randy's phone, which I've removed. The other phone's clean." The young officer returned Emery's phone. Smiling in thanks, she nodded then faced her parents.

"Mom, Dad … I think Randy and Goldie need to go home with you now. It should be the safest location at the moment. I'll wait here until there's some word on Tag's condition."

After a few hugs and kisses, they were about to depart when Officer Melendez, who would be accompanying the family home, motioned them to stop and wait for him.

"Captain, a word in private with you and Ms. Lawson, please?" Captain Jacovo nodded, as the young officer turned toward them.

"After questioning Randy whether he had lent his phone to anyone other than family members, he recalled his father's girlfriend borrowing the phone once. Obviously, that's how the tracking app was downloaded." Emery's expression was one of horror.

"Alex put our son in a dangerous situation. What the hell was he thinking?" She collapsed into a chair and Captain Joe quickly sat beside her, taking her trembling hand into his own.

"We're doing everything we can, Emery. Try not to worry." Looking up, he lifted his chin to Officer Melendez. "Take the family home. You have first watch tonight. Keep me informed.

Dismissed." Turning back to Emery, his eyes softened. "Officer O'Hara will stay with you until you are able to visit with Mr. Coleman. Afterwards, she'll escort you home. Your car is still at the scene, correct?" Emery nodded, a bit bewildered at the fact she had not given her car a second thought. Still holding her hand, he whispered, "Give me your keys. I'll have one of my men drive it to your parents' house. Get some rest, Emery. That's an order."

Ominous thoughts overwhelmed Emery; Tag almost killed, Alex in grave danger, her little boy targeted and almost kidnapped. It was too much to bear. The stalwart demeanor Emery had so carefully constructed for Randy's benefit instantly crumbled, and she frantically darted to the nearest ladies' room. Finding an empty stall, she collapsed in unrelenting sobs as grief and terror overtook her. Not only was Tag faced with an uncertain future, so was Alex, her long-time best friend and father of her child. Officer Jane O'Hara followed discretely behind Emery, standing a few yards away, on guard.

Three hours had passed since a nurse had approached Emery to inform her Tag had been taken into surgery. Pressing her for additional information had been fruitless; she had no comment except for, "Doctor Ambrosini is one of our finest surgeons; your friend is in good hands."

By this time, Emery and Jane had become instant friends, although the officer's eyes continued to scan the waiting room thoroughly on high alert if the need arose. The affable redhead had been with the PPD for fifteen years. Her soft-spoken voice belied her tough-as-nails exterior: tall, robust frame and hair pulled back in a severe, no-nonsense bun.

Four cups of tasteless hospital coffee later found Emery perusing the final text in response to the numerous terse messages she had sent updating family and friends.

TYLER: LET ROBBI OR ME KNOW IF YOU NEED ANYTHING. I CAN BE THERE IN A FEW HOURS. WE LOVE

YOU BOTH.

An attractive woman in her mid-fifties, wearing full hospital scrubs, exited a nearby elevator and approached Emery and Officer O'Hara. She held out her hand, and enquired, "Ms. Lawson? I'm Doctor Ambrosini."

Emery tentatively stood up, but her legs gave way and she collapsed back into the chair, eyes brimming with tears. "Please don't tell me ..." her voice broke with emotion. The doctor quickly sat down next to a trembling Emery, patting her shoulder in a comforting manner.

"He came through the surgery quite well," she assured, stroking Emery's forearm with her other hand. "The shot was a through-and-through. The bullet missed the heart by a few centimeters, fortunately no major arteries were hit and no bones were broken. He incurred some muscle damage, a nicked rib, and he will require physical therapy, but all things considered, Mr. Coleman is an extraordinarily fortunate young man."

Throwing her arms around the physician, Emery managed to stammer, "Thank you so much. Can I see him?"

"Just for a few minutes. He's in ICU and he'll spend the night there, but he will have his own private room by the morning if all goes well. We've given him some strong pain medication so he can rest comfortably. I'll take you to him."

Officer O'Hara followed the two women into the elevator. During the ride to the fifth floor, the doctor asked Emery for Tag's family's contact information. Feeling at a loss, Emery explained she didn't know his parents but was sure Tag had their information stored in his cell phone.

"I will bring Mr. Coleman's phone and personal belongings to you in a few minutes. He's in Room 515. You'll see a police officer posted outside. When you contact the family, give them my information so I can speak to them directly." Doctor Ambrosini slipped a business card into Emery's hand, and then pointed to the right as they walked out of the elevator.

Emery sat at Tag's bedside; his eyes were closed and his face looked extremely pale. He was connected to two IVs and a heart monitor. Gently taking his hand in hers, she pressed it to her lips, grateful for the warmth of his skin. Still gripping his fingers lightly, her cheek came to rest on his forearm. A nurse quietly padded into the room and placed Tag's belongings on the nightstand. Emery mouthed a silent 'thank you' and grabbed the phone with her free hand, scrolling through the contact list.

Feeling a slight movement of his fingers, her eyes rose to meet his as they opened dreamily. Emery was never so happy to see his striking green eyes in her life, even though they were heavy-lidded from the medication. Tag attempted to speak but there were no audible sounds. Pressing her forefinger softly to his lips, she admonished, "Don't talk, baby. You're gonna be fine. The injuries were not life-threatening and the bullet didn't cause any permanent damage."

Tag did not seem appeased by Emery's words; mildly agitated, his head began shifting stiffly from side to side. "Randy and Goldie are fine, Tag. You saved us. We're all just shaken up. The police are working the case and they have some good leads. Alex is involved somehow; he tried to warn us. He's the one who screamed for us to run. Until everything's cleared up, there will be a police officer posted outside your room. They'll be keeping an eye on Randy and me, too. So don't worry about us. Just rest, honey. Get your strength back." Emery sighed in relief when Tag's drowsy eyes reacted to her use of his favorite endearment.

"Tag, your doctor would like me to call your parents and let them know what happened. Would that be okay?" He gave her a slight nod. She held up his phone, pointing to 'Mom'. "Is this the right number?" Tag nodded again, as his eyelids fluttered.

"I'm gonna take your phone with me tonight, okay? Your

friends need to be notified, too."

Emery continued to hold his hand, softly kissing the mildly bruised knuckles. Again, there was a slight wiggling of his fingers. Although barely noticeable, the effort made Emery smile as thankfulness washed over her. She did not move her eyes from his until Tag was unable to remain awake any longer. She could have lost herself in his gaze forever, but the pain meds had other, more potent plans. After kissing his forehead and every other feature of his face numerous times, Emery tiptoed out and quietly closed the door. Nodding at the officer who was posted outside, she breathed a huge sigh of relief as she approached Officer O'Hara, who had been chatting quietly with her co-worker.

"He's sleeping comfortably. I'm so relieved."

Jane patted her arm, reassuringly. "Glad to hear it. Now let's get you home to your family."

During the ride, Emery nervously dialed Tag's mother's number.

"Hello, Mrs. Taggart? My name is Emery Lawson. I'm Cole's girlfriend. I'm also Randi Galloway's cousin. I have important news about Cole."

Chapter 26

"He who has a why to live can bear almost any how."
– Friedrich Nietzsche

Emery

Emery and Randy arrived at the hospital bright and early the following morning, accompanied by Officer O'Hara. Doctor Ambrosini was just leaving Tag's room.

"He's doing quite well this morning. He ate a decent breakfast. I just changed his dressing, and there's no sign of infection, so everything looks good. He needs rest, no exertion of any kind, and he might still be a bit groggy due to the pain meds. We can talk tomorrow about physical therapy. Oh, and thanks so much for contacting Mr. Coleman's family and giving them my number. I made sure he understood you were simply following my orders." The doctor winked supportively. "His father is out of the country on business at the moment, but his mother is on her way and should be arriving here in an hour or two." With a warm smile for them both, she quickly strode down the hall.

Randy couldn't hold back his elation at seeing Tag's welcoming smile. He was sitting up, stiffly propped against two large pillows, and connected to an IV. "Tag, you're okay! I saw all the blood, and I was so scared."

"Me too, buddy," Tag reassured the boy, reaching out his right arm gingerly to give him a weak fist-bump. Randy's expression swiftly changed when his eyes locked on Tag's left chest area and shoulder, which were heavily bandaged. Fear showed in the boy's eyes as his lower lip began to tremble. Noticing his reaction, Tag immediately reached out to ruffle Randy's hair affectionately, motioning him toward the bed before any tears fell.

"I'll always be here for you, Randy. Don't ever forget that." Tag patted his arm reassuringly as his eyes turned toward Emery. *Is he really okay, or just being brave for Randy's sake?*

"Are you in any pain, Tag? Should I get a nurse?" He shook his head, but his eyes revealed some deep-seated emotions.

"Nope. When I first opened my eyes last night and saw your beautiful face, I knew I'd be okay. And besides, these pain meds are pretty powerful."

"Tag, you still gonna be able to coach me?" The boy's innocent face scrunched up with alarm.

"Randy! Don't bother Tag with football stuff right now." He waved her off with an indignant snort, demonstrating he was far from being in a helpless, debilitated state.

"Hey! My throwing arm is still in great shape, ready to pass you a perfect spiral." Tag flashed a winning smile, although his attempt to raise his right arm caused him obvious discomfort, which he valiantly fought to conceal. *Just as I suspected, but he is going to be okay.*

Emery, glancing around the room, was taken aback by two large floral arrangements and several beer-bottle shaped balloons, which festively adorned one wall.

"Oh my! These must be from North Star," Emery exclaimed, laughingly pointing to the balloons. "Did they send over a few six-packs, too?" she teased, leaning over and pressing several chaste kisses to Tag's forehead. His nose brushed up her jawline past her ear, breathing in her scent.

"The flowers are from your parents and the gym staff," he clarified, as his right hand reached for Emery's. "Come closer. I need to look at my brown-eyed girl for a while," he teased affectionately as she pulled up a chair and sat. Randy leaned against her, with his hands gently resting on the bed, when Tag noticed the bandage on the boy's arm.

"You were hurt, buddy?" Worry laced his tone as his eyes probed Randy's.

"Nah. It was only a scratch. You shoulda seen the other guy. Goldie chewed off part of his wrist. The cops found his DNA in the blood on her teeth. It was so cool!" Immense pride filled her son's voice as he bragged about Goldie's heroics.

"Your dog's a tough one. She survived that nasty old coyote, right?" Tag gave Randy a knowing nod. Emery's curiosity got the best of her. "Tag, do you remember anything about the attack?"

He pondered her question then responded, thoughtfully shaking his head. "Most of it is a blur. I heard '*run*,' Goldie growled, and then I was lying on the ground. I saw you, Emery, and all I could think of was 'Please, God, let me see my girl's beautiful face again'." Tag smiled at her then seemed to experience another sudden reminiscence.

"I saw …" His right hand squeezed Emery's so hard she winced. "I saw Randi for just a brief moment. She told me I couldn't stay with her, because you were waiting for me."

Emery gasped upon hearing Tag's emotional words. *A dream? An actual 'Heaven is for real' encounter? It does sound like something Randi would say. She was the most unselfish person, always thinking of those she loved.*

Beautiful emerald eyes brought her back to reality. Nothing else mattered to Emery. He was alive. As they continued to chat quietly, Tag never let go of her hand.

There was a soft knock on the door before it opened to reveal Officer O'Hara as she peeked her head in.

"Mrs. Taggart is here."

Emery stood up and leaned over to kiss Tag softly.

"Randy and I are gonna go grab something to eat, okay? Oh, and here's your phone back, fully charged. Text me whenever you're ready for us to return." Tag nodded his assent. They had agreed the reunion needed to be a private one.

Emery greeted Mrs. Taggart out in the hall. She was a stunning blonde with the same eyes as her son, although a shade lighter. She immediately enveloped Emery in a warm, grateful hug.

"Thank you so much, Emery. We'll talk afterwards, okay?" Without even waiting for a response, she strode hurriedly into the room, pulling a carry-on suitcase behind her.

Emery and Randi strolled around the hospital grounds after having a light snack in the cafeteria. They found a comfortable bench and watched a small group of young children kick a soccer ball around. They all wore surgical masks, hospital gowns, and slippers; one little girl was in a wheelchair. Two hospital employees accompanied them.

"What's wrong with them, Mommy?" Randy's large brown eyes gazed up at Emery sadly. "Can I play with them?" Emery pulled him close, wrapping the boy in a fierce hug.

"I don't think so, sweetie. Those masks they're wearing protect them from germs. Usually that means they're seriously ill; maybe they have leukemia or some other kind of cancer. Perhaps they had surgery recently, like Tag." Randy nodded meditatively, digesting his mother's somber words. Emery watched his reaction intently; he was a sensitive child, but she and Alex believed telling the truth was always for the best.

Alex's plight had been a constant ache in the pit of her stomach since she had heard his scream of warning. Emery had been fearfully awaiting Randy's questions about his father, but there were none. A mother knew her son best of all; his fear lurked just below the surface. Emery could see it in his eyes.

"Randy, I want to talk to you about Daddy." The dam finally broke and his eyes brimmed with tears.

"I know he's in trouble, Mommy," Randy sobbed. "I can feel it. I'm scared!" He felt so small and vulnerable in her arms as he trembled.

"Baby, we don't know anything for sure. We need to have hope, think positive. Your dad has survived some scary situations in the past." Emery continued to hold him snugly, kissing the crown of his head.

"Mom, the last few times I saw Dad, he seemed different. He usually never talked about his job with me, but when he came to see us in San Francisco, we talked a lot on the plane ride home. He started telling me how dangerous it was and made me swear I'd take care of you if anything bad happened to him. He made me promise not to tell you. I'm sorry, Mom. I shoulda said something."

"Honey, it's okay. A promise is a promise; you didn't do anything wrong. What else did Daddy say?"

"Nothing really, except to apologize for bringing that woman, Claudia, along when we were supposed to be doing our guy things. That was when she borrowed my phone. I didn't like her. There was something mean about her and Dad acted weird when she was around."

"Oh, baby, I am so sorry I was away and couldn't be here for you. It was wrong for your father to put you through that, but I'm sure he had a good reason. You know how hard he works to catch all the bad guys, right?" Randy wiped his eyes as he nodded. Emery had always suspected Randy had knowledge of the dangers his father encountered, although a nine-year-old could never fully grasp the remote possibility of losing a parent.

The grave moment was interrupted by the buzz of Emery's phone. Her countenance visibly brightened when she gazed at the screen. Randy's expression perked up as well.

"That was Tag, right, Mom? Can we go back and see him?" Emery simply showed her curious son the screen.

TAG: GET BACK UP HERE NOW. I MISS U BOTH!

As they approached Tag's room, Emery had to make a split-second decision.

"Randy, would you mind waiting with Officer O'Hara for five minutes? I want to talk to Tag's mom for a bit before you meet her, okay?"

"Sure, Mom. Officer O'Hara is a Cowboys fan, so we have lots to discuss," Randy chuckled. Emery patted Jane's shoulder, whispering, "Thanks," as she turned to enter the room.

Tag had already given his mother the short version of his mysterious past twelve years, and was just completing the lengthy explanation of the recent four months, including how Randi's cousin had entered his life, and the revealing contents of the journal. Tag reached for Emery's hand as she carefully perched on the edge of the bed — far from his injured left shoulder.

"Emery, this is my mother, Lilly. Mom, Emery." He displayed a wobbly grin as the two women cautiously eyed each other. Emery was nervous, but Mrs. Taggart immediately enveloped her in an affectionate cuddle.

"Emery, it's so lovely to meet you. We adored Randi. You are so beautiful, just like she was. Cole has filled me in on how the two of you came into each other's lives. You know, I believe in miracles. I always have. The two of you finding each other? Well, it just proves my point. I have never witnessed a more perfect miracle."

Tag explained to his mother that only Emery's parents knew his true identity. With all the commotion of the attempted kidnapping, Alex's situation, and Tag's subsequent shooting, the shocking announcement had been intentionally put on the back burner. Emery was planning to divulge the secret soon. Possible negative reactions from her aunt and uncle preoccupied her mind, filling her with uncertainty.

After several minutes, Randy curiously poked his head in. "Can I come in now, Mom? I miss Tag!" Emery couldn't help but notice Lilly's emotional reaction to Tag's demeanor around Randy. *Seeing her son after so many years must be overwhelming. And now she's witnessing his happiness and devotion to us — a mother's dream she probably gave up years ago.*

Randy had snuggled gingerly in between Tag and Emery, careful not to jostle him. Tag deposited a kiss on the boy's head then made a casual introduction.

"Randy, I'd like you to meet my mother, Lilly." Randy reached his arm out at the exact same moment as Lilly.

"Pleased to meet you, ma'am." A genuine grin covered the boy's face.

"Likewise, Randy. I hear you're a pretty good wide receiver." Lilly was noticeably impressed by Randy's excellent manners, as she shot an approving wink in Emery's direction.

Randy beamed from ear to ear. "That's 'cause I have the best coach!" The conversation continued for another half-hour until Lilly began to gather her belongings.

"Sweetheart, I am going to check into my hotel and freshen up. We're staying at the St. Regis; I think it's just a mile or two away. Your father should be arriving tomorrow morning."

Lilly leaned down to give her son a loving hug followed by several kisses to his forehead. He held her close with his right arm and kissed her back with just as much affection. She then strode up to Emery, linking arms with her as they exited the room together. They embraced out in the hall, as Lilly cupped Emery's face with her hands.

"I can't begin to tell you how grateful I am. Not only did

you bring my Cole back to me, you have made him happy as well. Will I see you here later, dear?"

"I'm not sure. There's a lot going on right now, and Randy's dad is still missing, so …"

"Oh, Cole told me about that. I'm terribly sorry. I hope everything works out." After giving Emery a comforting pat on the cheek, Lilly turned and headed to the elevator, her stylish red pumps making clicking sounds on the tile floor. Emery breathed a sigh of relief and went back into Tag's room.

"Your mother is fantastic. I love her!" Tag's chuckle was the most robust sound he had made since the shooting.

"Well, that's because she genuinely liked you. You should see her around people she is not so fond off. Her older sister, my Aunt Ada, calls her Miss 3B — Randy, cover your ears — brash, ball-busting and bitchy." They shared a laugh, but then Tag's eyes clouded over.

"The next hurdle will be Dad. We haven't always had a warm and fuzzy relationship. I'm a bit anxious about our reunion." He paused for a moment, gathering his thoughts. When Emery nodded in encouragement, Tag continued, "Dad and I butted heads constantly about my future. He had always hoped I'd join the family's construction company. Although Dad constantly bragged about my quarterback exploits, he never fully supported my NFL goals. Growing up, I always worked part-time for him and my uncle during the summers and school breaks. I enjoyed it, but could not see it as my career. Instead of building housing complexes and shopping malls, I envisioned building bodies instead. Sports medicine or physical therapy was always my dream, if the NFL didn't pan out …" His voice wistfully trailed off. They were interrupted by a soft knock on the door, as Olivia and Sam poked their heads in.

"Hey! We just wanted to see how the patient is doing."

Tag gave them an enthusiastic thumbs up. "Thanks for the flowers. They're great."

"It's the least we could do for saving our daughter and grandson, Tag. We are forever grateful for your bravery." Olivia's heartfelt words brought a bit of welcome color to Tag's cheeks. Sam had his own thankful emotions to add.

"And, by the way, when you finally get sprung from this joint, you will be recuperating with us. We have a lovely guest room, the food is a helluva lot better than here, and I know you'll want your own private nurse." He chuckled devilishly, rolling his eyes at his daughter. "You know, for the sponge baths and —"

"Dad!" Emery sputtered, mortified at her father's bluntness. Tag and Sam shared an uproarious guffaw. It was good to hear Tag laugh so heartily, although at one point a slight wince marred his features as his right hand flew up to gently touch his bandaged shoulder. Emery's expression immediately morphed into a concerned scowl.

"All right, you guys, enough. Out. Now! You are disturbing my patient." Her smile returned as her father leaned in to kiss her cheek, whispering, "Visit with your fella for a couple of hours." Turning to Randy, Sam grinned. "Ready for an early dinner, kiddo? Alice Cooperstown?"

"Yay! You comin', Mom?"

"No, sweetie, I'm gonna stay with Tag for a while. You go have fun with Grandma and Grandpa, and I'll see you later. Make sure you bring a few leftovers home for Goldie, okay?"

"Okay, Mommy. Bye. Love you. Love you, too, Tag!" After kissing Emery and giving Tag a careful fist-bump, Randy skipped off in between his grandparents.

Emery snuggled on the bed, resting her head on Tag's right shoulder. "You okay, honey? Need anything? More pain meds?"

Tag shook his head, smiling as his mouth sought Emery's. It was their first intimate kiss since the shooting, countless terrifying hours for Emery as she imagined her life without him.

"Your lips are the only medicine I will ever need. More, please." His piercings had been removed before surgery and Emery thoroughly enjoyed nibbling his lower lip without fear of causing him discomfort. Their tongues were in the middle of a romantic duel when there was a firm knock on the door.

Tag gripped her hand as a somber Captain Jacovo entered the room. Emery's free hand flew to her mouth as she desperately tried to hold back her tears. It was obvious by the grief-stricken expression on his face what had transpired. Alex was dead.

Chapter 27

"The weak can never forgive.
Forgiveness is the attribute and the ornament of the brave."
– Mahatma Gandhi

Emery

During the days following the attempted kidnapping and subsequent gang takedown, details slowly emerged in the aftermath of the tragic events. Captain Jacovo visited Emery and her family to personally share confidential information that would not be made available to the news media. Alex Zamora had sacrificed his life for his family. The attempt to rescue him was not successful and it was surmised that he was murdered shortly after the botched kidnapping. The police, wearing heavy body-armor, stormed the warehouse where the gang was holed up and no gang members survived the heavy crossfire. An autopsy showed that Alex had died of multiple gunshot wounds — none from police officers' weapons.

Emery's grief was overwhelming, but her first priority was Randy. She did not want him exposed to any of the grisly details surrounding the tragedy. Tag, who was recuperating nicely in the Lawsons' guest room, had volunteered to keep Randy occupied during the police captain's visit.

Randy was inconsolable after learning of his father's death. He sobbed for days, being alternately comforted by his mother or grandparents. Emery mourned as well. Her best friend and lover for most of her adult life was gone. Despite her brave front for Randy's sake, she wept in Tag's arms when he held her during the night. Randy sought Tag out for solace, too. Emery suspected Randy was experiencing nightmares, first witnessing Tag getting shot, then learning his father died in a similar manner.

Alex's funeral and memorial service had been surreal. More than 1,000 mourners packed St. Andrew's Church, including police officers and elected officials from throughout the area. Next to the casket stood a blown-up color photo of a teenaged Alex holding newborn Randy in his arms, as an even younger-looking Emery beamed proudly. Captain Jacovo gave the emotional eulogy remembering a man whose passions included his friends, his work with the PPD, and most of all his family: parents Alejandro and Rosario, who were not in attendance due to illness, sister Valentina, Emery, and Randy, the light of his dad's life. Emery said a few words, then read a short letter Randy had written to his 'new guardian angel in Heaven'.

Dad, I always knew since the first time you held me in your arms, how much you loved me, and how proud of me you were. The truth is I was more proud of you. I know you're watching over me, but I still miss you. I love you, Daddy. You will always be my hero.

Afterwards, the procession of police cars and mourners followed the three-mile route from the church to the graveside service. Supporters hung signs from freeway overpasses that read "hero" and fire trucks were stopped along the route with firefighters holding American flags. Emery could see Tag struggling with his emotions at Alex's grave. *It's the first funeral service he's been to since Randi's. Me, too. We have each other's strength to rely on now, and Randy has us both.*

⊗

From the moment Tag entered the Lawsons' home after his release from the hospital, he and Emery were inseparable, with Randy not far away. Olivia made sure he was comfortable in the guest room, fussing over him every minute with offers of hot soup, a cold drink, or extra-fluffy, supportive pillows for his injured shoulder.

Aunt Morgan and Uncle Victor were back in town and had been invited to dinner where Emery finally divulged Tag's real identity and the circumstances of their meeting. Olivia and Sam had already welcomed him with open arms; Emery's explanation was irrelevant to them. Tag was a hero in their eyes. Sam spoke for the whole family when he praised Tag for his bravery in foiling the kidnapping attempt and protecting Emery and Randy with his life.

Much to Emery's relief, Aunt Morgan had a surprising confession to share; she had read Randi's journal the previous year and had long since forgiven Cole for his actions. In fact, both Morgan and Victor had always hoped for the chance to see him again and express their feelings of remorse at how Cole was treated during the aftermath of the tragic car accident. Overjoyed at seeing Cole again, it felt like a tiny piece of their beloved daughter had been returned to them.

Emery was grateful for Tag's strong male presence and protective nature where Randy was concerned. The loss of his father was devastating; Tag's unconditional love and support helped to ease the pain. Often no words were spoken between them. Randy simply leaned into Tag, as a strong arm would hold him close. Often Goldie would join them, nuzzling her snout under Randy's chin or licking his face in a comforting gesture.

Tag's injury was healing nicely with the help of a physical therapist, but his left shoulder muscles ached a bit and flexibility was hampered, interfering with his normal range of motion. Emery assisted him at first when he was in need of a shower or bath. She suspected Tag's discomfort was slightly exaggerated the day he proclaimed, "Getting a sponge bath from my beautiful, naked girlfriend is worth the pain of a bullet any day!"

Tag

Ever since making the monumental decision to build a life with Emery, Tag had been formulating plans to make his vision come true. With the assistance and personal recommendation of Bob Tomlinson, he had secured a position at a local college football program. Tag would be the quarterbacks' coach, in charge of strategy and strength conditioning. Coach Tomlinson also requested Tag join him in coaching the after-school football program for elementary and middle school students, in which Randy was enrolled.

With his career plans falling into place, Tag had one last decision to make — the final piece of the puzzle — his future family. He broached the subject as he was cuddling Emery after an exceptionally intense round of lovemaking that had resulted in multiple orgasms for each of them. Both were still breathing heavily and covered in sweat, spooning comfortably.

"I've been doing a lot of thinking, and I want to adopt Randy legally. My plans to move here permanently are falling into place and I want us to be a real family." It was obvious by her huge smile that Emery agreed.

"Randy adores you, honey. I know he'll be ecstatic, but there's one thing that might—" Tag covered her mouth with his in an all-consuming kiss, which threatened to put an end to the conversation, but Tag needed Emery to hear his intentions.

"I know what you're thinking, sweetheart, and if you can

guarantee your answer will be 'yes' when I pop the big question, then I am gonna get my ass in gear and make it happen."

"Yes, yes, a thousand times, yes! Let's tell Randy about the adoption plan at Dad's party on Saturday," Emery squealed excitedly. "But the other thing will remain our little secret. For now."

Emery and Olivia had organized an impromptu, low-key barbeque for Sam's birthday. Father's Day had come and gone with barely a mention, everyone agreeing that calling attention to the holiday would cause Randy additional heartache. He was adjusting as best he could to his dad's death. The evening's festivities were almost over, leaving only close family gathered around the remnants of the burning coals, toasting marshmallows. Goldie was happily gnawing on what was left of a Porterhouse steak. Emery signaled for everyone's attention as Tag came to stand beside her. Randy sidled up to them, squeezing in between, grinning up at Tag, and then ducking under his mom's arm.

"Hey, y'all," Tag drawled, his Texas roots surfacing. "I have a very important announcement to make." Emery cast a sidelong glance in his direction as she excitedly ruffled Randy's hair. The child's dark eyes were already wide as saucers. He motioned for his mother to lean over so he could whisper in her ear.

"You and Tag gettin' married?" The intended whisper was anything but, as every pair of eyes landed on Emery. Covering her beet-red cheeks with her hands, Emery murmured, "Someday, sweetie, yes." His face lit up, but Tag resumed speaking so quickly, there was no time for further discussion, much to Emery's relief.

"Randy, you know I would never try to replace your dad in your heart, but I want you to know that I love you very much." Tag squatted down so he was eye level.

"I'd like to adopt you, make you legally my son. I'd be your dad. For real. Would that be okay with you?"

Randy's lip quivered and Tag sat motionless for a moment,

not knowing what the outcome would be. When the child flung his arms around him, Tag released the breath he did not realize he'd been holding. Emery quickly joined the hug-fest as Tag declared with a fist-pump, "We're finally gonna be a real family, Emery, the three of us." Goldie interrupted with a loud, demanding bark as everyone laughed. "Sorry, girl," Tag was quick to amend, "the *four* of us!"

The party was winding down and people were starting to say their goodbyes. Emery's Aunt Morgan and Uncle Victor cautiously approached her and Tag. "May we have a moment? We have some news." Her soft voice held a tremor, causing her to sink into her husband's side for support. Victor continued in her stead.

"As you know, Randi was laid to rest in San Antonio, but"— he swallowed hard, and took a fortifying breath— "we live here now, and couldn't bear the thought of her being so far, so we had her moved to Resthaven Park Cemetery. It's only a few miles away."

Emery collapsed into Tag's arms, smiling through tears of joy and relief. He tucked her under his chin protectively, struggling to keep his own emotions in check. The idea of going to visit Randi's grave made his stomach churn, unsure if he could mentally withstand reliving the trauma of that terrible day. He knew Emery had her own heart-wrenching memories of the Texas gravesite, but hoped in time they would summon the strength to visit her together.

Emery

They talked for hours that evening, discussing the future as well as reminiscing past events. Suspecting Tag might be uncommunicative regarding visiting Randi's grave, Emery opted for the direct approach.

"Did you ever go back to visit her, Tag? I never did. I … I just couldn't find the strength." Emery sighed, as Tag shook his head despairingly. "I still miss her so much."

"I didn't have the courage back then." Raising his head, their eyes connected in silent understanding. "I do now, but only if we go together. I'll need you with me, Emery."

Their pillow talk eventually evolved into happier topics.

"Your speech today was so touching, Tag," Emery complimented. "Even Dad shed a few tears and he *never* lets us see his softie side." She had countless more questions to ask him about their future together, but preferred to tread lightly, letting him take the lead.

"There is no doubt in my mind you and Randy are the family I was always meant to have. I love your son like he is my own. I would be honored to become his father." Tag held her close as she gazed up at him adoringly.

"I plan to start the adoption process soon if that's okay. And, of course, if we're going to be a family, I will have to live here. Well, not *here* with your parents, obviously, but in our own home nearby."

Nodding cautiously, Emery's stomach was doing flip-flops. She was well aware how much Tag loved his lovely hilltop hideaway and would never demand that he sell it.

"I've been thinking for a while about a possible solution. I'm not selling my house. I'd like to rent it during the basketball and football seasons — team personnel, players, and so forth — leaving the summer months for us to use it as a vacation home. I have a real estate friend of mine workin' out the details. The only thing left for me to do is buy my best girl the house of her dreams."

"You are so beautiful," he murmured as he peppered featherlight kisses over her forehead, eyelids, cheeks, and finally her pert nose where he rested. Pulling out for a moment, he rubbed his piercing up and down her wet slit, and then plunged back in deep, where he rocked even further. As Tag started moving inside her, Emery met him thrust for pounding thrust, sending her plummeting toward the edge.

"Tag, I'm almost there. I just need …" She reached over her head, grabbing the headboard with one hand then brought her knees to her chest. Her free hand was buried in his hair, pulling his lips to hers in a blistering kiss.

"Baby, I'm gonna grab your leg …" Tag grasped one leg by the ankle and straightened it upward to the ceiling, deftly changing the angle of penetration, resulting in a scream of ecstasy which exploded from Emery's throat. "Ooooh, Tag. Please, don't stop!"

Afterwards, as he was tenderly cleaning between her legs, his lips traveled an invisible path up her silky thighs, pausing to savor the scent of her arousal. Resting his head on her lower abdomen, he began softly stroking her folds while lapsing into deep thought. Several contemplative minutes passed, when Tag's eyes sought hers.

"Baby, what if I don't know how to love? How to be loved?" Emery smiled warmly. "That's not possible, Tag. You had the very best teacher. Randi taught me a lot about love, too."

"You were right, Em. We *do* make love and I will never get enough of you. I love you, my sunrise girl," he said, barely a whisper.

"I love you back, Tag Coleman aka Cole Taggart, and *wow!* That's the first time you've actually said the 'three little words' to me!"

His lips curved upward and he chuckled. "Technically, I first said it in a letter that I never mailed to you." Emery's lips parted as a hand flew to her chest. Her heartbeat quickened.

"Remember when I first sent you those texts, before I read the journal? When you didn't answer right away, I thought I had lost you forever, so I wrote you a letter. But then I heard from you, so I never mailed it."

"Do you still have it?" she asked breathlessly, running her tongue nervously over her upper lip. Nodding, he rose from the bed, extracted a sealed envelope from his backpack, and placed it in her outstretched hand. Emery gently traced the carefully scrolled name and address with her fingertips before prying the envelope open.

Dear Emery, my beautiful, brown-eyed sunrise girl,

I miss you so much I can hardly bear it. I can't eat, I've hardly slept. Tyler's been taking care of me, which is not fun to say the least.

"Over You" is now on my iPod. I put it on 'repeat'. Fuck, those lyrics make me cry every damn time. Strangely, it reminds me more of you now. That's when I knew for sure. It's you, only you. I'm in love with you, Emery. When I first heard the lyrics, they represented the past, nothing but pain and loss. Now that song makes me envision the future — our future, together. I cannot imagine a tomorrow without you and Randy. When I'm with you, I feel like I'm where I'm meant to be. We fit together in so many ways, in every way. I don't know if I can live the rest of my life without having you by my side every day. Please, Em. Don't sentence me to another hour or minute without you. I will not survive. I've been a lost ship, caught in a hurricane in the middle of the ocean for years until you rescued me. You've become my anchor, my safe haven. I love you, babe. Tag. (Or Cole. You decide. We both love you.)

Chapter 28

"Doubt thou the stars are fire;
Doubt that the sun doth move;
Doubt truth to be a liar;
But never doubt I love."
– William Shakespeare (Hamlet)

EMERY

Before returning to ASU for the fall semester, Emery kept both herself and her mother busy house hunting in Phoenix and the surrounding suburbs. Alex had a hefty life insurance policy in place with Emery and Randy as sole beneficiaries, so Randy's future college education was taken care of, even if the football scholarship that Tag predicted he would earn didn't pan out. Tag still had a portion of his grandfather's money, so they were hoping to purchase a house in nearby Glendale, which was conveniently located near their places of employment, Randy's school, and Emery's parents.

Meanwhile, Tag spent a week tying up loose ends in San Francisco: finalizing rental agreements, and arranging transportation for countless household and personal items to Arizona. Also on the agenda was bidding farewell to his longtime friends at the gym and North Star Bar, where he would still appear occasionally as guest bartender. Emery laughed uproariously when Tag related how

Brew predicted those nights would be standing-room-only and suggested they charge admission. Even though he'd be returning every summer, Emery was well aware of what Tag was giving up, albeit willingly. His twelve-year escape from the real world had come to an end.

⊗

School was back in session for everyone. Randy was enjoying fourth grade immensely, and spent two periods per day, English and math, with fifth graders due to his advanced levels. Emery had been cajoled into teaching an "Intro to Sculpture" class at ASU, at the behest of the head of the Art Department, who had received a glowing letter of praise from Professor Luca Navarro. Emery was astounded and grateful that Luca apparently held no grudges.

Emery wasn't surprised that Tag was thriving at both his new endeavors, often unsure which provided him the most personal satisfaction: working with know-it-all college students or the always-hungry-for-knowledge middle schoolers. She suggested that perhaps the two groups could learn from each other, so once a month Tag would arrange for his college team to volunteer their time coaching his youngsters.

One afternoon, as Emery strolled across campus toward the parking lot, the sky darkened and she barely had time to duck into her car before the heavens let loose with a streak of lightning, followed by an ear-splitting barrage of thunder. Fat raindrops hit the windshield as she flipped the wipers on, their rhythmic pattern comforting her although an uneasy sensation invaded her ribcage. Random fragments of a faded reminiscence flickered through her mind. *Rain. Mud. Grave.*

Reaching into the glove box, her hand searched for a paper brochure. Upon locating it, she perused the contents, and then punched an address into MapQuest. Upon arriving at her destination, she was relieved to notice the storm had abated to a mere drizzle. Grabbing the paper, and an old blanket she used for transporting art supplies, she set out on foot, following the diagram, until she saw it.

Emery barely had a moment to spread the blanket on the ground before her knees buckled. Unaware of the passage of time, she had sobbed uncontrollably until her nose was stuffy, her throat raw, and her eyes had run out of teardrops.

Gathering what little strength she could muster, Emery got to her knees and reached up to trace the letters of her cousin's name that had been etched in the stone. Pressing her tear-stained cheek to the cool, wet granite felt comforting as her words tumbled out.

"Randi, I miss you terribly and have so much to talk to you about. You're always with me and I believe you can see everything here on Earth. I need to thank you for bringing me to Cole. He spent twelve long years in Hell, blaming himself, missing you, and still loving you. We're together now and love each other very much, but you will always be our first love. Forever. I'll be back soon, with Cole."

Lying in bed that evening with Tag snuggled in her arms, Emery confessed where she had been.

"Today's thunderstorm brought back the day Randi was buried so vividly. I was drawn to her, felt such a strong need to be close to her. You should come with me next time, okay, honey?"

"I'm not sure I can, but I'll think about it, Em," he whispered. Tag buried his face between her breasts, his lips trembling against her skin. Emery kept silent, stroking his hair while planting soft kisses on the top of his head. *He's not ready yet, Randi. Be patient with him.*

"I'll be honest with you. I dreaded going, but it was as if she summoned me. After a while, when I was all cried out, the rain abruptly halted and a random sunbeam broke through the clouds, illuminating this lone flower that had grown in front of her headstone. I'm not sure if someone purposely planted it, or it was a random seed that just happened to land there, but it was remarkable. I felt her presence as strongly as I feel you at this moment." His breathing had calmed to a steady rhythm. Emery thought he might have fallen asleep, but felt his large hand caress her belly. Pleading eyes gazed up at her as she continued.

"Honey, the enormity of what this life can offer us is so immeasurable. We have no choice but to focus on the tiniest portion; a single minute, a solitary day, perhaps a fleeting year that is gone before we even have time to buy a new calendar. We both have missed Randi every day for twelve long, excruciating years. But from the moment we came together, our hearts have been revived. Our souls recognized each other; together we have grown stronger and healed. I promise you, there will come a day when all you will remember is how you felt when you were in Randi's presence: filled with pure love and at peace." Tag nodded in agreement and exhaled a cleansing breath. His voice was husky with emotion, but steady.

"I believe Randi's love planted a lone seed in my soul that laid there dormant, bereft of water in solitary darkness, until you appeared in my life. Your warmth, my sunrise girl, enabled that seed to sprout into roots, which are now entwined around my heart. I simply cannot imagine a world without you in it. From the day we met, every sunrise has been more dazzling than the one before it. You taught me how to laugh, hope, and dream again. I am addicted to your loving heart and passion for life, and I need you by my side every minute of every day until I breathe my final breath." Her soft hands wrapped around him, feeling every subtle rise and fall of his chest. She felt a tickle on her neck; Tag was mumbling incoherently into her hair. "What did you say, Tag?" She continued to caress the skin on his shoulders. "I'm ready, Em. Let's visit Randi tomorrow."

*"What we once enjoyed and deeply loved we can never lose,
for all that we love deeply becomes part of us." – Helen Keller*

TAG

The day was picture perfect. A clear blue late-afternoon sky, a few random puffy white clouds, and traces of a rainbow that dissipated quickly after their arrival. Tag brought several items from Randi's wooden box: a few meaningful photos, a promise ring he had given her on their one-year anniversary, and a pressed flower wrapped in wax paper. Emery wore Randi's UT jersey and Tag had found an old, worn T-shirt from a Foo Fighters concert they had attended. A blanket was spread in front of the headstone, and after planting some daisies, they sat there for hours.

Tag brought his iPod and they listened to the melancholy lyrics of "Over You" as they clung to each other. Both had anticipated the visit would become a sob-fest but, miraculously, the opposite occurred as they took turns recalling happy events, sharing significant memories or relating personal anecdotes. Instead of mournful tears, genuine laughter resonated in the solitude. During the quieter moments, he simply pressed their foreheads together and gazed into the captivating eyes that now owned his heart.

"Do you believe Heaven truly exists?" Tag's simple, straightforward question belied the turmoil, which had tortured his thoughts and dreams for years. *Death. God. Heaven. Hell. Is any of it real?*

"I do, but it's not some distant, ethereal place where people go when they die. I think Heaven lies within our hearts. That's where Randi lives now. She's in every heart that ever loved her. She's always been there, since the day you first saw her in class.

She has been with me since the time I was learning to walk and she stood behind me, held my hands, lifted me up, and put my tiny feet on top of hers. We walked and walked until I became used to the movement and then she let me try by myself. Of course I fell down, but she laughed and said that falling was the best part, because it always gave you a second chance to get up and try again."

"Sweetheart, I believe, in a strange and mystical way, Randi brought the two of us together." Emery nodded in agreement, smiling and gazing upward at the cloudless sky. "Me, too. She can't be with us physically, but all the love she had for us still exists. Her love is ours to keep, to share, or to give to someone else. You were loved by Randi, as was I. Do you realize how blessed we are? We have all her love, plus our own, to share with each other."

The sun had long set but neither seemed willing to depart. Tag had his back to the smooth granite headstone, and Emery's head was in his lap, using her folded-up hoodie as a makeshift pillow. Their gazes rose to the stunning array of bright stars that had emerged. His head tilted and a tentative smile appeared.

"Remember the old guy I told you about who did my tattoo? I never mentioned Randi to him, but he sensed that I had suffered a loss and shared an old Eskimo legend with me. 'Perhaps they are not stars but rather openings in Heaven where the love of our lost ones shines down to let us know they are happy.'" They snuggled close, absorbing each other's warmth as their gazes returned to the night sky. The vast number of stars appeared to have multiplied as Emery suppressed a quiet giggle.

"Oh my God, Tag. Remember how obsessed Randi was with astrology? Always wanting to read everyone's zodiac chart and matching up couples according to their signs?"

"I know, right? She loved astronomy, but especially those damn constellations. What makes them so mesmerizing?" Tag mused, the stress of the day obviously taking its toll as he gazed skyward. "Stars only comprise a tiny percent of the night sky. A measly one percent or maybe even less, like one-tenth of a percent. The remaining 99.9 percent is pure black nothingness. Don't people understand the darkness is equally essential, perhaps even more so. Where would the stars be if not for the empty blackness in between them? We wouldn't even notice them; no one would give them a second thought."

Tag shrugged, then lowered his eyes to meet Emery's, realizing they were twinkling with amusement. *What the fuck have I been blabbering about when the most gorgeous girl in the universe is right here? I should be kissing the ever-loving shit out of her, or maybe even getting her naked ...*

Pushing her body off the ground, Emery turned to face Tag, straddled him, and then pressed their foreheads together. Her warm breath fanned his cheeks and his cock sprang to attention.

Her sultry, teasing whisper sent a shiver down his spine. "But I *have* noticed the brightest star, and he shines only for me in all that empty nothingness."

Tag's arms were around her in a flash, holding her closer than he thought was physically possible.

"*You* are the star in this twosome, and you are all mine. I love you so much, Emery. I've loved you since the first night you came into the bar. One look and my heart knew you were the real deal. A triple play: the Alaskan stout, the Cardinals hoodie, and the biggest, most beautiful brown eyes I had ever seen in my whole fuckin' life. It hit me immediately; I was a goner. I had jumped into the deep end. No turning back. Done deal. Going, going, gone."

Later that evening, after the emotional cemetery visit, Tag lay in bed waiting for Emery to join him. Something had been weighing on his mind for a while and it was time to let it go.

"Sweetheart, I am so sorry for those thoughtless, hurtful words

I said that night, about our baby and how I was undeserving, and every other unkind thing that came outta my mouth." His head shook back and forth, shoulders drooping, as a hand scrubbed down his face. Emery sat quietly as Tag regained control.

"I realize now I was in mourning. I had fallen in love with a baby that was taken away before we even knew if it was a boy or a girl. I never told you, but I bought a bunch of gifts for our baby. I still have them. Maybe someday we might …" Tag's voice grew soft as his thoughts trailed off.

"Yes, honey, someday we will," Emery affirmed as she dotted his face with kisses. "There's something I never told you as well. I went to your house to get my art tools and stumbled upon your baby gifts. After crying my eyes out, I fell in love with you even more."

He smiled, warmed by her heartfelt confession. Visiting the cemetery had given him a new strength and he was ready to share another small secret; one that he'd been holding onto for a while.

"Em, I'm going back to visit Randi again soon. That night when Robbi and I read her journal together, I didn't have the courage to look at the final entry myself. Robbi read it aloud. It's time I read what was in her heart — her final message to me — with my own eyes. I know she wants me to be with her when I do."

"Okay. Perhaps it's time Randy and I visit Alex."

⊗

Tag sat with his back against the cool granite headstone, Randi's open journal on his lap. It was late afternoon, and the violet-reddish hues of the approaching sunset bathed the surrounding grass in a vibrant glow. As his eyes lowered to the page, he crossed his ankles and a melancholy grin appeared. He had purposely worn his treasured old pair of burnt-orange Converse hi-tops with the UT logo that Randi had given him on their first Valentine's Day together. *I'm here, baby. Talk to me.*

Dearest Cole, I am so sorry I didn't let you explain. I just talked to Jake and I'm meeting him later so he can give me every detail related to what happened and why he set you up. He hinted it was all Clark's idea and there was more than just alcohol involved. It still makes my stomach turn, seeing you with that girl on the tape, but your eyes —nothing was there — they were empty. That's how I know you were not in control; you had no idea what you were doing.

I talked to Emma Marie today. After giving her the G-rated version, she told me I should give you the benefit of the doubt and forgive you immediately. Her exact words. Imagine, a fourteen-year-old giving ME advice on my love life. She always did have a soft spot for you, Cole. Truly, she is the best person I know, always sees the good in everyone. I'm going to call you the minute I leave Jake. I'll see you soon. I forgive you, Cole, but I have faith you already know that. You know me so well, better than I know myself sometimes. I love you, Cole. Always, Randi

He closed the journal, kissed it lovingly, and laid it against his chest. A barrage of tears was imminent, but a fast-moving swirl of color provided a welcome distraction. A swarm of Monarch butterflies was passing intermittently, several of them pausing to alight on various flowers, shrubs, or headstones. One particularly large Monarch landed on Tag's right sneaker, its wings fluttering gracefully for a moment before it stilled.

"I know you're listening, baby. I have so much to tell you, but you already know what's in my heart. Thank you for loving me, for believing in me, and helping me believe in myself. You taught me how to love and be loved. I'm sorry I forgot that lesson for a while, but that's why you sent Emery — to make sure I learned it once and for all. Until next time. I miss you."

After a quick flap of its wings, the butterfly took off and disappeared from his sight.

One Sunday autumn afternoon, Tag invited friends and family to attend the season opener at the college where he was working as quarterback coach. After the game had ended in a record-breaking shutout victory for the home team, and the field had been cleared, he led the group out to the fifty-yard line, under the pretense of taking a few photos with Randy. Sam hovered close by, with his camera poised and ready. Tag motioned for everyone to form a semi-circle, with Emery at the center. He stood in front of her for a moment, holding her hands in his, and then took a few steps back, as he demanded, "Do not move."

Tag proceeded to get down on one knee, and made a sweeping gesture reaching into his back pocket but oddly found it empty. Emery's eyes widened the minute Tag's knee touched the ground and her mouth had frozen in an incredulous 'O', as she leaned into her mother's side. Glaring at Randy in mock-confusion, Tag stretched his arms out in the classic 'What the hell happened?' gesture. Randy shrugged, shaking his head, then threw Tag the football he had tucked under his arm. Tag caught it deftly in one hand, then proceeded to break it open like an egg … it was plastic. Inside nestled a small black velvet box. As Tag's eyes rose to meet Emery's, happy tears were already streaming down her cheeks.

"Emery, my love and the light of my life. We share the same heart and soul. Will you be my wife, have my baby someday, and let me love you for the rest of our lives?"

Epilogue

"I would not wish any companion in the world but you."
– William Shakespeare (The Tempest)

HAPPILY EVER AFTER …

They often reminisced about the night before their wedding, when Tag shared his desire to use his real name again.

"I created Tag Coleman out of self-hatred and a desire to disappear. He was my badass, don't-give-a-fuck persona. I'm ready to let him go now, and embrace who I have always been. Cole Taggart. You made that possible, Emery. You allowed me to become the man I didn't realize I was. You gave me a life I never expected and didn't think I deserved."

Because it had never been changed legally, the process was not a big deal. Friends who knew him as Tag could continue to use the name if they wished, but he eventually hoped to put that part of his life behind him. Although Emery had known him as both, she felt more comfortable with Tag, the man she had fallen in love with. When they were alone, he was always Tag; out in public he became either, depending on the circumstances.

The wedding was a simple affair for close friends and family. Tyler, Robbi, and Brew flew in from San Francisco. Tag's parents also attended and all past grievances between him and Cole Senior disappeared. Emery walked down the aisle on the arms of the two most important men in her life: her father and her son. Later, at their reception dinner, Randy's adoption was formally announced. The legal papers had been signed that morning.

◈

Another vivid memory was seared into their consciousness: Tag, standing naked and proud, in the spacious master bedroom of their new home in Glendale. He was grinning like a fool while waving a box of condoms in front of Emery's face, declaring, "Sweetheart, we've been married for three months and I think it's time we made a baby of our own. What do you say we retire these for a while?"

They made love that night with no barrier between them. Tag sunk into her warm, wet heat and moaned in ecstasy. Every time was better than the last; every orgasm was an explosion of brilliant colors burning away the dark corners of his soul. Emery was on all fours, ass in the air as Tag took her from behind. It was primal, the pure hunger of two bodies giving and taking, each craving what the other lovingly offered. Two souls, desperately needing each other to become whole. Grabbing the small vibrator, Tag turned it on, placing it gently on her clit while his other hand teased her breasts. Shifting his hips slightly, he plunged in deeper and it didn't take Emery long to shatter. Her pussy clenched around him, and soon their orgasms hit simultaneously, as bodies, hearts, and souls connected, unleashing a tidal wave of emotion. Unbeknownst to them at that moment, a profound miracle had also taken place.

When Emery's pregnancy was first detected, Tag made sure the OB/GYN was aware of her previous ectopic experience. The doctor labeled her 'high risk' until it was verified that everything was progressing normally. During the first sonogram, Tag was closely scrutinizing the doctor's demeanor and when her face showed signs of consternation, he started to hyperventilate.

"Something's wrong, Doc. What's going on? Tell us, please," he barely choked out, while clutching Emery's hand in a near-death grip. Giving him a wide grin, the doctor smiled serenely, and pointed to the screen. "See this? That's your baby's heart beating." Waiting for their excited reactions to subside, she pointed to another area on the screen. "And right here? That's the second baby's heart. Congratulations! You're having twins."

During Emery's pregnancy, Tag was the textbook perfect Daddy-in-waiting. He became fiercely protective of Emery in every way: her wellbeing, comfort, and safety. In Emery's words, he was 'off the freakin' charts' and 'driving me crazy'. From the moment they had heard two heartbeats instead of one, he doubled his efforts, although that amount of extreme attentiveness didn't seem possible. They worked out together daily in the small home gym Tag had designed, with him closely supervising the exercises she performed. He read every pregnancy and expectant-father book available on Amazon and spouted his newly-acquired knowledge to anyone who would listen.

He massaged her feet and growing belly, and any other body part that appeared to be desirous of his touch, which was everywhere. He was grateful that her pregnancy hormones made her sexually insatiable, but with that perk also came the odd food cravings. String cheese and strawberries, bananas dipped in honey, and sour cream straight from the container with a few tart, dried cherries mixed in. If there were unhealthy items on her list, Tag would find a healthier substitute. Knowing coffee was on the banned list, Emery begged Tag for coffee ice cream, which he had readily agreed to procure. However, after extensive online research about caffeine levels in ice cream and chocolate, he was forced to break the disheartening news to his caffeine-deprived wife. He had found an array of alternative ice cream flavors for her enjoyment, and Tag thoroughly relished licking all of them off her belly, and other exotic southern locations where it managed to drip and drizzle. Emery's body, even pregnant, was his cherished piece of Heaven. Tag spent many evenings gently combing her silky hair; it helped relax Emery and a tranquil mom meant serene babies, which translated into a calm, restful night's sleep for them both.

Not wanting to know the babies' sex until birth, there were various 'baby pools' being run with quite a bit of money on the line. Tag bragged that he had the inside track, displaying adorable pink and blue onesies that he had purchased. Only he and Emery knew the heartbreaking story behind the items in question, but their shared memories of grief were replaced with pure joy when their beautiful, healthy twins entered the world: Daddy's little quarterback and princess, Cole Randall and Carlie Alexandra.

⋘⋙

The twins had just celebrated their half-birthday and a low-key, family picnic-style celebration was being held in Sam and Olivia's backyard. Tag and Emery were sharing a lounge chair — she was on top, her back to his chest, his arms snuggly enfolding her. Cole Junior, nicknamed C.J. by his big brother, and Goldie were enjoying a playful wrestling match while Randy was showing his sister how to properly hold and throw a miniature football.

Goldie's sudden, animated barks had every eye turned her way. She had grown to full size and matured into a reliable watchdog, a sweet, loving playmate with a fierce, protective nature where the twins were concerned. Goldie stood motionless as baby Cole grabbed onto her fur, pulling himself up until he was teetering proudly beside her. Time stood still for a moment as animal and human communicated in a language all their own. A second exuberant yelp from Goldie resulted in Cole losing his balance, plopping back down on the grass with a giggle. Goldie's snout nudged the toddler back into a semi-upright position, casting a confident glance toward the concerned onlookers, as if to say, "Relax. I got this." After gently depositing his sister on her mother's belly, Randy raced to his brother's side and gently steadied the baby, gripping his tiny hands.

"No worries, little bro!" he crooned. "Falling is the best part. You always get a second chance to try again. Right, Dad?"

Tag nodded his agreement, warmth flooding his chest every time Randy called him 'Dad'. Since the twins were born, it had become the norm although during football practice, Randy would revert to the occasional 'Coach' or 'Sir'.

Tag's embrace of Emery now included a half-asleep baby Carlie, and his hold tightened as they both gazed at the three precious lives they had created. His mouth found the sensitive spot behind her ear, and he rained kisses down the length of her neck.

"Hey, Tag? Let's visit Randi tomorrow. I want to tell her about our beautiful family."

The party continued around them, but their eyes were only for each other. Tag pressed his mouth to Emery's in a passionate kiss.

"Thank you, my gorgeous sunrise girl. You have given me a life I could never have imagined. I love you to the moon and back, brown eyes."

Not to be outdone in the romance department, Emery teased, "And I love *you* to the *stars* and back!"

Randy happened to be strolling by when he overheard his mother's remark. Rolling his eyes, he declared, "But, Mom. There's like a billion stars. That would take you forever and *ever!*"

A radiant smile lit up Emery's face, as brown eyes locked onto green.

"Forever sounds perfect."

The End

ABOUT THE AUTHOR

Teri McGill grew up in Queens, New York and moved to warm and sunny Los Angeles in 1994. She taught Mathematics to deaf high school students for thirty years, which explains some of the recurring themes in her stories. When she is not at the computer, either writing or beta reading/proofreading, she enjoys working out, golf, mosaics, math tutoring, and watching sports.

CONTACT INFO:

www.TeriMcGillAuthor.com

Teri@TeriMcGillAuthor.com

TeriMcG91604@gmail.com

https://www.facebook.com/Teri McGill Author

https://www.facebook.com/My Heart Is Yours Book Series

Twitter: Teri McGill @TeriMcGill

Made in the USA
San Bernardino, CA
02 May 2016